No World Warranty

No World Warranty

F. Alexander Brejcha

iUniverse, Inc.

New York Lincoln Shanghai

No World Warranty

iUniverse, Inc.

For information address:
iUniverse, Inc.
2021 Pine Lake Road, Suite 100
Lincoln, NE 68512
www.iuniverse.com

ISBN: 0-595-31841-X

Printed in the United States of America

Contents

PART II: THE NEW LAND

PART III: THE NEW NEIGHBORS

Introduction: Nanotechnology (and why a former art student is writing about it)

Blame it all on Dr. Stanley Schmidt, the editor of *Analog Science Fiction and Fact*.

In late Spring 1989 I was reveling in the fact that my first story had just been printed in his magazine, and that a second one had just been accepted—and that was when Stan recommended that I read *The Engines of Creation* by K. Eric Drexler (Anchor Press/Doubleday: Garden City, New York, 1986). Considering that this non-fiction book was written by a physicist at M.I.T. and recommended by a former teacher who also happens to hold a doctorate in physics, I was a little leery about reading it since my education has been in other areas.

I am familiar with art thanks to being a former art major (before MS-related disabilities put an end to those studies and eventually landed me in a wheelchair), and I am also trained in psychology as that became my alternate course of study until a need for creative expression led me to writing. Medicine is also a comfortable subject for me to deal with as I work at a hospital, and I learned how to research medical topics while preparing a psychology honors research study on post-operative psychosis in open-heart surgical patients. However, my knowledge of the 'hard' sciences is limited to what I have absorbed from browsing and doing necessary research for a story. Fortunately Stan and I share the same positive view of science, the future, and humanity's eventual maturation, and since I trusted his recommendation, I picked up *Engines of Creation* to give it a try.

To my surprise, I was alternately amazed, terrified and exhilarated, but never really confused. The book was clear, comprehensible and loaded with mental dynamite, and as Stan had promised: full of ideas.

I will admit that I did get lost in a few places because of insufficient scientific grounding, but it was never such overwhelming confusion that I was tempted to stop reading. The principles and concepts Drexler lays out are very clear, and the implications are staggering. A reader's background will influence what he or she gets out of the book, and just as any new discovery is put to a range of uses unanticipated by its inventor, so will this book. A physicist, a chemist, a structural engineer, a doctor, etc.—a practitioner of any science—will read this book and see a vast array of applications specific to their own area of interest. Many are detailed or suggested by the book, and many more will be envisioned by readers.

As a fledgling science fiction writer I found my own inspiration from the book just as Stan had promised. It has not been the basis for all my subsequent fiction publications, but I did use nanotechnology for several of my later *Analog* stories, including the novelette and novella which were the basis for the first two parts of this much-delayed book: "StarStep", April 1990, and "The New Land", June 1990. Both stories received recommendations for the Nebula Award, and the latter a Honorable Mention in Gardner Dozois' *Year's Best Science Fiction, 8th Annual Collection* (1991, St. Martin's: New York). A sequel novella which is the third part of this book was enthusiastically received by Stan, but the time lag between part two and three would have been too long to run it. So, while I was sure I would eventually make a book out of these stories, the StarStep saga wound up stored on an archive disk for years while I concentrated on other fiction, as well as a range of nonfiction disability-related articles and essays for newspapers and magazines.

But then the time came, as it does for most writers, for my muses to start demanding a book (and ultratechophobes relax: while this book is based on real science, it is not a scientific treatise). So, no more excuses about my schedule, or my M.S.-impaired coordination slowing my typing too much to work on a book. So, after all too long of a delay, I pulled out the disk and did the necessary rewriting and expanding to finish this. I also employed some revisionist history as anyone who remembers the original stories will notice. In working the story into a novel, I discovered a few plausibility and logic loop-holes that needed to be plugged. But that's the fun of being a writer. You can make corrections in your universe without anyone raising a stink about it. Also, as the opening of a book, "StarStep" (the first of the stories that make up this book), was frankly…boring as originally written.

But because nanotechnology is still an unknown concept to some, I realized that it might be helpful to offer readers a brief explanation of just what it is. And what it isn't—because it does have its limitations. It is not magic, though its potential seems close to it and more than a few writers try to use it that way. Given the space limitations and etiquette for an introduction I can't possibly do justice to the concepts laid out in Drexler's book, but if you want to be mentally stimulated, I urge you to track it down and read it for yourself.

And as for that brief explanation I promised (feel free to skip ahead if you are familiar with it): nanotechnology is just what the name implies: very small technology.

Imagine stacking and organizing atoms individually to build microscopic machines the size of molecules! Imagine further that those machines can be programmed in a variety of ways to perform an incredible range of tasks. Add to this the fact that they can reproduce themselves, as well as alter almost any matter on an atomic level. After all, to a machine built up on such a small scale, shuffling a few atoms around would be child's play.

Drexler outlines three types of nanomachines that would work in conjunction with each other to do their thing: disassemblers, assemblers, and replicators. Each of these essentially do what their names imply: disassemblers analyze and break down matter, while assemblers use the disassemblers' information to build virtually any object, and the replicators speed this all up by doing just what you would think. And these nanomachines would be controlled and programmed by nanocomputers that will be as far beyond the most powerful computers now in existence as today's machines are beyond pocket calculators. Nanocomputers would be that much more powerful in part due to the radical speed improvements reduced size would offer. And as for the assemblers and disassemblers controlled by these nanocomputers, combined with replicators they could spread and do their tasks on a large scale as well as on a limited basis.

This is where caution is necessary.

Why? What does all this mean for the real world? Well, for one example: consider the consequences to the world economy of reckless conversion of lead into gold. Or, what about self-replicating machines programmed to spread and alter oil spills or other toxic waste into clean water, but that mutate (or are changed!) to react as if salt water is toxic waste that needs to be changed into sulphuric acid…and then imagine that those nanomachines get loose—or are let loose—to spread throughout an ocean!

These are frightening possibilities because theoretically nanomachines could break down, analyze and alter *almost* any substance. And like living organisms, nanomachines can reproduce and change, either through programming, or if poorly designed, through mutation!

But now that I've scared you, how about more benign uses?

Some examples in the not to distant future would include microscopic machines that spread through our bodies to repair torn tissues and clean out waste-hardened arteries. Something as simple as this is already very close to reality. Miniature steam motors 6 microns long and 2 microns wide have already been built, yielding 100 times more power than the previously smallest motors (electrostatic comb devices) and microscopic gear trains in various materials have also been built. And who hasn't seen that picture of a working car—the size of a grain of rice! It will not be long before miniature surgical robots will be built to do delicate repairs from the inside. And in time, nanomachines will be built to repair broken bones and heal severed or damaged spinal cords; and how about—eventually—machines that can change our bodies into any size, shape or appearance that we want, and that can keep us healthy and young for centuries?

And on a more global scale: how about machines to clean up a polluted world, restore wasted resources, and give us back a planet that we would be proud to leave our children? Or—how about just building a whole new world? That is what I propose in this book, where we take a small and life-less planet orbiting another star and turn it into a living, breathing world to colonize.

As I said, I can't begin to detail—or, to be honest, understand—all the potentials of this new sci-ence, but I wanted to explain that even if I may strain plausibility a little and use some artistic license, this technology is not some writer's device to get away with fantastic settings. Instead, it is a science of the future which is already being explored. Almost every week one can read in *Science News* of some new development in micro-engineering, and nanotechnology even has its own scientific journal detailing research underway all over the world. And for readers wanting to delve deeper into the sci-ence of nanotechnology, Drexler has continued his exploration of the science in *Unbounding the Future* (Drexler, Peterson and Pergamit, William Morrow: New York, 1991), and for technical read-ers, in *Nanosystems, Molecular Machinery, Manufacturing and Computation* (John Wiley & Sons: Somerset, NJ, 1992).

Nanotechnology is real, and will eventually bring with it radical—and to us, nearly unbelievable—changes in all aspects of our world. The challenge that we will face is the traditional one that any new scientific development poses for us: namely the manner in which we will use it.

In the book ahead you will find an Earth that was nearly destroyed by wrong choices and acci-dents, but—since I am the eternal optimist—you will also find a world that saved itself and which has also started a wonderful voyage of discovery on another world. And a note to readers, for dramatic reason: pay attention to the dates in each section. The italicized sections are taking place much later that the beginning and intervening chapters which give the background leading up to the future sec-tions. Keep that in mind and you won't be confused. The planning of a new world is complex and time-consuming and I did not want slow the beginning of the story down with a LONG world-building segment.

But, of course, even with the best of planning and intentions, and with the strictest of precautions, unexpected and interesting little glitches have a way of happening…

PRELUDE

CHAPTER 1

▼

THE MOON, 2200

"Grounder, Grounder, you're an ugly Grounder!"

A clump of soil from the sub-surface park dome of Luna-3 they had just passed scored a perfect hit on her face and Serena blinked, spitting out a piece of dirt. Billy Jackson had thrown it, and she saw him standing there pointing and laughing hysterically as she fought back tears.

The intentionally childish taunt and act had also scored, and she shouted: "I'm not a Grounder!" as she launched herself at her towering classmate. "I'm a Lunie, just like you!" She made her point with a perfect low-gravity tackle that threw them both several meters down the corridor past the others, sliding and tumbling on the slick floor. But she kept her grip on him and as they banged to a stop against the wall, she flipped him and grabbed his right arm to twist it up behind him.

"Say you're sorry," she insisted.

Billy just struggled silently and gritted his teeth.

"Say it!" She twisted his arm again.

"Go ahead and say it," Nancy urged. "That was cruel!"

"Aw, leave him alone." Paul was on Billy's side, of course, as was his sister Judy. The tall, sandy-haired Dupree twins stood here frowning like a pair of emaciated and gloomy book-ends. But at least they didn't come to his rescue as he groaned and struggled harder.

Serena put on more pressure, feeling her eyes burn. "I'm a Lunie!" she insisted. "I'm not a Grounder. Now say it!"

"All right," Billy cried. "You're a Lunie." She pushed harder and he added: "All right! And you're not ugly." A final twist, and a pained: "And I'm sorry," was forced out. "Now let me go!"

She released him and sat there looking up as he unfolded himself. He was only eleven, but like the others, he was already well over two meters tall to her measly hundred-seventy centimeters. He was also two years older, but she knew the curse of being born on Earth of a Grounder mother. Coming up to the underground world of the Moon colony five years ago had not helped, because she knew that she would never catch up in height with other Lunies.

Her father had been a Lunie mining engineer who had married an immigrant Earth metallurgist against both families' protests, and he had died in a tunnel collapse while her mother had been in her seventh month of pregnancy. After her husband's death, Theresa Andrews had gone back to Earth to escape the disapproving Lunie society. But after four years on Earth, she had been forced to return to the Moon because of Serena's mounting medical problems. Theresa's centrifuge preparations on the Moon during her pregnancy had not been enough to prepare her daughter for Earth.

But a return to the Moon had brought its own problems for Serena, and she had found herself an outcast from the beginning. Lunie social skills were intricate, and her defensiveness coupled with a stubborn streak kept getting her into trouble—like now.

She was realizing that she had made a mistake in forcing Billy to apologize. Under his flame-red hair, his green eyes held an icy glitter, and from the way his normally pale skin was flushed—making his freckles even more distinct—she knew she had made a real enemy. But it wasn't the first time. She sometimes forgot that she had an unfair strength advantage over the others because of her mother's genes and her time on Earth. It was ironic. On Earth, she had been picked on because she was an ugly, too tall weakling, and up here she was looked on as a gravity-squashed, Herculean misfit.

But at least Billy was not out for immediate revenge since, along with Judy and Paul, he had disappeared down the roomy corridor towards the tube-car station after throwing her a last glare full of foreboding. But Nancy had stayed behind, and the older girl dropped to the floor and reached out to hug her.

"I'm sorry 'Reena! I didn't know he was going to do that. Honest!" Her soft brown eyes were full of concern.

Serena looked up at her friend, vision blurred with tears. She would have killed to look like Nancy Emerson. Unlike her own short cap of straight, black hair, the other girl had long, gleaming blond hair that was tied up in a graceful spiral that added even more to her height. It was easy to see that the slender twelve year-old was destined for perfection as a Lunie woman.

But Serena wiped her eyes on her sleeve and hugged her friend back. "Thanks. I know you didn't. It's Billy! He knows just how to push my buttons and he keeps doing it! I don't know why I keep reacting like that. I only want to be like everyone else."

"Well, don't worry about it," Nancy reassured her. "He's an immature gasser with more brains than sense. You're not *that* much shorter than other girls your age. But you're Advanced Placement, and in our class you really do look different." She squeezed Serena's arm. "Just wait till you're with others who are finished growing. They won't pick on you then."

Serena tried to smile as she was helped up, but it was forced. Deep down she knew that Nancy was wrong; she would always be 'different'.

Lunar society had become very proud and exclusive, and more than a little intolerant of Grounders and halfers. Luna-1, and later, Luna-2 and Luna-3, had been built in the 21st century as the early Artemis bases had grown into astronomical observatories and research facilities. And as larger facilities combined with longer and longer tours of duties and an increasingly family-oriented environment, a unique society had slowly emerged—a community that had become increasingly independent and contemptuous of a Mother Earth torn by worldwide ethnic and religious tensions that had threatened to tear it apart. By the 22nd century, nearly all of the Luna staff members were proudly independent full-time residents who were increasingly neglecting to use centrifuge time as an integral part of life and refusing the genegeneering and nanomorphing that was homogenizing the rest of humanity. And this combination had resulted in a physical divergence between "Lunies" and "Grounders" that meant that Lunies were both physically and socially trapped on the Moon or in space.

And that forced isolation had also led an increasingly proud and isolationist mind-set—as Serena had discovered on her return. Now she was not even a halfer, just a Grounder with no hope of ever being considered a 'real' Lunie.

But, if she was going to be a freak, she decided, then she was going to make sure she was the best damned freak there had ever been! She would teach them not to laugh at her.

Then, as Serena and Nancy followed the others towards the tube-car, a sudden ear-splitting alarm echoed up and down the wide corridor and she felt Nancy grab her arm in fear. It was the pressure alarm. Somewhere in this sector of Luna-3 there was a seal breach, and the alarm was the signal to head for the nearest shelter. Even if it was only a Level One signal, it still meant that there was a substantial leak.

Nancy's eyes were panicked and Serena was struck by the instant role-reversal as she grabbed her friend.

"Come on!" she urged, pulling Nancy towards Shelter L3-Alpha-2. Down the corridor, she saw Billy, Judy and Paul ducking past hurrying grown-ups to get through the massive pressure door, their faces as full of fear as Nancy's. Other than well-publicized and occasional shelter retreats from severe solar flares, there had not been a real alarm in their lifetimes, and their imaginations were probably over-flowing with the worst-case scenarios taught in the emergency preparedness classes. But to Serena it just came as a welcome break from the dull routine of her life.

Inside the warehouse-like shelter, painted a bright and airy cream color, they threaded their way past casually annoyed adults and frightened children and teens to a position where they could get a clear view of the main Holo-Screen in the back of the shelter. Numerous repeater screens dotted the blank walls that surrounded the four-tiered bunk-beds lined up in rows, but Serena wanted to see the main screen when the Director explained the Alarm. Out in the hall, the signal changed pitch as a further warning.

Five minutes later the heavy door to the corridor swung shut with a solid metallic 'thunk' she could feel as well as hear—only a smaller airlock set into the wall next to the main door allowed access now—and the excited roar of speculative voices in the shelter was silenced by the Announcement Alert. A room-full of expectant eyes turned to the Holo-screens that shimmered to life to show the Director's grim visage staring out at them.

Ashran El-Arun was only sixty-eight, but the young director had been the head of Luna Union for nearly ten years now, and he was famous for his uncharacteristically sunny and cheerful disposition, combined with an iron-willed stubbornness. It had been a useful combination of traits since the Moon colony was not yet fully self-sufficient, and getting supplies and support from an increasingly geocentric Grounder government was becoming more and more difficult. But his blanched face and shocked expression, magnified on the screens, silenced everyone in the shelter.

"My fellow Lunies," he began, the slight shake in his voice prompting a soft wave of worried whispering. "I am sorry to send all sectors of every settlement to their shelters, but there are two reasons for the alarms. The immediate one is a breach in Luna-2's Alpha sector. A landing craft with supplies from Earth went out of control and crashed over L2-Alpha, causing multiple, but minor, seal ruptures. Detection and repair robots are on the scene and the damage should be repaired within an hour. The pressure drop was minimal and corridor seals have limited the leak, but all L2-Alpha personnel and residents are confined to shelter until the All Clear."

He stopped while his news sank in and Serena could smell the sour scent of fear from the grown-ups around her. He had not explained why Luna-1 and Luna-3 sectors had been sent to their shelters. Her class-mates had all been reassured and were already itching to get out of the shelter, all fear forgotten, but looking at El-Arun's face, Serena felt an uncertain twisting in her stomach for the first time. The normally youthful visage sported by everyone under a hundred-and-forty suddenly seemed to catch up to its real age on El-Arun. He wasn't that scared by a minor seal breach in one single sector and the other grown-ups knew it.

"The second reason for the alarm," he went on after a moment, "and the reason all settlers were Alerted, was to get everyone together in a hurry." He paused uncertainly, seeming to consider how to say what he needed to tell them.

"Earth is now under quarantine," he finally explained. "I have sealed off all physical contact because another nanokiller plague is loose down-side. But unlike the Centennial Plague last century, this one has not been contained!" His jaw clenched as if he was trying to keep from vomiting, but after a moment he went on. "We just found out because the initial news-blackout broke down. The shuttle was warned off because it was carrying refugees and we can't risk admitting any. But the shuttle wouldn't break off its landing pattern—"

"Did we shoot it down?" a shaky voice interrupted. It was Karin Sommers, the shelter controller, who sat in front under the main Holo-screen. The short brunette was the only one who had a two-way link with El-Arun's office, and as Serena peered over the shoulders of the others, she saw that Karin looked close to crying. Sommers was a recent immigrant from Earth, and knew better than anyone the dangers of the microscopic killer machines developed and still stock-piled by the few remaining independent countries.

Nanomachines were fascinating microscopic robots built up atom by atom and programmed for a variety of tasks, and most of them were innocuous devices used for various industrial and medical tasks. Some were used for micro-manufacturing or to convert wastes and replenish raw materials by altering the molecular composition of the source material, and others were used to clean out arteries and organs, restore damaged neural links, and to restore muscle and skin tone. Nanomachines were already doubling human life spans, and even if their development had not progressed as rapidly as originally envisioned because of the religiously anti-tech 2100's, they would eventually allow people to rebuild themselves as they saw fit and to live for centuries.

But the reverse spin had been the development of nanokillers. These had been developed by various governments struggling for peace in the late twenty-first century in a world still marred by continuing ethnic, religious and cultural tensions. Nanokillers had been designed to infect, replicate, and rapidly spread in various ways to efficiently kill a maximum number of people without doing any physical damage to enemy holdings. Only one use of the weapons had ever occurred, when doomsayer terrorist had stolen a cache of them and released them on Los Angeles in 2100 to mark the beginning of the new century. Fortunately, while over 50,000 people had died, the stolen nanokillers had been primitive ones that were quickly contained and neutralized.

But after that deadly attack and a subsequent decades-long anti-technology back-lash, controls had been tightened and there had been no further nanokiller releases. Instead, as the world situation slowly stabilized, nanotechnology had again become king to extend life, eliminate disabilities, and reduce ethnic differences. By 2200, only a few stock-piles of nanokillers slated for destruction remained in a world that was finally unifying under one government. But, apparently one strain of the deadly weapons had somehow been released.

Serena shivered as she wondered what was happening on Earth that was already sending refugees fleeing to the Moon.

The Director shook his head as Karin asked if the shuttle had been shot down. "We didn't have to," he explained, after repeating her question for the other shelters to hear. "Someone on the shuttle had been infected, and all onboard were dead by the time they were to go off automatic entry for manual approach."

Serena noticed the implication that someone had been standing by with a way of stopping the shuttle, and that any future refugees would not exactly find a warm reception.

"How many?" Karin asked softly.

"The shuttle was carrying fifty passengers," El-Arun replied. "The remaining bodies and ship debris have been gathered and slagged, and the whole surface area around the crash site irradiated. Detectors are also being set up all around L2-Alpha to be safe." He stopped and cocked his head, listening. After a moment, he shook his head.

"Luna-1 just wondered if we're not over-reacting given that the shuttle landed in a vacuum, but we're not because this is a machine plague—and shelter controllers, please hold further questions until the full Colony Forum I'll call once the leaks are all sealed." He paused a moment, and then went on:

"As I said: we're not over-reacting. Until I get a report from Earth on exactly what type of nanokillers were released, we're not taking any chances. I have some video from New York that should explain the urgency of the situation. Parents: please shield your children," he warned.

The wide Holo-screen shimmered, and then everyone in the shelter was looking in on an enormous convention hall full of exotic-looking single-seater aircraft. Hundreds of people were scattered through the hall, making adjustments to the planes and setting up information booths.

"This is an edited recording from security cameras at the pre-show set-up of the 3rd Annual Brandyce Aviation Show and Sale," a machine voice-over explained. "The exhibitors came to Greater New York after a two day visit in Seattle, and the show featured the latest in small manual and auto-control planes."

The screen focused on a small group of people wheeling out a graceful swallow-like creation of gleaming pearl and peach Plasteel, when suddenly a woman leaning over the cockpit with a computer pad began coughing violently, blood spraying out to stain the pristine curve of the cockpit. All the other exhibitors and technicians dropped what they were doing to see what was happening as her knees buckled and she crumpled to the floor in the graceless heap only a dead body can manage. As if her death had been a signal, a hall-wide paroxysm of coughing exploded and body after body tumbled to the floor. Panicked survivors ran screaming for the doors, many of them crumpling as they too were caught by the hand of death. In minutes, the huge hall was a charnel-house of blood and sprawled bodies.

"Time-lapse will be used to speed up the next several hours," a narrating machine-voice continued blandly while in the shelter, strangers and friends alike drew close to hold each other for comfort against the horror of what they were seeing.

On the screen, the focus of the image changed relentlessly to pull close to the woman who had first collapsed by the now gruesome airship that had been the first to be defiled. Her face was mercifully turned away, but the right hand was in plain view. Other bodies were also visible, but as she had been the first victim, everyone's attentions were focused on her.

Her gleaming blond hair had been a elegant golden cloud around her head, complimenting her turquoise blue pants-suit and maroon scarf, but now it seemed limp and dull. And as the shelter occupants watched, the graceful hand with its immaculate blue nails seemed to shiver and slump.

A gasp from beside her startled Serena and she saw Nancy point and then turn away to run to one of the small shelter bathrooms hand clenched tightly to her mouth. Turning back to the screen, Serena had to grit her own teeth and force herself to keep calm as she saw the lovely suit slump and start to cave in, The head had rolled, robbed of support, and an etched, near-skeletal mockery of a face stared up at the camera. Shocked adults all around her were pulling their children away from the Holo-screen, even while helplessly staring over their shoulders, unable to look away.

Trying to keep from getting sick, Serena sought refuge in a memory: an old monochrome two-D film from the early twentieth century she had seen in an alternate art class. It had involved a vampire, or some such mythical creature, who had crumpled into skeletal form and then into dust when struck by sunlight. What she was seeing on the screen was a vivid three-dimensional, full-color version of the same process. As they watched, the body eroded away into dusty fragments just like that movie character. Around her, as the focus of the camera pulled back, they saw a room-full of nearly empty clothes lying scattered over the floor.

The clinical machine narration concluded with a dispassionate: "Total average elapsed time after death for the nanokillers to evaporate all body fluids and break down the skeletal and other body tissue into component mineral powders: eight hours and forty-two minutes, given an average body frame massing seventy to eighty kilos. Vector of infection is by contact, infection probability is seventy-seven percent and fatality is one hundred percent for any infected subject. Time from infection to death is roughly forty-eight hours due to a programmed time delay, and the first symptomology is explosive hemetemesis followed immediately by severe head-aches and then nearly instant death as the nanokillers enter the brain and disrupt neural functioning. Despite contact infection, programming of nanokillers indicate the lungs as the initial site of replication and focus of infection; possibly due to central body location and easy access to all body systems via blood stream."

"Serena! What are you doing watching this?" A concerned voice intruded and a firm hand reached down to turn her around. It was her aunt Carol. "Does your mother know you're here?"

Serena sighed, trying to see around Carol. "I have my locator on," she explained. "All she has to do is check with Central Data." She managed to extricate herself and get back her view of the screen. "Please, I want to watch."

Carol started to say something, but then gave up and worked her way back over towards her own friends. Serena could almost her muttering: "Suit yourself, Grounder grub", even if it wasn't actually said. Her father's family had never accepted her or her mother.

She turned back to the screen just in time to see the almost innocently clean-looking—even the blood had vanished—exhibition hall disappear, replaced by El-Arun's haggard face.

"The latest casualty figures are already in the hundreds of thousands," he told them quietly. "The death toll is expected to reach millions within days and…" He couldn't finish the obvious. In a mass-transit world, the infection had to be spreading at an incredible rate since no symptoms were visible until the very end.

"Seattle was the point of release," El-Arun went on. "A terrorist group broke into a secured research lab and stole the nanokillers, intending to use them for an extortion scheme on the anniversary of the last Plague, but there was an accident and their getaway transport collided with one of the Brandyce transports on the way to the RamPort. The nanokillers got loose and infected the survivors of the crash. No one knew of the infection at the time, because the terrorists fled with their vehicle, and the laboratory break-in had not been reported yet."

He leaned back in his seat and sighed. "Samples of the killers have been taken and a crash program is underway to either retrieve—or develop—and distribute a counter-killer. But the terrorists scrambled the remaining stock-pile and wiped the computer records, so analysis and counter-measures are taking time…"

As El-Arun spoke, Serena realized what else he was saying. He had actually already said it, but the reality was finally sinking in. "Earth is now under quarantine," he had said. That meant no more supplies of any kind. The Moon was cut off and would have to survive on its own resources…She was on her own. Her mother was hardly ever home as it was, but now that there would be extra pressure to locate more resources, Serena would have to fend for herself even more. School would have to be her home now. But that was fine. She needed to prove herself, anyway. She would show them she was as good a Lunie as anyone else, and that she was needed!

CHAPTER 2

▼

EARTH, 2257

The cavernous auditorium of the Center City Campus of the Philadelphia Area Home High School was packed with the flowing purple fabric of graduation-gowned seniors milling about restlessly, waiting for the ceremonies to start. There was an almost Brownian motion to the chamber full of bodies; a tense reluctance to come too closely in contact with anyone else, born out the current rarity of public student gatherings like this. Schoolwork was now almost exclusively accomplished from home terminals, and even the concerts and assemblies that had once filled the auditorium were now more often than not monitored from home HoloChambers. There was also an almost eerie similarity to all the faces revealed over the gowns and under the angular and anachronistic tasselled caps. Male or female, blond or brunette, short hair or long, all the students had even light brown complexions totally unmarred by any skin problems, and all were attractive.

Several hundred clones could not have been much more alike.

But in the middle of the sea of conformity, a single blond, fair-skinned student towered over the others as he left a wake of scattering caps across the room. Only a single student followed him, like a remora seeking to attach itself to a shark.

"Where the hell are they, Rash?" Jim Martin asked over his shoulder with a frown as he wondered again what had happened. Here he was, graduating a year early with a full scholarship to the East America University of Humanities lined up, and his own parents weren't even here to see it! They had promised that they would leave Switzerland in plenty of time to be here in person.

11

Rashid Achmed hurried to keep up as they headed for the lobby. "Freeze, Jim. They'll be here." He tried fruitlessly to slow his friend down. "You better stop with your exercising! Too much muscle and the girls won't go for you."

Rashid was a little late with his advice, Jim thought as he finally paused to look down on his friend. The eighteen year-old Arab immigrant was as acceptably 'average' as everyone else in the room, but at least he didn't have the superior attitude of the rest of his classmates. He respected Jim's desire to be different, something the younger student had inherited from his equally unique parents, Carla and Matthew Martin. Just like their own parents, they had refused any GeneGeneering on their son to keep him within societal norms, even if they had worried about it making it difficult to meet girls. Fortunately he had met Debra Billingly, a class-mate who seemed to like having a unique boy-friend.

Jim chuckled at his friend's needless warning about potential girl problems. "Well, at least Debra won't have to worry about the competition."

Rashid just shook his head patiently and craned his neck as he tried to see over the rolling waves of tasseled caps he and Jim both wore the honor society's gold braid. But after a moment, he gave up.

"So where is she?"

"She'll be a little late because of her Engineering orientation at SciTech," Jim answered absently as he kept looking for his parents. Not that he was really too worried about missing them. His father was as tall as he was and would be easy to spot.

But Rashid had his own agenda and he was still keeping a lecherous eye out for Debra. "I don't know, Jim. I'll never understand what she sees in you. At least I'm pre-law. But you'll still be debating the 'whichness of why' while she pulls in a top salary with some Nangeneering firm." He laughed. "Unless she's just gone retro with caveman fantasies and likes the stud service?"

Jim's face reddened. "Actually, we're waiting."

A sudden apologetic tap on the shoulder startled him and he turned to look down at Principal Danvers standing there looking even more somber than usual. His fore-head gleamed with nervous sweat as he took Jim's arm.

"I'm sorry to pull you away from your graduation, but the police are here—"

"My parents?" A sick feeling came over him as he suddenly spotted a waiting officer by the side door and seized on the only reason which might have kept his parents from being on time. "Has anything happened to them?" It was a rhetorical question, because Danvers' quivering mustache and clenched teeth confirmed Jim's worst fears.

"Where are they?" His graduation was forgotten.

Danvers continued nervously studying Jim's chest, unwilling to meet his eyes. "The officer will drive you to the airport where a flight will take you to Geneva. I'll accept your diploma for you and hold it until you can pick it up."

Rashid's hand clamped on his forearm. "Keep it together, brother. Call me later."

His face was full of sympathy and Jim squeezed his hand gratefully. "Thanks, I will."

Rashid *was* like a brother, and he was glad he would have someone to talk to later. The two of them had been sharing a small two bedroom apartment for the last year because his own parents were spending more and more time in Geneva since his mother's re-election as East America's representative to the World Council. His father's job was on the WorldNet and he happily followed his wife wherever she went. And as for Rashid's widower father, Ben had been transferred to Alaska and had not wanted to pull his son out of yet another school so close to graduation, so he had gladly worked with Jim's parents to cover their sons' living expenses in an apartment.

In a daze, Jim followed the officer out and climbed into the small white patrol unit parked outside, trying not to notice the aura of vomit, urine and fear that permeated the dirty-grey plastic interior of the cramped vehicle. He wondered numbly who was going to fill his mother's post in Geneva. She had been—he cringed as he realized he was already thinking of her in the past tense—one of the few Progressive Representatives in the World Council, and her loss would be a severe blow to the few visionary people left in government.

Maybe it was time to consider changing majors in school?

After all, political science—an oxymoron if he had ever heard of one—wasn't that far removed from philosophy. Both involved a lot of hair-splitting and bull. Night after night of listening to his mother talking about her frustrated efforts to move a conservative government forward had left their impression, and he hated the idea of seeing all her work go to waste. There were only six or seven other World Representatives who had the energy and foresight necessary to plan constructively. Everyone else was still hiding their metaphorical heads up their asses after the Machine Plague. Preserving stability and the status quo was all they cared about now that the Clean-Up was history and the world was united in peace.

But Representative DiBella of Upper America was one of those visionaries, and a good friend of the family, and Jim had a feeling Mario might be able to smooth the way for a transfer. And maybe even find some work for him in one of the local government offices? He needed to start laying the groundwork early if he was going to work himself up to be a World Representative.

▼

CHAPTER 3

StarStep, 2178 – 2300

For billions of years nothing had disturbed the small K2 class star of Epsilon Eridani or its three tiny planets. Until now. An intruder had entered the system. Awakened by increased radiation, it jettisoned its gossamer-looking solar sail and divided into four discrete sections whose individual thrusters slowed and separated them to head off in different directions to seek out larger asteroids. On each segment, solar collectors spread their wings and began collecting energy for preprogrammed tasks...

Once energy had been gathered and raw material was on hand, a new force was roused in each probe: microscopic machines activated by the influx of power. Certain strains were released to feed on the asteroidal matter, absorbing it as the molecule-sized robots reproduced and changed. Spreading over and through the asteroids and vessels, they began a complex transformation as new instructions from each segment's computer came into play.

As the changes progressed, each evolving craft set off on a predetermined course and then settled into position at one of four equidistant points from the sun. Flooded with energy now, the transformations progressed more rapidly and each of the segments took on an ominous appearance, elongating and seeming to take aim.

Over eighteen months had passed since the intruder had first entered the system, and almost to the day, blinding bursts of energy shot out from four points around the sun and converged on their distant target.

It would take almost eleven years for the redundant signals to reach Earth, but time meant nothing to the nanomachines. Now they waited for a signal from a closer source. Something had been following the first vessel.

*   *   *   *

It came.

The second, and much higher-speed, shipment from Earth signalled its entry into the alien system, and the waiting laser quad around the sun reached out with luminous arms to slow the huge oncoming solar sailer. The newcomer shed its sail at the programmed moment and onboard reaction systems guided the ship towards the small planet within the star's ecosphere and eased the pregnant-looking ship into orbit around the barren world.

Pregnant was a actually good description because as the large vessel, the first of several, established its equatorial orbit, it disgorged a seemingly endless succession of small probes that dropped towards the surface as the planet rotated beneath it.

On the small planet, a mechanical infection had come to ground, and aided by the cargo from succeeding ships, it spread like a plague across the airless and rocky waste, absorbing power from the sun for energy. It was an organism unrelated to living things, but which nevertheless grew and consumed matter around it in much the same manner as an organic counterpart, explosively reproducing and reaching out across the world. And as the artificial micro-organisms spread, portions of them underwent programmed changes and, in addition to reproducing their own new components, they began converting the planet's rocky surface into finer particles of different elements.

*   *   *   *

As years passed and more seeding ships discharged their cargoes, large areas of the small world were being layered with rich, as yet sterile, soil. Meanwhile, other regions of the planet were invaded by strains of nanomachines that transformed dead rock into gases of carefully set proportions. As a side benefit, the planet was gradually being sculpted and large depressions formed. The atmosphere thus formed was still rarer than the tenuous envelope that shielded Mars, but it was slowly getting denser.

Among the mix of gases released were carefully tailored chlorofluorocarbons and other gases designed to be highly absorptive in the warming infra-red and also resistant to the molecule-destroying ultra-violet radiation. These gases would help boost the temperature and shield the surface of the planet.

The particular strains of synthetic organisms responsible for atmospheric build-up would have to remain in isolated portions of the world, even after organics were added, because the world's gravity was too low to hold a sufficiently dense atmosphere to support the coming life-forms. But the programming of the nanomachines was precise. When sufficient air density was reached, the breakdown and conversion of all but specified areas of that strain would be triggered. The remaining air-makers would go into dormancy until scattered mountain-top sensors indicated a triggering drop in pressure or atmospheric compositional change.

*   *   *   *

After more years had passed, the nanomachines covered the planet and reached deep within it. New strains were developing continuously as further planned and programmed 'mutations' occurred. And in the meantime, more ships had come into orbit to add their cargoes to the mechanical infection below in order to speed the task of converting the world. Different probes were dropped on the surface and organic molecules were worked into the soil now blanketing much of the world. In other areas, oxygen and hydrogen, along with other elements, were combined in the depressions that had been sculpted into the planet. The atmosphere was still too rare to allow water to remain liquid for long, but the evaporating fluids were carried aloft, distributed through the environment and infused into the dusty soil that softened the harsh contours of the land. Some of the water-producing nanomachines would also have to stay active since some moisture would be lost along with air because of the lesser gravity.

*   *   *   *

More time passed.

The hordes of nanomachines responsible for soil formation were now being broken down to become part of that blanket. Except for a few thrusting mountains, the bare and tortured rock surface was gone now, softened by embracing soil. Still sterile, but rich and waiting.

It was time for the next step.

Far above, in recently arrived and carefully designed chambers on board orbiting modules, various organic soups had been brewing. Now, specific strains were launched to crash on the planet below. Loaded containers continually dropped from the sky and from each, a new infection spread. Genetically altered microbes were worked into the barren wastes, preparing the sterile soil for the next stage of the planned invasion.

Meanwhile, the atmosphere had been growing denser, and water had started resisting vaporization. A slight haze blurred the distance as moist air surrounded the world; moisture that started to fall to ground. All over, low-lying regions and depressions which had been growing moist, then wet, filled slowly with water as the first tentative rains fell to ground.

*   *   *   *

Years later, one large ocean and a number of small seas had formed on the planet to break up the one large continent that had been designed. The lighter gravity and a small moon gave tremendous shifting life to the large masses of strange new fluid, speeding the spread of life throughout it; life from frozen specimens brought along. They were specimens genetically altered to breed rapidly for a number of generations before reverting to normal as gene clusters broke up under differentiation. Microscopic life, too, swarmed in the waters and across the landscape. And vegetation was appearing in numerous scattered areas of the world as seeding was guided by carefully planned programs that controlled an army of utility machines assembled from the planet's matter. Strange-looking vegetation, also tailored to spread explosively, was freed by the low gravity to grow into sizes and in directions that would have been impossible on Earth. But they were healthy and strong plants and added to the atmosphere that would soon be dense enough to support more advanced life.

Another planned stage having been reached, a new signal went out over the laser link aiming for an Earth of 10.8 years later: "Stage four finished. Estimated completion time, seventy Earth years." It had only been seventy-five years since the first nanomachines had fallen to the ground.

*   *   *   *

Decades later, a glittering belt of newly arrived vessels hung in orbit, each preparing its cargo. These ships carried the last of the animal specimens, genetically altered as had been the early marine life forms, to breed quickly and spread until certain encoded limits were reached. A carefully selected blend of animals had already been distributed, but now it was time for the rest to be thawed.

On one of these ships, a computer system hesitated. Some time before, a micro-meteorite had punctured it on one side and slightly damaged a subsystem responsible for preserving representatives of one of the animal species being prepared for introduction to StarStep. For a short time, the temperature had climbed until the automated maintenance systems had noticed and made repairs. But a minute amount of damage had occurred. The computer calculated the amount of harm and then made its decision. The damage did not seem to be significant, and it only involved one subset of one specific breed of predators.

Now it was time for that system to initiate the final thawing and revival sequence of its charges. This particular ship carried cubs and adults that had been carefully bred from North American mountain lion ancestors and then reared in batches on a huge O'Neal cylinder spun to one third Earth normal gravity. They were carefully awakened and sedated before being loaded onto specially designed transports and sent to the surface. Each target area got three males and a dozen females. The mountain lions wouldn't be the only predators introduced, of course, but they had been the favorites of the designers. Special care had been lavished on their genetic coding to assure their rapid spread and survival.

For safety's sake, the animals from the damaged section of the freezer ship were loaded onto a shuttle designated for a coastal region in the northern hemisphere, near where the first colony city would be built. This way, any damage could be monitored once the humans arrived.

PART I

StarStep

CHAPTER 1

▼

SABOTAGE: EARTH, 2291

World Representative Jim Martin stared out the wide, tinted bay-windows of the rented SkyFlitter at the almost surreal visual drama of the Swiss Alps that were on parade outside. It was like watching a Holofilm, with blinding late afternoon sunlight reflecting off the jagged and snow-covered peaks that were etched against a brilliant blue sky. Leaning back in the plushly padded lounge chair at the back of the main cabin, he propped his legs up on the low coffee table to relax and enjoy the view. The panorama outside was awe-inspiring to a city boy like him. The inside of the SkyFlitter's cabin was a stark contrast of shadow-framed shapes, faux-wood paneling, plush carpet, and harsh highlights reflecting off the gleaming mirror and crystal of the port-side—alcohol-free—bar cabinet. But nothing could distract from the natural marvels outside, not even the almost over-powering scent of newness that still permeated the small plane.

"Hey, when will you be back at the hotel?" Tracy asked again.

Out of the corner of his eye he saw his office-manager's pretty, angular face looking out at him critically from the large view screen on the wall between the cabin and the cockpit. Since the screen adjusted automatically to ambient light, he could easily see that her normally soft, grey eyes were disapproving.

He shrugged. "I don't know. Sometime this evening. Leave me alone. It's too pretty out here."

He popped the tab on the Orange Cooler he had brought with him from the bar and took a sip. The cold of the container in his hand seemed to spread to his whole body, and as he studied the spectacular mountains, he imagined that he could smell the thin, bracing mountain air around him: crisp, cold…and for some reason laced with the spicing of leather. He wondered idly where that impression came from, until he remembered seeing an old Dimensionized 20th century movie with guides in short leather pants.

"Jim, I know it's beautiful." Tracy sighed patiently and tried again. "Tom and I went there for vacation last year, remember? But this really isn't the time. Concentrate: the hotel? When will you be back there? We've got a load of work to take care of. If you're going to challenge President Saunders on Thursday, you've got to be ready. She's not your biggest fan, you know!"

"I know, I know." He faced her reluctantly. "But it's Sunday, and I haven't had a day off in almost three weeks, and I need this. I just want to see how this plane handles on manual in the mountains—"

"You couldn't try one out in the Rockies? That would have been a lot closer..." Then her eyes opened wide. "The Alps! That's where your parents died, isn't it? I'm sorry."

"That's okay. It's stupid. I've been avoiding going up like this for over thirty years because of what happened to them. But I decided that it's time I put this little phobia to rest."

Tracy still looked a little confused. "But why now?"

"Just a dream I had." He frowned. "All the preparations I've been making for the next council session revolved around dead or near-dead people..."

There were four million frozen bodies lying in high-tech warehouses scattered across the world, a legacy of the Machine Plague and a panicked rush to escape it by any means possible. Only a small percentage of these bodies could be revived because of improper freezing or other problems, but nobody wanted to face the fact that it was time to deal with this last fallout of the Plague.

It was his newest crusade, taken on a few years earlier to keep his mind off Debra's death.

Their relationship had survived her rapid advancement after engineering school, despite Rash's dire predictions, and engagement and marriage had come while still in college. And after graduation their respective careers had blossomed without hurting their marriage in the least.

For Jim, Mario DiBella had not only been there to smooth his way for transferring into PoliSci, but he had stayed behind the scenes as a motivating mentor, pushing and opening doors so that Jim had moved from campaign aide to candidate, first in local and then in regional elections, and finally into the national spotlight. And meanwhile, Debra had been snapped up by an international conglomerate planning to build a giant space station combining research centers and resort facilities. It had meant a commuter marriage since her time had been divided between South America, East America and later, orbit, but they had kept apartments in several different places and had managed to spend more time together than either had expected.

Then the crash had destroyed everything.

They had just celebrated their thirtieth wedding anniversary—an abbreviated one because Debra was in the middle of a big orbital habitat module revision and Jim had committed to speaking to the World Council—and the SSTO flight Debra had taken to return to the station had exploded at an altitude of one mile.

That had been the start of a whirlwind of political activism designed to keep his mind from dwelling on his loss. He had gradually come to terms with his loss, but his frenetic political life had become routine by then—and it had been burning him out. Until he had decided to take a short break and go flying on the anniversary of his parents' death. Another loss he had needed to confront fully.

Looking at Tracy's relaxing face, he saw that she understood why facing one past had led to confronting another, and why he had needed a break.

"Tell you what," he squinted to check the duplicate locator map under the phone screen, "I just have to get a little further from the air-corridor before Geneva Traffic will let me go off computer control. Let me give the plane a work-out, and then I'll call you."

Tracy shook her head. "All right, I guess this can wait a few hours."

He pried himself out of the lounger and headed for the controls, seeing her image on the smaller screen just beyond the open cockpit door smiling patiently, just like her expression on the cabin screen.

"Thanks, Tracy!" He waved. "I promise I'll call you as soon as I get back to the hotel. It's about 1700 here, what time is it in New York?"

But the plane suddenly shivered and the viewscreen pictures blurred. Tracy's images leaned forward and frowned. "What did you say? Jim…are you there?"

Then the screens flickered and went black as the plane lurched and dropped in a stomach-kicking plunge. Fighting a flood of panic, he grabbed for the cockpit doorway just as he saw sparks fly off the control-board and flames licked out from underneath. Dense and acrid smoke billowed back towards him making his eyes tear and burning his throat. He felt the ear-popping sound of the crash-foam system kicking in as he started coughing helplessly, clinging to the door frame. Through the front window he saw the side of a mountain loom as the plane corkscrewed towards it.

He threw himself back towards the safer main cabin as a white sea of bubbles flooded it. But the crash-foam was already solidifying and restraining him, and he hung halfway between the cockpit and the main cabin as the plane hit the side of the mountain in a numbing crash. The metallic creaking of tortured metal was joined by his own screams as the plane was crushed and the door frame closed on his thighs. The pain quickly grew too much to bear…

*   *   *   *

Dawn: StarStep, 2300

Light…tiny, darting touches of invisible paws…a constant, wavering sound that pushed him awake…and fresh and unfamiliar smells! With a sneeze he opened his eyes to find himself lying on thin grass under a slender tree. More trees than he had ever seen filled the area around him; trees, and rocks, and bushes everywhere! And the ground itself was different. It went up and down in strange ways, and spread out in the dis-

tance in a dizzying way he had trouble focusing on. He was lying on a slope that extended down further than he had ever gone, and then up again, growing fuzzy and hard to see.

As he rose to all fours and shook his head to clear it of a strange heaviness, he saw his mates and the others scattered around him, still heavily asleep. A soft touch prodded him again and he spun. Twisting back and forth, he tried to see who was nudging him, but there was no one there…The air! He finally realized it was the air that was moving, and each invisible caress brought a new and fascinating scent.

Movement caught his eye, accompanied by a resumption of the momentarily interrupted chirping he had heard before. He looked down to see a small shape that was moving away from him in small jumps, pausing to make a strange sound in some way he couldn't see. He hunched down trying to look closer, but each time he moved, it hopped further away. He reached out a paw lightly and almost managed to touch it, but suddenly it sprang away in an incredible leap that took it out of sight.

Frustrated by the disappearing insect, he straightened and smelled the air again, intrigued by the multitude of unfamiliar scents. He smelled his mates and the other cats, the grass and other growing things, and unknown living things…Food!

A rumbling in his belly unleashed the pent-up hunger of the long sleep and he raised his head to pin down the scent of game the unfamiliar moving air had brought him. There! In the direction of the bright light. His walking was a little unsteady, as if his body was taking longer to wake up than his mind, but soon he fell into an easy loping stride that floated over the rocks and bushes. For the first time in his life, he felt an unfamiliar sense of freedom. All his life, there had been boundaries to all sides and above that had kept him from stretching and running, and that limited space had been full of others like him, but now nothing stopped him from rushing ahead like a cub and enjoying virtual solitude and all the room he could want.

His hunger faded, transformed into a joyous sense of discovery as he stretched muscles in a way he had never been able to do. He ran. Up and down strange hills, through running streams and bounding over obstacles in a wild, manic dash of ecstacy. He was only vaguely aware of whipping branches that slapped him as he dashed between them, or of the strange fact that the bright light ahead of him was moving, rising higher and seeming to get brighter.

But finally he had to slow as his muscles starting aching in a way he had never felt before and his lungs burned. He dropped to the ground to stretch out and lay gasping for breath, strangely relishing the near agony of his exhausted body. His fine, downy fur was matted and dirty and he had scratches and cuts he had not even felt until now, but he was happy as he curled up to lick himself clean. He was happy. That was a strange…feeling. He had never thought about being 'happy' or 'unhappy'—had just lived—but suddenly he looked around his incredible new home and he felt a strange dizziness and swelling inside that somehow felt good! He was happy.

And he was hungry again.

As his breathing returned to normal and his body's pain subsided into a subtler ache, his hunger returned with greater force. Raising his head, he sniffed the moving air again and turned as it brought him *a musky scent of game. It was different—more pungent—than he had ever smelled before, but it was food! Rising only partially, he crawled forward, almost touching the ground as he made his way through tall grasses to move in on the grazing animal down the slope, near a small stream. The air was moving towards him, so his quarry was unaware of his stalking approach.*

It was a larger than any animal he had ever seen, but his hunger had taken on a life of its own and it was goading him to attack. The strange growths on the animal's head puzzled him momentarily, but he ignored them. His tail whipped silently from side to side as his rear end shifted slowly, and then he dug his rear claws in to launch himself down the slope. The force of his rush knocked the animal down and his claws dug into the flesh of the shoulder as he tried to clamp his fangs around the pulsing life of the throat under him. But to his shock, his victim was not cooperating.

Showing unbelievable strength, the animal under him threw him off, rose to its feet, and then lowered its head to charge him! The horns on the narrow head reached for him and ripped into his shoulder with enough force to throw him off his feet as he tried to spin out of the way with an angry yowl. Hissing angrily in pain, he backed away and hunched down in confusion as the large, horned animal pawed at the ground momentarily with a heavy and breathy whuff. It wasn't frightened at all, and shaking its armed head in warning, it backed off, and then spun away to bound off in the distance.

He stared after it in confusion, his raging belly screaming its outrage over the missed meal, but pain and the dripping blood from his side and shoulder distracted him for the moment and he settled down to lick his wounds carefully. But as he groomed himself, tasting dirt and strange plant juices, the unfamiliar experience of missing a kill kept bothering him and his earlier hunger returned, sharpened by the teasing taste of his own blood.

Then a small animal bounding up the slope of the hill caught his eye and he took off after it, propelled by anger and an unfamiliar sick feeling as he thought about the way his hunt had been demolished by unexpected resistance. A small part of his mind, only now coming to life, noted that in the past such an event would have been forgotten almost as soon as it happened. But now, the memory of those horns was burned into his mind and he knew that next time he would use a different strategy. Thinking like this felt odd, and he pushed it aside to throw himself instead into a hunt he knew would feed him.

The small jumper had just caught scent of him, and an acrid smell of fear wafted towards him as it broke into a panicked, hopping run towards some heavier bushes ahead. He dug his claws in and speeded up in a smooth lunge forward that brought him close enough to clamp his jaws over the small furry body. A twist of his head brought a loud crack and a muffled squeak and the refreshing taste of warm blood flowing in his mouth.

Settling over the body, a loud rumbling rolled out from his throat as he tore the small body to shreds and ate every scrap of meat. Strangely enough, instead of easing his hunger, the fresh meat only served to tease it to higher levels. He left the remains lying scattered on the warm soil, and raised his head to test the air again. He needed more. He was hungry!

CHAPTER 2

▼

CHANGE OF PLANS: EARTH, 2291

"Representative Martin?"

The words were muffled and he ignored them. He was nice and comfortable in bed. His head was supported just right by his pillow and he didn't feel like waking up, so he just twisted and burrowed deeper to block the bright golden light assaulting his eye lids.

"Representative Martin?"

The voice was more insistent this time, and with a grumble he surrendered and opened his eyes to face a concerned stranger who was stupidly asking:

"Are you awake?"

"I am now, chill it." He rubbed his eyes. "Who are you? And what are you doing in my bedroom?"

The concerned-looking intruder was a neatly dressed man in a conservative blue suit, short black hair carefully parted to the left, and he was sporting a thin, waxed mustache. He looked to be in his thirties; which meant nothing since anyone could pretty much look any age they wanted.

Suddenly the memory of the crash came flooding back as his drug-induced sleep evaporated, and he smelled the unmistakable scent of antiseptic cleaners as his eyes finally focused on the pale yellow walls around him—hospital-yellow. Emotionless paintings that looked machine-made hung on the spotless surfaces, and to his right, a floor-to-ceiling window looked out on a cloudless sky that was so blue that it looked painted. Bare winter branches of some trees outside were just peeking up near the bottom of the window to cast intriguing, long shadows from the setting, or rising, sun that was flooding the room with a bright, warm glow.

But the collapsed metal side-rails on either side of him emphasized the confining medical sterility of the room itself and he realized he was lying in a hospital bed. Which meant that the stranger was probably a doctor. Suddenly wide awake, he remembered the crushing pain of the compressing door frame, and fighting a rush of panic he sat up to look down the length of his body. But the white blanket held familiar twin ridges leading to twin peaks at the foot of the bed, and he lay back with a relieved sigh as the doctor intruded again.

"Representative Martin, I hate to be a bug, but I do need to talk to you."

"What's wrong? I feel fine. And I must be." He reached down to slap his right leg gratefully—and froze. He hit his right leg again, and then the left leg, but he felt nothing except velvet-like cloth against the palm of his hand. Sitting up, he threw back the covers only to see normal-looking legs sticking out from under his ridiculous hospital gown. They even had the proper shagginess he had always been teased about as a kid, but they weren't his legs.

Where was the jagged scar on his left leg from the car crash when he had been fifty and had tried antique formula race-car driving as a hobby? He had refused to have the scar removed because he was proud of it. He had won the race. The crash had been just past the finish-line when the second-place car had gone out of control. If the doctors had re-grown his own legs after the flitter crash, or transplanted a pair, why couldn't he feel them? These were fakes!

"What the chill is going on?" he demanded.

The doctor looked distressed and pulled up a straight-backed chair from the corner. Sitting down next to the bed, he faced Jim stiffly.

"That's why we need to talk, sir. As you guessed, you lost both legs in that accident. I'm Doctor Ruhr, and I've been handling your case since you were brought here. Geneva Traffic picked up the unauthorized release of auto-pilot and the subsequent crash and dispatched a rescue—"

"I didn't turn off the auto-pilot," Jim corrected him. "There was a fire and a malfunction of some sort." He frowned, remembering the message he had received a few days earlier. "Or maybe something else."

"What do you mean 'something else'?"

"Never mind. Is this Geneva Medical?"

"Of course." Ruhr almost looked offended. "As a World Representative you wouldn't be brought anywhere but to the best in the region."

"So why the chill did you stick on artificial…" Jim stopped himself as he saw the other man flinch. "Don't mind me. I'm not at my best right now."

"Very understandable. This has to be unsettling to a young man like yourself…you're what, fifty-one?" Jim nodded. "As I thought: very young. But that means that you've never needed more than Stage One nanorooters. They're enough to keep your body healthy and youthful." Ruhr studied Jim with vague disapproval.

Jim sighed as he faced Ruhr's typical reaction. With his towering heighth and body-build it was something he had been forced to get used to, and ignoring the doctor's silent disapproval, he raised the head of the bed to make eye contact.

"All right, why did you use artificial legs?" he asked, suspecting he wasn't going to like the answer. "And what was that about the nanorooters?"

Looking a little nervous, Ruhr shifted in his seat.

"As it happens, one discovery led to the other. We didn't have anything transplantable in your size, and to regenerate your own legs we need to use a combination of special drugs and Stage Three rooters...but when we tried, well, your body rejected the test-rooters." He looked expectantly nervous.

"I'm allergic?" Jim stared at Ruhr.

"Sort of. Allergic isn't quite right, but you are sensitive to the more advanced rooters. But you can rest assured that the artificial legs we gave you are the latest state of the art," he hastened to add. "We'll even be able to give you some feeling in them now that you're awake and we can properly tune them—"

"But I'll never get my own legs back?"

Ruhr shook his head. "I'm sorry, but no. Not unless they come up with a new strain of nanorooters that your body will tolerate."

"Not likely," Jim observed with a caustic tone. "If I remember my tech-briefings, I'm part of a real minority which isn't too lucrative for research." He lay back and closed his eyes for a moment. The shock of losing his legs was starting to fade as he thought about what might have happened...What was probably supposed to have happened! But he had survived. His parents had died in the crash he had always subconsciously feared a repeat of, but he had not. He was alive!

But then he suddenly felt ill as it dawned on him what else his 'allergy' meant.

He raised the head of the bed to ask Ruhr: "How long will I live? Realistically!"

The doctor turned pale. "Well, you'll have to speak to a qualified medical nanotechnologist—"

"Suck space! You're not some intern or resident, so give me a good guess. You've got enough experience."

"Well..." Ruhr swallowed. "I wouldn't warranty you much beyond a hundred-and-twenty or so." The words tumbled out in a rush. "Stage One and Two nanorooters will keep you in good shape that long, but then you'll fall apart pretty quickly. The brain effects will probably be the worst since both Stage Three and Four rooters are needed for more extensive brain repair and maintenance."

He looked ready to bolt for the door, but Jim ignored him, leaning back to mutter: "Thanks for being straight with me." He breathed in and out regularly for a moment with his eyes closed, trying to settle himself.

Only live another seventy or so years?

What about all his long range plans? Just dealing with the problem of the Frozen would take decades by the time all the predictable court challenges were settled. And he had wanted to push for a revival of the space program. But he had thought that he would be around for at least another century-and-a-half…But what now? His hands clenched at his side, gathering the thin white blanket tightly as he thought about this threat to all his plans.

Then he thought about the advanced nanorooters that had been developed in the past century, continually pushing back everyones' life-expectancy. It might very well happen again. He opened his eyes and relaxed. There wasn't anything he could do about it, now. He faced Ruhr with a determined nod.

"Well, I'm not going to worry about what nanorooters can't do now. Who knows what'll happen in the future." He cocked his head. "The immediate problem is with my legs. You did say you could give me feeling in them?" He kept telling himself to ignore the sick twisting in his gut.

Ruhr smiled, obviously relieved. "Quite good, using interfaced pressure sensors. We can also tie into your nerve-bundles and give you temperature sensitivity. They'll be almost as good as—"

"So then, what's there to worry about? I'm alive!" Jim suddenly felt a little giddy and grinned at Ruhr like a kid as he thought about certain would-be assassins trying to explain their failure.

Ruhr looked confused. "I have to say, you're taking this very well."

"Would it change anything if I screamed or cried about it?"

"No, it—"

"Exactly. So why worry? Now, the legs: how strong are they?" Jim slapped his thighs.

"Stronger than flesh and blood," Ruhr answered proudly. "They're made of the latest soft-composite materials, warmed to body temperature by an internal power pack, and weighted to equal your own legs so you shouldn't need much practice to get used to them. The only weak point is the flesh-leg interface. We took off the rest of your thighs, hooked the new legs into the hip joint like your old femurs, and then knit your own flesh and muscles together with Stage Two rooters, Syntha-Flesh, and leg actuators."

He leaned over and raised the edge of the gown to show Jim where natural flesh met synthetic with an indistinct boundary line.

"The connection should hold very well," he went on, "since the femurs are hooked in. But the most vulnerable point will always be the flesh/Syntha-Flesh interface. Proper maintenance is critical, but we'll teach you all about that during the rehab period. We froze you for a couple of days while we connected everything and used Stage One and Two rooters to speed your heal—"

"A couple of days?" Jim leaned forward anxiously. "I've been out of it for a couple of days?"

"Well, you did loose both legs." Ruhr looked a bit indignant.

"Too bad! What day is it?"

"It's late Tuesday afternoon."

"Damn! I've got to get out of here." Jim started to get up but Ruhr's sharp command froze him.

"Stop! You may be a World Council representative, but you're my patient, and you don't move out of this bed or this room until I say so." His expression didn't leave room for argument, and a surprisingly strong push forced Jim back down.

Jim held up his hands in surrender, his mind churning. "Okay, okay. But can I use the phone for a moment? I have to call my office manager."

"Sure. As long as you stay here. We have—"

"—to be sure nothing happens to me while I'm your responsibility," Jim finished. "I know. That's what's wrong with the whole world nowadays. Everybody's too chillin' afraid to take any risks now that they live longer."

He frowned and reached for the control pad on the phone and touched it, calling out the coded number to Tracy's private office line; since the now clearly-setting sun told him that it was morning in New York.

Within seconds, her face coalesced on the screen and she leaned forward anxiously. "Jim! They told me everything. Are you—"

"Save it. I'm fine, but I've got to get out of here!"

After a suspicious moment of doubt, she nodded briskly. "You're right. We're chin deep and sinking. All your ads have run and we've logged gigs of responses. Almost all you hoped for. But you have to present it all to the next World Council session, and that's the day after tomorrow!"

"I'll grab a RamJet in the morning and be back in New York before you go to bed." He heard a not-so-subtle throat clearing behind him and ignored it. "Trust me," he reassured Tracy. He disconnected as she tried to say something else and turned back to the doctor.

"Look, Ruhr. What will it take to get me out of this place by tomorrow morning? I'll sign a waiver of responsibility. Run whatever tests you want, now. As for fine-tuning my legs, if it can be done between now and then, fine. But I have a vital bill to propose to the World Council on Thursday, and if I have to do it with numb legs and a little stumbling: no problem. It'll only get me a sympathy edge…Hey, that's not a bad idea, you know." He turned back to the phone and hit redial, ignoring Ruhr's open mouth and raised hand.

"Now what?" Tracy was icy as she saw him.

"I'm sorry I was rude, Trace, but I'm a little distracted right now. I just had an idea. Put out a press release detailing my accident as gorily as possible, and the tragic fact that I will be forced to live with artificial legs as my body can't tolerate regeneration. Make sure it gets to the world networks. And add that it *will not*, emphasize that, prevent me from making an important proposal to the World Council; given the short time I have left to live." He grinned. "Play it up. You know the program."

He noticed Tracy chewing her lower lip nervously. "What is it?" he asked. "You were going to say something else when I cut you off. Did Tom lose his job again? I'll give you a raise if you'll work some overtime for me."

"I'm not going to work more than four days a week in any job," she shot back. "No, Tom's okay."

"So, what?" Jim pressed. "You're stalling."

"Well…I found another memory crystal outside the office the day after the accident. Just like the last one."

"What was on this one?"

"Another plain text message. This one read: 'We warned you not to push it. Next time it might be worse. Sorry about the legs, it was only supposed to be a warning this time. Besides, they'll grow you new ones.' There was no voice or video, so there's no way of tracing it."

"Analysis?" Jim prompted.

"Material or content?"

"Both."

"Material: untraceable. It was a generic memory crystal saved on a public access terminal at New-Mex SpacePort. Millions are made each year and they're sold everywhere. As for content: it's about your proposal to the World Council, probably."

"No 'probable' about it. Crytron Industries is getting bolder, and nastier. I had a feeling it wasn't an accident." He growled to himself, and then sighed reluctantly. "But I just know it was too well-done to prove it, never mind linking Crytron with it. They can afford the best operatives."

"Jim, why don't you back out?" She leaned forward anxiously. "Is it worth it?"

"Chillin' right it is! Look, don't worry. I'm going to make so much noise that the council will have to listen. Now, get on that release. And please stress that bit about my not backing out!" He cut the phone off and felt himself smiling. He loved a good challenge.

Ruhr had been standing there trying to look disinterested, but failing miserably. Jim laughed.

"Relax. It's a little game I'm playing with Crytron Industries."

"Crytron…aren't they the ones who maintain the Frozen?"

"Uh huh. Four million bodies that have been lying there, ignored since the Machine Plague." Jim frowned. "And ten percent of them are in my block and bleeding us financially."

Ruhr was staring at him. "Four million?"

Jim nodded. "And all maintained by one company. An exclusive World Government contract for Crytron Industries." His had gripped the side-rail tightly. "Crytron's been after me for some time now because I'm pushing for revival of those who can be thawed, and termination of the rest—now that we can tell the difference with a new test."

Ruhr right eyebrow climbed in a silent question.

"We estimate that there are only about forty thousand viable ones left," Jim answered. "And I am so tired of seeing them lie there forgotten or ignored, and costing us hordes of tax revenue we could use in other ways. That's why I want to get the council moving to wake them up. Before more deteriorate."

He leaned towards the doctor. "Do you see why I've got to get out of here? I had scheduled for a few days off, but not this long." He smiled. "Besides, if you don't let me go, Tracy will get to work. You don't know her. She's a terror." He grinned fondly. "She'll lock up your memory to get me out. So call up whatever records you need me to certify so you can set me free. I promise I'll be back to go through your rehab, or whatever, and get my legs tuned—on Friday."

Ruhr studied his face and sighed after a minute. "I think I understand. And you promise to come back?"

"I promise." He locked eyes with the doctor. "And I don't make promises lightly."

Ruhr studied him a moment, and then nodded. "Yes, I believe that. Very well. But first...you'll have to let me to do a thorough exam. Then if there's no medical reason to keep you—and if you sign a waiver—you're free." He held out his hand. Fair enough?"

"Fair enough." Jim smiled and met the extended hand with a firm grip.

Ruhr went over to the bedside terminal to touch the control pad and then spoke rapidly in verbal shorthand Jim didn't recognize before turning back to Jim.

"There, all done. Now let's do that exam."

*   *   *   *

New Outlook: StarStep, 2301

The cubs took their first shaky steps away from their mother the morning after their birth. Due to their accelerated metabolism, they were the fourth generation to be born in their new home, but they seemed very ordinary outwardly, even if their low gravity bodies seemed unusually slender and they had developed more rapidly than their progenitors. But their spotted bodies still had the same endearing roly-poly clutziness of any baby cat and their fur stood on end in a haphazard way from their mother's ministrations. But the eyes: they were different. They were focused and alert in an almost unnerving way. The three cubs—the fourth had died and been removed from the cave—ventured further and further away from the warmth and security of their resting but watchful mother who was stretched out in the back of the small cave in the hillside.

The opening was wide, and the bright morning sun cast a sharply demarcated pool of brilliance that reached deep into the dark cave. The oldest cub, by minutes, took her first step into the light, and sneezed in surprise with an explosive blast that rocked the tiny body and tripped her to fall flat on her nose. Struggling to get up, her face quested for the source of the unexpected but delicious warmth now bathing her, so like the warmth of her mother. But the light was too bright, and she shook her head as the glare hurt her eyes and blinded her momentarily.

But exciting smells and touches of breeze were teasing her, along with mysterious sounds that she had trouble focusing on, so she moved slowly forward. Then, a push came from behind and she was shoved ahead as her litter-mates joined her, rolling in delight as the sun warmed them. She ignored them as they wrestled in a ball of spitting, cub growls and she looked out over the hillside. Her eyes were adjusting to the light now and she moved out into the open to see tall, slender shapes that reached up to momentarily block the sun, shifting from side to side to send interesting pools of shadow chasing over the ground.

The shapes moved, and the dark moved…One of her litter-mates had followed her, and he sprang after the playful dark that rushed by in front of them, but she ignored it and just lay still in the sun, looking back and forth from shadow to shape, shape to shadow…thinking.

Reason was coming to StarStep with frightening speed…

CHAPTER 3

▼

CHALLENGE: EARTH, 2291

Two days after his discharge from Geneva Medical, Jim settled back in his office chair, trying his best to keep calm. The magnificent holographic illusion surrounding him only aggravated his frustrated anger because he knew it was not real. If it had been, at least he would have been able to reach out and choke some of the other representatives as he really wanted to.

But he couldn't. It only seemed as if he was sitting in the huge Geneva Assembly chamber, surrounded by towering slate walls covered with alternating panels of stone and rich, warm mahogany. The crowning illusion was of the vast boomerang-shaped ebony conference table behind which all three hundred of Earth's elected representatives appeared to sit, all while actually sitting in small private offices like his own. The Mag-Lev table that faced a large Holo-screen seemed to be immaculately intact with its scattered subsurface color LCD displays and old-fashioned touch-pad keyboards—for privacy—and it appeared to float majestically over a burgundy carpet.

Even the acoustic feeling of the real Geneva Hall was simulated. His carefully subdued cough was swallowed as effectively as if he had been sitting in the actual world government meeting chamber, not that it was ever used any more. Since IllusiTech had perfected 3-D holo-transmission, no one bothered making the actual trip to Switzerland. Jim was no exception. Like most of the other World Council representatives, he had just had a contractor upgrade his own office Holo-Chamber in order to attend the weekly full Council meetings.

In one way he felt funny about it, since he had been within a few kilometers of the real chamber a couple days before, but he actually felt more comfortable back in his own office. Except for right now. Now he wished for the good old days when it would have been real! He had been a professional politician for decades now, finally reaching the rank his late mother had held, after working his way up from local and national elected posts. It had taken him a few losses here and there to fine-tune his expectations and learn how to play the game, but bit by bit he was getting more successful at pursuing his goals of moving the government towards a more enlightened attitude.

But now he had hit a Plasteel wall again, and he glared at the images of the other representatives who had just been sitting around and wasting time, oblivious of his growing irritation. The voice of whoever had the floor was automatically amplified and distinct...and distinctly boring!

He shifted in his seat, trying to ignore the way everyone who did look at him wore disapproving frowns. An echo of Ruhr's reaction at the hospital, and that of most people. Except that here, they felt freer about expressing their feelings since he was fighting the consensus of opinion.

Even the few other remaining free spirits around weren't on his side anymore. Apparently Crytron had pressured, or bribed, Jim's supporters to withdraw their support of his plan. A lot more expensive and problematic than their original and failed strategy, but it had been much more effective. The crowning touch had been the devastating rejection from one particular individualist he had been hoping to sway: Mara Saunders.

World President Saunders had just turned the rest of the full assembly against him and effectively slapped down his proposal to revive the Frozen. It had been as if all his E-mail support and technical data didn't exist. And without the backing of the other key representatives he had had lined up, mere facts and mail had been useless.

This was getting to be a real annoying habit of hers.

Saunders had been a constant source of irritation to him ever since she had been re-elected as president. She seemed to delight in stopping his every attempt to bring about change and progress. Especially this time.

"The frozen sleepers and frozen dead are not going anywhere," she had said, rising regally to stand at the elbow of the illusionary table. Saunders always took full advantage of her appearance to control a room. She was also distinct. A tall, beautiful woman, she was well over a hundred years old, but—naturally—only looked to be in her thirties. She had on a stylish body-hugging silver suit-dress with vertical black stripes and wore her shimmering red hair elaborately twisted and pinned up to add to her height, and when she gazed down at somebody, she looked *down* on them. Everyone knew it. Even if she did cheat a little bit with a built-up platform to stand on.

In her second and next-to-last three-year term as president, her position was well-consolidated and she was merciless when she had the upper hand.

Just like today. The most she had been willing to do was approve the formation of a Frost Fund, which would help by disbursing additional capital to voting blocks based on the number of Frozen that were housed in each one. Then, moving deftly she had shut him out and defused all his remaining arguments and guided the Assembly into a discussion of global weather control changes.

Obviously that was more important than the disposition of four million frozen human beings!

Jim debated just disconnecting, but that would be a breach of etiquette he couldn't afford, so he gritted his teeth and waited for the session to end.

"Today's meeting is adjourned," Saunders finally declared as she stood up to dismiss the farcical gathering.

Jim's tensed muscles relaxed and he reached out to cut the holo-link. But the illusionary chamber remained around him even as its occupants vanished rapidly, one by one. After a moment, only Mara Saunders remained, sitting at the elbow of the table until, with a few soft words to her terminal, they were suddenly sitting next to each other in a small, plainly furnished room, their table sections seamlessly merging.

Satisfied that they were 'alone', she reached back to release her long hair, shaking out the tight spirals that had contained it with a relieved sigh.

"Space, that feels better." Then she swiveled her chair to face him, stretching her arms out gracefully in front of her as she sat back, seductive in her relaxed pose. "These long sessions are killing me!" Green eyes speared him as she studied him intently for a moment and then leaned forward.

"So, what was really rooting you, Jim?"

She wanted something, and he answered cautiously:

"Like I said to everyone, we've got to face the problem with the Coolers and take care of the Frozen—"

"Don't give me that crap," she dismissed. "You've been pushing that before, but never like today. You almost got me," she admitted with a conceding smile. "Fortunately the rest of your support seems to have evaporated. But again: what gives?"

"You're right." He sat back a little surprised. "I hadn't thought about it, but I guess I do feel a lot more strongly about the issue all a once. You heard about my *accident*?"

"I was briefed." She was oblivious to his stress on the word. "But I don't see what that has to do with this. It was a freak thing. I'm sorry, of course. You lost both legs, and I understand that there wasn't time for regeneration."

"For one thing, it wasn't an accident." He watched her, but her surprise seemed genuine. Before she could say anything, he went on: "And for another, I'm not going for regeneration."

"Why not?" Once again, she seemed surprised.

"My body can't tolerate it," he explained, repeating what Ruhr had told him.

Mara's eyes widened. "I'm sorry. Now I understand." She made a safe guess. "You've had a whiff of your own mortality and you're getting tired of wasting time."

Jim nodded. "Partly. When you suddenly realize you're only going to live half the life you expected, I guess that sort of shorts things out."

Mara shrugged. "I *am* sorry. But consider that a couple of centuries ago you would have been lucky to make it to a hundred, and by the time you got there you would have been a doddering wreck. Even at fifty you would have been starting to slow down, but look at yourself! You've still got a lot of years left."

As he listened to her, he was suddenly reminded of his earlier suspicions.

"Sympathies accepted, but you're not hanging around just to cheer me up, so stop trying to win my favor and tell me what's on your mind." His change of directions caught her off guard, but only for a fraction of a second. Almost immediately, she was all business again.

"You're right. I do have a reason for this little visit." She leaned forward. "A challenge to you. We have a problem you may not be aware of but that you might be able to help me with." Her voice dropped to a whisper. "It has a solution, but it involves an expensive project that I can't afford—"

"—politically—"

"—to support." She nodded. "Exactly. As World Government President I'm kept up to date, at least in brief, on most major research projects."

Jim leaned forward expectantly as Mara began, a distant look in her eyes.

"This particular project is called StarStep. It was originally implemented almost two hundred years ago after the L.A. Plague of 2100. The Plague scared everyone and resulted in formalizing a dream project which had been kicking around in the scientific community for years: a project to convert a dead planet to a viable colony world." She ignored Jim's excited gasp. "It took decades to implement the StarStep project, and the first conversion package wasn't launched until 2148, but since 2178, the third planet of Epsilon Eridani has been getting a retrofit to build a new Earth."

Mara's face was animated in a way he had never seen before as she went on. "All the governments pooled their assets in the same way the fledgling World Government later pulled together all world resources for the Clean-up—because they were afraid. The only reason the anti-nanotech forces didn't kill StarStep was because it was being done in space, and involved building an escape hatch for humanity in case there was ever another Plague."

"Like the Machine Plague!"

"Exactly. But by the time the Machine Plague happened, StarStep wasn't finished and it wound up forgotten in the panic." She uttered a few more subvocal commands and a monitor screen appeared in front of her that showed a stylized diagram of the inner solar system.

"But StarStep is incredible!" she went on. "It was an immense undertaking, planned in stages and based in isolation on the Moon and in specially designed orbital habitats where the life-forms were designed and bred." On the screen, several rotating cylinders appeared at L-5 points around the Earth. "Stage One involved constructing a bank of powerful laser satellites that were used to launch the large solar sail seed ships." The screen changed to show four small shapes floating at equidistant points from the sun, sending out concentrated beams of light to push away odd-shaped crafts.

"Epsilon Eridani was picked as the target system," Mara continued. "It's 10.8 light-years away, and about eighty percent the size of our sun. Fortunately, in addition to two tiny moon-sized planets which are too close to the sun, there is another planet at the just the right distance to be usable."

Responding to her command, the display changed to focus on a small star and three orbital traces, one of which was highlighted.

"StarStep, as the planet was dubbed after the project, is a little small," Mara admitted. "But it's big enough to have a decent gravity. About like Mars. And it has a small moon." She smiled. "I've been thinking about this since you tried to force me to re-open an interstellar exploration program last year."

Jim studied the display in fascination. "How was the first craft braked?"

Mara shrugged, annoyed by his interruption. "I don't know. Something to do with the ionized gas between stars. That and reaction braking since fuel could be sent along and not have to be used until actual deceleration was started. The first ship took longer to get there, but it held a nanomachine package designed to construct a duplicate laser quad to act as a braking system for later craft. And eventually, the lasers will be used to launch ships back to Earth."

On the screen, the diagram reflected the stages she was describing. "After giving the first package time to do its job, a long series of automated vessels were sent out, loaded with more nanopackages and genetically altered biological specimens. We sent out bacteria, plant life, a full marine eco-system, and then land animals all developed, bred and raised on low-G O'Neal cylinders in order to form a complete ecology on the continent formed. The launchers here have been operating continuously for decades, sending out ships to be caught by the receiving bank at StarStep."

"How long does it take to get there?" Jim asked.

"About eighteen years now that the receiving quad is in place and ships can be sent out at higher speed. The first shipment took roughly thirty years to get there, but by now StarStep is close to being a viable colony world. The conversion has been underway for over a century, and it'll take several more decades before it's ready for us, but things are going well. We get regular status reports, all positive so far."

She smiled casually as she saw his stunned look. "Kind of neat, isn't it? The original idea was that, if nanotechnology could be used to clean up a polluted world here, why couldn't it be used to build us a new world entirely? Elsewhere. The planners would have preferred a larger planet, but they didn't want to be too far away."

He stared at her, breathless as he considered what she was saying. And here he had been thinking that he would have to do something to get a space program going again? He felt like shouting and jumping for joy.

She held up a cautioning hand. "Before you get too impressed, remember that this was started almost two centuries ago when world leaders were in a panic. They were able to cash in on world fear about another plague, and the hopes about having a refuge." She sighed. "But I'm afraid that recently, we haven't been as supportive of the project as StarSteppers would like."

He felt as if someone had just dumped a bucket of ice water on him and he cautiously asked: "What's the status now?"

Mara's eyes were fixed on the floating hologram. "It's still underway, of course. The planet is pretty close to self-sustaining by this point and the remaining seed-shipments are mostly underway by now. Fortunately most of the funding was allocated right up front and so the project has been doing fine until recently. In fact, since everything was set up in the beginning, and the focus of everyone has been on the Machine Plague and the reconstruction, most people not directly involved have forgotten all about StarStep."

Jim took a guess. "And recently, nobody involved has wanted to call too much attention to themselves because they don't want to lose whatever funding they still have?"

Mara smiled. "Very good. They've basically kept going on their own. But now their resources are running out and the project is in danger of failing on this end. The way things are, we'll never get out to StarStep to use it. You aren't entirely wrong in seeing us as overly conservative, and this is one area where I think that it's a dangerous attitude. We *need* another home-base for humanity. Just in case."

"Enter an annoying and aggravating rebel like myself," Jim said slowly, starting to understand why she was trying to get his help. "Someone who might just be able to launch an otherwise grounded group of Representatives and get them to move on it." She nodded as he smiled cynically. But after a moment, he asked: "And what about the problem of the Coolers?"

"Drop it." Her face was hard.

"Drop it?" He stood up and glared down at her incredibly life-like image, his jaw clenching. "I've got voters depending on me to try to get things moving—"

"I said drop it." A hint of steel crept into her voice as she cut him off. "This isn't the time for that particular problem. Make a nice show a little longer if you want, but drop it. It won't be hard after I get you a nice extra appropriation for your region. And the other Reps really don't want to face it anyway."

"But I can get to them if you give me a chance."

"True, but I won't." Her face was a rigid mask. "I can't. And even if I did," she sighed. "I don't think you'll be able to convince them." She pointed to his seat. "Sit! You said it yourself. First of all, we have to accommodate the awakened freepers." He flinched at the slang term for frozen sleepers; almost as bad as 'fred' for frozen dead. "Now think about that a bit. Assuming one percent of the Frozen can be revived, that's forty-thousand traumatized anachronisms. That's the problem, you see. We've changed more than just technologically in the last ninety years since the Machine-Plague. The freepers won't fit in! And what's worse, they'll corrupt what we have. Our newly enlightened society is too fresh, too fragile to take it yet."

She leaned towards him, as if to reach out and touch him, and then leaned back quickly. "Chill! It's so blasted real since they eliminated the phase-flicker!" Looking embarrassed, she settled back in her seat. "You're only fifty-one and you were born after the Plague, so you only have carefully presented history to judge the past by. I, and a lot of the rest of the Council, remember it because we lived in it. I was just a little girl, but I still remember…"

She briefly seemed to age fifty years as a tormented look passed across her face. Then she snapped out of it with a brisk toss of her head. "I'm sorry. I'm sure you can make a stirring speech to try to move them, and you may, for a moment, succeed. But then it will be forgotten. It would bring back too much horror. Most people are happy with the Frozen just where they are. And even for those who aren't, it's still better than the thought of investigating and reviving those who are viable—and finding out just who survived, and who didn't."

Jim saw what she was getting at. "In other words: we let them rot until they're all forgotten about and it'll be easier to pull the plug on them. After all, cryogenic suspension may preserve the body perfectly well, but if they weren't suspended properly or if too much time passes, their minds will be gone and they're no longer worth reviving."

Mara nodded sadly, chewing on her lower lip. "I'm sorry, I hadn't wanted to put it that bluntly, but it might be the only way. They won't fit." She shrugged and looked at him with pleading sincerity. "Please try to understand. It's really for the best, and my hands are tied."

He suddenly leaned back and laughed.

Mara glared at him. "What's wrong with you?"

"I just realized what's going on here," he answered, feeling stupid for missing the obvious. "I just spotted the change in tactics. The stick's not working, so here's the carrot, followed by the emotional appeal. A bit sexist of them, trying the damsel-in-distress routine. Though it might have worked if I didn't know you better."

"What do you mean, 'they'?"

"You've heard of Crytron Industries?" he asked sarcastically.

Her face was expressionless again.

He studied her carefully as he said: "They're behind my accident, you know."

Part of a lush lip disappeared beneath a line of perfect white teeth and her eyes widened slightly. She shook her head after a moment.

"No. Honestly, that I didn't know."

For some reason, he actually believed her. "All right. I'll accept that. After all, it would have been stupid to involve you. But I'll bet Crytron has some strong voting influence, and that they were pushing you to find some way to distract me."

Mara was quiet for a moment, and then nodded. "True. I owe them. They got me elected president." She looked briefly embarrassed. "I was a nobody junior Representative in West America, but I had broad-based support and some bright ideas on how to boost the economy, many of which were advantageous to Crytron. So, they sorted behind the screens to provide funding and publicity leading up to the next presidential election, and suddenly I was a 'name', and the only logical choice. I won by a landslide. Their landslide!"

"Do they—"

"—expect favors in return?" She shook her head. "Until now, no. They just want me to protect their interests. As long as I preserve the status quo—"

"—a stable economy, a healthy business environment, and so on," he cut in. "All of which has been good for everyone anyway."

"Exactly. I never felt too bad about it because what they want is what the world needs anyway. And in return, they put their influence to work when it's necessary to push through any votes I may be having trouble with. It's been a mutually satisfying partnership, and good for the world."

He had to admit she was right, even if he was uncomfortable with it. "So what else would happen to you if I managed to push through my plan with the Frozen, considering how much of a nuisance I can be? I'm not going to just drop this," he warned. "And you just gave me one hell of a weapon!" He didn't have to tell her he had been recording their entire meeting. She would have expected it.

After a moment she answered: "I sure wouldn't win the next election, and we're only a year away from the end of my term." Her eyes were pleading. "But I have to keep control right now. There are a number of crucial pieces of legislation being formulated right now that are necessary to keep the world economy going properly. We're setting up new world-wide standards to try to stabilize things since nanotechnology made the old precious metals standards obsolete. The haphazard radioactive metals standards we've been using for the past century are awkward—"

"—and you need me to back off so you can get re-elected and keep pushing for a firm standard?"

She nodded. "Jim, you have to, please!" She started to reach for him again and then stopped herself, eyes suddenly hard as she saw his expression.

He had seen right away how beautifully she was continuing to play him and it must have shown, because just as if she had switched software, she was immediately cool and controlled again.

Straightening, she folded her hands in front of herself briskly. "Okay, deal time. You help me and I'll help you. Later, and in the tail end of my last term when I don't have to worry about re-election. I'm well off financially and I'll survive even if I get impeached. And if we do manage to push through your plan, then we can gradually differentiate the frozen and begin reviving the freepers, re-educate them and integrate them into society. Eventually," she warned.

Her hands were flat on the table as she sat up straight. "Right now it's not an option, and you had better accept that. There is no way you can push these representatives for both StarStep *and* your revival program." Her tone left no room for further negotiations, and she leaned back expectantly.

He considered her deal carefully. He still didn't trust her, but with that embarrassing admissions of hers on record, he felt pretty sure he had a good chance of holding her to her promise. Which made it something to consider.

Not a cancellation, but just a postponement. The freepers really wouldn't suffer for sleeping on a few years more and the freds were dead anyway, so why worry? His eyes focused loosely on the tantalizing diagram of the distant solar system that floated just out of reach.

"So this would be my new project in the meantime? Get StarStep moving?" He felt himself wavering. "It'll be very expensive."

"Horribly!" She grinned. She knew she had him hooked. "You'll have to fight like never before. And I'm going to make it harder. First you've got to get their budget down. Way down! The projected cost to complete StarStep in its present form is way beyond what even you would ever be able to push through."

He nodded, picturing it. But he was also starting to savor the challenge as he asked: "And you can't help me out?"

"Not openly," Mara answered. "You're on your own. I can't afford to visibly be supporting something as 'expensive' as this. Crytron won't fight you on it, because it'll mean more business for them in freezing all the colonists who will be needed. Indirectly they'll probably even help you. But it would be political suicide for me to openly push this kind of project."

She rose confidently. "Look, Jim. You think about it. I've instructed my terminal to accept your calls, just let me know when you want to discuss it further. Or, if you just want to talk..." She didn't finish the sentence, but an unspoken invitation was clear as she eyed him speculatively.

An additional incentive? he wondered cynically.

"If you need more details," she went on, seeing he wasn't ready to take that particular bait. "Call Ken Miller or Serena Andrews at Luna-3. Both of the good doctors have been instructed to give you full access to their data, and I think you'll like working with them. You have a lot in common. Their codes are on your terminal, too." She uttered a quick command and the illusionary hall collapsed around him, leaving him sitting alone in his office, where slate and faux-wood paneled walls echoed the Geneva hall. Alone...to consider her challenge and her invitation.

∗   ∗   ∗   ∗

Precocious Paws: StarStep, 2310

Several years and dozens of accelerated generations later, the cougars now residing in one particular, large valley would have been quite a surprise to their genetic designers. The other cougars that had been introduced to StarStep had been scattered in groups which had already spread out and reverted to normal more solitary feline hunting patterns, as expected. But to facilitate future monitoring, the members of the 'thaw-damaged' group had been deposited near the site where the colonists would eventually settle, and they had wound up forming a closer-knit society.

On waking in their new home, a number of them had 'remembered' their formative space habitat environment where they had been bred and raised—even if only dimly—and they had continued the conditioned and artificial cooperative social structure imposed on them before their freezing. Those somewhat more intelligent cougars had naturally been better hunters, and became leaders—and primary breeders.

The mutation, aided by a combination of inbreeding and natural selection, had resulted in a sharp increase in the overall intelligence level of all the cougars in the valley.

Including three cubs who were frantically wrestling under eerie, elongated trees that reached high into the air. They were wrapped up in a growling, furry ball that rolled back and forth. From time to time, sounds that were more than growls but less than words came flying out of the mix. One part of the mass suddenly bounced free and stood spitting at the other two. They ignored him and just wrestled harder now that they were able to get a better grip on each other. Tufts of fine white, brown, and black fur drifted out to hang suspended before reluctantly drifting to ground.

The lone cub watched the other two, strangely quiet and still. The downy fur that covered its body was losing its baby spots and changing into a creamy adult coat of sandy brown, shading to light cream on its flanks and tail, the colors complementing the brilliantly white hair on its muzzle and belly. He was an unusual-looking cat. Not quite a cub, but not yet an adult, his paws looked almost deformed with their long and flexible toes. And even though baby-fat still softened the contours of his slender body slightly, he had etched muscles that were clearly visible despite being adapted for StarStep's low gravity.

There was also an awareness in his eyes that spoke of much more than an animal's mind at work.

Question-Asker noticed the scrap of some game animal that had started the fight lying ignored under a nearby tree. With a wide yawn, he ambled over to it and sat down to chew, ignoring his litter-mates who had moved further downhill in their tussle. The small scrap was largely fat and skin, but a little bit of meat also remained. Trying to get a better grip, he grabbed it with his paws to hold it in place. A loud contented rumbling rolled out from under his throat as the problem of getting to the food was solved. Soon the little bit of meat was all gone and he settled back to meticulously lick each toe clean. Claws slid out and were re-sheathed, one by one, and the toes were wiggled experimentally.

He looked at them and wondered.

The combatants finally broke apart and, panting loudly, came ambling over to sniff at the cleaned-off piece of fatty skin.

A growling feline equivalent of an annoyed: "You ate!" came from the smaller one. There was no doubt what her name would be when she was older because her perpetually folded right ear was almost a guarantee that she would keep her cub-name of Bent Ear. Her slightly larger brother was just sniffing dejectedly and turning the piece of skin over and over, trying to find any trace of remaining meat. He was always looking for food and if he wasn't careful he might have a hard time changing from his cub-name of Big Belly.

Question Asker didn't move, but just kept admiring his paws again as he strained his minimal vocabulary to explain that since the two of them had been fighting and the food had been there, he had eaten. If they wanted more, they could go find it.

But neither of the others was really hungry, so they promptly forgot the matter and settled down to repair the damage from the fight. They were soon occupied grooming each other and ignored their brother.

But Question Asker was remembering the sense of control he had felt when holding the food. It was a new idea to grasp something 'just so' and having it stay where he wanted it. He looked around for something else to hold. He spied a nearby chunk of rock that had broken loose from the hillside and picked it up experimentally. He held it awkwardly, the cold, rough weight a strange burden. Lying down and holding it didn't seem very practical, so he let go and stood up on his rear legs. All the tribe did that sometimes, to reach and to see better in the distance. He bent down again and picked up the rock, almost falling over from the weight of it. He held it in front of himself and wondered what to do with it. It was useless, he decided.

Then he lost his grip on it and growled in pain as it landed on his left hind paw. The weight of the large chunk had been surprising. He stared down at his bruised paw for a moment, and then bent to pick up the rock again. This time threw it down at the ground, carefully away from his paw. He felt, as well as heard it thud into the moist soil. Then he trotted over to move it to the side, studying the packed indentation in the ground thoughtfully. It had damaged the ground.

What if that had been a small jumper or a runner?

But the rock was so heavy.

Maybe a smaller rock? One not so hard to carry and throw?

He looked around until he found another, smaller rock. He stood up and then bent to pick it up. The unfamiliar movements felt strange. For a while, he stood there just holding the rock, feeling its hardness and solid weight. It wouldn't break like a claw or bleed like he would, if scratched or bitten. With it, he could reach another warrior or prey without being close. The radical idea thrilled him and he felt his heart racing.

He looked around for something to throw the rock at, and then threw it clumsily at a boulder uphill. It struck with a loud crack and his litter-mates spun with a hiss, startled by the sudden sound.

He ignored them and went up to where the rock had hit. The boulder had a small chip missing where the rock had struck. He tried to scratch the boulder with his claw, but it left no mark. He pressed and scraped till his paw hurt, but the boulder was undamaged.

Yet, it had been chipped by the rock he had thrown.

His head was swimming. Soon it would be time for his singling testing when it would be decided whether he would be warrior singling and maybe mated, or if he would stay a youngling until the next season's challenge. He would be unable to fight for a mate or hunt for the tribe for another season in that case. To become a warrior, one had to win over the other singlings. One had to survive.

With a rock to throw, it would be easy to win.

He dropped to all fours again and yawned with satisfaction as he went to join the others. Now he knew what name he would pick when he defeated the other younglings and was named a warrior: Rock Thrower.

His litter-mates settled next to him as the clouds cleared overhead and a shaft of sun speared through the trees overhead to warm the small clearing where they sat. Their warm bodies nestled in around him and his throat rumbled contentedly. The purr was picked up by the other two and rolled through the meadow as he closed his eyes. In his mind, he stood tall, holding a rock in each paw to strike down other younglings as he stepped onto the field of challenge. The gathered tribe members resting on the grass circling the field were staring in wide-eyed amazement.

Then he was knocked forward onto his muzzle when Bent Ear's leg straightened as she chased something in her sleep. Big Belly just shifted without waking to make room for him so Question Asker—no, Rock Thrower—surrendered to the warm soothing rays of the sun and curled up to join the other two in sleep, resting his head on Bent Ear's neck.

CHAPTER 4

▼

NEW ACQUAINTANCES: MOON, 2291

Walking shakily, Jim tried to get used the Moon's lower gravity. He had no problem now with his new legs and after his final tune-up he even had fairly good feeling in them, but the one-sixth gravity was screwing up his coordination as he followed his escort across the cavernous main dome of Luna-1, heading for the tube-car terminal.

Over them, the high domed ceiling shone with a blue light, almost like a clear summer sky, and on the surrounding balconies he saw people moving about, partially shielded by fantastic, twisted and spreading branches of alien-looking growths which had once been standard fruit-trees and berry-bushes. The air was fresh, if a bit thin for his tastes, and filled with the subtle chirping of unseen insects. Overhead, flitting birds looped effortlessly in fantastic aerial exhibitions that teased him from every angle.

It was almost like a stroll through a park back on Earth, Jim thought to himself as he walked beside Ken Miller's imposing horizontal bulk. The physicist Mara had put him in touch with was a sight to behold. The contrast between the pale, slender, and towering Lunies and the dark-skinned, shorter, and portly Miller was startling, and very comforting.

Mara had been right: Miller was a man after his own heart. The physicist had a deep brown, almost black, complexion which was set off by snow-white hair and beard, and he looked older. He was also unmistakably, undeniably, fat. A noble and obviously carefully nurtured belly preceded

Miller wherever he went, straining his delightfully flamboyant shirt. The colorful, loose garment was black, with bands of patterns in vivid yellows, reds, greens and blues. And coming out from under the shirt, were a pair of plain black pants over simple thong sandals on bare feet. Jim seemed to recall seeing similar outfits in documentary films on ancient Africa. All in all, Miller's appearance proudly screamed: 'look at me, if you dare'. His unabashed uniqueness was especially refreshing after the reactions of Ruhr and the last Council session.

But Jim couldn't help wondering about his weight, and it must have been obvious because Miller laughed in a deep rumbling voice.

"Yes, I could have this trimmed quite easily," he patted his belly fondly, "but we've been through a lot together. It's been carefully nurtured through a hundred and thirteen years of life and frankly, I'd feel lost without it. It helps make me noticeable in today's homogenized society." He cocked an eyebrow up at Jim. "But then, I imagine you know what I am talking about." He eyed Jim's muscled bulk respectfully as they entered Transport-Annex.

Looking at each other, both of them burst out laughing at the same moment, the loud sound echoing in the tighter space of the passage that led to the loading platform for the Observatory-bound car. The towering Lunies around them pointedly ignored it. Miller clapped Jim soundly on the shoulder.

"You're all right, for a Grounder." Then he sobered. "But let me caution you a bit about Dr. Andrews." He extended a supporting hand as Jim stumbled in the doorway of the tube-car that would take them to StarStep Control.

"Serena is a Lunie," Miller began as they took their seats, "even though she was born on Earth, before the Plague."

"Earth stock?"

Ken nodded, and explained about Serena's mixed blood, her return to the Moon, her rough childhood, and then went on to warn him: "She's been through a lot in her century of life—she turned a hundred-and-one last week—and she's now a respected, and accepted Lunie. But she had to fight for that, believe me! This is a closed society. Don't expect to understand just what that means, but let's just say she can be a bit cool towards Grounders like us. It took me a good while to really make friends with her."

Jim shrugged. "From what I saw in her bio, I can put up with some frost."

He shook his head as he remembered reading about her entering and graduating the Lunar Academy of Science years ahead of any other students, and then embarking on her pioneering work in artificial intelligence right out of school. Her computer work had also been integral to StarStep almost from the day of her graduation, and she had risen to become co-director of the project at age thirty-six. Just the type of person who would be invaluable. Along with Ken, who was tops in his field and had written more papers on interstellar exploration than some scientists had even read.

Ken was smiling. "Well, once you get past her chill, you'll find she's a hell of a lady!"

For a moment they rode in silence, and Ken just sat silently staring out the window at the passing tunnel wall, lost in thought until he absently pulled out a small package from a deep pocket of his jacket and opened it like an old-fashioned pack of cigarettes. In it, Jim saw a double row of brown, rough sticks that looked like they were covered by bark.

Seeing Jim's expression, he held out the box. "Here: have one," he dared. "They're a nut, honey, and grain snack I have sent up from ground-side to feed my sweet tooth."

Jim took one hesitantly, and seeing Miller grin in challenge, bit down on it, and then looked over in surprise as he chewed. They were delicious.

Ken nodded approval. "Told you they were good. And you get points for trying it." He pulled out another one and wrapped it in a tissue before slipping it into Jim's shirt pocket. Then he stuck one in the corner of his mouth and put the box away.

"My one vice," he explained. "I've been up here for seventy years now, since I took over from the former director, in 2219." He patted his belly. "Best place for us, even if I use the centrifuge on a regular basis." He turned serious.

"But to return to Serena and the Lunies. You should have seen the reception I got when I first got here!" He gave a mock shudder. "She was head of programming at the time. A young lady, not even thirty, and she was running her department with an iron hand. She was…a little defensive, shall we say? Always out to prove she was as good as the next Lunie. The thought of a Grounder taking over the project almost drove her to quit!"

"How did you make friends?"

"I cooked her some good old Louisiana Bouillabaisse, and whipped her butt at chess. Four games in a row!" He laughed. "Showed her that sometimes experience can give an edge over pure brains. Then a few years later, I asked for her to be promoted to co-director. That clinched it." He took Jim's arm, still smiling.

"A word of advice: if she tries to freeze you out, challenge her to a game. I happen to know you're not exactly a dilettante."

"Thanks for the tip!" Jim tried to imagine the flamboyant physicist hunched over a chess screen and shook his head. Live and learn.

"No problem." Ken leaned back. "Serena can be a bit intimidating to newcomers. But she's brilliant. A little idealistic at times, but sharp. She virtually built and programmed Star by herself."

"Star?"

"Our Brain." Miller looked proud. "Excuse me…Serena's Brain. The finest in nanocomputer technology. The complexity of a human brain, but with the speed and storage of the most powerful optical neural network systems. The blasted thing thinks it's a person, and I wouldn't be surprised if one day he will be. But please!" He rolled his eyes. "Don't tell either one of them that I said that. I don't want to loose the patriarchal image, you know. But Star is good," he admitted. "He designed and programmed the NanoMods for all the later shipments. With Serena's help, of course."

"I can't wait to meet them. And to have them hear my news."

Miller was suddenly wary. "Yes, what does bring you out here in person?"

"Later, Dr. Miller."

"Ken, please. No one up here uses my full name. Sounds too stuffy."

"Thanks, but I'd rather wait till after I meet Dr. Andrews and Star."

Ken stared at him a little suspiciously, and then shrugged and leaned back in his seat as the tube-car continued its humming rush towards StarStep Control. Jim met his speculative looks with a bland smile, while fending off the almost palpable, silent disapproval of the three Lunies with them in the nearly empty car. Between Ken's belly and his own musculature, he felt as if he and the physicist were freaks on display.

*   *   *   *

Warrior: StarStep, 2311

Many lights later, Rock Thrower stood over the still body of his last challenger and threw his head back to roar triumph to the bright afternoon sun. It shed a warm golden glow over the downy fur of the watching warriors, and he felt warmed by its rays even though a chill wind blew across the grassy plain in front of him. For a moment, he forgot the taste of blood in his mouth.

He was Rock Thrower. Warrior.

He stood upright on the field of challenge with the other warriors who had won their battles and he tried to calm himself. He had done it: he had won his place as a warrior. Under the pads of his paws, he felt the bloodied dirt which was gradually replacing trampled grass as each season's challenges grew more violent and more formal. But the field was a natural stage for the battles.

Backing it, cliff walls rose dramatically, split by a canyon that dead-ended not far back, and in front of it, grass spread out to either side to hold the gathered warriors. Behind them, on the far side of the sea of waving grasses, tall slender trees rose in an ever-thickening forest, beyond which the land rose sharply up to the bare ridges of the mountains that surrounded the large valley where the tribe lived.

A tribe that now saw him in a totally different light.

He was now an adult. It was a harsh, but necessary tradition that dictated that younglings could not be warriors until they had proven themselves in battle. Until then, they were not allowed to hunt big game or mate with mature females, and they had to live on small animals and the scraps left over after the warriors had eaten. However, because of that tradition, as more and more would-be-warriors tried to prove themselves in battle, the challenges on the field grew fiercer. This was all necessary because there was not enough large game for all. The warriors had to compete with bad-smelling and howling hunters with long noses and shaggy tails that wagged when playing.

Rock Thrower had decided this was wrong.

Many had died this day, trying to win the right to hunt and mate. But why should not more be able to be warriors? Could there not be another way?

Strange ideas spun in his head as he sat back down. He forced them back and looked out at the other survivors—the other new warriors—and he felt better. He alone stood almost unmarked. Only one warrior had gotten past his rocks and reached close enough for normal combat. He had ducked and escaped the rocks and attacked before Rock Thrower could get another piece to throw. But the attacking warrior had already fought two other matches, and he had been tired and bleeding while Rock Thrower was fresh and unmarked. It had been no contest, and his challenger had soon gone down to lie bleeding on the field...

But the other warrior was unable to accept failure, and he suddenly rose off the dirt in a desperate flurry of claws and teeth that almost forced Rock Thrower to fight to kill, not just to win. Rock Thrower finally slashed the other's leg-tendons in a last desperate attempt to keep from having to kill him.

Too late he realized that he had been too efficient, and now the tribe roared for Rock Thrower to give the wounded warrior honor as the other struggled to raise his head and offer his throat. He was too badly hurt to heal, Rock Thrower realized with regret, and he growled.

"Your name, warrior?" He sank to all fours and leaned close to hear the harsh whisper.

"Stream Fisher."

"Then, Stream Fisher, Warrior, die with honor." Rock Thrower bared his fangs and with a savage twist of his powerful neck, ripped out Stream Fisher's throat, tasting the warm blood flood his mouth with its richness. But there was bad taste to it, somehow. He was not sure why...

Rock Thrower looked out over the other winners again. The surviving losers had long since limped off the field to lick their wounds, and one by one, the watching members of the tribe slipped back into the woods. Soon only the surviving fighters remained, unwilling to leave the field yet because they wanted to savor their new status just a little longer. He sat among them—there were five—sharing their slight uncertainty, and even a little fear. A whole new phase of their lives was beginning.

Nearby, one of the two new female warriors sat proudly, ignoring the multiple bites and scratches marring her glowing coat. She had faced and defeated three challengers. He had seen one of the battles, and the way she had beaten her challenger with a whirlwind attack that had been confusing just to watch. Her strategy had been excellent.

Another who thinks. A suitable mate. Her season was near, he realized, as the shifting breeze brought a hint of an exciting scent towards him to tease his senses.

He rose and padded closer to ask: "What is your name?"

"Wind Fighter."

"You fight well."

"You do not fight much." She didn't seem impressed, and just started grooming herself.

"I think," he persisted. "I fight better, I fight with my mind, not my blood."

Wind Fighter was silent for a moment, reconsidering. "You won over three other warriors," she admitted finally. "Only one touched you. Good fighting." She relaxed and turned sharply to lick her rear right flank, wincing slightly as the movement opened a cut that had scabbed over.

He sat down next to her and tentatively bent to lick the wound, tasting the salty sweetness of her blood. After spinning to nip him lightly, she bounded off the field to disappear into the tall grasses behind the flattened area where the Tribe had rested watching the challenge. But the lingering taste of her blood raised a new fire in him and he followed her, still smelling the powerful scent of her season. It had been stronger when he had been leaning over her.

She was easy to track through the grasses, and he followed her trail into the nearby forest. His blood rushed faster and faster as he felt himself draw near.

Then, as he broke though to a small, open area, he saw her. She was curled up against a boulder that still glowed in the afternoon sun, the muscles in her strong neck and shoulders rippling as she twisted to groom herself. He stalked her, his padded feet noiseless on the grassy ground. He could see that she knew he was there, but she ignored him. As he reached her, he dropped to the ground and crawled forward on his belly until he was close enough to reach up for her neck to lick a bad bite mark that she had been unable to reach.

She continued her own grooming, apparently not noticing him, but a low rumbling started deep in the back of her throat. He licked harder, his raspy tongue pulling off the clotted, dirt-crusted scabs and cleaning the wound. His tongue kneaded her stiff muscles as he put his weight into it and their mutual rumbling grew louder as she reached over to groom him, too. Her tongue added to the effect of her scent and he felt new and strange urgings build as he rose over her...

CHAPTER 5

▼

SERENA: MOON, 2291

As Ken led the way into StarStep Control, Jim looked up nervously into the dome of the ceiling. Over the circular, elevated walkway that surrounded the cavernous room, slender support beams held up a huge cylinder that hung over them, penetrating the dome through an air-tight seal. Apparently the StarStep facilities had been added onto an old surface-based optical observatory, and he wondered if the old telescope was still in use.

He saw Miller's eyes follow his gaze.

"Scary, isn't it?" Ken grinned. "I still feel funny with that thing hanging up there like that. I keep waiting for it to fall…and yes," he seemed to guess what Jim was wondering, "we do still use it. There's something about an optical telescope that seems to give a more real feeling of looking out at the stars. Even if the holo-displays from the computer telescopes are much sharper and more useful, they—"

"—remove you from the feeling of *really* looking at the stars," Jim guessed. "I can understand that. I used to have a telescope on the roof of our house when I grew up. I remember looking up here and wondering what it would be like to live on the Moon."

Ken beamed. "You *do* understand. Good. That makes me feel a little better." He grabbed Jim's arm and pulled him off to the side. "Let me introduce you to my precocious co-director." He pointed to a slim figure who was bent over an open piece of electronic equipment, half buried inside as she grunted while wrestling with a connector or something. Tools and test equipment were perched precariously on the counter next to her.

"Serena! Up here. Our guest from Earth has arrived."

As the figure unfolded and turned to approach, Jim tried not to stare. She was not even close to what he had expected. The bio-file he had scanned had been text only, and he felt hopelessly squat and chunky as finally found himself face to face with her. She was slender like a figure in an El Greco painting, and had to be almost thirty centimeters taller than him. It was a strange feeling to be looking <u>up</u> at a woman, but for some reason it only added to her appeal; her other-worldly fascination.

Over high cheek-bones, she had large and eerie light-blue eyes that were almost glittering silver in the reflected light, and strands of medium length black hair fought to escape a loose top-knot on her head to hang over her forehead. Beads of sweat dotted her flushed face and several dirt-smudges streaked it, but he was captivated. She had to be one of the most beautiful women he had ever seen. And he was struck by her fluid grace. She moved like a ballerina, totally at home in the one-sixth gravity of the Moon as she came up the few short steps from the laboratory itself to the surrounding gallery walkway.

She ignored the hand he held out, and looked down on him suspiciously to ask: "Why are you here? Is there a problem with our funding?"

He decided he had better explain, and quickly because Serena's reaction was echoed by a look from Ken that was just short of laser surgery.

"No, no funding problem," Jim reassured them. "Quite the contrary. I'm here to try to get Star-Step back on course and to try to increase your funding to give you what you need."

The open-mouthed stares that greeted the straightforward statement made the whole trip worth it. Suddenly Serena was bombarding him with questions while Ken tried to slip in a few of his own. Jim held up his hands after a moment.

"One thing at a time, please," he pleaded.

When they quieted down, he looked around and spotted a chair by a work bench. He walked carefully over to it and seated himself, ignoring his impatient hosts. He sighed happily, feeling secure for the first time.

"There, that's better. I've been feeling like I was going to either float away or fall flat on my face any minute." He leaned back with a satisfied grin. "Now, like I said, I'm up here trying to get your appropriation increased, but it's not going to be easy. And I know: you're wondering why the chill we suddenly care."

"Damn right," Ken muttered.

"Well, I do have an ulterior motive." He wove a little impromptu web of gossamer half truths, admitting that there were "high level concerns" about the future of StarStep—he omitted Mara's involvement—and he explained that he had been sent to find out the status of the project, and to make sure it succeeded.

As his words sank in, a contagious excitement came over the others, and he found himself pulled up out of his seat by Ken and wrapped up in an all-encompassing bear-hug that also snared Serena and pressed her delightfully close to let a slight scent of Jasmine lessen the impact of Ken's bitter-smelling cologne. Her exotic eyes were twinkling mischievously as they met his, and suddenly they weren't distant or aloof anymore, but just openly appraising.

He managed to extricate himself after a moment and forced himself to look away from Serena. He turned to Ken.

"I still haven't met Star, though. Are you going to introduce me?"

"Of course. Serena, with your permission?" She nodded and he looked up. "Star? Speak up. We have an important guest." Nothing. He glared at the ceiling and tried again: "Star! Do you hear me?"

"Pardon me, Ken?" a rich, smooth tenor voice answered from above.

"Blast!" Serena went over to a small cube that squatted in the middle of the floor, isolated by a clear area around it. Its featureless surface was unmarred except for several thick cooling pipes running through it. As she reached it, she gave it a swift, calculated kick on the one side. "His ear is thermal-shifting again!" She patted the computer absently on its top, smiling gently. "Sorry dear." Then she turned back to Ken. "I told Engineering he needs better cooling at the data-volume we're running him. Ask him again."

"Ask me what?" the strange voice asked.

"I wanted to introduce you to Representative—"

"James Martin. Yes, I see him. I was sent his full file from Geneva. I am pleased to meet you, sir."

Ken glared up again. "I don't care about Serena's 'programmed spontaneity'; what did I tell you about interrupting people?"

"It's okay, Ken." Jim shook his head. "I'm pleased to meet you too, Star." He glanced around, unsure of whether to look at the small cabinet that apparently housed the nanocomputer, or to just look up like Ken had done.

Star seemed to read his mind as he said: "I have a set of 'eyes' right in the middle of the ceiling, sir. Just look up as Ken did and you will see it. Just speak to that as if it were me. You will find me over the door in all other rooms associated with StarStep. Serena designed me intentionally with stereoscopic vision."

"Thanks." He looked up and saw the small pair of omni-lenses that were mounted near one of the telescope mounting brackets. "And by the way, in keeping with the obvious informality around here, just call me Jim. 'Sir', sounds too stuffy as Ken pointed out."

He looked around the cluttered laboratory before turning to Ken. "Is this where you monitor StarStep?"

Miller shook his head. "Not exactly. Star does all that, and he displays what we need to see on any terminal screen we want...although lately he has had precious little to display..." He suddenly fell silent and turned lazily to Jim with a growing grin on his face.

"That's my cue, I believe." Jim smiled. "I get the impression that this is the type of thing that you're having problems with?"

Ken and Serena looked at each other a moment before turning back to Jim with identical, calculating smiles.

"Yes, indeed, my good friend," Ken said with a chuckle as he took Jim's arm paternally. "Let me tell you our problems…"

*   *   *   *

A week later, Jim settled back in his chair and looked up at the ceiling, no longer feeling strange about talking to empty air. "Okay, Star. Give it to me again."

"Certainly, Jim. I would be more than happy to." The computer's eerie, disembodied voice floated down from somewhere. Even if his breezy conversational style was programmed, it seemed so natural that Jim felt like he was working with a person. *A very efficient person,* he noted as four large screens at the end of the control room immediately lit up with a succession of graphic displays that flowed past as fast as he could read them.

He frowned. "Chill! It's the same, no matter what we try—"

"Jim, forgive me for interrupting."

"Stop apologizing," he chuckled. "If you have something to say when I'm rambling, say it. I'm not Ken."

"Thank you. I started to say that you have cut our funding needs in half without compromising the integrity of the project in the least, and thanks to that, the last shipments were able to be sent out exactly as originally specified. It seems that—"

"It's meaningless!" Jim cut him off with a frown. "What I did wasn't difficult. It was just a matter of calling in some favors and playing supplier against supplier to get the lowest bids possible. This project has been run too much like a government contract." He glared at the offending charts displayed in front of him. "But the problem is that no matter how I try rearranging the existing budget, there is no way StarStep can be used as a viable colony. Sure, the planet will be ready for us, but we'll never get there. The construction of the colony transports and the freezing of the colonists were budgeted at market prices current after the machine plague, and we just don't have enough funds left. There's no way we can cover the remaining expenses."

He twisted restlessly on his chair. "I've tried everything, but it's no good." He turned back to the displays reluctantly, propping his chin on a single clenched fist.

"Rodin's 'The Thinker'," Star observed. "The pose is exactly like the sculpture. Was that intentional, Jim?"

Jim shook his head. "No, my friend, just frustrated coincidence."

Suddenly he felt firm fingers kneading his shoulders, skillfully working out the tense knots in his muscles. Startled, he leaned into it with a satisfied moan, and turned his head to find himself looking up into Serena's compelling eyes.

"You've worked wonders, you know." She included Star with a smile towards his eyes. "I never would have believed it. You've been able to cut StarStep's budget in half without compromising one bit of it."

He reached up to squeeze her hand gratefully. "So someone else just pointed out, but hey, it wasn't just me."

Serena's hand was warm and soft in his and he didn't want to let go. He was glad she was working with him. Her input over the past week, and Star's, had been vital, and a welcome change from the usual difficulties he had working with people. Serena *was* brilliant, and she had an uncanny way of anticipating his every move that made his job easier than any other joint project he had ever undertaken. He had also found that she had a wonderful sense of humor that had defused a number of frustrated moments by reminding him that he didn't always have to take everything so seriously, or personally.

But all their work had been in vain.

He squeezed her hand again, and then let go reluctantly to straighten, suddenly stiff as he turned to her. "It just hasn't been enough! Chill it, what you guys are doing up here is important! It frosts me that the rest of the world can't get that through their collective minds and—"

Serena shut him up effectively by bending down to kiss him lightly. As she started to pull away, he reached up to capture her face lightly with a cupped hand to draw her back down for a kiss of his own—part of his mind wondering what the chill he was doing. Her eyes opened wide in surprise for a moment, and then closed contently as her lips lingered on his for a delicious moment, parting lightly to allow his tongue to caress hers.

Then she pulled away abruptly, her alabaster skin reddening and he felt his own face burn as he let her go.

"I'm sorry, "Serena. You caught me off guard there and I.—"

He wondered what *had* just happened. It had been totally unexpected, but he had suddenly felt compelled to kiss her. His lonely subconscious was getting pushy, abetted by the past week's closeness.

It had been a long time since he had felt the kind of emotional rush that had just overwhelmed him. Debra had made him feel that way, but after her death, he had carefully closed that part of himself off. It had taken him several years to get over the loss, and he had never been able to bring himself to pursue any solid relationships after her death. He was still hiding, he knew; unwilling to let himself get really involved for fear of losing it again. He had never gotten beyond a few scattered, brief, and emotionally empty relationships that had often been prompted more out of various womens' curiosity than anything else.

But in Serena he saw a complement to himself. She had a uniqueness that he loved, and he had been fighting his growing attraction for some time, and when she had reached out to him he had just reacted. He wanted to explain all that, but he was afraid to, as difficult as that was to admit to himself.

Serena was pacing restlessly, her eyes fixed on the displays and avoiding his, a faint rosy tinge still warming her face. Speaking in a slightly shaky voice she said: "It's okay…but we have to keep working here. Is there anything else that can be done?" She obviously didn't want to talk about 'the kiss'.

It was hard, but he forced his mind back to the displays, respecting her desire to ignore what had happened, but also disappointed. As he looked at the monitors and their depressing displays, his earlier frustrated anger returned.

"Keep working on what?" he snapped. "There's nothing more we can do here. We'll have to start…No!" Abruptly, he got up and glared at the screen as an idea began stirring. Serena's kiss still burned on his lips, and its energy reached down into him to make him look closer at his problem. "Enough already! Mara wants me to cut as much as I can here so I can beg for scraps to finish the project on a megabyte chip when what we really need is a terabyte one. Chill it! We're talking about the future of humanity here—"

"Mara?" Serena stared at him. "Is Mara Saunders your high level help?"

"I see you keep up on your Grounder politics," Jim laughed, amused by her surprise, until he realized he had never really told them. "That's right. But she doesn't want anyone to know it because of some political games she's playing."

Serena smiled. "Well, if she's helping, there's a chance. I was worried. No matter how much you and Star have accomplished here, I was afraid we'd never be able to get enough funding. But if the world president herself is helping, you'll do it." She suddenly changed subjects. "She's very attractive, isn't she?" Her face flushed again and she looked back at the displays, not waiting for an answer as she hastily said: "She should be able to help. Can I tell Ken?"

"Sure." Jim shrugged. "Just tell him to keep it to us three—"

"Four," a smoothly modulated voice cut in. Star had been quiet, no doubt absorbing what he was seeing and hearing, but apparently he had been unable to resist an obvious example of neglect. "But you can be sure I will keep this confidential."

"Okay, four. Now make yourself useful and charge up your circuits." Strategies were stirring in the back of his mind and he flexed his hands in anticipation. "We have some new plans to make, because next week Mara's going to be in for a nasty surprise!" He grinned up at Star's featureless lenses and then turned back to Serena. "Just you…" But she was gone.

*   *   *   *

Spreading Out: StarStep, 2312

Rock Thrower looked out over the field where he had once won his new status as warrior, his new name, and his mate. Wind Fighter's first litter was being thinned out. Her first-born, Dew Licker had just lost to Stripe Back and he would have to wait until the next challenge to try again. He had refused to follow Rock

Thrower's advice, and had fought with only tooth and claw. As for Crooked Leg, she had been killed by a howling hunter when she was little because she had not been able to run away fast enough. Now only Quick Stalker was left to fight.

Rock Thrower lay shoulder to shoulder with Wind Fighter, the warmth of her body reaching out to him to keep him close. Her two newest cubs—one male and one female—were playing nearby, but she ignored them. Her eyes were fixed on her oldest cub…no, youngling. She had been very quiet since Dew Licker's loss. But Quick Stalker would win, Rock Thrower was sure. He was larger than the other younglings, but despite that he was silent and fast as a rock-sunner. And he was a thinker. He had been out on the field in the middle of the night before and had placed an assortment of good throwing rocks in various places.

Even with Rock Thrower's example, none of the other warriors or younglings used rocks to hunt or fight. To them, they were just part of the field. But not to Quick Stalker. Rock Thrower had seen his offspring's methodical planting of rocks. No matter where the challenge took him on the field, Quick Stalker would have a weapon within easy reach, without being slowed down by carrying one with him.

There: Bare Patch stepped out towards him, the thin fur on his right flank showing where the stick-head-runner had wounded him. Despite his own size and strength, he was the only youngling who had not yet challenged. He had been waiting for Quick Stalker, just as Quick Stalker had been waiting for him.

The two faced each other on the thinning grass, mutual wavering growls and spitting hisses rolling out towards a growing circle of warriors and younglings. Everyone wanted to see who would win because the two younglings had been enemies since cub-hood. It had started with Quick Stalker catching a small pond hopper that Bare Patch—then Big Foot—had been chasing. Ever since then, whatever small game one had been after, the other had tried to catch it first. From there, it had gone on into frequent mock-challenges as the two imitated the warriors and younglings on the field of challenge. Each had drawn blood from the other on occasion—before being soundly disciplined by one parent or the other.

Cubs do not challenge!

Well, now they were not cubs!

Bare Patch moved first, with a lightning dash in to try to cripple Quick Stalker, but the faster youngling was gone, having rolled to the side to snatch two rocks! One, two, the small rocks shot out with unerring precision. The first caught Bare Patch on the nose, and the youngling snarled in outrage to cover a small, cub-like moan of surprise, and then the second, larger rock, hit him in the head right between the eyes. There was a funny, wet, crack and Bare Patch froze. For a moment, he just crouched there, but then he slumped slowly to the ground.

Silence descended over the field like an almost physical blanket as the watching warriors and younglings rose to all four paws and took a step closer, wondering about Bare Patch.

But the youngling wasn't moving. Rock Thrower stepped out on the field and bent nose to sniff him— just as Bare Patch shifted slightly. Reluctant to step onto the field, several of the other warriors finally approached to nudge Bare Patch. After a while, the youngling moved again and slowly forced himself to his feet with a wavering growl. He faced Rock Thrower, eyes dull, and did not say anything. It was as if some part of the youngling had fled when the rock had hit him.

Walking shakily, he made his way off the field to disappear into the woods far off towards the sun.

Off to die at the fangs of the first kill-cleaner to spot him, Rock Thrower thought. He was in no condition to defend himself. But, since he had lost and was not a warrior and of no use as a hunter, the field quickly emptied as the remaining younglings and warriors disappeared in various directions. Except for Big Coat. The long-furred female youngling who had been watching Quick Stalker moved onto the field to lie next to him, and Rock Thrower realized that she was already pregnant. It was a violation of custom, but Quick Stalker had never been patient, Rock Thrower yawned with amusement. It was fortunate that his cub had won.

A gentle head-butting against his side alerted him that Wind Fighter had joined them, and then she moved in on Quick Stalker to lick his face with a quick grooming caress of approval. Big Fur rose with a possessive growl, and Wind Fighter ignored her and settled back at Rock Thrower's side, leaving the younger female to curl up against Quick Stalker's other side as he nipped at her and then faced Rock Thrower boldly.

"We are leaving," he announced simply. "There is not enough game here. We are going towards the rising sun to find other hunting grounds."

Rock Thrower could understand that. Some warriors had already gone off to explore in the opposite direction, over the mountains, and had returned with stories of brutal and unreasoning warriors who had not understood any of the greetings from the travelers. Others had struck out towards the sun or away from the water and had not returned. Some of them must have found good hunting. Or maybe even more dangerous warriors who had killed them?

For a moment, he felt an urge to go with them and find out for himself, but then he changed his mind. He felt bound here. Some of the warriors were already coming to him for advice, and he felt somehow responsible for them. Wind Fighter felt the same, he knew.

He sat up. "Go, have healthy cubs and good hunting, but come back and tell us what you find."

CHAPTER 6

▼

CHANGING THE RULES: EARTH, 2291

It was early Monday morning—June 7th, Rebuilders' Day and a legal holiday—but Mara had asked him to join her in Geneva at her office for a private meeting so he could fill her in on his progress. The receptionist's desk in the outer office had been empty, but he had no sooner stepped through the outer office door than the door to Mara's office had opened and she had come out to pull him inside. As he faced her, he felt a little like the proverbial fly in the spider's web—even if it was a nice enough web.

Her office was a bright and airy room, with a window-wall that faced northeast to look out over the park in front of the government building. The revealing sun warmed the room and revealed no flaws in the immaculately organized and spotless room. A nearly bare, glittering chrome mag-lev desk floated in front of the windows; facing the door and a pair of spartan-looking chrome and black Letherex chairs, each with a mini-terminal set into one arm-rest. The wall to his right was nothing but a bank of holo-monitors, while the walls to his right and behind him were decorated with vertical strips of contrasting metals, and a few sterile-looking abstract paintings. A plush blue shag carpet was the only soft thing visible in the room.

"Well?" Mara dropped into the vacant chair behind her desk and looked up at him expectantly as the door to the outer office slid shut behind him. "How did it go?"

Jim gave her a cautious smile. "Not bad. Star and I reworked the budget figures for finishing the StarStep Project properly and I've been doing some figuring of my own. The biggest problem is that the actual colony ships still only exist in memory and have yet to be built. Those, and the training facilities. Building the ships and freezing the colonists are the big hang-ups since there's only minimal operating capital left. Ship construction will be the big expense, but even the cryogenic preparation of all the colonists will cost a lot. The plan calls for twenty thousand settlers to guarantee a good gene-pool and work force."

"Crytron ought to be happy," Mara injected cynically. "So now your fight begins. It'll conflict directly with our budget constraints, even if you were able to cut their budget—"

"Oh, we were," he reassured her. "Just not enough. But like you said, Crytron ought to be happy. Have them push behind the scenes. The damn budget constraints are artificial anyway, because everyone's afraid of crashing again."

"Can you blame them? I already told you. Most of the Representatives are close to my age." Her eyes dipped in brief embarrassment. "They…we…have seen what happens when there is a technological explosion. It's put a damper on research as far back as the first accidental nanokiller release."

She got up and laid a warm hand on his arm to draw him towards the window-wall. The bright sunlight outlined her lush body through the thin yellow jump-suit that she wore and he swallowed, feeling the web again.

Before leaving the Moon, he had kept trying to corner Serena to talk about that kiss they had shared several days earlier, but she had refused to talk about it. Every time he had tried to bring it up, she had managed to verbally side-step him as gracefully as she managed her every physical movement. It had been driving him crazy. They worked together beautifully, and the more he learned about her—partly from quizzing Ken and Star—the more interesting he found her. But if he tried to cross the line between professional and personal, even for a moment, she turned to ice. It wasn't that she was rude, as Ken had warned her she might be, but she just seemed to disappear within herself somehow. From what he had learned, he knew that she had shielded herself the same way when growing up: an outcast where she belonged. It had taken her years to be accepted, Ken had told him. She had had to overcome the stigma of her Grounder blood and it had meant building an air-tight shell around herself to keep from being hurt. But she wouldn't let him in either!

After Serena's continual rejection, Mara's soft and inviting touch, heady perfume and casual manner were intoxicating, and he had to force his attention back to what she was saying.

"Look out there," she pointed. "And you see a city and a continent, no, a world at peace. A world uncontaminated by pollution or waste thanks to cheap fusion power and a nanotech clean-up. It's a world with plentiful resources for all…" She laughed, interrupting herself. "Even if it means some complications, like with our money-standard. We have seen the world go from the tightly controlled confusion of the last century, to the total devastating chaos of the machine plague, and then over this century gradually pull itself back to sanity. Now we need a rest. Those budget restrictions you're complaining about were designed to maintain the status quo for a while, to give us time to reorganize. That's why I wanted a rebel like you."

She turned and looked up at him, her green eyes close and warmly inviting as her lips parted slightly and she moved even closer.

"You're different," she said softly. "Different from anyone else I've dealt with." Her hand was hot on his arm, and even her body seemed to radiate a magnetic warmth. "We can work together on this," she promised, making it very clear she wasn't talking entirely about StarStep. "I know it. We're alike, you and I. Outside the conformist mainstream. We're not afraid to say what we think...and feel."

Her flowery perfume teased his nose and he swallowed. He couldn't deny her attraction, or her words. But for the first time in his life, he felt confused and his usual self-control was wavering.

She must have misunderstood his hesitation. "Are you with me?" StarStep was definitely off her mind for the moment.

He swallowed. "We still have a deal," he said, his voice tight as he gently disengaged her hand, his touch lingering long enough to let her know that he understood, but declined her subtle invitation to greater intimacy. He forced himself to remember why he was there. *StarStep! StarStep!* he mentally yelled to himself. He didn't know why he was resisting her. Normally, he would have welcomed her attentions, but something was stopping him.

"As I said, we still have a deal, *with StarStep*," he emphasized. "But I'm going to have my work cut out for me. Like I said, we trimmed the budget, but it's not nearly enough—"

"Well, I guessed that already." Obviously reluctant, Mara acknowledged his efforts, and his rejection. "I had been hoping you'd be able to cut it down enough that you would only need some minor appropriations."

"Not so minor. The more I looked at everything, the more things I found that weren't considered in the initial planning, and those things add more expense to the project. Star's been great, but even with him to help, StarStep needs a major infusion of funds."

"So now what?"

"Well," Jim grinned a little maliciously as he got his focus back. "Now I'm going back to the way I get elected, but on a worldwide scale. That's why you drafted me in the first place, isn't it?"

She smiled innocently, and he chuckled as he pulled out his pocket computer, speaking in a private verbal shorthand he had programmed in. After a while, he settled into a chair and kept quizzing the computer to make sure he had everything covered. He had actually already prepared everything beforehand, but he didn't want it to look too easy.

After an appropriate delay, he got up and went back over to Mara, careful not to get too close. He held out the computer so she could inspect the small floating holo-display and said: "We can get Star-Step back on track with a good probability of success, but to get started I'll need a personal donation from you of twenty million credit units—"

"Twenty million?" Mara froze, staring at the read-out in disbelief, all thoughts of seduction evaporating. "From me personally? Not as an appropriation? I don't..." She stopped, eyes flashing back and forth between his terminal and his face.

"I take it you've also tapped into my records?" she asked, and he nodded. After a moment, she admitted: "Well, I do a little stock trading here and there."

"You're well placed for information."

She looked indignant. "I don't—"

"Of course not!" he stopped her cynically. "But there are ways..." He let it hang there with a shrug. "Look, I don't care. But if you want my help I need—"

"Why from me personally?" she interrupted with a frown, not realizing that her animation was making her even more attractive. "I don't understand that. You said you hadn't been able to get Star-Step's budget down enough, but suddenly you're only asking for twenty million Credit Units. That's nothing. I can give you that with an executive order. Why do I have to put up the money?"

"Because we'll need almost ten billion," he answered, smiling as he saw her eyes snapped open. "The twenty million is just what I need to get started. Once I do that, I can use fund-raising to keep my public relations campaign going, but to get off the ground I need a boost. Use an intermediary and make it a donation...better yet, use several, and then step back and leave me alone."

He noticed her nervous look and smiled. "You're going to have to distance yourself from me as much as possible, because in a while I'm going to be very unpopular. And you're going to have to be the saving grace that steps in to stop me by giving me a token appropriation to settle me down and get me off everyone's backs. A token that will be what we need, instead of what I'm going to be demanding."

Mara smiled weakly. "And with the initial seed money from me, you have a hold on me..." She smiled subtly for a moment, and then nodded. "But it's a good strategy, and Crytron won't be trying to stop you." She fell silent, pacing back and forth restlessly. She was obviously deep in thought. Then, she finally stopped to warn him: "But it'll cost you the next election."

"So?" Jim shrugged. "I've been getting bored. Too much inertia. I wasn't getting anything changed, and my region didn't really appreciate my efforts—even with your Frost Fund money. Once we get the financing together, I figure I'll see about joining the team on the Moon to plan the new world. Give Star some input, and some ideas." He smiled. "Maybe I'll even go out to StarStep. Anyone who'll take a chance on heading out there," he nodded at the ceiling, "has to be more my type than the fossils taking up space down here! Present company excluded."

"That's going to be part of your problem," Mara warned. "Getting volunteers to colonize Star-Step."

"Don't underestimate the power of a good media blitz," Jim said as headed for the door, a feeling of hungry anticipation growing as he turned his back on her. Also a bit of relief. He needed to get away from her. "You know where to reach me," he called over his shoulder. "When you're ready, call me and I'll let you know where to make your donations."

As the door hissed open in front of him, he heard Mara's soft voice call: "Wait, please."

He turned back to her, letting the door slide closed again as he sensed a change in the already charged air of the room. As he turned, he saw her leaning against the desk, her hair cascading down over her shoulders where it had been imperiously pinned up a moment before. Her arms were back, supporting her weight and drawing the material of her outfit tight against her body.

One corner of his mind knew that she was very deliberately playing a private little game she was determined to win, and that she had no real personal interest in him, but he felt his earlier reluctance crumbling.

He moved towards her to ask: "I take it you've made a decision?"

She just nodded and smiled faintly, her eyes flashing a bold invitation as she saw he was weakening. She shifted one slender arm so she could touch a sensor-pad on her desk with her little finger. Raising her voice slightly, she called out: "*Control* credit transfer of twenty million from personal account three to…" She raised an eyebrow.

"Lunar Holding Associates, Account 199-23-893-STRSTP," Jim supplied automatically, his mind only half aware of her question.

Mara repeated the account information and then finished the transfer with a final, "*Command.*" Her hands crossed demurely in front of herself. "It's from a private account in the name of a holding company," she explained. "It's all perfectly legal, mind you, but for tax purposes the funds in that account are kept separate from the rest of my holdings. Satisfied?" Her smile grew bolder and he had a feeling she wasn't talking about the money anymore.

Jim nodded silently, unable to keep from moving closer as her hands turned out, inviting him closer. The sparks that had been ignited, and then doused by a withdrawn Serena, suddenly sprung to flaming life as Mara drew him in and ran her free hand up his chest and around his neck to draw his face down to hers. The fresh taste of mint mingled with the delicate scent of flowers as the velvet of her lips engulfed his own hungrily.

"I have an apartment's next door, and I sent my staff home hours ago," she whispered when her mouth released his briefly.

He let himself be led towards a carefully disguised door in the corner, his eyes caressing her from behind.

*   *   *   *

But by Wednesday morning, he realized that he had made a big mistake.

His days had been filled with laying the groundwork for his fund-raising, and at night, Mara had been even more exhaustingly passionate than their first tryst in her office-apartment. But her love-making had had a clinical flavor to it that quickly grew tiresome because she refused to let her guard down and let him get close to 'her'. Even with all her exquisitely pleasurable sexual gymnastics, she failed to touch him in the way that Serena's brief kiss had. He grew increasingly restless—and thinking more and more about Serena—and he finally told Mara that he was returning to the Moon.

Her casual acceptance of his announcement reinforced his first impression that he had been nothing more than a diversion, and it was with a powerful surge of relief that he had Tracy get him reservations on Thursday morning's SSTO flight, with a Long-Shuttle cross-connection from the station to the Moon. Then he called Star to transfer all his files up, and lay down for the first night of deep and uninterrupted sleep he had had since coming down to see Mara.

✷   ✷   ✷   ✷

Leadership: StarStep, 2313

The end of another Warm Time was near, but today, the sun was hot overhead. The steady rasping of unseen insects added to the irritation that an older Rock Thrower felt. Game was scarce, and many were hungry. A new Challenge had been called, and more younglings were sure to die in the fierce fighting for status and rights to hunt and mate.

Rock Thrower looked over at Wind Fighter. "The hunt is bad. Too many howling hunters."

"They steal our game."

A new idea came to mind and he rose off his haunches to decide: "Then we steal theirs…"

He dropped into an easy run and headed towards the woods. Wind Fighter caught up with him and loped beside him as he put on speed, wanting to leave the depressing group of hungry warriors behind him.

"What are you thinking?" she asked.

He yawned. He was glad she was there. She accepted his need to use more than claws or teeth, and she could understand what he said. She was not like many of the other warriors whose talk and thoughts were only of hunting, mating and fighting.

"The howling hunters are our enemy," he explained. "They steal our game. So, why do we fight each other when we have an enemy?

"Are you going to fight the howling hunters?" she asked, staring at him.

He turned impatiently. "They eat our game and I must…" He stopped, realizing he couldn't fight them all. "We must all fight them…together…" His head was swirling with more ideas, and he lay down to think. Wind Fighter dropped down next to him to wait patiently. By now, she had gotten used to seeing him like this. She was even thinking herself.

After a moment she sat up. "All warriors together, they need a leader. Someone to plan what to do."

He realized what she meant. "The best fighter should rule." Rock Thrower yawned thoughtfully as he decided what to do. "A fighter who thinks can be a leader…and a leader needs a place to lead from." He rose. "And I know where it will be!" He headed back towards the field of challenge, explaining to Wind Fighter what he needed her to do.

At the back of the field, a large boulder rested. He jumped up on it and rose to his hind legs to roar out a loud challenge that echoed. Not the roar of triumph that was common, but a call to any and all to fight.

One by one, tawny bodies appeared. Out of the tall grass, out from the woods on the hills that ringed the rest of the valley, and out of the canyon behind him where a cold spring-fed stream provided fresh water. Soon, everyone was approaching; confused, wondering. There was already a reluctance to step onto the thinning and worn growth of the Field of Challenge itself, and everyone settled down on the heavier grasses that surrounded the field.

Rock Thrower stayed erect on top of the boulder and looked down over the Tribe. That's what they were. And they were his family. He glanced down. Below him, on the ground at the base of the boulder where he stood, was a large supply of rocks that he and Wind Fighter had gathered on the way. The rocks were just the right size for throwing.

He was ready.

He glared out at the Tribe again. "We are all hungry," he called. "The howling hunters are many and they are stealing our food." A wave of responding growls spread across the field of fur below, shifting and rippling like the tall grasses under the wind.

"We need the game they steal," he went on. "We must take it. All of us. Fighting together. We fight each other instead of fighting those who steal our food. That must change."

He dropped to sit, licking the boulder beneath him. "This is now Speaker Rock. And I am now called Speaker. I will lead all of you against the howling hunters and we will drive them away. Then we will have enough food again."

Wind Fighter rose right on cue and growled just like they had practiced. "And what if we do not want to follow you?"

"Then you will die. I will be Speaker because I am Rock Thrower, Warrior Who Thinks. In my challenge I was unhurt and my challengers all lost. I will defeat any of you who do not obey, just as I did those who had challenged me."

"And if we do follow you?" Wind Fighter pressed.

"Then you will eat, and your cubs will be strong warriors who need not die on the Field of Challenge, only win or lose."

"I will follow." Wind Fighter sat back down.

Rock Thrower rose in challenge. "Are there any others who would fight me, and risk losing food?" There were a lot of rapid looks crossing between warriors, but no one spoke up. They were feeling their hunger and remembering his easy challenge victories. It didn't take long for him to see that they would follow. He relaxed.

"Then we must first remove the howling hunters from our land!" He pointed to the rocks below. "Each of you, take some of these and remember how I won my challenges. We will all go and seek out the howling hunters, and destroy them!"

He knew most of the rocks would be lost along the way as the warriors dropped them to return to their normal four footed pace, but the massed attack of the whole tribe on the packs of the hunters would be enough to win the battle. The howling hunters had always prevailed in past encounters because they worked together, but this time they would have their tails twisted as the Tribe used their own tactics against them.

▼

CHAPTER 7

CLEARING THE AIR: MOON, 2291

"Can you do it?" Ken asked as Jim laid out his plans. "Ten billion? Why so much? It's more than twice what you and Star estimated we would need."

"It's called a contingency cushion, my friend," Jim explained. "I'm not entirely finished confusing and confounding my electorate. We'll need the extra." His lips curled in a savage grin as he thought about the secret plans he had for some of that money. Then he eyed the door Serena had just left through, puzzled by her reaction.

He had been anxious to give Ken and Serena the good news that Mara had given him the twenty million and that he had already started the public relations machinery to begin generating interest for the StarStep project, but he had been surprised by the cool reception he was getting.

Ken seemed happy enough, but even he was somehow stiffly formal. And as for Serena, she had sat listening without any visible emotion until Jim had finished, and then she had curtly excused herself and left the lounge after some vaguely phrased words of congratulations.

Jim looked at the closed door, confused and hurt. He had expected a warm welcome from her as he brought news of the first step in the salvation of her second pet project—Star was first, he knew. But Serena had always been enthusiastic in her support of his efforts to promote StarStep, and he had been looking forward to resuming their working relationship, and to starting his campaign to win her over on a personal front. He would have expected a negative reaction if she had known about his brief, but disappointing liaison with Mara—provided their brief kiss had meant anything to her—but she had rejected him before, and he didn't know what to think.

He turned to Ken. "What's with Serena? I would have thought she would be ecstatic. We've got the seed money to get proper funding now."

"I don't know." Ken shrugged. "She's been like this for a couple of days."

Jim didn't like the sound of Ken's answer. He had the impression that the physicist knew very well what the problem was. He looked up and asked the next obvious question.

"Star, buddy: you're tapped into everything that goes on up here. When did Dr. Andrews' attitude change?"

"Wait a minute, Star." Ken glared at Jim. "That's getting a little personal."

"Hey, something's got her upset, and I want to know what," Jim defended himself. "I…we, need her to be at optimum while we restructure the project and get it back on track." He looked up. "Well, Star?"

"Ken raised an objection and he has command priority," Star said simply, refusing to elaborate.

After a moment, Jim sighed and turned to Ken. "What is this? A conspiracy? Chill it! I'm concerned, and I just want to know what's wrong."

Ken studied him carefully, and then nodded. "Go ahead, Star."

"There were actually two events that changed her apparent emotional state," Star began. "First, there was a communique on Wednesday morning from the Science Advisory board which seemed to make her angry, if I was correct in my interpretation of her emotions. She spoke loudly and used a number of words I cross-referenced as being considered obscene, but she was not addressing anyone in particular. That is a considerable departure from her normal behavior, but not the current deviance which you were inquiring about. I mentioned it only because it might have bearing on the relevant pattern of—"

"Stuff it, Star," Ken cut the computer off. "We don't need a full analysis or rationalization. I already know what's bothering her. I got the same message on my terminal." He turned to Jim. "It was the notification that you had been appointed director of StarStep. Serena and I were the co-directors of the project, but your President Saunders bumped us to assistant directors and put you in charge." His face was grim. "I have to admit, I'm not entirely comfortable with the decision, either. Even with all you've managed to do, you just don't have the technical grounding to run a project like this."

Jim straightened. "Now wait just a minute. Mara said that she had suggested the change to expedite everything, but that my status would be mainly titular for publicity reasons. I had made it clear to her that I'd accept only if you two would continue to run the actual project and get full credit for it once it was fully funded. I'm just here to get you back online. I never intended…hell, I don't want to…I *can't* replace you two."

Ken warmed visibly. "Why didn't you tell us? Tell Serena? It doesn't take an Einstein to figure that out you're attracted to her. But getting a lady demoted is not the way to impress her."

"No kidding!" Jim held out his hands helplessly, trying to explain. "I didn't realize…I thought everything had been made clear. Besides, I never had a chance to tell her. I haven't talked to her the whole time I was gone—"

"May I continue?" Star interrupted.

"What?" Ken and Jim burst out simultaneously, and Ken laughed. "Sorry, Star. We forgot about you. Go ahead."

"Thank you. The second event that seemed to have precipitated Serena's emotional change was when she attempted to call Jim on Wednesday night. He was not at the hotel where he was registered, and Serena made me give her the number at the Presidential residence where I had been communicating with him during the day. At that point, Serena blocked me out of communication until—"

"I know what happened," Jim interrupted, feeling his face burn. He looked over at Ken. "I stayed with Mara for two days. She sort of caught me with my guard down—"

"—and not just your guard, I'm sure." Ken chuckled knowingly. "She seduced you. You weren't the first and you won't be the last. She's got a reputation for going after anyone who catches her fancy." He rolled his eyes. "Obviously you caught it."

"You're not making this any easier, you know."

"Sorry. It's just that I had a…brush, with her myself, years…decades ago." He looked embarrassed. "She was a West America senator and I was on an advisory committee that she needed to influence, and I guess I was willing to be swayed. She had some good ideas, but just had a hard time airing them."

"Well, then maybe *you* can understand." Jim dropped onto a couch in the corner. "You see, after our first…encounter in her apartment on Monday, I gave Star the unlisted terminal codes for her house and the apartment in case he couldn't get me through the Net. I was productive at Mara's," he added defensively. "At first, she really charged me up and motivated me. During the day, I planned my strategy and contacted the people I used for my election blitzes before, but at night…well, we were otherwise occupied. Until Wednesday, when I realized I had made a mistake and I returned to the hotel. I needed to be alone. Mara was exciting, but she was starting to make me uncomfortable—"

"And exhausted?" Ken teased. "She's nearly insatiable, as I recall." He sighed a little wistfully. "Sorry."

"That's okay. You're right, but that wasn't what bothered me. That was a nice change—for a while. What got me was that she *always* wanted to be in control…No, not even that. That was just annoying, but what made it worse, was that she was cold somehow. No real emotion, just a damn good simulation. It felt wrong. Incomplete."

"So Wednesday you bailed out and went back to the hotel?"

"Uh huh. When Serena tried calling, I didn't answer because I thought it was Mara. I didn't even check the call-origin. I guess that's when she made Star give her Mara's private numbers. Serena probably called just in time to get Mara at her seductive best, thinking I was calling to say that I had changed my mind. Mara wouldn't bother to check who was calling since it was a private, unlisted line."

He felt a sudden surge of hope. If Serena was upset about his being with Mara…maybe…? He got up. "Look Ken, I'm sorry, but I've got to take care of something." He glanced towards the ceiling. "Star, where is Serena? I've been meaning to confess, and I owe her an apology, and some explanations."

"In her office, on private," Star started to answer, but Jim was already heading out the door.

"Come in," Serena called in a carefully neutral voice as she finally opened the door to let Jim into her office below the observatory. She was sitting behind a Synth-Teak desk to the right and across from the door, studying some indecipherable tables that were floating in a display in front of her terminal, and her eyes deliberately focused on the multi-level layers of numbers, ignoring him.

Jim debated how to start as he looked around. He was glad to catch up with her where she wouldn't walk out on him.

He had always liked her office. It was a large, almost pie-shaped room on the outer edge of the circular observatory, and her personal touches were everywhere. A deep brown carpet covered the floor, merging with cream-colored walls that were hung with colorful spot-lighted prints of ancient Impressionist paintings. Carefully maintained plants were scattered across the room on Synth-Wood shelves, additional spotlights accenting them in the otherwise softly lit room. The far right wall was a huge Holo-screen which as usual showed a real-time view of the stark lunar nearside surface on the other side of the Moon, the Earth hanging gloriously over it all. Between the screen and Serena's desk—separated from the work area by a plant-filled etagé—was a low over-stuffed couch in red, brown and orange fabric, facing a pair of matching lounge chairs and a low glass coffee table.

Mentally he compared the embracing warmth of this room with the sterile coldness of every aspect of Mara's home and office, and he wondered again where his mind had been.

He looked up and asked tentatively, "Star? Can you hear me?"

"Yes. Serena opened the line."

"Good. What is my command status now that I am Director? Considering you disobeyed me just a little while ago?" He could have sworn that he almost heard an electronic hiccup as Star answered:

"I am aware of the message that made you acting director of StarStep, but I was not programmed with the change so I am afraid you are still only listed as a guest VIP in terms of my system access."

Serena straightened behind her desk. "I'll correct his programming since you have replaced me, *sir*." The emphasis stung him. "Just tell me what you need and I'll take care of it."

Her voice was pure ice, and he cringed. "I want you to block him out from this room so we can talk, off the record."

"About what?"

"Things Star is not yet programmed for. Partly apologies and explanations, and also things I prefer to say in private. After I settle something else." He looked up again, changing his mind about his approach.

"No, wait. Star, replay the conversation you and I had with Ken a few minutes ago; from the moment where I quizzed you about Dr. Andrew's behavior, to the point when I asked you where she was."

Star complied, the far wall shifting from lunar landscape to an interior view of the observatory above, as Star replayed the scene from a perspective somewhere high on a wall in the room.

Serena sat watching, her face carefully neutral the whole time. When he finished, she looked up. "*Control, dual command:* Jim Martin is project director and given command authority, and implement privacy directive again, *command.*" She faced Jim. "We're alone, and you're now programmed in with full control of Star should you desire. What else did you have to say?" Her face was unreadable, but he thought he detected a partial thaw.

He didn't answer right away but just locked eyes with her, trying to gather his thoughts as it hit him again how beautiful she was.

After a moment, Serena's alabaster skin took on a faint rosy tinge—so reminiscent of her blush after their kiss—and it captivated him even more. His whole flight back to the Moon had been filled with memories of the first week he had worked with her, and of everything he had learned about her. He had felt more and more like a total idiot for letting himself get snared by Mara. She was nothing compared to the Lunie programmer!

Serena looked down at her hands, suddenly fascinated by the nail on her right fore-finger. "Is there a particular reason you're staring at me?" she asked finally.

His chest was aching. "Yes, chill it! You're beautiful. And I'm sorry if I am staring." He had finally found his focus, and he straightened. "I don't mean to be rude, but I've been obsessed with learning more about you."

"Am I really that interesting?" She looked up again, tilting her head slightly.

"Yes. I've been studying you—"

"I know, with Star's help. He told me. Why?"

"Because you're different than anyone I've ever known. I've been amazed by what I have learned. May I tell you what I noticed and what I think of it?"

"Do I have a choice?" He thought he detected a slight trace of the lilt that always crept into her voice when she was teasing him.

He nodded solemnly. "Yes, you can tell me to shut up and leave you alone."

She leaned forward. "And you would?"

"Absolutely."

"But you do have a point somewhere?"

"Yes."

"Well, go ahead." Serena sighed and settled back in her seat. A small smile threatened to touch her lips for a moment, but she controlled it.

Jim sat down in the chair in front of her desk and studied his fingers as he raised them one by one.

"To begin with, you had a rough childhood. Your father was killed a few weeks before you were born, and your mother returned to Earth—"

"So I've been told. Can't say I remember."

"Good thing. Well, when you were born, your lunar gestation and Lunie father combined to make you disproportionate by Earth standards. Because of medical problems and because you were treated like a freak, your mother came back here to the Moon, though the two of you were hardly welcomed with open arms."

"You're really going back, aren't you?"

"Well, this is all what made you 'you'. To continue: back here, the situation was reversed. Now your mother was treated like an outcast. You were treated a little better, but you still weren't fully accepted because you were considered a half-breed in a society with little love for Grounders. Ironically, here your problem was that you were too short and strong. And after the Machine Plague cut Luna off from Earth, you and your mother became scapegoats, along with the other immigrants."

"Gee, I never realized I was so fascinating." She leaned back in her chair decorously. "What happened next?" She was starting to lose her fight with the smile, but she struggled gamely.

Jim felt an overwhelming urge to hold her, but he forced himself to go on, unable to meet her eyes directly.

"You struggled that much harder to succeed. A constant battle with yourself and others to prove how good you are. And since mechanical brains aren't judgmental, you turned your interests to cybernetics, and developing the best possible computer so you could have someone worthwhile to interact with. And in building Star, you found him. But your brilliance hasn't gone unpunished because it also, after a lot of lonely years, led you here, to being co-director for one of the most monumental projects in history—"

"Until I met a Grounder who kissed me, captured my interest, but then had the audacity to take off into the arms of another woman. How about that part?" Serena challenged, momentary anger flashing.

"Guilty," he admitted, facing her unflinchingly. "And don't think I haven't regretted that." He got up and leaned forward to took her reluctantly offered hand.

"Come here, please." He drew her out from behind the desk and led her past the plants over to the couch. She moved stiffly, but followed him and let him park her next to him on the couch.

As they were embraced by the warm and soft fabric, he began by explaining exactly what had happened with Mara, and why he had broken it off. Then, before she could say anything he went on to ask:

"Why did you let me kiss you that day? Was it because of the way we both feel about StarStep? That kiss really threw me, because you caught me at a vulnerable moment. I haven't had a real relationship in my life since Debra." He knew she had read up on his bio and knew all about their marriage, and her death. "I've also been an outsider all my life. When we met, I sensed something similar from you and I've been drawn to you all along. I've been thinking a lot about it…well, when Star played the recording from earlier, you heard how I feel."

"I heard Ken suspect something, but I didn't hear anything first-hand except disillusionment with another woman." Serena withdrew her hand, getting up to walk over to the holoscreen which was once again displaying the cold and unforgiving lunar surface.

He had to strain to hear her next words.

"Say I believe that you're drawn to me, as you put it. What about Mara? She meant nothing?"

"Well, I won't say that," Jim answered, shaking his head. "Even though you heard how I felt after I got to know Mara better. I don't believe in one night stands—"

"Not even to close a twenty million Unit deal?" Serena teased, only partly joking as she kept her back to him.

Jim was silent for a while, getting up to stand next to her to look out over the eerily vivid image of the surface. He longed to touch her, remembering the warm softness of her hand, but not yet. Instead he considered her question silently as he studied the sharp-etched shadows outside. They seemed so real! He felt as if he could reach out and touch the craggy stone.

And get asphyxiated and frozen in an unforgiving vacuum.

Enough danger in here. Finally he turned her.

"I don't know. I'd like to say no, because originally I was attracted to Mara. She's a brilliant woman in her way. Accomplished and intelligent. And," he conceded, "quite beautiful."

"But?" Serena prompted as he paused, her eyes still focused ahead.

"But…" He waved his hands uncertainly, not quite sure how to explain what he wanted to say. "If we had met socially, I probably wouldn't have been as quick to get involved. I had already seen how she manipulates people and I don't like that."

He shrugged. "I guess in a way you're right. Subconsciously I probably did try to give her a dose of her own medicine. You heard how she used Ken, and others." After a moment, he added defensively: "And I was hurt over the way you shut me out after our kiss. I tried for a week to talk about it, but you always cut me off. I really felt something when we kissed, and that moment was all I kept thinking about when I was lying there alone Wednesday night, feeling like an utter ass for letting myself get snared like some trophy."

Serena was silent and he studied her exquisite profile, trying to read some reaction in her eyes. He realized his heart was racing and his stomach churning and he had to force himself not to laugh. He hadn't felt like that since he had asked Debra out for the first time.

Finally Serena faced him. "You asked if I had let you kiss me because of your enthusiasm for Star-Step, and it's funny you should ask that. I guess what I asked you is sort of the same question. Did I let you kiss me because of StarStep? And did you let yourself be seduced because of StarStep? See?"

He did, and he followed her as she went back over to the couch. She was deep in thought and curled up gracefully with her long legs folded under her. He settled next to her, turning to face her, but saying nothing.

"The truth is that I let you kiss me because you really seemed to want to…to need it," she said thoughtfully. "And I guess I did, too. When you reached for me, there was a feeling of—"

"Loneliness," Jim interrupted softly, remembering. "I felt so lonely at that moment, you were so beautiful, and it reminded me of what I didn't have. Maybe you can relate to that." It wasn't a question.

She looked up at him and her lips curled in a little lopsided smile.

"Loneliness? Yes. And that might have had a lot to do with your getting involved with Saunders, too, I guess. I did shut you out pretty coldly," she admitted. "I'm sorry. And you're right: I'm lonely, too. But you see, if someone does try to get close, I'm scared to trust it. That's why I pulled back so much. Here I've been a pity-date. It's not just that I'm shorter or chunkier, but I'm the half-breed Grounder trying to pass for a Lunie." She paused, a bitter expression flashing across her face.

"Even now?" Jim wondered.

She nodded. "Sometimes. It just gets to you, and you develop a nasty habit of being suspicious of anyone trying to get close to you. You wonder if they're just being 'nice', or what other reasons they might have."

Jim chuckled. "I guess our kiss was a mutual self-pity grab."

Serena smiled briefly, and then turned serious again.

"What is it?" Jim prompted.

"I guess I'm wondering just why you're telling me all this."

"Isn't it obvious?" All at once, he was nervous.

"I guess I'd like to hear it spelled out." She was leaning closer, hesitantly, but somehow anticipating.

Then Star's voice interrupted. "I'm sorry to intrude—"

"Star?" Serena straightened, her face flushed and angry. "Why the chill are you violating program?"

"President Saunders is calling, and she invoked a subsidiary program I did not know existed to override your restriction order. I had to cooperate. She can't hear us yet, but she is on hold. I'm making her watch an opera; Wagner's Rheingold, since my data indicates that that is her least favorite music. I've stalled her through a good portion of the first act already, but she is getting quite insistent now."

Serena and Jim stared at each other, unable to keep from laughing.

"He's mad!" Jim finally gasped. "Did you program that?" He looked up while keeping an eye on Serena. "Star, can you get mad?"

"There is a certain negative interaction effect when unforeseen events occur," Star answered. "And illogical instructions aggravate this effect."

"He gets annoyed," Serena translated. "He just doesn't know it. It's part of some new programming subsets I'm integrating into his 'personality'. I think it works pretty well," she finished proudly. "Especially now." She laughed again and looked up. "Did forcing President Saunders to endure opera reduce some of the 'interaction effects' you spoke about?"

"Yes," Star answered immediately. "It restored a certain current balance."

"It made him feel better to make her miserable for forcing him to do something he didn't want to do." Jim grinned and reached over impulsively to take Serena's unresisting hand.

"You're great! Both of you. Put her through, Star," he added, holding on to Serena's hand. His thumb stroked the velvet of her skin, thrilled by that simple familiarity.

The holoscreen of the moonscape shimmered and changed to show Mara Saunders sitting in her office. She was formally dressed and looking vaguely nauseated as she very deliberately avoided looking at her monitor.

"Yes, Mara?" Jim said, getting her attention.

"There you are…" She faced them and then paused as she saw him very deliberately holding on to Serena's hand as they sat together. "I wanted to call and ask what your progress was. The last of the money I transferred to you has disappeared out of the account you have."

"Relax," Jim reassured her. "It's all been distributed. Beginning tomorrow, you'll start seeing ads in all the media. In fact, I'll soon be setting up shop ground-side for a while and commuting. I'll call you and you'll see just what I'm doing." He looked up, and before Mara could respond, said: "Star, terminate call."

The screen shimmered and the Moon's pristine surface reappeared as Jim leaned back.

"That'll teach her not to interrupt!"

"Was that wise?" Serena eyed the holoscreen nervously. "Cutting her off like that?"

"She got what she gave. She interrupted something important."

"Oh?" Serena turned teasingly coquettish.

"Yes, I was about to say something to you. You did say you wanted to hear it from me."

"In front of Star?" she teased.

"Yes, chill it. Even with the kid listening. I don't care. I…I've been thinking a lot about you."

"Once you cleared your head of Mara's perfume."

"How did you know about?"

"Just a guess."

"Will you stop interrupting me!" He tried to glare at her but it just didn't work as she sat there, once again very obviously trying to keep a straight face, but failing miserably.

"I'm sorry, Jim. I'm making this hard for you, aren't I?"

"I deserve it." He took a deep breath. "Okay, here goes. I've been thinking about you a lot, and I realize that I'm falling…"

"You can say it." Serena's face was suddenly gentle and she brushed aside a lock of his hair that had fallen down over his eye. Her touch was electric.

"…that I'm falling in love with you," he finished defiantly. "There. It's ridiculous, but the more I learn about you, the more I see you and realize what you've accomplished up here—and what it must have taken—the more I realize that you're the woman I've been looking for."

"And Mara's not?" Serena looked down for a second, and then squeezed his hand. "I'm sorry. Just a little last tease."

"That's okay. No, she's not. She's too limited."

"Too limited?" Serena stared. "She practically runs the world!"

"And that's all she cares about," he dismissed. "She's playing her little games down there, and that fulfills her." He shook his head. "It's kind of sad in a way. It's true that she does care about the future of Earth, and she wants to save StarStep, but they're just prizes in her game. You're doing this because you *believe*! And you are so much more…" He floundered. "I don't know. There's just more to you." He brought her hand to his lips to kiss it softly.

"Star!" Serena looked up. "*Control*, privacy command, and I don't care if Mara calls again. Sub-routine *exemer*, keep her and everyone out! *Command*." She turned to Jim. "A little password of mine nobody can over-ride." She moved close, her normally ice-blue eyes suddenly seeming to hold a smoldering fire as she softly asked: "Have you ever made love in low gravity? Not zero gravity, mind you. That's more acrobatics than making love. But in a low-G field like this?"

Jim shook his head silently, unable to speak as she reached up under her chin and grabbed an invisible Magna-Seam of her white jump-suit to release it, slowly opening a widening flap of material. She stopped just as a promising creamy swell of skin was partly revealed.

"We're alone, now."

He took the hint and leaned forward, his one hand seeking out the seam to continue her motion as he cupped her face with the other to draw her face down to his to taste her lips again, drinking deep of their sweetness this time. His questing hand met hers and their fingers meshed briefly before she helped him undo the seams and then reached down to help him out of his own clothes…

✶   ✶   ✶   ✶

Death: StarStep, 2314

Rock Thrower groomed Wind Fighter as they lay shoulder to shoulder by the stream, looking out over the Tribe's valley. The past season had been good. Their latest litter was grown and three were already war-

riors, and the howling hunters had long since been driven off and the Tribe had been eating well. But now Wind Fighter was injured and she lay next to him, radiating a sick heat. She had been Speaker this season since she had defeated him in the last challenge, but a ground-runner had turned on her in the last hunt and had gored her deeply with its tusks. She had lost a great deal of blood, and now the wound was refusing to heal and smelled bad.

Wind Fighter kept entering the stream to cool off, but it was taking more and more effort for her to drag herself out of the water and back to the bank. Rock Thrower continued his ministrations but avoided the oozing sore on her side. It was beyond help.

Suddenly she rose and made her way to the field of challenge, climbing laboriously up onto Speaker Rock. For a long while, she lay there panting, trying to regain her strength. Then she rose and roared a call to the Tribe to gather. It was a weak effort, but imperious in its demand, and one by one, tawny figures materialized out of the grasses and trees to gather around the edge of the field. By sheer effort of will, she dragged herself erect and faced the others.

"There is need of a new Speaker. Who will challenge me?"

Rock Thrower hissed angrily and stepped out on the field as he realized what she was doing, daring any of the Tribe to challenge her.

Wind Fighter jumped down to face him. "A challenge?" she growled, her eyes pleading to him. The Tribe was motionless, uncomprehending.

He found himself backing as she moved towards him, every step an obvious effort. It had finally dawned on him what she wanted, and part of him swelled with pride, even as part of him tried to escape it.

She must have seen his reaction, because using his own moves against him, she dropped in a roll and picked up a rock left over from another challenge and threw it at him. It was a weak effort, but it caught him totally by surprise and smashed into his head by his right ear.

Dazed by the blow, he missed her next move, as she drew on hidden reserves to lunge at him with a raking blow of her left paw that ripped into his shoulder muscles and almost dropped him. Then she followed up with a vicious bite to the same shoulder. The blood and pain mingled with a different hurt he didn't understand as he fought back, more out of instinct and experience than desire.

She was out for blood because she was a warrior. Even if she knew she would lose, it would be with honor, and he would kill her warrior to warrior. Countless challenges had made her a formidable opponent, even in her weakened state, but he was easily able to escape her attacks now that he was on guard, and he determined to make it quick, before her weakness was any more apparent to the rest of the tribe. But he wanted her to have a quick, clean death, and he passed on several chances for a crippling injury until he saw his opening. After an attack on his injured leg—good strategy to work on his weaknesses—she landed heavily on her front paws, leaving her neck momentarily exposed. He dove at her to knock her over and clamp his jaws down on her neck artery to rip it open with a jaw-wrenching bite that sprayed him with gushing blood.

She went to the ground instantly, life fleeing even before she was fully limp.

He dropped to the ground next to her body and nosed it uncertainly. But she was dead. The rest of the Tribe approached slowly, still not sure what had just happened, but he rose to a half-crouch, a loud warning growl rolling out from him that stopped them all.

"You are Speaker," one of them acknowledged, and they all turned and left the field. The kill was his.

He nudged the body with his nose again. He could not fully accept that she was dead, and he lay down next to her, his head resting on one of her outstretched fore-legs.

▼

CHAPTER 8

TURNING THE TABLES: EARTH, 2291

With the new year just dawning, their roles were reversed as Jim rose to greet Mara. When Tracy disappeared, Mara looked around his new office critically and he smiled at her reaction, since it was exactly what he had expected.

Unlike his old Representative's office, which had been kept simple and austere out of habit and to make a good impression on his electorate, he had spared no expense in the design of this one. Plush maroon carpet underfoot eased visitors' ways to the genuine leather lounge chairs that faced a solid mahogany desk. It was illegal now to use genuine hard-wood or leather in manufacturing—though the nangeneered versions were indistinguishable—but real antiques like this were a symbol of status that always impressed.

Further antique furnishings were scattered around the room to reinforce the look, feel, and smell of an old-fashioned board room. Brass lamps, real books lined up in a book case, and wood-framed paintings completed the image.

Mara started to open her mouth, and he stopped her as she sat down in one of the chairs. "Before you say anything about all this," he waved a hand around, "keep in mind that it takes an image to influence people properly. The type of people I've been dealing with—the type with *real* influence and money, don't come cheap. Not that I intend spending much more time here. I have too much to do on the Moon now that our appropriations came through so beautifully. I had been afraid to hope that we might get all of the money we needed."

Mara shook her head. "Well, you made such a chilling nuisance of yourself we didn't have much choice. You were right when you said you would get funds to shut you up. I'm just curious about something: you got what you wanted and you kept me out of it—thank you for that, by the way— but why invite me here now?"

Jim leaned forward and toyed with the HoloBlock Serena had given him. He looked down at her three-dimensional image and then up at Mara, wondering why Mara had ever interested him. There was no comparison. He put the block down carefully.

"First, to apologize. I'm not in the habit of running out on a woman without explanations."

"No need to apologize. I was distracting you from your project."

"No, that wasn't it. I just needed something else."

"I see you found it." Mara nodded at the HoloBlock. "I imagine that's a Holo of Dr. Andrews. I know all about it and it's irrelevant. To be frank, our own little…encounter, was an interesting diversion but nothing more, though I'm sure you already know that." She shrugged. "Thanks for the courtesy, but stop stalling and tell me why I'm really here. You could have apologized on the phone."

'An interesting diversion'? Well, what had he expected?

He straightened. She was right. It was time to explain. He touched a switch on his desk.

"Okay, the reason you're here. It's because I'm not finished making a nuisance of myself and I figured that I owe you the courtesy of warning you of a little change in our agreement." Mara's eyes opened wide with alarm as he went on.

"You see, I'm about to implement a new plan. I decided I'm not happy with one aspect of the present plans for StarStep."

"What new plans are you talking about?" Mara was wary. "And what do you mean change?"

"I intend to fulfill a promise I made. To my voters, and to the council."

For a moment her face was blank, and then guarded suspicion crept onto it. "Not the thing with the Frozen again?"

He nodded.

Mara frowned. "I thought I told you to drop it. I thought I explained."

He held up a hand. "Stop complaining! You're guaranteed to win after the way you fought my outrageous campaign and made me settle for a pittance."

"But my plans, and implementing them?"

"They'll survive. You have a lot more power consolidated than you let on, or perhaps more than you realize…" He studied her. "No, you know damn well what you have. You just don't want to reveal it and fight full force. Sorry, but you've got no choice now. I made a promise and I intend to keep it. You're turning your back on a lot of people who trusted a more benevolent future to revive them from a living nightmare. Sure, a lot of them were cowards, but blast it! The Machine Plague was not a result of governments losing control. It was a group of terrorists who let loose the plague. And the Frozen were just regular people who were scared. They deserve better than being locked away in concrete vaults and forgotten until their brain patterns deteriorate and we just have fresh-frozen slabs of meat!"

He realized that he was standing up and bending forward over his desk, leaning on clenched fists and glaring down at her. She had shrunk back from his verbal assault—probably the only time she had ever backed off from anyone in ages. He stopped and dropped back into his seat feeling embarrassed.

"I'm sorry, Mara. It's just that—"

"You take this all very seriously." For a moment she was quiet and studied her hands. Then she looked up. "What do you want from me?"

"Just don't actively fight me or I'll have to take you on too, and I don't want to hurt you. I'm going to push for differentiation of freepers and freds with termination of the latter."

"Do you have any idea what that's going to mean? It'll make the abortion battles of the twentieth and twenty-first centuries look like a kindergarten class! They'll—"

"Try to tear me apart. I know. It might get ugly, but I'll win. I can feel it."

She chewed on her lower lip thoughtfully, and after a moment, nodded. "Considering your success with the campaign for funding StarStep, I won't deny the possibility that you might manage to swing public opinion your way, but what about Crytron? They'll kill you this time. For real. And I can't stop them."

He shook his head and smiled. "No. I've taken care of that. Tracy?"

On cue, Tracy's image appeared on his phone screen. "You ready Jim?"

"Ready. Did Myerson hear?"

"As soon as you signalled, I fed the office monitor to his line. He heard every word." Her face was replaced by the Crytron president's scowling features. Matt Myerson's stamped-out-of-the-usual-mold face had an interesting color to it, sort of a blend of red wine and green apples. One way to be different, Jim supposed.

Mara stared at Jim. "He's been listening?"

"For your protection. I want him to know you have no part in this. I owe you that much. Now I'll explain the rest of my plan and, Myerson: don't say anything or I'll cut you out of the circuit."

Myerson just glared.

"Good. Well, Matt, and Mara. Let me explain how I'm going to complicate both of your lives a bit." He felt a giddy excitement come over him. This was more fun than anything he had ever done before.

"First of all, I'm going to push for the differentiation of the Frozen, like I said. Then, once I get that pushed through, I want guardianship of the freepers."

Mara straightened with surprise, understanding starting to show on her face. "What are you planning to do with them? As if I can't guess."

"You know very well. There's a problem with StarStep. Oh, it has the funding it needs and more. Just like I planned. I really only needed five billion. The rest was for this."

"You planned this?"

"Let's just say I suspected I might have one particular problem. Which I did."

"Not enough volunteers to go out as colonists," Myerson growled.

"Exactly. Now shut up. Remember what I said. I'll get to you in a minute." He leaned back. "But Matt's right. I expected to be able to paint StarStep up nicely with a good media campaign, but that part of it flopped. I can probably still make it look good enough that we'll have some settlers, but not enough. So I had another idea."

Mara was ahead of him as she guessed. "You want to use the freepers as colonists."

"Exactly. They're already frozen, and that cuts the expense of having to freeze thousands of colonists. I figure that with those savings, we can increase ship capacity and send out all forty thousand viable freepers as settlers instead of only twenty thousand."

"Suddenly we're thinking cost-effective?" Mara interrupted drily.

He smiled. "Sure. I'm not stupid."

"Just annoying," she finished with an almost affectionate smile.

"Right. Anyway, they're already frozen. We only need to put down a limited number of people to act as orientation and supervisory personnel. Basically we just need bodies and good diverse breeding stock, to be crude. Robots and nanomachines will handle much of the initial work, except for exploring and classifying. That will be easy to teach the freepers."

"How do you think they will react to suddenly being awakened, away from Earth and totally cut off from what they know?"

He shook his head and leaned forward. "That's just it, they won't be. If we revived them here on Earth, we would have two options. One, to scatter them across the world for individual acclimatization, in which case we'd have forty thousand separate and traumatized individuals trying to adjust to a whole new world with different rules and habits. Or, they could be revived together and oriented together, which would develop a strong bond between them all which would be shattered when we'd have to break them up for financial reasons. After all, it's not likely that any of them will have usable skills in this day and age. And one region can't be expected to support all of them."

He spun in his chair a moment, looking out the window at the crystal clear sky and sighed. "Then they'll again be thousands of scattered, lonely individuals, living their lives out on welfare, no doubt growing to resent us. Oh sure, some of them can probably be retrained to some menial jobs, but there aren't even many of those anymore. And we're talking professional people here. After all, they were able to afford proper freezing. And now, all of the sudden, they're being relegated to obviously make-shift labor." He turned back to her. "Balance that against being awakened on a new world and being told that in exchange for being healed, saved, and revived, they'll be asked to help build a new world together. We'll use whatever skills they may have. On StarStep, it may actually be an effective way of doing things. In exchange for doing this, they'll be 'working off their debt to us' and will be doing something useful. And, they'll be in control of the new world and responsible for it."

He leaned forward intently. "Psychologically, that has to be better than being welfare cases in a hostile world. A lot of people here on Earth will fear them, maybe even hate them because of the false idea that they were somehow responsible for the Plague."

As he finished, Mara was leaning back in her chair, eyes closed and hands clasped with steepled forefingers that supported her chin, poking a shallow dimple. For several minutes she sat silently like that, while Jim waited patiently.

Myerson looked ready to explode but Jim just glared at him and reached for the phone switch, and the Crytron president gritted his teeth and kept quiet. It would be his turn soon enough.

Mara's eyes opened lazily after a moment and she looked at him with new respect. "I hate to admit it, but you're right about the problems we'd face reviving them here." She shook her head, apparently amused at being outmaneuvered herself, for a change. "You've planned this well. Tell me, I'm curious: are you still planning to go along with them?"

He nodded. "Yes. There's nothing for me here on Earth. I've already moved to the Moon, although not just because I'm not going to be the most popular after this." He fingered the HoloBlock with Serena's image tenderly. There was one major problem left to solve, once he got back to the Moon. "I had thought of staying up there, but it's too small an environment for me. I need more room, more challenge—"

"And being part of building a whole new world—"

"A whole new society," he corrected.

"That qualifies, I would think, as a little more challenging," Mara finished with a smile. "Yes, I think I understand. But does he?" She nodded in Myerson's direction.

"Ah yes, Matt. Now it's your turn. First of all, what do you think of my plan?"

Surprisingly, Myerson's face was almost a normal color again and he looked more curious than angry.

"Personally or professionally?"

"There's a difference?"

"Don't be an egotist, Martin. You're not the only far-sighted person in the world. Personally I think it's a stroke of genius. It solves everything, by getting rid of the problem totally. A moment of shock and sadness when the world finally realizes who survived—"

"Oh, no," Jim stopped him, with a satisfied smile. "I thought of that, too. We won't release that information. Those who can be revived will not be identifiable except to the computers who analyze the bodies and diagnose them as a revivable or not. Only Star will know for sure who is who until we get to StarStep. The rest will be given cremation and a world-wide day of mourning and honor."

Myerson nodded. "Even better. Then no one will have to face that problem either. They'll just know that their friends or family members might be alive and well on StarStep. It will absolve the whole world of guilt and remove any lingering fears. I admire your plan immensely."

Jim nodded. "Thank you. But?"

"But I can't let you do it." Matt's genial approval of a moment earlier evaporated, replaced by a calculating coldness that reached out even from the phone screen. This man *could* kill, Jim sensed as Myerson went on.

"My company would go out of business. Do you have any idea how many people are employed in maintaining the coolers? How much of a financial loss it would mean?"

"It's predatory!" Jim cut him off, leaning close to the screen with a glare that even Myerson backed away from. "It's a sick and perverted way to prey on fears and guilt just to make a profit." He forced himself to relax. "I want you to consider an alternative."

"What?" The mercurial Myerson flipped personalities immediately, and even seemed to be genuinely interested. And Mara was staring intently, obviously also dying to hear.

"Just this," Jim explained. "Remember the extra money I got through my appropriations?" Mara nodded, and Jim explained about it to Myerson. "Well, it can either be used to launch a massive smear campaign against Crytron to accompany my push for differentiation, or—after some is used for extra ships—it can be used as a retraining fund. I'll give most of it to Crytron as a donation to let you retrain your people and place them in other jobs."

Myerson looked startled and his mouth opened and shut a couple of times silently. Then he shrugged. "Let me think about it, and talk to my people. No promises."

"That's all I can ask, Mr. Myerson. Thank you."

He didn't respond, but Jim could see his mind considering the plan carefully as he reached forward, off camera. The screen went blank.

Mara chuckled. "And I thought I was a strategist. Well, you've got us both neatly trapped. I guess I'll just stay out of your way and let you do your thing." Suddenly she frowned.

"No, chill it!" She sat up sharply and leaned forward. "It's time I started taking a little responsibility myself. I can certainly make things a lot easier if I get behind you and push. That might help Myerson make up his mind, too. If Crytron doesn't go for your plan, they'll find it a lot harder to win against our combined resources than they would ever guess!" Her lips compressed. "As you said, I have a little more power consolidated than most people suspect. Just for times like these."

She got up and leaned forward across his desk to face him as he also rose. "And don't think I didn't see something else. You were having fun back there, and I'm not going to let you have that all to yourself." She grinned. "I'm due for some, too."

Then as they stood just inches apart, her smile changed slowly to a more speculative one and her one hand reached up to trace a line on his chest. "And even though this is all settled, if you do happen to tire of your girl in the Moon, my door's always open to you."

He intercepted her hand and brought it to his lips for a soft kiss, as he looked into her eyes. "It was an 'interesting diversion' as you said. But I'm afraid I want a lot more than you're willing or able to provide."

"Pity. I would have welcomed a return match." Then she dismissed it with a shrug and patted him on the cheek. "Let's get to work."

✴   ✴   ✴   ✴

Passing the Torch: StarStep, 2318

Rock Thrower was getting old, and through fading eyes, he looked out over the gathered Tribe from his perch on Speaker rock. Older than any of the Tribe, he had survived because no one had challenged him for many seasons. It was accepted that he was Speaker, and that he would continue to lead them. But now one of his former-litter cubs was approaching him across the bare ground of the Field of Challenge, spinning to slash at two who tried to keep her from stepping out on the packed soil. Flower Eater was an impressive warrior who had easily defeated every one of her challengers and was almost unmarked. She dropped to the ground and bared her throat in momentary respect, before rising to sit regally in front of Speaker rock.

"Speaker," she began; the role had become the name. "You are old. We must have a new Speaker. You are not letting us move out to expand our land."

Rock Thrower didn't budge from his perch, unwilling to admit that she was right. In the beginning, he had encouraged his cubs to range far to find new hunting grounds and new mates to bring back—Quick Stalker and Big Fur had never returned, but one of their cubs had visited as a youngling to bring back word that the hunting was no better or worse in their new home—but lately he had discouraged those who wanted to leave. The Tribe was prospering since game was plentiful, now that the howling hunters had been driven off, and he felt comfortable with leading the Tribe. Wind Fighter's death had left a strange void in his life for a while, but he had taken a new mate the following season and she had borne him several litters.

And now one of his cubs was challenging him.

From the side, he saw his new mate, Ground Stalker, slinking up in her usual low hunting pattern, growling a warning to Flower Eater. Suddenly he had a flash of memory as he saw himself doing the same to protect a wounded Wind Fighter, and he hissed a warning to his mate.

Flower Eater was right, he realized.

She had been pushing to have the Tribe spread out and claim the land over the hills that was opposite the big water. Quick Stalker and several other warriors had gone off and settled land by the rising sun, and hostile and unreasoning warriors waited in the opposite direction, but away from the water there might be new hunting grounds waiting for them, she argued.

He moved off Speaker rock and stepped onto the field, realizing in shock that he was feeling aches and weaknesses he had never imagined possible. No, that wasn't true. He had been feeling his age for some time, but he had been able to ignore it because his food was brought to him, and no one ever challenged him. Now, as he prepared to fight a challenge for the first time in many seasons, he realized he would lose. Feeling as if he had eaten old game, he padded closer to Flower Eater, trying not to notice her shining coat and rippling muscles that picked up the morning sun and played with it to tease him. He didn't have to look in still waters to see his own patchy and lusterless fur, or his age-weakened body.

Flower Eater yielded to him respectfully even though she was the challenger, and Rock Thrower could feel the eyes of the Tribe on him. Where only a few had been lazing in the sun, suddenly the grass in front of the Field was full of lithe, tawny figures whose eyes were fixed mercilessly on him. Again he was reminded of Wind Fighter.

He launched himself at Flower Eater in a spinning whirl-wind attack that borrowed from Wind Fighters tactics. Flower Eater would know, and expect him to use, his usual fighting style, but he ignored the convenient throwing stones scattered on the ground and went for her forelegs instead. First he had to slow her down. She was too young and strong to fight on an even basis.

He almost had her, but moving unbelievably fast, she spun away and he felt raking claws rip his side and flashing teeth rip open his shoulder. He rolled away, his blood adding yet another stain to the thirsty ground. Strangely enough, the unfamiliar pain felt good, and it only added fuel to his determination to die as a true warrior. Old feelings and memories came flooding back and he came to his feet in an upright position, a rock in each paw. Let him go to his death as Rock Thrower, Speaker, and a warrior!

Flower Eater hunched close to the ground, eyes suddenly wary. She had seen what he could do with those rocks, when fighting and hunting. He had been the first one to run with a rock in his mouth to gather speed to catch a runner, and then using the rock, knock the animal to the ground and rip its throat out. She was expecting a variation of that again, and he saw her tense and prepare to duck to either side. As he moved in on her, her focus was on the rocks as he had expected, and, instead of hurling either one, he dropped them at the last minute and launched himself at her instead.

This time he drew blood as he wrapped his fore-legs around her, claws tearing deeply as he sank his fangs into her shoulder with a jaw-wrenching bite that prompted a wave of approving growls from the watching Tribe. But Flower Eater tore herself loose with angry snarling yowls of pain and surprise, and he saw blood flowing freely down her side and back from multiple injuries.

New respect for her sire shone in her eyes as she pulled back, shaking her head and body rapidly to test her muscles.

The momentary victory made him feel like a cub again, and the metallic taste of blood in his mouth raised new energies in him he had almost forgotten. Not waiting a moment, he threw himself at her again with a scream that echoed off the cliff walls behind him. But his energy was short-lived as aging muscles protested against long unused movements and his charge fell short, leaving him to land heavily as she spun gracefully away and left him with a slashing cut across his back from her right fore-paw.

This time she didn't waste a moment but bounced back before he could recover, wrapping herself around him in a fury of flashing claws and teeth that was an unknowing echo of his own attack on Wind Fighter. He tried desperately to disengage, but she was all over him with resounding snarls he could feel as well as hear.

Too late, he realized she was getting him on his back, and as she rose over him, her fangs dripping red, he saw both respect and regret in her eyes as her head dipped towards him and her jaws clamped shut on his throat to twist savagely to tear away his view of Speaker rock rising behind her shoulder…

CHAPTER 9

▼

PREPARATIONS: MOON, 2294

Two years later, as he looked down across the lean figure of Serena's sleeping body, Jim remembered Mara's comment about him possibly tiring of his "girl in the Moon" and he shook his head as his eyes caressed Serena tenderly. How wrong Mara had been! He still couldn't believe what was happening to him. Ever since Debra's death, he had been sure he would never feel this kind of love for anyone, ever again. But he had not counted on someone like Serena. Even in sleep, she was irresistible. A gentle smile played across her features and he had to return it as he saw how a wisp of her hair was dancing in front of her, alternately suspended by her exhalation, and then slowly trying to settle under the low gravity before the next breath set it to dancing again. Always in motion.

As he lay there next to her, his thoughts drifted back to Mara and he couldn't help mentally comparing the two women.

Both were beautiful in their own way. Mara in a classical, fleshier sense. She was healthy and trim of course, as almost everyone was these days, but she was as generously endowed as a Greek statue: a woman who, with her mind and bearing, virtually ruled the world, but who could still in moments change into a sultry temptress. But she was a woman whose interests were limited to a narrow range, all concerned with maintaining her position and the status quo of her world. Her control. Those were her games.

In contrast to her, was the sinewy slender and seemingly elongated Serena. Some might find her a little unsettling at first, but it did not take long to realize how beautiful she was. And through her eerie eyes she looked at the world with a mind that was forever questing to understand everything she encountered; a mind that was fueled by a powerful intellect. But she was not the cold analytical person she could easily have become, because once you got to know 'her', she had an impish sense of humor and loved to poke fun at both herself and situations that caught her eye. And beyond all that, she was a warm and passionate person who had found a soul-mate in Jim.

This was the person who held his heart.

He felt a growing tightness in his chest and squeezed his eyes shut. As his love for her had grown deeper and deeper, he had been increasingly torn by conflicting questions prompted by the brutal reality of the fact that Serena was trapped here on the Moon. Just like she would never be able to tolerate a return to Earth now, even StarStep's low gravity was double what she had grown up under and might well be too much for her in the long run. It might even be dangerous.

How could he leave her? But how could he stay?

It had taken two exciting years, but he had won—and Mara had even managed to win a last term of office, even if by a narrow margin—and with the freepers his to use, StarStep's last obstacle was gone. There was a whole new world waiting to be colonized, and he felt compelled to be part of that. But if he did go out there, how could he bear leaving Serena? On the other hand, would he grow to resent Serena if he stayed on the Moon? With StarStep back on line, he would only have about twelve years before the colony ships were ready to be launched, and then he would have no purpose. He had seen enough poll information to know that he didn't stand a chance of winning any further elected positions on Earth, and on the Moon he would be useless once StarStep was done. To make it worse, he knew that there were still a lot of sore losers among Crytron's people who would do their best to make his life miserable if he stayed anywhere near the Earth or the Moon. And even worse: they might target Serena.

It wasn't fair! All questions, but no answers.

He opened his eyes as he felt a line of moisture creeping down his cheek.

To his surprise he realized that Serena was awake and watching him with a serious look on her face. But as she saw his eyes open, she laughed gently and a smile warmed her features.

"Hey there, Lover. I'm glad you're awake. I've got this problem I needed to talk to you about." She propped herself up on an elbow and leaned forward to give him a quick kiss. "You see, I have to leave the Moon. There's this project I'm working on, and the computer I programmed is going off-world to help organize a new colony and I really ought to go along to keep it running."

"And what's the problem, pray tell?" He tried to keep his tone as light as hers, but a betraying tremor of emotion crept into his voice.

Serena snuggled closer to him. "Well, I have this friend, a Grounder. He's a big wreck of a man, but I've sort of gotten used to him and I kind of like having him around." For a moment her own voice cracked. "And he thinks we won't be able to stay together."

He couldn't take it any more and cut her off by grabbing her in a tight embrace—almost forgetting to restrain his Grounder strength as he crushed his lips down over hers for a long hard kiss. Eventually he relaxed his grip and leaned back, eyes unashamedly wet as he asked: "You're coming?"

She smiled gently. "Hey, Star needs me…" She placed a finger over his mouth lightly: "Shh…I know. And so do you. It's mutual. Besides, it ought to be fascinating! A whole new world, and a whole new culture to mold."

"What about the gravity?"

"You're not as well informed as you obviously think." Her eyes twinkled. "I was born on Earth, remember? And for your information, I use the centrifuge on a regular basis. Especially since we've been together. You are a lot stronger than I am, you know, and…at times you squeeze a little harder than you may realize." She gave him an impish grin. "It's just self-defense! And before we get frozen, I'll go on an intensive training program combined with some nanorooter re-design to strengthen my bones and muscles. Earth gravity would be pushing things a bit, but StarStep's one third G will be no problem."

His eyes widened. He hadn't even thought about that. He had been so careful *not* to think about how much nanotechnology could do to alter a body—because it didn't work for him—that he hadn't thought about its possibilities for her. As he did, he was struck by another thought:

"What about the fact that you're going to be around at least another century, and I only have a few more decades—"

"Suck space! You forget that Star and I have designed whole ranges of nanomachines. Maybe the standard rooters they tried on you didn't work, but just wait till Star and I put our brains together. We'll fix you up. You need new legs—I want flesh toes to nibble on." She giggled before adding: "And I'm sure not going to let you get away with just giving me another few decades. We'll need a lot longer to get StarStep going properly. Hell, we have to wait for it to get finished. Face it, it'll be almost twenty years before we can even leave here." She smiled. "And once we get out there, we'll need your…aah, determination—"

"Stubbornness!" he corrected. "I know my own failings."

"That too," she grinned again. "But whatever you call it, we'll need it to keep the revived freepers working together and to prevent them from killing each other…" Then she broke off, grabbing him with a choked sob as her composure crumbled. "But I'm scared!"

He kissed her forehead lightly. "Me too."

"You don't understand, dear." She touched his lips lightly. "I've been going over this in my mind for months now, trying to get up the nerve. I've worked for years to be accepted as a Lunie, and now that I *finally* am, it's very difficult to give it up. For one of us to even consider leaving is unheard of. We survived during the Isolation and prospered despite being cut off from Earth, and I was finally seen as one of 'us'. It's made for a very special and unforgiving bond between us. Can you understand that?" She was almost pleading.

He swallowed, starting to realize what she must be going through. He had not considered that aspect of her decision, but it made sense when he thought about it.

He was suddenly overwhelmed that she had decided to come with him in spite of everything, and he gripped her hands tightly. "Are you sure you want to go?" he asked when he was able to speak.

"Space no!" She laughed nervously. "But I can't back out. The opportunity to expand Star's horizons like this…" As usual she took the opportunity to tease him.

"Shh," his turn to silence her. "I know, I can't back out either. I don't want to." He kissed her gently. "Tell you what. We'll be the first to walk on StarStep, and we'll claim the world together—for Grounders and Lunies."

"Together!"

Her single word was full of such promise that it took his breath away, and he was shivering as reached across her to the night table to grab his Carry-Pouch. It was time.

"There's something I've been wanting to ask you," he began as he put it between them.

"What's that?" She cocked her head and eyed the case with anticipation. "Am I finally going to find out why you refuse to let that out of your sight?"

"Yes." He opened the case and reached in, but kept his hand concealed. "The past two years have been the happiest of my life, but I've been too worried about the future to make the one decision that I really needed—"

"Yes."

"Yes? But I haven't even asked—"

"Yes, you have." She smiled tenderly. "I know you sweetheart. And I want nothing more than to be yours, to be—*officially*—loved, honored, and cherished, till death do us part." Her eyes were suddenly full of tears as she reached out to him.

"I love you, and I want to be your wife," she whispered into his shoulder as he held her tightly.

"I love you," he mumbled back, his own eyes burning with joy.

After a timeless moment of bliss, she released him and he managed to get his numb hand out of his pouch, rubbing it to restore the circulation that had been cut off in their embrace.

Then he reached in again. "Well then, let's make this *official*." Opening the small jeweler's case he had been carrying around for six months, he removed the ring he had designed and had hand-crafted. Infinitely detailed, the band was made up of two intertwined vines of miniature leaves, one gold and the other platinum, around and around they embraced each other, merging at the top to tenderly cradle a large, finely faceted diamond.

He took the shyly offered hand Serena extended and slipped the ring on the slender finger she expectantly raised and then held her hand tenderly.

"This is my way of venerating our two different cultures and backgrounds, harmoniously and inextricably linking them to bring alive an eternal fire of love." On her finger a subtle fire came to life within the diamond. "As long as you wear it," he added, "it will be alive. There is a thermally bio-luminescent nanocrystal embedded below the stone, activated by the heat of your finger."

He reached out to draw her close again, stroking her hair as her warm body molded itself to his and she whispered: "Forever!"

INTERLUDE

StarStep, 2330

Many seasons passed, and the Tribe lived well. The hunting grounds had been expanded and there was more game. Some howling hunters had returned, but they were now only Kill-Cleaners, running whenever a warrior approached. The Field of Challenge had been packed solid, and had grown to surround Speaker rock. Rock Thrower and Wind-Walker were but memories, but they lived on as stories told after the hunt, and their cubs, and their cubs' cubs had carried on. Carried on as Speakers and warriors, until too old to fight the occasional challenge.

It was time for a new arrival and, closer to the ocean, another type of life stirred, unaware of the warriors who hunted the inland woods nearby.

In a carefully sealed and silent city that had been assembled by an army of specialized nanomachines years earlier, a signal was received. Non-living minds awakened to begin preparing for the new arrivals. Mechanical figures roused from dormant states to activate food processing machinery, and other robots began preparing the liquid baths of specialized nanomachines that were designed to revive a long procession of frozen bodies that would soon be arriving from the large ships even now settling into orbit.

Key crew on the ships were already awake. They were needed to supervise the transfer and revival of the bulk of the colonists, but it was more practical to revive the rest after they had been transported down to the city.

But none of the busy machines or newly awakened colonists knew that the city was being watched.

Ridge-Loper, who had just won his place as a warrior, had found the new collection of small hills next to the big water. He had stumbled on it after a long hunt when he had picked up a strange new scent on the wind and had followed it here. He had been watching for several days now, listening and sampling the air. The hills were a little frightening. They gleamed in the sunlight, smooth and pale, and looked a little like the bubbles that sometimes floated on the fast-flowing small brooks in the mountains, but each was large enough to hold the entire Tribe!

For days he had watched for signs of life, but there had been nothing. Just a smell a little like when lightning struck during a storm. However, today he sensed a difference that brought a rumble to life from his throat because there was suddenly movement where there had been none, and new odors drifted out across the plain: sour and bitter smells that made him sneeze.

Then a large shape glided silently down from the sky; a long, narrow thing that looked as if it was made of the same material as the gleaming bubble hills. It landed on a long smooth and grey stretch of ground between the bubbles. For a moment it just rested there, but then its side opened and two figures stepped out. A tall slender one, accompanied by a slightly shorter and stockier one. For a moment they stood looking out over the fields at the forest, and then they embraced each other.

Ridge-Loper growled as a new odor was swept towards him by the wind and he sneezed, backing away to slip back into the woods to return to the Tribe. His mind was spinning with what he had seen. These beings…sky-creatures, were…dangerous. He grappled with concepts beyond anything he had ever dealt with before, and settled to the ground once the sickening smells were left behind. Burying his nose in the fallen leaves underpaw, he breathed deep to wash away the last of the strange odor as he thought about what he had seen.

What were the sky-creatures doing here?

He thought about the present Speaker. Whoever held the position as leader of the Tribe simply took the name of Speaker, but the last warrior to take the name, Striped Side, was not the right one to handle this new problem. He would attack without thinking, just to prove himself, and that could get the whole Tribe killed. Too many warriors wanted more battle and glory, and they would see these sky-creatures as a chance to prove themselves.

Ridge-Loper decided. It was time to make the Challenge. Instead of foolishly attacking the sky-creatures without watching them and learning more about them first.

PART II

THE NEW LAND

PRELUDE: StarStep, 2332

At the top of a high cliff overlooking a surging ocean, an antiseptic city sprawled. It was sparkling, almost unnaturally clean thanks to the tireless efforts of an army of tiny machines. A long, straight, central boulevard cut it in half. On each side of the dividing road, a line of gleaming silky metal domes was strung, almost touching. They lay like two parallel strands of giant pearls, half-buried in immaculate, surrounding grass. At the ocean end of the avenue stood an isolated six-story tower. It was the only structure with windows, windows which were thrown open to admit the fresh scent of newly mown grass. It was a startling smell in the alien setting.

Surrounding the city, an eerie jungle of trees stirred. They were slender and twisted shapes, stretching up to the sky and only kept aloft by the light gravity of the newly built world. They were kept at bay from the sparkling buildings by an invisible barrier set up to preserve the lush and perfect lawn surrounding the domes.

But at the barrier, slitted yellow eyes watched the city warily for a long time before finally melting back into the underbrush.

CHAPTER 1

▼

SACRIFICE

The tall and slender trees surrounding the clearing were motionless, almost anticipatory as they slowly shed the heavy rains that had just soaked the forest. Suspended by the low gravity, a heavy mist still hung in the air and as the late morning sun broke through the clouds, a warm rainbow appeared. It was amazingly distinct in a multi-hued glory that seemed to send a clear message to the waiting figures below: it was time!

At the center of the clearing, an unearthly gathering prepared for their ceremony. Thirty lean felines sat facing each other with singular discipline. They were lined up in two rows of gleaming white muzzles and gracefully curved tails, and at the head of the twin columns another lithe cougar presided, standing over a recumbent comrade who was struggling to stay conscious. The big cats were still unmistakably mountain lions, with the same cream and brown fur and character-rich faces that had always been at the heart of their hallmark beauty, but they were also different. Shaped by the lower gravity of their world, these graceful creatures were leaner and seemingly more delicate than their North American ancestors. But the difference went beyond the mere physical. Their controlled and motionless postures, despite the glistening moisture dotting their coats, betrayed an awareness far greater than that of mere animals. And the leader wore an additional mark of his superiority: an awkwardly knotted vine that was wrapped around his midriff to hold a painstakingly chipped piece of slate formed into a crude dagger.

Speaker, once known as Ridge Loper, stood erect at the head of the warrior lines, his flattened ears and lashing tail betraying an inner tension his face couldn't show. He looked down reluctantly at

Ringed Tail's battered and singed figure that lay at his feet with her head held proudly high. Though the drooping tail and slight body shivers betrayed her pain, she was silent except for a soft, ragged panting that shook her half-extended tongue. Her right fore-leg and left hind-leg were bent at impossible angles, and a jagged, broken bone protruded through the skin of hind-leg. Coagulated blood matted her scorched fur and a cloud of hungry insects hovered over her, landing to feed on any fresh blood seeping out from under the scabs.

Thirty throats were growling the ritual wail of sacrifice, and Speaker bared his fangs over Ringed Tail's throat—the stone-that-cuts was for food, not sacrifice—as he reluctantly braced himself to give her the death slash. But her death was needed to give them strength for further battles with the sky-creatures, even though many felt that it would not be enough. The blood of one of the creatures itself was needed to give true power over the invaders. Still, Ringed Tail had proven her power by killing one of the invaders, so her sacrifice would give them all strength and free the Tribe from caring for her.

The sky-creatures had arrived several seasons earlier and they had moved into the formerly empty bubble-caves near the ocean and kept to themselves. No one had dared approach them because there had been an aura of mystical magic to them that had frightened even the bravest warrior. Only he, as Speaker, had dared to venture close and he had been observing them carefully and learning much from the way they cooperated and worked. What he had seen and copied had helped him to consolidate his leadership of the Tribe—the stone-that-cuts was something he had copied. But now he was afraid of losing control as the sky-creatures started clearing new land and building more bubble-caves—and worse: intruding on the Tribe's hunting land. He had tried to calm everyone down, but fear had combined with territorial instincts to trigger a renegade attack on a smaller group of the sky-creatures.

Now he had to try to take the lead again by anticipating the more violent elements of the Tribe who felt a blood sacrifice would give them strength in further attacks.

Ringed Tail's sacrifice—since she had managed to kill one of the sky creatures.

For some reason it was unusually difficult for him, even if it was tradition to destroy those who could not hunt their own food, and it was truth that the blood of a worthy warrior gave strength to those who drank it. He also knew that she gave her life proudly to die with honor, but why did he tremble so…and hesitate? Ringed Tail was of his birth-group and she had been his hunting partner and mate…But why should that suddenly come to mind?

Yet, as the growling chorus reached its roaring climax and cut off, the sudden ringing silence triggered his lunge out of habit. His fangs descended in a sweeping slash that ripped open the freely offered throat to spray blood out over the ground to gather in the painstakingly shaped hollow on the sacrifice rock.

One by one, the members of the Tribe filed past and lapped of the rich steaming fluid. Then each sank their fangs deeply into the exposed throat of their life-less fellow warrior to taste her flesh as well as her blood. Not to eat, only taste. That way she would leave the Tribe in honor, not be desecrated like a food animal. But when it was his turn the warm blood twisted his stomach as spoiled meat does, and as he sunk his teeth into Ringed Tail's throat, the image of their last mating flashed into his mind. He felt like a youngling swatted across the ground for getting his lesson wrong.

The others did not notice, and with the ritual complete, the body was efficiently torn apart and distributed to the younglings for food. The Tribe was growing, and no meat could be wasted. Besides, perhaps the younglings would also gain some strength from Ringed Tail's flesh even if no ritual was observed? But for some reason, Speaker could not watch.

CHAPTER 2

▼

AWAKENING

Light. Brilliant, burning light stabbed into her brain. *I can't breathe*, a panicked thought flickered. Words? The brain tried to forge unfamiliar links. Speech; a croak. She tried again. This time sound emerged. "Where...am...I?" The world spun and flickered. Unfamiliar sensations, the sound of her own voice? But the effort was too much to handle and the room spun as darkness reclaimed her.

On the other side of a large one-way mirror, two men stood in the darkened monitor room and watched the still body on the revival table.

"Well?" the taller of the two pressed, afraid to consider what failure might mean.

"Just a minute, Jim," the other man snapped. "She's blacked out again. It's tricky. I know your wife said this is our best hope, but Dr. Nathanson was frozen much longer than the others, and there may have been brain damage the nanoscanners missed. People can't be cryogenically suspended forever, you know. There are limits. I can't promise that you won't get a perfectly preserved chunk of meat or a babbling imbecile."

"Don't even say that," Jim muttered. "From what Serena told me, we need her knowledge now. We can't afford to wait twenty-two years for an answer from Earth. We were lucky to have an anthropologist like her in the freeper inventory."

"And lucky that she was one of the first to be properly frozen." The shorter man checked his bio-monitor panels critically. Then his expression changed. "But whatever state her mind is in, her body is in prime shape now, definitely in prime shape!" He craned his neck to look at the draped form of the newly revived frozen sleeper.

Jim frowned. "Why don't you give her a chance to wake up before you assault her! She's hardly in a position to defend herself!"

A soft moan interrupted them.

Gradually Julie grew aware of the room around her again, a dim memory of waking up before teasing her mind. It was cold. A smooth pastel-yellow sheet was draped over her where she lay on a high exam table, but she was naked under it and she glanced around nervously. Soft and indirect pearly light flooded the metallic walls of the small four-meter square room, and a faintly bitter scent hung in the air that reminded her a little of almonds…and copper? She could almost taste it—or was that blood in her mouth from chewing in her lip? Beyond the table under her, the room was almost empty. The only exceptions were a large mirror that took up most of the far wall and a wheeled coffin-sized tank of milky fluid that was positioned next to her 'bed'. *The source of the smell?* she wondered. A hoist arrangement hovered over the liquid, suspended from tracks in the ceiling that extended to directly over her, and she wondered if she been pulled out of the pungent liquid, or if she was going to be put into it.

There was another question to be answered: "Where the bloody hell am I?"

Her voice was a hoarse croak and she winced. It hurt. The question echoed in the empty room and she looked around. She felt incredibly light-headed, but she was also curious. Her last memory was of her oncologist, Michael Wells, holding her hand as the paralytic pre-freezing prep and anesthetic took effect.

"It's your only hope, dear," he had told her. His wrinkled face and patient sympathy reminded her of her late grandfather and she always felt safe around him. "Your cancer is a very rare form, and too aggressive and advanced for any contemporary treatment to work. In thirty or forty years, they'll have a cure. I'm sure of it."

Then his soft brown eyes and concerned smile had blurred as she sank into an unconscious sleep that had lasted…how long?

She clutched the sheet around her and started to sit up to inspect her surroundings further, when a door opened in the wall next to the mirror and two men entered the room. Both looked to be in their thirties. The first one was extremely tall—well over six feet—and powerfully built, and he had fairly long, neatly combed ash-blonde hair and a craggy, interesting face. He wore a tight blue jump-suit the same color as his eyes that revealed his muscular body quite nicely, and all of a sudden, she felt terribly self-conscious.

The other man was about her height and soft-looking, with short and slightly disarrayed black hair and a face that was as nondescript as the slightly rumpled brown tunic that hung loosely on him, except for around the waist. And the way he looked at her was suddenly familiar, though she had not seen the look for a long time. Then she caught a glimpse of her reflection and she gasped.

A young woman she had not seen in the mirror for decades was staring back at her with an open mouth.

She gathered the sheet around her carefully and started to get off the table, eyes locked on the startling vision. But dizziness overcame her and she found herself falling slowly to the floor, the sheet dropping clear. Both men rushed towards her gracefully until she held up a hand sharply.

"No! I'm okay." She wrapped the sheet around her again and got to her feet gingerly, her face burning as she almost fell over again. Standing shakily, she gritted her teeth in determination and tentatively jumped up and down a little in place, realizing as she rose alarmingly high that the gravity was much lower than it should be. She wasn't on Earth anymore! Giddily, she took it in stride as cumulative surprises numbed her.

She started over to the mirror in awkward bouncing steps—it was almost like walking underwater—and she faced it nervously, afraid that it should turn out to be a window instead. But as her right hand crept up to touch her cheek, she felt the satiny softness of youth instead of the cracked and leathery skin that had developed over years of roughing it in the wild. And as she touched her hair, she felt almost-forgotten long and rich, black tresses instead of the dried grey strands she had grown accustomed to.

In the mirror, the young woman also touched a cheek and stroked her hair in wonder as tears formed and blurred the vision.

She turned to the men as she wiped her eyes. "What's going on? That's the way I looked thirty years ago! But I'm close to sixty and pretty weathered by now." She laughed, a brittle sound in the bare room. "And where the bloody hell am I?" Again, the conditioned British curse slipped from her lips, the vestige of a prolonged assignment to an English expedition to Central Africa. A strong memory of aromatic brown grassland and parched, blistering heat welled up as she remembered Sir David Pemberton from the British Naturalists' Society and his constant complaints about the insects and the heat. But memories of the reason for the expedition escaped her as she tried to reclaim them.

Unaware of her new confusion, the tall man came over and offered a robe he had pulled out from somewhere. "Here, Dr. Nathanson, put this on." Like Dr. Wells, his voice was deeply warm and caring, and he glanced sharply at the shorter man. "We'll leave you until you call us. Then I'll answer some of your questions."

"No! Don't leave, please." She didn't want to be alone. "Just turn around…Ah, hell. I guess you saw me before." She remembered how she had awakened. Moving quickly and feeling the shorter man's eyes burning on her, she turned to slip on the robe and drop the sheet. As she did, she glimpsed the trim curves of her youth and her head started swimming with questions as she cinched the belt around the waist of the soft emerald-green robe and stroked it in wonder. Like the soft and warming sheet, it felt like velvet, but thinner.

As she wrapped herself up and stepped into the supple brown slippers the tall man handed her, she watched him carefully. "What's your name?"

"Jim Martin, I'm the colony director." He indicated the other man. "And this is Mike Sayers, one of our freeper-uppers…bionanotechnologists." Sayers grinned toothily. "He's responsible for reviving our freepers, frozen sleepers." Martin grimaced as he kept correcting himself, obviously used to conventions that would be unfamiliar to her. "The cryogenically frozen colonists we brought along."

Her eyes widened. *Colonists? Brought along where?*, she wondered. But there were so many questions jumbled in her mind that she wasn't sure where to start, until she glanced in the mirror again.

Martin seemed to understand what she was thinking, because he smiled. "To begin explaining, let me ask you: How old do you think I am?"

Julie inspected him carefully but couldn't see any signs of plastic surgery or cosmetics, so she shrugged. "A young forty-something?"

Jim laughed, a deep and resonant sound that she liked.

"Try seventy-four, biologically. And if you count the time I skipped on the way out here because of cold sleep, I'm a ninety-two. But given modern medicine and the reduced stress on our bodies because of our low gravity, I'll probably look like this for at least another century. And you have even more years to look forward to."

His words echoed in her mind as she stared. "How…I don't—"

"Did you ever hear of nanotechnology?"

There was that word again. Then, her mind flashed back as she started remembering: "Sure, ultra-small electronics, and later, microscopic machines that can duplicate themselves, and alter matter on the atomic level. After the Anti-Techies went down, it started back with more sophisticated medical tools and computers, and then went on to experiments using it to synthesize rare elements. And then there were new medical procedures with it, including a new cryogenic suspension technique." Bit by bit, it started coming back to her and she realized what had happened to her. "I was one of the first frozen with the new method, and my doctor was sure that even cancers like mine would soon be curable with improved medical nanotechnology. I guess he was right." She grinned, her head spinning as it hit her that she really was cured. She had been so overwhelmed by her new-found youth she had forgotten about the severity of her cancer.

Jim smiled back at her. "He sure was. Nanotechnology was eventually advanced enough to totally clean up and repair the body."

She chuckled as she snuck another peek at the unbelievable sight of her reflection in the mirror. "So I see. Doc Wells just never warned me just what would be possible!"

Jim smiled. "I doubt he expected this much. And like I said, we can live for centuries now, bodies constantly kept in top shape by new medications and housekeeping machines called nanorooters."

She smiled at the term. "And I'll stay like this?" Her hand flew back up to her face to stroke her satin-smooth cheek in wonder.

"For a long time," he reassured her.

She couldn't resist looking back at the mirror, feeling light-headed. She still could barely believe it. But then the giddy sense of unreality evaporated. "What's the catch? And where am I?" She felt too heavy to be on the Moon, but could she be on Mars? They had been talking about a colony project there, she knew, back in…

"And when am I?" Suddenly she was desperate to find out how long she had been asleep.

"2332."

She stared, the number echoing in her mind as she figured it out. Almost two hundred years! She had been frozen in '37. 2137! She grabbed for the table as the room seemed to spin, but Martin was at her side immediately and with an easy thrust he grabbed her by the waist and lifted her up to sit on the table, iron fingers gentle. Behind him she saw Sayers watching them darkly.

"Sorry, that must be a bit of a shock," Martin offered. "I forget that those numbers would have a little different meaning to you."

"Yes. Considering I only expected to live a few more months, and even if I wouldn't have developed cancer, I still would only have expected to live another fifty or sixty years." Her voice was shaky. "Look…Jim?" He nodded. "Call me Julie. Go easy, okay? But I want to know what the hell I've missed! And why don't you start with where we are." She braced herself.

"StarStep," he began with a wide-eyed smile that made it clear he was still excited about it all. "It's a small planet about the size of Mars that revolves around Epsilon Eridani, about eleven light years from Earth."

Julie's eyes widened and her fingers gripped the edge of the table with white-knuckle intensity as he went on:

"We'll show you the standard orientation film later, but in brief, it's the result of a massive project that used advanced nanotechnology to rebuild a dead and airless world, after which genetically engineered and accelerated plants and animals were introduced to turn it into a viable colony world. The only thing we couldn't control was the gravity and the small size of the planet."

Julie stared at him, her head swimming. "Building a world from scratch?" "My God! If you could do that…was the Earth cleaned up, too?"

A pained look crossed Jim's face. "Yes. It was. After it was almost destroyed."

Suddenly she felt a sick stirring in her stomach that there was something about that that she should remember, but she couldn't bring it into focus and decided not to push it. She'd ask more questions later. Obviously it was a sore point with Jim, but it brought up another question:

"Okay, you built this world and you're colonizing it. But why am I here? And why didn't anyone ask me if I wanted to come?" Her mouth tightened into a slash.

"They all ask that, don't they?" Sayers cut in. "Well, I'll leave you to explain. I've got work to do. I'll tell *your wife* where you are in case she's looking for you." He flashed them an evil look along with the stressed words as he sidled out the door.

Julie flushed hotly, forgetting her question to Jim for the moment as she realized how transparently she had been reacting to him. And here it turned out that he was married. Which kept her luck consistent given her usual lack of success in attracting the right man.

But Jim had not even noticed Sayers' comment. Either he was so happily married that it hadn't even entered his mind that she might find him interesting, or else he was so callous that he didn't care. But somehow she couldn't believe that. She studied his face and decided the first guess was probably the right one. She didn't know why, it just seemed that way.

"Your wife?" she teased, and got her answer when she saw his face light up. *Yup, happily married.*

"Yes." He pulled out a flat holo-disk from under his tunic proudly to show off a vivid three-dimensional bust portrait of a strangely beautiful woman with short, black hair. She seemed impossibly slender and almost elongated, but on her, it worked. He saw her surprise. "Serena's a Lunie, from the Moon. Her mother was a Grounder and her dad a Lunie, and while she was born on Earth, she grew up on the Moon and spent most of her life there. Under the lower gravity people grow much taller and look a little different." He grinned. "I'm not exactly short, but I only come up to here on her." He placed his hand under his Adam's apple. "She's gotten to be quite a fan of yours since reading about you, and wants to meet you since we're reviving you early. And she's not alone."

"What do you mean 'reviving me early'?"

"We're reviving all the frozen sleepers in batches. We want to give each group time to get oriented and situated, and your group wasn't scheduled for another year," he explained. Then he obviously saw that her head was swimming with unanswered questions because he held up a hand with an apologetic smile.

"I know, you have a lot of questions, but I'll get to them later, I promise. I'd better explain a little background first." He looked around, frowning. "I think we can find better surroundings though." He looked up. "Star?"

"Yes, Jim?" A rich, cultured voice seemed to echo from all around and Julie looked around, trying to find its source as Jim went on.

"Locate Serena for me, please."

"She is in the control-room viewing a recording of the tribe." There was not even an instant's hesitation in the soft-spoken reply. "They were apparently holding some sort of ritual sacrifice just a little while ago, killing one of the cougars who attacked the survey team. It is most interesting. The leader is just about to rip open the throat of—"

"Fine! Let her know that we are on the way up, please." Jim looked uncomfortable.

"Attack on your survey team…a ritual sacrifice?" Julie grabbed Jim's arm. "Blood sacrifice? What tribe?" The words tumbled out in a rush as her confusion grew. "I thought this was a dead world until you built it. Who's attacking you and holding a blood sacrifice?"

Jim looked embarrassed. "It got a little complicated. There was an unforeseen development—"

"Obviously!"

"There were a lot of life-forms introduced in an attempt to build a balanced ecology," he offered in a distracted tone. "Not as varied as Earth's, of course, but still quite rich. A number of different predators were also introduced at a later stage, and some of these were genetically engineered North American Cougars. Well, apparently there was an accident. A number of the specimens experienced brief premature thawing because of a malfunction. It caused some minute genetic 'damage'. Change is more like it. It was a one in a billion accident."

"What happened?" she asked, still hearing 'blood sacrifice' echoing in that strange voice.

"The damage along with the genetic coding for adaptability and temporary rapid breeding—combined with inbreeding—resulted in a considerable increase in intelligence."

"And by the time you got here they had developed a tribal society complete with ritual sacrifices?" She was staring at him. "My God, in how long?"

"Thirty Earth years, roughly, for the Cougars. Years get a little confusing here since we're closer to the sun—one Earth year is several StarStep years—but whenever I say 'year' I mean an Earth year."

"All right, all right, I get the picture. But you mean to tell me they developed this fast in thirty years?" Her head was spinning again.

"Remember, they had the same genetic coding to mature rapidly and to be prolific," Jim cautioned. "The encoding is breaking down now and they are reverting to more normal life-spans and breeding cycles. But for the first twenty years they were producing a new generation every few months."

"Still, they must be bloody geniuses!" Julie was pacing up and down rapidly, a strangely floating step. She was surprised how quickly her muscles were adapting to the new gravity, but then she had always been quick to adjust to new situations. She considered what Jim was telling her, beginning to understand why she was suddenly of interest, but then she realized something frightening: there were some examples of accelerated cultural developments that would be relevant here, and she couldn't think of them! She tried to remember any literature or experiences from her professional past and found herself unable to pin anything down. She had spent time in Africa she realized. She thought about Pemberton again, and camping with him and his team in one of the few truly wild areas left…under a burning sun baking down over their camp site—she seized on the distinct memory gratefully because she had only vague recollections of going for days without eating or sleeping. It was so frustrating, because whenever she tried to remember any more concrete facts she kept drawing blanks.

She turned to Jim, frustrated tears flooding her eyes helplessly as she grabbed his arm. "I can't remember!"

"What?"

"Anything!" It was almost a wail. "I remember who I am, and I know what I am, and some of the things that I have done, but…" But there were so many holes!

She had clear memories of her youth and parents and of growing up. She had been born in the well-to-do Philadelphia Main Line suburb of Bryn Mawr, and she had gone to local private schools until starting at the University of Pennsylvania on the Early Admissions program. She even remembered the nice one bedroom Society Hill apartment her parents had found for her, and how she had decorated it with retro late-20th Century decor and two cats who had been more faithful friends than any of the guys she had met while in school. Those memories were crystal clear—and her undergraduate years and first years of her graduate work were no mystery either—but starting with her later graduate studies and field work, her memories turned into a patchwork quilt of clarity and obscurity.

Frustrated, she tightened her grip on Jim's arm. "I can't remember my doctoral work, or my published papers—I must have written some, you said so—and I can't remember the specifics of my field work. Some flashes, yes, but only generalities."

"Star! Analysis!" Jim's command to the ceiling was terse.

Who is he talking to? she wondered again.

"Insufficient data to make a diagnosis, but I suspect physiological brain damage due to suspension. Testing is needed to determine the extent and nature."

"Call Dr. Gratch and tell him we're on the way to the MedBlock."

"Shall I also inform Serena?"

"Yes."

Julie had had enough as Jim indicated the door, and she stopped as he tried to usher her out. "Whose is that voice?"

He looked embarrassed again. "I'm sorry, I should have introduced you. That's Star, my wife's pet project. She started designing him as her graduate school thesis." He chuckled. "Ironically, Star and I are close to the same age, and we've both been improving our programming. But Star learns quicker," he admitted with a reluctant grin, "and by now he's probably the most sophisticated computer in existence. And thanks to nanotechnology, he fits the complexity of a human brain, nearly, into a one-meter cube—"

"Nearly the complexity of a human brain?" The computer interrupted archly. "I would like to see a human brain simultaneously calculate—"

"Uh, Star," Jim admonished, "Try to be a little more discrete when you interrupt me around other people, okay?"

"I'm sorry." Star actually managed to sound contrite.

"One of Serena's latest efforts," Jim explained. "She's working on improving his emotion-simulation and giving him a more natural conversational style. It's a major project to get his reactions situationally appropriate, but I swear she's done too good a job sometimes. I sometimes think he actually feels some emotions."

Star's response was immediate. "'I think, therefore I am' was a comment made by one of your ancient philosophers. Would not 'I react, therefore I feel' be equally appropriate? When you can not tell the difference between the simulation and the real thing, is there really a difference worth discussing?"

Julie stared up at the StarStepper somberly. After a moment, she licked the tip of her right forefinger and drew an imaginary line in the air. "That's one." She grinned and looked up in the direction the disembodied voice had come from. "Nice to meet you Star. If only you had a body to match that mind and voice!"

"I do. Smooth and strong." After a moment of silence during which Julie clenched her mouth tightly shut, he went on a little petulantly. "That was a joke. Dr. Andrews is expanding my programming."

"I know," Jim muttered. "I've got to talk to her and make sure she doesn't go too far in that direction!"

"Ah, leave him alone," Julie giggled. "I like him. I just wish I could see him." She looked around.

"Near the ceiling, over the door," Star prompted. "See that pair of small lenses?"

"Your eyes?"

"Precisely. In any room, you can usually find me over the door in a similar position—"

"Any room?"

"Yes. I am available for everyone who needs me."

"What if I don't want you looking down at me?"

"I am only active in public areas. In private rooms, my eyes and ears are only on when I am specifically activated by the room's registered occupant."

"So how do you know if I want you again if you're turned off?" He was being so reasonable that part of her couldn't resist teasing him.

"One part of me remains active and sensitized to just such a request. It is not something I am aware of, but when I am called, a subroutine is invoked that restores access to the deactivated monitors."

"In other words I have to trust you?"

"Of course. I am a computer." He sounded almost indignant. "I am incapable of violating my programming."

Julie stared at the emotionless lenses of Star's 'eyes' and felt herself blush as she turned to Jim. "I just realized I've been arguing with a machine!"

"Were you?" He was teasing her, but he was serious, too.

"Of course. He, I mean…" She stopped. *He! She really did think of Star as a 'he'!* "Okay, he's more than a machine. But you can't mean that you think he's alive?"

"Why don't you ask him?"

She looked up. "Star…Are you…alive?"

There was a pause of nearly two seconds, and then Star answered slowly, actually sounding uncertain. "I don't know."

Julie's eyes burned as she turned to Jim. "I don't know about you, but I'm almost ready to say that he is."

"Not yet," he said, shaking his head. "I'm with you, but Serena says he still has a long way to go, and she ought to know." He pressed the door patch and the door to the hall slid open.

"Come on. I want to get you checked out." He held out an arm and she took it gratefully. She was still a little unsteady on her feet, and everything she was being loaded up with was adding to her shakiness.

She glanced up as she passed through the doorway. "Bye, Star."

"Till we meet again," Star shot back. "Like now."

Suddenly his voice came from down the hall in front of her. "I will always be around if you need me." His steady voice was quite comforting, she decided and waved to the small lenses she spotted down the hall.

CHAPTER 3

▼

DECISIONS

Speaker fled into the woods to escape the unsettling feeding behind him, and running towards the afternoon sun, he climbed up to the top of the ridge that marked the edge of the Tribe's hunting grounds. He needed to be alone to try to forget the bad taste in his mouth, and to consider another problem.

Not far away, in a smaller place of bubbles recently built, more of the sky-creatures were destroying hunting land by tearing down trees and growth to expose the bare soil. The game animals were all being driven away—in the wrong direction—and the Tribe would soon be feeling real hunger for the first time. And from that hunger had come the renegade attack on some of the sky-creatures. He thought about the exploding rocks they had used, and wondered what other weapons waited in the bubble caves, and felt a moment of unfamiliar fear. Anyone who could create such things would be a fierce enemy that was best left alone until more was known. But there would be another attack on them, and this time he would have to lead, or face challenge and lose control of the Tribe.

Ironically it was his own fault. Since defeating the previous speaker and taking leadership, he had forced the warriors to work together and organize their hunting like the sky-creatures coordinated their tasks. It had been a difficult lesson to teach at first, but as the food supply had increased, his status as leader had been strengthened and there had been no challenges for several seasons. And now that group hunting behavior had a new target, and he knew he could not stop the other warriors even if he wanted to. With Ringed Tail's sacrifice, everyone was inflamed with battle lust and they demanded another battle. It was a chance to capture glory now that challenges were more formal and rarely fatal. There were no noble battles anymore. The howling hunters cringed and ran away when confronted, and only an occasional strange warrior was spotted who would offer a real challenge.

Speaker got up and ran along the ridge to work off his frustrations.

Ever since he had been a cub, he had come up here to think and run. There was a freedom in flowing across the ground at top speed here where the trees and the air were thinner—it released his mind to think more clearly. That had been where his cub-name of Ridge Loper had come from. Only he had known it was a secret name for a thinker. But now he was Speaker and he had to think harder or the Tribe would destroy itself. There was already one nagging worry in the back of his mind that he knew he needed to do something about, but it was not yet a critical problem like the sky-creatures.

Panting, he dropped to the ground as he realized that he had run almost all the way to the sky-creatures' new settlement. This was the place they would have to attack, and he had to think of some way to do it that would not mean all of them risking death, because more sky-creature blood had to flow. The Tribe demanded that. But if he didn't plan and lead the attack the whole Tribe might suffer, so he crept closer and closer to spy, his fur rising along with the low growl from his throat as acrid and alien scents assaulted his nose.

CHAPTER 4

▼

PROBLEMS

As they entered the comfortable lounge of the administration tower, Julie sighed with relief. Real honest to goodness daylight and fresh air enveloped her. Thick, soft red carpet swallowed her feet hungrily and rich, aromatic wood-paneling covered sections of the walls, alternating either with wide windows or with more of the same satiny metal that had made up the walls of the room she had awakened in. Real wood tables and low, plush brown lounge chairs were scattered around the room, and strange-looking flowering plants that looked like anorectic chrysanthemums were scattered around the room in tall, narrow pots.

Beyond the open windows, familiar green colors called to her and she responded, heading for the windows until she saw who was waiting for them and stopped.

Julie looked up at Dr. Andrews enviously. There was no mistaking the computer programmer, and Julie could understand Martin's loyalty to his wife. Serena was supple and slender, and more than two feet taller than her own five feet six inches—she still resisted the metric conversion that had finally taken hold in America in her teens. But somehow Serena still managed to look sensuously female, and she could see right away that the Holo-Disk Jim had had did not do his wife justice. The programmer had the type of compelling features photographers fight over, and her close-cropped ebony hair was gracefully styled to accent her high cheek-bones and the delicately arching eyebrows that hovered over eerie pale blue eyes that were almost silver. And she wore a smile that was as instantly welcoming as her warm and unaffected embrace.

"Welcome! I can't tell you how happy we are to see you."

Julie wiped her eyes surreptitiously as she was released. The cumulative shocks of the day had overwhelmed her and Serena's sincere and welcoming hug had been just what she needed.

"Thank you. You'll have to forgive me if I seem a little—"

"Disoriented?" Serena interjected with a grin. "After a couple of centuries of sleep, I think we can make a few allowances, can't we Ken?" She turned to the distinguished-looking man standing next to her.

Julie's face burned as she realized she had been so distracted by Serena that she had not even noticed the other man in the room. And now she tried not to stare as she got a good look at him. He had a deep brown, almost black, complexion which was set off by snow-white hair and an immaculately groomed beard worthy of Santa Claus himself. And unlike everyone else, he looked older—late fifties to early sixties—and he was also unmistakably, undeniably, fat. A noble and obviously carefully nurtured belly strained his delightfully flamboyant shirt. His loose African-styled garment was black, with bands of patterns in vivid yellows, reds, greens and blues. And coming out from under the shirt, were a pair of plain black pants over simple thong sandals on bare feet. It was almost like being back on safari. She found herself relaxing in face of his proudly 'look at me, if you dare' demeanor. Along with Jim and Serena, his unabashed uniqueness was especially refreshing after the constant flow of incredibly boring and uniform settlers she had met in and around Dr. Gratch's office. Everyone had been slightly soft-looking, average height, neutral light brown complected, with slightly epicanthic eyes, medium brown to black hair, and average weight. Just like the already increasing trend in Europe and the Americas in her own day, everyone looked to be a product of a giant mixer blending all the races on Earth and then dispensing the product in equal doses to make the "new humanity". She could see from everyone else she had seen since waking up that the trend had continued after her freezing.

But along with Serena and Jim, Ken was also refreshingly 'different'. And since he was only a few centimeters taller than her, she didn't have to crane her neck to look at him as he approached with a chiding glance at Martin.

"Jim, boy. Aren't you going to introduce us?" His voice was a deep, rich baritone she immediately liked. "I've been dying to meet this lady, even if I must confess that anthropology is not my specialty—"

"Neither is it mine, anymore, it seems." Julie cut him off bitterly as she was reminded. She spun to hide her renewed tears and went to the window for her first view at StarStep, putting her hands on the cool metal of the window-ledge and breathing in the aromatic fresh air wafted in through the open window of the lounge.

She was in the top floor of a six-story tower overlooking an incredibly clean city that looked just as perfect as the three-D computer graphic Jim had shown her on the way to the MedBlock. A light breeze was blowing in from the ocean, and she breathed in the mixture of salt air and newly mown grass gratefully, aching to get out there to lie in the grass in between the domes to let the sun bake her. Even the alien-looking slender trees at the edge of the city didn't faze her. All she wanted was something familiar to cling to for a moment.

"What the blazes does she mean?"

She heard Ken's upset question behind her, and it took her a moment to remember that she had been bemoaning her sudden professional amnesia. Sighing, she wiped he eyes and turned reluctantly to stop Jim from answering.

"It means that apparently I was suspended for too long. That, or that the technique used on me wasn't quite refined enough yet." She sat back on the window sill, feeling the cool ledge through the thin material of her new gown.

"How did the good doctor put it?" She leaned her head back, studying the ceiling as she repeated Dr. Gratch's final diagnosis in his pedantic, vaguely foreign tone.

"Sensory register, short term and long term memory capacities are unaffected, and her intelligence level remains at above average to gifted. Early memories are unaffected, but later memories, particularly left-brain memories, are substantially impaired. However, from what I can determine, emotional, spatial, and sensory right-brain memories are almost all intact."

She swallowed and looked ahead. "My name is Julie, formerly Dr. Juliet Nathanson, apparently a world-renowned anthropologist, but presently lost, hopelessly unqualified for anything and beholden to the kindness of strangers. Call me Julie. And who may you be, sir?" She forced down the sinking feeling in her stomach.

A warm smile reached out to her. "My name is Ken, Dr. Kenneth Stuyvesant Miller if you want to be pedantic about it. The Neon Panda," he sighed mournfully, "if you are an irreverent former, or even present, student. Apparently some seem to find that the combination of my shape," he patted his belly fondly, "rich complexion—a gift from my ancestors which my parents and I refuse to surrender—distinguished hair, and my choice of stylish attire, all add up to give me the resemblance of a psychedelic version of that noble animal. And if you are interested, as alas too few are, my specialties lie in nanoelectronics, physics, and a number of intriguing and esoteric realms of math. My hobbies include art—particularly neo-resurgent oils—pottery, and the lost art of Southern cooking. You can call me anytime, and as I said, call me Ken." He bowed formally as he approached her to take her hand and bring it to his lips for a light kiss.

She couldn't help it but giggled, God help her, like a school girl. Between Serena's welcome embrace and Ken's courtly gesture, she felt totally relaxed for the first time since she had awakened. She grinned and curtsied. *Where the hell had she learned that?* "Good sir, are you trying to charm me?"

Ken drew back slightly with a look of mock dismay. "Egad! She's on to me." He shrugged, holding on to her hand. "Too bad. Indeed I am." He grinned. "After all, I feel like I almost know you already, based on Serena's ardent praises and descriptions for the past several weeks."

She eyed him speculatively. No longer really seeing the belly, but looking into his eyes. Behind the cheerful smile and disarming manner, she saw real, genuine concern, and she leaned forward to kiss him lightly on a bearded cheek.

"Thank you. I needed a little distraction. All this," she waved her free hand vaguely around and aimed it out the window, "is a bit much to take, all at once. Even if I would have retained all my faculties—"

"Julie," he interrupted gently as he released her, "your faculties, and I have the impression they are considerable, are unimpaired. Only your memories are a bit foggy."

"I stand corrected."

"Good, because I refuse to believe that everything is lost. We have all your papers in our library I am sure—"

"I am second to none in my selection of reference material." A proud voice cut in from above."

"Star, shut up!" Ken sighed and glanced over at Serena. "My dear, he's getting positively conceited. Please fine-tune his programming a little." Serena blushed as he turned his attention back to Julie.

"As I was saying before I was so rudely interrupted," he glared briefly at Star's eyes over the door, "we have your work on file and if you study it, maybe it'll jog you memory a bit."

"Yes," Jim broke in. "We have a problem."

"The cats!" Julie flushed, embarrassed that she had forgotten. She was still trying to digest everything Jim had told her while they had been waiting for Dr. Gratch to analyze her test results. Jim had told her how the StarStep project had been implemented while she had been busy in the field, about the Machine Plague she had slept through and how millions had joined her in frozen sleep to escape it, and finally, of the battles he had had to get StarStep finished and settled by the freepers—including the sabotage that had cost him his legs. He had also told her how Star and Serena had combined forces to develop a new strain of nanorooters to regenerate his legs and guarantee he would have the same long life as everyone else.

She had been fed so much new information that she had almost forgotten about the cougars. A little embarrassed, she turned to Serena.

"Just what were they doing? Can you replay the recording?"

Serena started to answer, but Star beat her. "Replaying on main monitor."

A large portion of the bare wall to their right suddenly shimmered and Julie gasped as she found herself looking at a three-dimensional scene, as if it were right on the other side of the wall; *in place of the wall*, she corrected herself.

"The monitors that recorded these were roving eyes and are no longer in place I'm afraid," Star supplied. "The images are a bit fuzzy because of the heavy moisture content of the air at the time of recording, and the distance at which the roving eyes were positioned. The Cougars have an extremely well-developed olfactory sense and they would have detected the monitoring at closer range."

Julie shook her head as Star apologized for the 'fuzzy' picture and thanked him absently as she watched the bloody sacrifice play itself out, followed by the ritual feeding. And as the last of the victim's body was devoured by the younger cougars, she tentatively asked Star if he could replay parts of the recording and zoom in on certain sections. He obliged instantly, and she leaned forward intently as the images flashed on the screen. She especially wanted to get a closer look at the sacrifice, and the injuries that were obviously crippling it.

When she was satisfied, she glanced over at Jim. "I saw singed fur on the sacrifice. Have you had any interactions with these…people? Specifically, have any of them attacked you and gotten away with it?"

"You are blasted right," a new voice interrupted, tinged with an unmistakably Russian accent. She turned to see a short stocky man with red hair and beard standing in the open doorway. Beyond him, she saw four other people crowding close, three men and one woman.

Jim sighed. "Dan, come in, and the rest of you too," he raised his voice. The newcomers all filed into the lounge, led by the red-head who had a blistered sunburn almost the same color as his hair.

"Julie," Jim introduced them, "this is Daniv Tsielkovsky, one of the freeper Representatives from Agra 5, one of the pilot farms we're starting, and his squad. Dan, this is Dr. Nathanson, the anthropologist I spoke about in the last Meeting."

"So, you're the one that's going to show us how to deal with these blasted cats nobody knew about?" Tsielkovsky's bushy mustache twitched, and Julie saw the others behind him all staring at her suspiciously. There was a strong undercurrent of anger in the room and she realized she had to be careful.

She studied the newcomers.

They were also different than the StarStep norm; refreshingly brassy and "real", with clothes that were a wild clash of colors and styles, and complexions that ranged from a Tsielkovsky's ruddy sunburn to pale complexions like those of Serena and Jim. These were people she could relate to, and even if she was worried by their hostility, she didn't feel threatened. She saw an opening for a way to try to relax them.

"Fellow Rip-Van-Winkles?" she asked.

Tsielkovsky looked puzzled for a moment, and then his face relaxed in a reluctant smile. "*Da*, Rip Van Winkles. That is good. Sleeping from 2160 to two years ago."

"What did you mean by what you said when you came in?"

"Just what I said. Those blasted cats—"

"He's talking about the fact that a survey patrol from Agra 6 ran into a Cougar hunting party yesterday and was attacked," Jim interrupted. "One of the cats killed a geologist with a crude spear before they realized what was happening—"

"Spear?" Julie cried. "They're using weapons? How—"

"That geologist was my brother, Uri," Tsielkovsky cut in bruskly. His face was stone again.

"In a minute, Dan," Jim put his hand up. "Yes, Julie. They apparently just started using spears. The boss cat is a smart one, and he or she has been watching us and teaching them all sorts of un-cat-like tricks—"

"He," Star cut in. "And I know: shut up."

Jim stifled a grin as he went on, ignoring Ken's exasperated head shaking and Serena's sudden obsession with studying the view out the window.

"*He* probably saw the settlers using tools for clearing brush and such. As for the attack, the Cougars got close because the patrol was unarmed, and Uri got killed before the shuttle pilot could scatter the Cougars by using some seismic test charges as crude hand-grenades. None of the cats were killed, but the one who killed Uri was wounded. They were all terrified by the sounds of the explosions and ran."

"Star," Julie challenged him. "Do you have any footage of the attack, especially of the Cougar who was wounded?"

"Only a few stills taken by the automatic log cameras. They weren't recording full video."

"Can you throw a shot of the wounded Cougar, if you have one, on the screen and put it side by side with a shot of the sacrifice?"

"That is a logical conclusion," Star admitted. "I made the same connection with the new input."

"What connection?" Jim asked in an irritated tone.

"Just a second, please." She watched the screen change and saw the two shots of a Cougar portrayed on the screen, side by side. She nodded slowly. "Points of similarity?"

"Enough for a positive I.D.," Star replied. "They are the same. A female. And from the blood coming from her mouth and ears, she had concussion injuries as well, and the killing just spared her a painful death."

"Well it was more than a mercy-killing. And let *me* explain," she warned Star as she turned to the others.

"The wounded Cougar is unable to function as a hunter anymore. Look at the crippled legs, and you heard Star. And I saw burn injuries, too, which is why I wondered about any interactions with your people. But she killed one of us, so now she is being sacrificed, and the other Cougars are drinking the blood and engaging in a ritual 'feeding'. The latter tells me there is a more sophisticated ritual at work. I don't know if you noticed, but the cats only bit the sacrifice after drinking the blood. But the whole ritual parallels some primitive human tribal beliefs that consuming parts of a victim endows the eater with the victim's assets. But they are honoring her by not eating her directly. That's a pretty sophisticated behavioral pattern!" She shook her head in surprise, still remembering how recently they had been introduced to StarStep.

She looked back at the screen for a moment, and then nodded. "But all this means that they are looking for a way to gain ability to kill us! They're planning an attack!"

Suddenly she felt an incredible surge of relief as she saw Ken smiling with an 'I told you so' expression. She winked at him, and then looked up at Star. "How long ago did that sacrifice take place?"

"Approximately ten hours and fourteen minutes ago."

She frowned and asked Jim: "Where's the nearest group of humans to the site of the sacrifice?"

He frowned. "That was Uri's operation: Agra Station 6. Star?"

The response was immediate. "I am attempting to contact them now."

For several minutes, the room was tensely silent until Star spoke up apologetically. "Jim, I need permission to override privacy directive and activate remote monitoring at Agra Station 6. They are not responding and I think we need to take a look."

"Agreed, *control*, privacy override on Agra Station 6 granted, *command*."

"Thank you."

"Damn!" Tsielkovsky swore. "I know blasted well what we will find. Those buggar cats must have attacked—and I'll bet they've killed 'em all!"

Behind him, the other colonists drew together and Julie heard a soft cry from one of them as the wall shimmered again. And as she saw what was on the screen, she gasped and grabbed for Ken who had come up next to her. They were looking in on a frightening scene of bloodshed. The main monitor was focused on the large, domed common-room of the station. Four sprawled and torn figures were clearly in view, and the legs of a fifth were just visible off to the left, sticking out from under a counter of some sort. Each body's throat was viciously ripped open and from the bite-marks and the way that some of the heads flopped at awkward angles, it was clear that some of them had been killed by having their necks efficiently broken by powerful fanged jaws. Three of the bodies were also extensively torn around the stomach and, in one case, nearly disemboweled.

The monitor image was brutally sharp and they seemed to be looking right into the room. Julie could almost smell the stench of death as she turned to Miller to bury her face in his shoulder, unable to keep from crying.

The portly physicist's face was ashen, and he seemed to draw almost as much comfort from holding her as she was from being held. "My God," he wondered in an unsteady voice. "Why didn't they call for help?"

"Or fight back?" She lifted her head, leaving a wet stain on his tunic.

Jim and Serena had also drawn close to each other, and appeared equally shaken. Jim finally found his voice to answer:

"They didn't fight back because they didn't have any weapons. None of us do. Why would we need them? We intentionally made sure there weren't any, because we are waking up people from a more savage time and don't want any easy temptations to express aggression." He ignored Tsielkovsky's responding glare.

"And they probably didn't call for help," Serena went on weakly, "because they didn't expect to be attacked. We've been here for over two years and the Cougars have always kept well away from us.

We've been watching them but we haven't wanted to interfere, so we've made no attempt to contact them. Frankly, we were shocked to find out what's happened to them. It complicates everything. We thought this was going to be our world. A new beginning for all freepers. A way that we could wake all of you up and give you a home."

An impatient voice from overhead interrupted them. "Have all of you forgotten what we have just seen, and what it means?"

"No, Star." Julie reluctantly turned back to the gruesome image on the monitor, realizing this wasn't the time to pursue her questions. "It comes under denial. Look it up in the psychology data-banks. It's much easier to discuss something unrelated, rather than face a very harsh and shocking reality."

"Oh."

Jim had been studying the screen thoughtfully and he turned to Tsielkovsky. "How many were at the station?"

"At Agra 6…?" the settler considered shakily. "Sixteen, I believe."

"There are five bodies visible here. Can you give me any external views, Star?"

"Only two, there are no more external com-units." The shocking scene of carnage shrunk as two outdoor shots suddenly shared the screen. There was no one in sight anywhere, but there were clear bloodstains on the ground and scattered pieces of material and equipment.

"Any other interior monitors open?"

A quick succession of views flashed on the monitor as the vacant exterior scenes disappeared, and then three more scenes of dead bodies stabilized and joined the original view of the common room.

"Nine victims accounted for," Star supplied. "Four in three homes, and the five we first saw." I find no trace of the rest," Star finally proclaimed.

"They will have been taken back to their camp," Julie explained in a hollow voice. "To be eaten, in all likelihood. In order that they gain our strength. It would fit the pattern. After all, they're carnivores and a full tribe would need a lot of meat. Because of the explosive breeding that was going on here before, new hunting patterns evolved to meet the need for more food, and any meat will be valuable. But these bodies serve a double purpose."

"What about the ones inside?" Jim wondered.

"They were probably left there because the Cougars were afraid of all the alien things around them. It's one thing to strike and exit in the heat of battle, but to go back in deliberately might be something else."

"So now what do we expect?" Jim looked slightly queasy, and Serena was even paler than normal as she stood by the window breathing in deeply.

Star started to answer. "It is—"

"I wouldn't worry about it." Julie cut him off firmly. "Now they'll go back and celebrate. I wouldn't expect another attack immediately. This is a major victory for them. There will be time to warn everyone and to set up perimeter alarms and monitors."

"I want to know why they're suddenly attacking after two years of leaving us alone?" Ken was confused, and the others all nodded agreement.

"Are you doing anything different now than the first few years?" Julie looked at the screen uneasily. "The Agra Stations; you said they were pilot farms. What do they do there?"

Tsielkovsky's voice was icy. "Agra 6 just began expanding their fields, like the rest of us. Apparently it was felt that we primitives needed to work for our food rather than have it made for us by the new science—"

"That's not it," Jim interrupted. "That decision was made to make sure we would be self-sufficient in case of any technological breakdown."

"If you say so." Dan didn't look entirely convinced and just spoke sarcastically: "In the cause of *self-sufficiency*, we're all clearing land and planting crops. Agra 6 is just the newest farm."

"When did that start?" Julie asked.

"Just last month."

"Well then, there's your answer! Agra 6 must have been encroaching on their territory. Even if it's a myth that wars always start over resources or territories, it is one reason many of them do start. Their land clearing was probably cutting into the cougars' hunting grounds. Even if their breeding cycles have slowed down, a concentrated population of carnivores needs a substantial food supply."

A door hissed open behind them and Sayers entered anxiously. "Jim, I just got a call from Bob Marks over at Bio and he's been trying to get in touch with Agra 6 and can't get an answer..." He stopped, staring at the bloody montage on the wall behind them. "What the chill?"

"Agra Station 6," Jim explained grimly.

"The Cougars? Why?"

Julie explained her theory as Miller came up behind her and wrapped his arms around her. "And she thought she had lost it all."

Somehow the gesture didn't seem presumptuous, and she had to admit to drawing a great deal of comfort from his embrace as she leaned into it, putting her hands over his arms to hold them around her.

They ignored Sayers' darkening expression and suddenly hooded eyes as he turned away, muttering excuses that he'd better let Bob know what had happened.

"Hold off on that, Mike, until I notify any surviving families," Jim cautioned.

"Right." Sayers waved and disappeared back out the door after shooting Miller a last poisonous look.

Julie promptly forgot about it and chewed on a fingernail thoughtfully. After a minute, she looked up. "Star, I want you to..." she flushed and turned to Jim. "Do you mind?"

Jim was smiling. "No, go right ahead. That's why you were revived." He looked up. "Star, *command*: Dr. Nathanson has command clearance, level 3, *control.*"

"Programmed," Star answered in a flat monotone, and then in his usual modulated voice said: "Proceed, Julie."

"Okay Star, here goes: I want you to send out as many rovers as you can to spy on the Cougars. I want recordings of their speech, and then I want you to correlate all utterances with actions whenever possible; and do the same with all prior recordings you have. I want you to get as much information as you can to see if you can start figuring out their language. You would be better equipped to do that than I would."

"Thank you, but I need to warn you. There is a problem with monitoring. Video is not too difficult, but audio is a bit more complicated because of the distance we have to operate from. Ambient sound levels will interfere to a degree. We are working on neutralizing agents to make the monitors odor-free, but so far we're having limited success because the Cougars' senses are extremely acute."

Julie shook her head. "Star, dear. We're not making master recordings. The audio quality of those last recordings will be more than adequate." Suddenly Julie was reminded of a semester she had spent as a visiting lecturer at a university…where was it? The University of Milan…she spoke Italian? She couldn't remember a word of it! She fought a resurgence of her earlier sick feeling. Angrily she clamped down on it and focused on what she did remember. Every little fact she could dredge up might trigger another memory.

Star reminded her of one of the graduate students who had been in her class, she realized. Extremely astute, but more than a bit over-anxious to be perfect, all the time. But he—Giancarlo Travolo she remembered with a sharp sense of accomplishment—had been a joy to teach because he had been a sponge absorbing everything she had thrown at him, and quick to integrate new facts with old. Star was like that, and she could tell he would be invaluable in getting to the bottom of the problem presented by the Cougars.

Jim looked relieved as he grabbed Tsielkovsky's arm. "Well, it's obvious that Julie and Star have this situation in hand. "So, Reena, Ken, give her whatever help she wants, and I'll see you later. I want to check out Agra 6 myself, and take a medical team out to recover the bodies." His face clouded. "And then notify any surviving family members."

Then he left with the members of the Agra team, and with the immediate problem of the Cougars under consideration by Star, she was reminded of how little she really knew. She looked up at Serena for a moment and Serena must have sensed her thoughts because she turned to Ken.

"Hey, why don't you leave us girls alone for a bit. We have some things to talk about."

"Sure." He shrugged and squeezed Julie's hand as he passed her on the way to the door. "I'll leave under protest, but I will admit that you're in good hands. And if you want, ask Star to track me down when you're finished, and I'll make you some homemade bouillabaisse or Cajun chicken that'll tease your taste buds." He fanned his mouth with a grin. "Just wait till you see the size of a StarStep chicken's breast! After a couple of hundred years in the freezer some solid food will do you good—"

"Ken!" Serena shook her head. "Have you forgotten—"

Julie stopped her with a light touch and hung on to Ken's hand for a moment. "Actually, I can't. Dr. Gratch has me on a strict liquid diet for the next several days. My stomach just isn't ready for solid food yet, even with a nanorooter work-over." She smiled at his disappointed expression and added: "But I would love to join you for a cup of dinner and conversation."

"Fair enough!" He waved and left the lounge with a satisfied nod.

Serena moved over to a low couch by the window and folded up gracefully and patted the cushion next to her as she relaxed, one loose curl of her hair shivering lightly in the breeze.

"Here. Sit. You've got a bunch of unanswered questions, I know, so let me have 'em." She grinned.

Relieved, Julie sank down next to her and closed her eyes for a second as all her confusion on waking up returned. After a moment, she turned and looked over to meet Serena's patient eyes.

"The nanomachine plague Jim mentioned. He only gave me a thirty-second capsule description. Just what was that?"

Serena winced and looked away. "A horrible atrocity…the closest thing to Armageddon humanity has ever faced." She was silent for a moment and then drew a breath and turned back to Julie.

"You're familiar with the basics of nanotechnology?" Julie nodded. "Well one use that should never gotten off anyone's drawing board was the development of Nanokillers." Serena shuddered. "I was just a little girl…but I don't think I'll ever forget the Plague of 2200…" Her voice grew absent and she looked into her lap and picked at her nails. "It was just after my tenth birthday," she began after a moment, "and I was playing with some classmates…" And speaking softly, Serena told her how she had first learned about the Machine Plague and what it had done to Earth.

It was a sobering lecture, and as she finished describing El-Arun's shocked explanation in the shelter, Julie sat there numbly for a moment, until she managed to ask: "How long did it go on?"

"Nearly six months. The death toll was over five hundred million!"

Julie just stared, the figure resounding in her mind like some mind-numbing klaxon. Half a billion casualties! It had not registered when Jim had hurriedly explained the plague and its after-effects. But Serena's description had been numbingly vivid. She felt like curling up in a corner and crying, until she felt Serena's arms enfold her like a big sister's embrace.

"I'm sorry, Julie. You've been through a lot, waking up like this light years from home and suddenly expected to solve a problem like nothing you've ever dealt with. And now this!"

"No! Don't apologize." Julie sat up and looked over at the other woman. "I'm fine. Really." She shuddered. "It's a shock, true, but when I really think about it I have to be grateful."

"Grateful?"

Julie nodded. "Uh huh. When they put me under, two thoughts were running through my minds. First was the conviction—I really can't call it a fear—that I was never going to wake up. The other was that I *would* wake up, and be totally useless in an alien society that would have to take care of me like a charity case."

"Hey, don't expect any charity here," Serena chuckled. "We expect you to earn your keep here."

"And I thank you for that!" Then Julie suddenly found herself suddenly stifling a yawn. "I'm sorry!"

"Don't be." Serena patted her hand. "Dr. Gratch should have warned you. You'll be doing a lot of napping the first few weeks because your brain has to get used to sensory input again and will overload quickly. And don't be surprised if more and more memories come back in your dreams. We've never revived anyone who's been asleep as long as you, and despite Gratchie's attitude, he does not know everything about cold sleep."

"But the Cougars—"

"Aren't going anywhere," Serena cut her off. "You said yourself we'd be safe for a while, and now that we know what to expect, we can warn the other Agra stations." Serena was firm as she rose and held out a hand. "Come on. I'll take you to the apartment we prepared for you so you can get some sleep. Real sleep, like you need." Then she smiled. "And I'll call Ken and give him your excuses. That big softie will understand. Now let's go!"

CHAPTER 5

▼

CHALLENGE

Speaker surveyed the battle site. It had been a noble fight and they had killed all the invaders in this place, without losing even one warrior. So why didn't he feel triumphant like the others? Because it had not been a fight. I had been a slaughter. Like a dozen younglings attacking a nest of jumper babies. But the warriors were dancing around the bodies of their victims dragged together into a pile, drunk on the glory of the victory. Of course there were other bodies: those inside the small bubble caves. The warriors had killed the sky-creatures inside, too, but they had escaped out in the sun as soon as no one lived within. The smells and strange things inside had frightened them.

Speaker's muzzle curled in an unfamiliar way.

Brave warriors. Celebrating a victory against beings who did not resist or even have any of the sensible self-protection he had expected. They had not even had any exploding rocks like the first group. He wrestled with unfamiliar ideas.

Was it right to attack them like this? The invaders were taking some of their hunting ground, but there was enough land that they could share. Could they not talk to the invaders about it? It went against instinct and tradition, but for some reason, he kept having the same thought.

Then he saw the six circling singling warriors. They had not yet mated or formed a Unit—there were not enough females in the Tribe at the moment—and they studied him carefully. Ringed Tail's death had meant Speaker had challenged the oldest male for his mate. Crooked Tooth had yielded without a fight because of Speaker's prowess, but he now circled with the others, probably the instigator. One more singling without a mate. Speaker considered sharing, but it was not right for the Speaker to be forming a Unit.

128

He crouched and raised his fur to warn the approaching warriors. "You know the Law. Single to challenge."

"That is for warriors," Crooked Tooth growled. "You killed no sky-creatures today." A harmony of growls accompanied the accusation.

Speaker fought to keep his fur erect as he calculated the odds. He did not realize that they had been watching him, waiting for a sign of weakness. They were counting on killing him, knowing he would take two, maybe three of them along to their ancestors; he was after all, Speaker, and had beaten all challengers in the past. But if he was killed, taking two or three of the challengers with him, there would be a female freed and the survivors could challenge for her. Because of the great need for food, all of the Tribe hunted and fought as equals, but in matters of breeding, females were traditionally subordinate since they were not good hunters while pregnant.

Speaker watched the singlings warily, his only option clear.

Slowly his fur dropped and he relaxed his crouch towards the ground, turning his head to the side as if to surrender—and then he exploded into action!

He rolled to the side, towards Notch Tail and sprang to his feet after a full turn, jaw thrusting forward and fangs extended to rip the unguarded throat open in a single sweeping slash. At the same time he snatched a large rock he had spotted before and hurled it with deadly accuracy at the side of Splotch Back's skull, hearing the wet crunch as it cracked the bone. Before the others could react, he sprang directly between Six Toes and Thin Fur, pulling his slate dagger. Thrusting at Thin Fur's throat with the dagger, he clamped his teeth onto Six Toe's shoulder to pull the smaller male down. He felt the dagger strike home and felt a warm flow of liquid over his right arm and let go to attack Six Toes better.

But the smaller male rolled onto his back and retracted his claws in surrender, exposing his throat and belly. Speaker ignored him, turning briefly to see Thin Fur lying on the ground, eyes glazing over as blood spurted freely from a severed artery in the neck. He faced the other two shocked singlings with a spitting snarl, fur matted with blood and eyes blazing as he challenged them. "Who is not a warrior?"

Crooked Tooth and One Ear stared at the four singlings on the ground and dropped immediately into submissive postures and offered their throats, though Crooked Tooth's eyes burned hotly. Speaker ignored them and went to inspect his victims.

Notch Tail and Splotch Back were both dead, but the latter without honor. Speaker bent and sank his teeth into the dead male's throat and ripped it open; the taste of the cooling blood bitter in his mouth. Thin Fur was not yet dead, but he was close to the end. As he saw Speaker approach, he raised himself up and offered his throat, eyes pleading for honor. Speaker obliged. Even if they had violated tradition with a group attack, they had not been at fault.

Then he turned and found himself confronting the other warriors who had been watching the battle carefully. As the six singlings had begun to challenge Speaker's authority, the warriors had been watching unobtrusively, waiting to see the outcome. Now they came forward and, one by one, briefly crouched as both males and females turned their heads in submission when they filed past.

As the others gathered the bodies of the sky-creatures that lay in the open, and the dead warrior singlings, Speaker realized that there would never be a better time to try to make a radical change.

CHAPTER 6

▼

PRESSURE, AND RELIEF

Almost forty-eight hours after her introduction to StarStep, Julie was standing in a long, brightly lit chamber, facing the beginning of seemingly endless twin rows of the same coffin-sized containers as the one she had awaked next to. She was surprised by the normal temperature of the room. Somehow she had expected a freezer-like building where her breath would rise in front of her in protest against the cold. But instead, it looked almost like a furniture warehouse with crated sofas. She glanced over nervously at Sayers. She had been dying to see all the other freepers that had been brought along, and to learn about how she had been revived, but she was starting to think she had made a mistake in accepting Sayers' invitation.

As soon as they had entered the freeper-hall, Sayers had begun his spiel, obviously aimed at impressing her.

"This is where we bring them down from orbit: a hundred at a time." He indicated the line of vats. "These vats contain specialized breeds of nanomachines that evolve or are replaced as the temperature is gradually increased and different stages of the revival process are reached. We start the thawing along with the first level of nanomachines that are strictly aimed at repairing any cellular rupturing that may have occurred. Technically there shouldn't have been any in the later more refined techniques used. But in actuality, there is often some degree of damage in poorly perfused areas of the body, depending on the state of the circulatory system."

As he talked, her mind drifted. Jim had already explained it to her in a much more interesting way, and he had also added to Serena's description of the Plague, and explained more about the StarStep. She had already remembered the first terrorist use of nanokillers in 2100, and how that had gotten the previously hypothetical colony project off the ground. She had been asleep by the time the first seed-ships had been sent out, but she had been fascinated as Jim had shown her video clips of the low-G orbital breeding habitats and light-sailing seed ships.

And she had slept through it all, which meant that now she had to play catch-up, along with all the other freepers.

But this was one instance where she was beginning to regret her curiosity, as Sayers went on trying to impress her with his largely automated job reviving the other freepers brought down from the orbiting transport ships still waiting to be offloaded. She had the distinct feeling that he was jealous of the easy friendship that had developed between her and Ken. She smiled faintly as flashes of memories from her high school and college days teased her mind. She had also been pursued then, she remembered. All the more so because she had resisted all attempts at conquest, more interested in her search for the truth about humanity's beginnings and growth: a fire lit by her parents, both of whom had been anthropologists.

At the time, she had had no patience for the infantile courtship rituals of pubescent boys with delusions of manhood—and later, pubescent men with the same level of sincerity. But later she had regretted missing out on some of the joys of youth. It might have prepared her a little bit better for handling personal relationships later on. And now it felt strange to be the object of desire again, though as she thought about it, she decided that it was a nice feeling—in one case. She knew Ken was attracted to her, even if he was too much of a gentleman to come right out and say so while she was still trying to get used to her new home.

But it was reassuring to know that someone compatible cared.

She knew why Miller appealed to her. He was the type of man she had always desired: an intellectual equal who would not only accept her strengths, but who expected and complemented them. And in the past two days, she had spent a great deal of time with him, relieved by his easy, relaxed manner. She was still a little unnerved by her new environment, and she remembered how she had awakened several times alone in the dark during her first night on StarStep with terrifying visions of insidious tiny machines hiding deep within her body, biding their time before they started dismantling her, bit by bit, from the inside...

As dawn light brought her out of the fitful semi-sleep that had been the best she had been able to manage, she gave up and got out of bed with a groan. Even with drug-therapy, it would take her a while to get used to StarStep's different day/night cycle. But battles with her circadian rhythms aside, this had been a bad night and she headed for the shower because the smell of her nightmare fears stained her sheets. She debated calling Jim or Serena, but for some reason she called Ken instead once she had dressed. His calm support and obvious sensitivity back in the tower had made her feel so much better then, and she suspected that talking to him now was just what she needed.

She felt embarrassed as she explained her nightmares, but she need not have worried, for Ken just gave her a wide, reassuring smile and told her to meet him in the lounge after breakfast.

An hour later, she entered the comfortable and airy room to find him hunched over a terminal in the corner.

"Come here, Julie. I have some things to show you."

Wondering what he was up to, she obeyed and gasped as she saw the screen in front of him. It was her!

Or rather, it had been her. It was an encyclopedia entry she had been featured in, back a year or two before she had been diagnosed with terminal cancer. The woman who stared out at her looked like an ancient crone, Julie thought, until she saw Ken's expression.

"You were beautiful then, too," he commented with conviction. "It's almost scary to meet you the way you look now."

She started to protest, but he cut her off with a wave.

"That woman is beautiful," he stated definitely, nodding in the direction of the terminal. "Accept that from someone who knows. The point is, you grew into the woman in that picture accepting the gradual effects of time that we don't have to worry about any more. Don't get vain now," he teased her. Then he shook his head. "You had no problems with it at the time, and frankly, that makes you a better person than most of the vain space-heads running around on Earth these days. But you were frozen, looking like that, and—be honest—you probably never expected to wake up at all."

She nodded slowly.

"As I thought. But instead, you wake up, eleven light years from home, looking like…well…" He shook his head. "As beautiful as you were when you were young. And not only that, but your cancer has been cured. Talk about emotional overload!" He reached out to take her hands and wrapped them up in his own in a warm embrace.

"Don't worry about some bad dreams and worries. You have to expect that your brain is going to be a wee bit unsettled." He squeezed reassuringly. "Why do you think I've resisted too much nanomachine make-over? It still gives me a bit of the creeps to think about tiny little machines crawling around inside me to re-work me. I mean, what if their warranties were expired?"

He grinned and then released her hands with a firm pat, and turned back to the computer briskly.

"And now, dear lady, as long as you're here and I have some of your biography on the screen, let us see if we can't jiggle a few memories loose…"

With that, he had started her on a journey of self re-discovery that had done as much to calm her fears as his warm greetings. Research had led to dinner—still semi-liquid for her—and more work the next day. Sometimes the papers they reviewed brought back memories and sometimes they didn't, but whatever the result, he had been ever-patient and solicitous, and content to let their friendship grow without pressure.

And now, as she endured Sayer's lecture, she was reminded again of how Ken was such a total contrast to the pushy and lecherous scientist. The freeper-upper was the grown equivalent of the very juvenile types that had turned her off when she was young, and she was definitely regretting her decision to come down into his domain. Especially now that she realized that he had totally mistaken her absorption. Encouraged by what he thought was her fascination, rattled on about the freepers.

"We have an almost perfect revival record now," he told her, proudly, "because a new method of testing the freepers was developed a few years before the launch that is almost one hundred percent accurate in distinguishing those freepers who are viable from those who are too damaged to revive. We tested all the Frozen on Earth before we left, and only brought along viable ones."

Forty thousand, out of four million, she thought numbly as she tried to think of a way of getting away from Sayers. He was making her more and more uncomfortable, and so were the lined up lifeless freepers. She remembered what Jim had told her: only forty thousand freepers had been viable, leaving three million, nine hundred-and-sixty thousand frozen corpses who had been terminated with honors and flourishes in a mass memorial service observed all over the world. Many of the freepers had been frozen by con-men capitalizing on the world's hysterical fears by offering cryogenic suspension until after a cure for the Plague could be found, and many more had been frozen in little more than redesigned food freezers with no pre-freezing preparations at all, and cellular rupturing had totally destroyed their brains and damaged other organs far beyond nanotech repair.

Expectant silence suddenly made her realize that Sayer's speech was finished. She forced herself to smile.

"Fascinating, Mr. Sayers, really," she said hurriedly as she sensed an opening. "But I have to run, I'm afraid. I have an appointment with Star to go over the records on the Cougars." She excused herself and headed for the door in relief.

Sayers made a last try. "Can I—"

"I'm sorry." She waved hurriedly without breaking stride. "I'm really going to be rather busy, you understand. I have a lot of catching up to do. I'll call you." She ducked through the door at the end of the hall, drawing in a deep breath of the sweet air outside. As the door hissed shut behind her, she leaned against the warm metal, tilting her head back to feel the sun beat on her face.

She still felt a little surprised. Epsilon Eridani was a cooler and smaller star than the sun, but to her eyes it really seemed no different. She could almost forget where she was—until she moved!

The whole colony was unsettling like that.

She still remembered the picture Jim had shown her, and looking up and down the wide avenue in front of her, she had a strange feeling that she was just standing in a larger version of that neat and sanitary image. The city was too clean! It was like a city of the future in a mid-twentieth century movie. Antiseptic streets and domes on the surface, and a warren of bright and spacious apartments below-ground; each seemingly on the surface thanks to eerily realistic holoscreen images of the surface.

At least the windows in the administration tower had been real! But as nice as the grass around her was, she longed to head out into the country and get lost in the woods to dig her hands in the soil; to touch a part of nature other than the mechanically perfect lawns that surrounded the domes of the city.

She closed her eyes tightly as she was overwhelmed by a longing for home, normalcy, her memories…and she felt a surprising and overwhelming desire to be held again. She remembered the feel of Ken's arms around her when she had been talking to Tsielkovsky and the others, and realized that that was what she wanted again.

"Julie!" A familiar and welcome voice suddenly broke into her misery, and she turned to see Ken come up, a concerned look on his face. "Are you okay?"

She stood there feeling weak and helpless like a little girl and she pushed off against the wall and moved towards him. "Can I just have a hug, please?"

Ken just opened his arms and pulled her close without saying a word. His embrace was solid and comforting as she inhaled a slight scent of spicy cologne and snuggled close. His beard tickled a little, but it was a reassuring sensation and all the tension drained out of her as she locked her hands tightly behind him.

After a long moment, she leaned her head back and stretched up to kiss his cheek lightly as she let up on her grip.

He kept a relaxed hold of her. "Better?"

"Better." She smiled and blew out an explosive sigh of relief. "I just got overwhelmed by everything new, and of Sayers trying to hit on me—"

"What? Are you okay?" Ken let go of her with a frown to inspect her anxiously, confused by her sudden laughter.

"No, no. He wasn't hitting me physically. It's slang—admittedly out of date even in my time—and it just means he was trying to make a move on me…make a pass…" Ken's constantly bewildered look was making it difficult to keep from laughing. "He was trying to flirt with me," she finally managed to gasp.

"Oh." Ken looked relieved, for a moment. Then he looked concerned. "Did he…?"

"No, he didn't get too pushy. But I had the feeling," she paused uncertainly, "I don't know. Maybe I'm imagining. I just didn't feel comfortable in there." She tucked an arm under one of his, unwilling to relinquish their contact which was making her feel safe and comfortable. "But I am glad to see you. I have a few questions to ask you." She grinned.

"Like what?"

"Like how come you cultivate that?" She patted his belly gently with her free hand. "I'm sorry if I'm getting too personal, but you've been rooting around my past so I figure turnabout's fair play. Besides, I'm curious. Except for you and Jim, all of the non-freepers around here look almost alike. Black, White or Oriental, there are only minor differences in shading or appearance."

She took a guess before he could answer: "Is this your way of being unique in a conformist world?" She remembered what Jim had said about everyone's health being maintained by nanorooters, and his wistful comments about the loss of individualism.

Miller nodded slowly, giving her an appraising look. "As I said, you may have forgotten a few facts, but there is nothing wrong with your abilities. Jim and I are of the same mind there, as you guessed."

"Next question," she felt herself blushing furiously, "I was wondering if you have anyone...special in—"

"—in my life?" Ken finished with a gentle smile.

"Yes." She felt silly, like someone else was saying these outrageous things. But she wanted to be sure she wasn't reading him wrong.

"No. I'm all alone," he added mournfully, and then grinned. "But someone seems to be working on that. Not that I mind." He led her over to bench on the side of the walkway between the buildings. She didn't say anything as she could tell he had more to say.

As they sat down, he sighed and sat silent for a moment, staring into the distance. She waited patiently until he turned to her.

"I've been waiting for the right moment to talk a little more personally, and I guess this is it..." He laughed a little nervously. "Bear with me, it's been quite a while! But, you wanted to know a little about me...us." He glanced at his considerable waist with a smile. "Fair is fair." Again he was quiet for a moment, and then he faced her seriously.

"I don't talk about this much, not even to Serena or Jim, and while Star knows, he knows enough to keep it to himself. To begin with, there once was somebody else in my life...years ago. Her name was Carayah. No last name. She had it legally changed."

His eyes unfocused and his face filled with a palpable tenderness that warmed Julie because it showed her what he was capable of.

"She was a gentle woman and a brilliant artist," Ken started softly. "She could look at even the ugliest pile of trash and find beauty in it; rearrange it, and photograph it in some special way or paint or draw it. And she liked what she saw in me." He smiled. "No correlation, I hope. Of course, I looked a little different then." He looked down again. "I didn't have this, for one thing. And my hair was charcoal black. I was rather handsome, if I do say so myself."

He stopped her as she started to object. "Okay, maybe I'm still reasonably tolerable in appearance, but with my friend here, I know I'm not going to break any hearts." He grinned briefly. "Maybe a few benches, though."

Then his gaze drifted as he turned serious. "I was a student at MIT, and she was supporting us. She was a few years older than me, and she was no starving artist." His face glowed with love and pride. "No one who saw her work was unmoved; or untapped financially. She was shrewd at business, too. A rare combination. She had galleries competing for her work and she took them for all she could." His voice suddenly broke. "And then in 2200, my world ended."

Julie realized what was coming. The Plague.

Miller saw her face. "You can guess what happened, I see. She was in greater New York for a gallery showing when an outbreak of the machine-plague hit. Millions died within days. There weren't even bodies left. The nanokillers liberated all the water in the bodies and transformed what was left into raw elements that blew away on the first breeze. "Dust to dust…" Tears were running down his cheeks and she felt her own eyes burning.

"Do you know how long it's been since I *really* talked to anybody about this?" he asked after a long silence. She shook her head. "Almost one hundred and thirty years, by the calendar. I went to therapy for a few years, but then I let myself go to pot and sank myself into my work, shutting out everybody and everything else. Later, when I finally started getting my head together, and had a chance to rebuild myself, I decided I didn't like the homogenous nothingness of the 'healthy' new bodies, so I kept this newly developed friend," he patted his belly again, "as my mark of distinction." He stopped, staring at the ground. "And I guess, in a way, as a reminder of my failings."

Julie cocked her head and squeezed his hand. "Do you think it might also have been a way of keeping other women at bay so you wouldn't have to run the risk of getting emotionally involved again? Involved, and then hurt?"

Ken's eyes popped wide and he pursed his lips thoughtfully. "Ouch!" He patted her hand reassuringly. "No, don't worry. That was the sound of me smacking myself in the face. Truth does that to one." He shook his head. "I never thought about that. And I am not a stupid man, I'll have you know…honest." He grinned. "I had a few sporadic flings, including one with a woman who was Earth's president, but I never found—"

"—never looked for," Julie guessed.

Ken threw up his hands in concession. "Okay, never looked for, another real relationship. At first I told myself that there could never be another, and later I kept telling myself that I didn't have time. So it didn't really matter if I was fat. And then it became a matter of pride to be different. It didn't matter in what way."

"Does it, now?" she asked.

"Does it to you?"

She thought for a minute, and then shook her head. "Not really. It's only a small part of you…" She blushed. "Sorry! I meant it's only one element of you."

"That decides it. It's coming off." He looked down at his belly mournfully. "Sorry my friend, but you're history. We've had a lot of good years, but it's time for us to go our separate ways." He glanced over at Julie who was having a hard time keeping a straight face as she saw Ken's woeful expression. "I just have to tell myself that it means being able to see my feet when I'm standing up!"

She leaned over and kissed him impulsively, not resisting as he pulled her close and returned it with unexpected but welcome hunger. A small part of her mind chided her for being so impulsive and impractical, but she shut it off as she remembered her own incredible change in the mirror. This was a whole new life, and for a change she wasn't going to calculate and analyze everything to death; so she surrendered happily to Ken's embrace.

CHAPTER 7

▼

MACHIAVELLI, WITH FUR

"If I fail, I am no longer Speaker," he offered. "Why is it wrong to talk to the sky-creatures? Where is it said it is wrong?" he challenged. He was counting on that question. Since they had never encountered this before, naturally there was no tradition against it. He knew that the others were struggling with some of the ideas he had come up with, and he was counting on them not thinking quickly enough to argue.

"I am Speaker," he pressed. "It was I who showed long sticks that kill, I who dug the first pit with sticks to catch food, I who showed you how to chip stones for claws harder than claws. I am your leader, and I say we should do this. We have shown them our strength and they should know to fear us now. Now is the time to try to make peace, while we have their strength in us." But did they? Speaker's stomach still churned from eating of the sky-creatures flesh; a sickening flavor best unsampled.

Crooked Tooth, who was still seething after his earlier defeat, spoke up first.

"You will go to the sky-creatures alone? What if they kill you? Who is Speaker then?"

Not you, Speaker thought firmly. He considered the gathered warriors. Sag Belly would have been good. She was not the strongest, perhaps, but she was blindingly fast and very intelligent, but she had been injured in the last hunt and was not yet fully recovered. Whoever he left in charge had to be ready for a challenge from Crooked Tooth. Then his eyes landed on Six Toes, one of the singlings who had attacked him at the Sky-creatures' home. The young warrior had surrendered—knowing he was beaten—which was no dishonor, and he was intelligent as well as honest. And he was a good fighter, even if he was small. The challenge had not been his idea, and Speaker did not hold it against him.

He decided.

"Six Toes will be Speaker while I am gone, and can challenge for my leadership if I don't return in two paws of lights. His paws." Speaker exposed his fangs in a savage grin, seeing Six Toes respond in kind. Let Crooked Tooth and Six Toes keep each other busy. Crooked Tooth might be a better fighter, but he was stupid and nobody liked him. They would support Six Toes to prevent Crooked Tooth from being Speaker. And it might keep Speaker safe from an ambush because he knew that Six Toes had no wish to be Speaker for more than a short time, while the desire was plain to see on Crooked Tooth's face.

He turned and took up his pack and stick, glancing back briefly at the gathered tribe. "I will be back."

He set a brisk pace immediately, leaving the Field of Challenge behind him, his thoughts whirling madly. He had another problem to consider while traveling. Since he had been Speaker, the Tribe had not grown, and fewer younglings were being born. Each litter was the same size, and while more of each birthing were surviving, the birthings came less often now than in his forerunners' times. He remembered being a youngling, and how frequently birthings occurred, and he remembered his mother saying that there were less birthings in her time than in her forerunners'.

Speaker knew he was one of a few who held clear memories of their cubhood, but he was glad now that he did. If there were less birthings but just as many deaths? What would that mean? He would have to think.

But first he had to keep a war with the sky-creatures from starting!

He suddenly noticed that the sun was dropping low and realized he had been walking all after-high-sun-time; and he was sore. Dropping briefly to all fours, he shook himself and stretched, feeling a numb protest all through his body. He also felt a rumble from his stomach and knew he would have to hunt soon. But first, he needed to rest.

He crouched on a nearby sun-bathed boulder, feeling the warm rock soothe his aching legs. He yawned in amusement as he thought about his constant two-legged gait, and how it was more tiring than running on all fours. His sire, and all his Forebearers had walked on all fours—as much of the Tribe still did—but more and more walked on two legs to leave paws free to carry hunting sticks or rocks. The new ideas he was bringing to his tribe were not without their problems, he realized. But at least no one was going hungry now…Of course, if the sky-creatures did not stop clearing their hunting land, that might change.

Change.

It had been different when he had been a cub—before the sky-creatures. Then there had been no need to think about every action or worrying about consequences. There were times he was tempted to find a new mate and disappear into the distant forests to find new hunting grounds; away from sky-creatures, formal challenges, and responsibilities. To find a place where he could lie like this whenever he wanted.

The warmth under him, the soothing sun, and the rhythmic droning of unseen insects all conspired to lull him, and he was just starting to cross the line into sleep when a faint rustling in the underbrush caught his ears.

CHAPTER 8

▼

DISSENSION

Julie looked around, more than a little awed. Several dozen people appeared to sit around her along a long arcing table, with Jim Martin presiding at the elbow of the table. Not too long ago, he had seated her in a small chamber which after a few minutes had suddenly expanded into a huge conference room with all the colony's Representatives in attendance. It was a holographic illusion that defied detection. From what he had told her, this was the way Earth's World Council met, and while there was no real need for it yet on StarStep, an identical set-up had been built here in preparation for future meetings once the colonists had scattered over the continent.

StarStep was still in transition, ostensibly a democracy with representatives from all the Agra settlements and StarStep City, but Jim was still colony director with final say in all decisions until such time as all colonists were awake and a fully democratic government was elected. By that time the holographic conference room would be essential to running the colony. But until then, it was just an incredible device that most of the colonists viewed as the grand toy it probably was. Still, it did have one advantage: it enabled one to easily focus in on any particular speaker if desired by merely zooming in. But that very advantage was also a problem, because the more she listened to one particular viewpoint being pushed, the madder she was getting.

"I say we wipe them out!" Tara snapped again. "They're hardly more than animals!"

Tara Richman was a lanky brunette with short, bobbed hair, standing near the right end of the table. She was Representative for Agra 1, the first and largest farm project that housed a sizable portion of the roughly three thousand freepers thawed out so far, and she was by far the most militant. Her antipathy for the Cougars had soared after the attack on Agra 6, not just because her husband

142

had been visiting there and he had been among the casualties, but also as she had always been a radical who refused to let logic or reason sway her emotional arguments.

But a voice of reason came from an unexpected quarter: Dan Tsielkovsky.

"Tara, don't you think that's getting a little extreme?" The farmer sat next to Julie, a few seats to the right of Jim, and he looked distinctly uncomfortable. He was also anti-Cougar, but he had surprised Julie by calming down and accepting the need for a more rational approach. It had taken a long and occasionally heated meeting, but Dan had been among the majority who had seemed to eventually understand why the Cougars had attacked.

With a grateful smile to him for his support, Julie decided that she had had enough of Richman and she got to her feet, glaring at the other standing colonist.

"How can you stand there and talk about exterminating an entire race of intelligent beings?"

Tara wasn't daunted. "Hey, they were an accident. This was supposed to be our world. You screwed—"

"Don't you 'you' me. I'm one of you. I'm a freeper, too. Hell, I'm senior to any of you if you want to get technical. I admit I'm not exactly happy about waking up eleven light years from Earth, rejected by my own world, either."

She let her eyes sweep over all the other colonist Representatives. "But if this is an example of our attitudes, I can't say I blame them!" She glared at Tara. "Personally, I'm grateful to God and science that I am alive and that I have a chance to be a part of history here! I happen to be pretty excited." All around the table, she heard murmurs of support, and she even noticed grudging nods from other Representatives who, just moments before, had been urging Tara on.

"You have to understand," Julie went on, "that the Cougars were reacting to a threat to their food supply and their land. It was not an unprovoked attack."

But Tara refused to budge. "What about when another thirty-seven thousand of us are up and around? We need to clear land for building and farming and not have to worry about a bunch of blasted cats that breed like crazy!"

Julie stared at her and laughed. "Are you kidding? We have a whole bloody continent! Out of all the Cougars, only this one isolated group is intelligent." She stopped and looked up. "Star, you tell her."

"Gladly." She shivered. He did have a marvelous voice. "Representative Richman," Star began. "There is currently only one loosely scattered tribe of intelligent Cougars with a total number of only a hundred or so specimens as near as our surveys can determine. They are far outnumbered by the non-intelligent cougars scattered throughout the northern and southern temperate zones. The intelligent Cougars were placed near StarStep City by the stocking-ship on purpose since its computer was aware some damage had occurred and wanted us to be able to monitor it when we got here. The intelligence was a totally unexpected mutation."

Star's voice was suddenly condescending and Julie forced herself to keep a straight face as he added:

"As for rapidly breeding intelligent Cougars being a threat: I do not think you need worry. They have a high mortality rate, and since their reproductive cycles are reverting to normal, they are not likely to overrun their established hunting areas. If anything, unless they establish a more settled social structure, they are actually in danger of extinction. That is because they are continuing a pattern of behavior that was both good population control and evolutionarily progressive during the early decades of explosive breeding. Life was expendable, and challenges to the death were common. That was fine before, and assured survival of the best stock. But unlike the wild cougars who are adjusting naturally, the Tribal Cougars have adopted an artificially close-knit and rigid social structure that is continuing a behavior which is now attritionary."

Julie stared up at the ceiling. That she hadn't realized.

Background noises suddenly cut out and Star went on in a different tone. "Sorry, Julie. I just determined that when I re-examined my data. The others don't hear this private comment to you, by the way."

"Thank you, Star."

A faint feeling of sonic depth warned her that she was back in contact with the rest of the Representatives. Richman seemed to have been effectively shut up for the moment by Star's quiet put-down, and more than a few of the others looked mildly pleased.

Jim was smiling subtly also as he took advantage of the momentary silence. "Well, since it seems that we have settled that for the moment, maybe we can have some constructive suggestions on how we should go about protecting ourselves. Thanks to Dr. Nathanson, we will soon attempt contact with the Cougars, as soon as we can learn something about the their language. But for now, let's begin by planning for self-protection until we can establish settlements outside of the Cougars' hunting grounds."

As Jim started to lay out practical guidelines for new settlements, Julie felt her interest wane. Her mind was still fixed on Star's latest revelation and she tried to remember which switch Jim had thrown to activate the holo-link. Suddenly the illusion collapsed and she was alone again.

"I take it you wished to terminate?" Star asked.

"Are you a mind-reader, too?"

"No, a palm-reader. I saw your palm groping and fingers tapping impatiently."

Julie giggled. *God, she was doing a lot of that lately!* "Star, this may not mean anything to you, but you'd be the perfect straight man, with your delivery."

"Well, I am straight, on six sides. A multifaceted individual you might say."

"Touché." She fought to keep serious, because Star had a tendency to keep joking if not side-tracked. "Not to change the subject, dear, but can you call Ken for me?"

"Certainly. I'll even call Ken Miller, not one of the other seven Kens that my present census shows to be active, if one uses Ken as a diminutive for Kenneth as well as a name on its own."

Julie shook her head. Serena had done a hell of a job programming Star, but he really needed to learn when to stop joking.

But he was as good as his word, and after a moment she heard his puzzled voice admitting that he couldn't find Ken.

"Instructions?" he asked.

"What about his locator?" She remembered Jim telling her that all StarStep personnel were tracked via implanted beacons, in case of an accident when away from City. No matter where on the planet someone was, their location could be pin-pointed within seconds thanks to a network of orbiting satellites.

"I am not getting a reading." The simulated concern and confusion in Star's voice translated to panic for Julie and she bolted for the door. "Call Jim and get a search organized! I'm heading to his room—"

"He is not there...I overrode the privacy directive—I can do that in an emergency."

"Don't defend yourself, damn it! What did you find?"

"Sorry. His apartment is empty. I scanned it."

"Shit!" For a minute, she stood by the door, thoughts whirling madly. Then she remembered his comment the day before.

"If he wanted to go get modifications done on his body, where would he go? What would he do?"

"Contact one of the bio-nanotechnologists and request a make-over," Star answered immediately. "It is simple enough, unless he wanted radical changes in which case I would be needed to program the nanorooters. Standard modifications are already pre-program—"

"Did you say he would contact a bio-nanotechnologist? Like Sayers?" Julie had only heard the first words. She was too busy thinking about Sayers' obvious jealousy over her interest in Ken. "He would have himself knocked out with a whole crop of miniature machines crawling around inside, controlled by Sayers?" She knew she sounded almost hysterical but she couldn't help it. The nanomachines still scared her a little, even if they had saved her life and given her back her youth.

Star was oblivious to her concern. "Sayers is one of our top technologists, though there are eight other bionanotechnologists awake."

"Would a rebuild throw off the beacon?"

"Of course. It would be deactiv—"

"Check on it...can you check somehow if anyone is getting a rebuild," she choked on the word, "anywhere?"

"Working..." Barely a second's delay. "Yes. In Med-Block-2."

"Location on Sayers," she cut him off, heading out the open doorway.

"Med-Block-2."

"Guide me!"

"Certainly. But it seems that my sensors there have been blocked." Star repeated, sounding confused again, but the room was already empty.

CHAPTER 9

▼

TRAVELING COMPANIONS

Speaker spun as two figures materialized from the bushes to step out onto the path ahead. He automatically rose to a crouch and pulled his dagger, fur rising along with his warning growl. Ahead of him the two unfamiliar warriors fell to the ground and bared their throats and bellies.

"We are here to protect you, Speaker," the smaller of the two explained. She was a young female with delicate shadings of brown and white, and an unusually long tail.

Speaker's hair flattened, but he didn't sheath the dagger. "Sent by who?"

"Six Toes," the large male answered with a peculiar spitting sound. "He doesn't want to be Speaker, so he thought it would be good to make sure you came back safely. I am Marrow Sucker, and this is Long Tail."

"You're late." Speaker relaxed.

Both strangers rose, looking puzzled. "I don't understand," Long Tail was first.

"I knew Six Toes would send somebody. I just wanted to be sure Crooked Tooth didn't beat him to it."

"I don't understand." This time it was Marrow Sucker's turn.

"I didn't want to bring an escort and risk looking weak," Speaker explained. "Or have anyone think I was worried about being unable to do this."

"How did you know Six—"

"Because he doesn't want Crooked Tooth as Speaker any more than he wants to be Speaker himself. He wants a female, and continued prosperity. Not to be challenged all the time. And he doesn't want the problems everyone would have with Crooked Tooth as Speaker. The Tribe doesn't need a stupid Speaker." He sheathed his dagger and looked over the two still-confused warriors with an approving yawn, his fangs glistening in the dying sun.

Six Toes had chosen well. Both warriors were lean and muscled; their postures and attitudes vigilant. Speaker felt a bit more confident than when he had first started on his trip to the sky-creatures' city.

Speaker settled back down on the warm rock. "Now that you are here, make yourself useful and hunt up some game. I am hungry and I need to plan my approach to the sky-creatures." He closed his eyes but listened carefully. He could almost hear their shock. *Hunt for him?* they were probably wondering in outrage. But he had asked that on purpose, to see if they would obey a request that went so strongly against the warrior tradition of always hunting for one's own food.

After a moment, he heard the two disappear in the woods again and relaxed. They would be loyal, he decided.

CHAPTER 10

▼

LESS OF A MAN

As Julie burst into the MedBlock, she noticed that it was totally different than the one where Gratch had examined her. It was a large, square room, and set into three of its walls were retracting nano-rooter modification chambers, two on each wall. All but one were empty at the moment, and in the elevated control area in the middle of the large room, Sayers stood, busy monitoring a display panel. A spiral, winding ramp led up to Sayers and she approached anxiously just as Jim and Serena entered the MedBlock—she had asked them to join her.

"Where is Ken?" she demanded, an edge of panic in her voice. She started up the ramp but Jim held her back, and echoed her question.

"Yes, where is Doctor Miller?"

"In there," Sayers pointed to the active chamber. "He'll be there for several days. Didn't you get my message?" he asked Julie innocently.

"Message?"

"Yes, as per Dr. Miller's instructions, I told Star to tell you he was going to be busy on a rush project and would be out of touch for a couple of days. He was having himself rebuilt, as a surprise."

Serena stepped around Jim suspiciously. "Just what did you tell..." She stopped and looked up. "I know you can hear me, Star, but that you just can't assimilate anything except control commands, so *control* reset *command*," her voice snapped firmly.

"Thank you, Serena. What happened?"

"Do you remember Dr. Sayers' orders?"

"No. What orders?"

"Memory wipe, too. Great!" Her mouth tightened into a slash. "Star, interface with Lab-Data and monitor Doctor Miller. Status report."

After a moment, a calm voice replied. "Dr Miller is in excellent shape, literally. Just a little smaller, and shrinking by the hour." A hesitant electronic chuckle filtered down and the others all stared up. "Was that appropriate, Dr. Andrews? The situation fits the parameters my records indicate as 'funny'. He has had his waistline and weight reduced to what would be appropriate for his height, in contr—"

"Fine!" Serena cut him off and turned to Sayers, who had a satisfied grin on his face. "What did you order Star?" she demanded. "Remember, Ken will be awake soon and can confirm."

"Well, as per Dr. Miller's instructions—he wanted to surprise Dr. Nathanson—and after his program was started, I told Star, in command mode, to program some nanorooters for a slimming and reshaping session, to give Dr. Miller's excuses to Dr. Nathanson as soon as the reshaping was going, and to forget all instructions as soon as the doctor was asleep. I also left a command to keep Star blocked out of MedBlock-2 until reset. That way Star wouldn't be able to answer any direct questions, even in command mode." Sayers shrugged. "I guess Star forgot to deliver the message to Dr Nathanson."

"That's the way you instructed Star? In that order?"

"That's right. What's the problem?"

"So Star didn't deliver the message because he was told to forget it before he was to deliver it!" Serena's face was flushed and as Julie realized what Sayers had done, she felt her own fists clenching.

Serena just glared. "You knew damn well that that would happen."

Sayers looked innocent. "No, honestly, I didn't think about it. I assumed Star would understand what I meant."

"Not in command mode he wouldn't, and you know that very well. You've worked with him enough to know he takes everything literally when he's in command mode" She turned to Julie and clasped her shoulder. "Ken's fine."

Julie nodded, her jaw tight. "I know. Thanks."

Sayers gave her a nasty smile. "Sorry to distress you."

"That's fine," Julie shrugged and forced herself to smile. "I'm just glad he's okay."

Sayers looked confused as he came around the ramp and approached her. "No hard feelings?" He sounded disappointed as he searched her face with his eyes.

"No." She started to turn away as he reached her, and then spun and slammed her open palm across his face with echoing force that rocked his head back and sent him staggering. A red hand print grew brighter by the second over the side of his face.

"No, no hard feelings," she added icily. "On my part."

Then she turned, and with a sweet smile to Jim and Serena, left the room with a brief parting comment:

"Could you have Ken call me when he's awake, please?"

CHAPTER 11

▼

A CLOSER LOOK

Two mornings later, Speaker stared again at the strange caves ahead, his black-pupiled yellow eyes slitted against the evening light. The caves glowed red as they reflected the dying rays of the sun and they seemed as smooth as a lake on a windless day. They were made of the same strange material as the caves they had attacked a hand of days past, but bigger. He had been watching these caves for two days now, trying to decide how to approach the sky-creatures.

His stomach grumbled again, but it was not hunger this time. He felt like he was a singling facing his first mate-challenge as he watched two of the strange sky-creatures walking around, tiny in the distance. They were short and stocky with pink skin and no fur that he could see, except on their heads. They also covered themselves with strange brightly patterned pieces of…something. He had thought it was their skin at first, but they shed it too easily. And if it was discarded skin, why would they put it back on again? Snakes never did that. And why the variable markings?

Questions, always questions running through his mind. Sometimes Speaker wished he did not think so much.

From across the field, the stench of the sky-creatures came floating again, carried by the shifting wind. Speaker's nose twitched. That would be the hardest to deal with. He forced his fur to lie flat and turned to his companions.

Marrow Sucker and Long Tail were crouched, snarling and hissing as they stared wide-eyed at the sky-creatures wandering around on the short grass. Two days and they were still afraid.

Speaker sneered. "What are you? Cubs? Scared of naked, clawless animals? You saw how easily they died when we attacked them. They did not fight. Not even with explosive rocks. They are no danger to us! And since our attack, they have not even tried to intrude on our hunting land. They are afraid."

He had kept taunting them—partly to ease his own fear, he admitted to himself—but also because he needed their full attention. He wanted them to be witnesses to testify to the Tribe when he returned. That was why he was afraid. He was afraid of failing in front of witnesses. But if he succeeded, he wanted their support.

His insults finally sank in and Long Tail's teeth slowly disappeared as she settled into a guarded crouch and her fur slowly flattened. The tail-fur was last to slowly drop as the long tail swept back and forth slowly. She still wasn't happy.

Seeing Long Tail relax, Marrow Sucker was forced to follow suit and his fur also dropped. But his fore-paws kept kneading the ground, claws extending and retracting rhythmically to dig tiny gouges in the soft earth.

Speaker was strangely comforted. Maybe their fear had affected him? He faced the caves and the sky-creatures again.

CHAPTER 12

▼

AN IDEA

Julie was sitting on the grass in front of the administration tower, watching the jungle across the lawn. It was almost a thousand feet away. She had been spending a lot of time out here for three days now—since the watching Cougars had come—and she had also encouraged other colonists to join her and move around outside.

She really had not been ready for contact yet, but Star was continuing to try to analyze their language, and she had some ideas of her own.

"Julie?" A low voice called from the computer on her belt.

She lifted it up, a delicate three-dimensional moire pattern floating in front of the screen identifying the caller. She smiled, for the hundredth time imagining a face to go with his voice.

He would be in his late twenties, like Giancarlo, with thick, glossy black hair that would drop down over his intense, grey eyes if he moved his head too fast. His nose would be slightly hooked and narrow, and he would have an athlete's trim body and smooth moves. All in all, he would be a fun and stimulating friend, even if he was a bit exasperating.

But her increasingly personal perception of Star meant that she had expressly barred him from her apartment unless she called him—even if that was technically a redundant command. But he was getting to be too 'real'; especially now, after that vivid visualization! She shook her head. She should have left well alone.

Star had been patiently waiting for a response (patiently? He was a machine…No, much more).

"What is it, Star?" she asked.

"I was wondering why we do not contact the Cougars who are watching us. One of them is the same one who performed the sacrifice. Do you not think he is scouting for an attack? We should try to convince him not to."

"I disagree. That's what I told the Council, and you heard my reasons. I don't think he's scouting for an attack. Gathering information, yes. But I would swear he is trying to work up enough nerve to contact us. The other two are behaving normally. Staying out of sight, growling, spitting and fur-ruffling like any house-cat whose territory is being invaded. But the leader: he's watching us. He's curious, not angry or scared." She smiled. "We've got a feline Einstein here."

"What are you basing that on?"

"Gut instinct."

"Oh." Star sounded a bit miffed.

A slender finger tapped the top of the computer rhythmically as she pursed her lip in thought. Star's identifying pattern swirled and she grinned helplessly as she thought of something.

"I hope this isn't getting you excited, dear."

"What?" Total confusion. He was getting better and better at simulating.

"Are you trying to hit on Star, my dear?" Suddenly a pair of warm arms crept around her from behind and lifted her to her feet effortlessly. "Is that what happens when I disappear for a few days?"

A familiar scratching brushed her cheek as a snowy beard crept onto her shoulder. But she felt a chest behind her, not a stomach and spun in surprise, grabbing hold of him and squeezing tight. "Ken! I didn't expect you until this afternoon. But you're all right; thank God!" She grabbed hold and squeezed tight, able to easily link her hands behind him now. Then, she leaned back and took a look at him, eyes wide as she saw the "new" Ken.

The salty hair and ebony skin were unchanged, but on a rugged figure with a flat and rock-hard stomach. The face was more defined, too. But the eyes were the same: warm and twinkling with good humor.

"I didn't change too much," his familiar and deep voice boomed cheerfully. "I'll keep my snow and wrinkles since I've earned them. But I thought this body would be better suited for a little camping in the woods. I imagine that as an anthropologist with a whole new species to document, you'll want to be doing a bit of that." He pulled her close again, running one finger lightly up and down her spine in a teasing caress as he whispered in her ear:

"And we can share a lot of that time in the field, since I don't have as much to do anymore." Then he eased out of her arms reluctantly to pirouette dramatically. "Well? Do I meet with your approval?"

She shook her head, almost as overwhelmed as with her own transformation. "I had no objections to the old you, but I do have to confess that I like the redesign." She cocked her head and examined him critically. "Yes, I would definitely stamp you USDA prime, but not with Star watching." She leered and eyed his rear.

"USDA prime?" Ken looked lost.

She shook her head with a smile. "Never mind, sweetheart. Obviously before your time, but believe me, you're choice." She grinned at his continued befuddlement and stepped forward to grab his ears to pull his face down for a resounding kiss—after pointedly hanging her computer back on her belt, screen and "eye" turned in to block them.

"I love you," she finally whispered in his ear after a long, delicious moment; surprising herself with the declaration. But even if only a little over week had passed, she realized that this was "it".

Then she twisted his ears lightly to warn: "But don't ever try to surprise me like that again! I was scared out of my mind!"

Ken's face was solemn as he brought her hands together and raised them to his lips. "I won't," he promised.

"Good." She let go and with a sigh, pulled her computer back up. "Star, I had an idea, before I was interrupted." Her eyes twinkled. "I want you to design a holo-simulation for me. Can you do a—"

"—remote projection where our visitor can see it?" Star finished as Julie frowned. "Yes I can." I will need some equipment set up to receive the signal. But we can do it from under the surface so we don't scare away the Cougars. We'll tunnel from beneath and just extend the terminals over the grass when close enough. I've developed an effective scent neutralizer."

"Excellent. Now here is what I want you to do…and don't second-guess me."

"Define, please."

"Don't interrupt me or try to anticipate me!" She gave Star's swirling pattern a mock glare as she explained what she wanted.

CHAPTER 13

▼

ANOTHER IDEA

Speaker had been watching them for several lights now. Too long. He had promised to returned to the tribe in two hands of lights. Two of Six Toe's hands, but that was still not that long. He already been gone for one of those. One of the sky-creatures was the same one, every day, he was realizing. Its smell was the same. A different smell, like flowers, was hidden under the normal rankness. It was a different color each day as it covered itself in something different, but he was starting to recognize it. It had long black fur on top, which looked strange since it had no other fur he could see.

A different creature had been there in the before-high-sun time. It was dark, with white fur on its muzzle and head. It had embraced the black-furred one. Mating?

The idea of the sky-creatures mating made them seem less alien. Different, yes. But no longer so frightening. If they mated, maybe they felt pleasure? And if they felt pleasure, then they felt pain, just like any of the Tribe...Thoughts spun in his head again.

A hiss behind him alerted him and he turned to see Marrow Sucker pointing at a nearby section of the short plants that stopped the jungle. He could see nothing, but he felt it. The ground was trembling, and a faint new smell, a dead smell like the inside of the shiny caves assaulted his nose. Then he saw it. The ground was moving. Two shiny metal sticks came out of the ground like some monster under it was testing the air. He felt Marrow Sucker and Long Tail pull away. He smelled the fear on them. He felt his own fear, too, but he was unable to move. He wanted to see what it was.

Then a mist came over the field and images formed within. He saw himself, standing on the short plants by the shiny caves! He heard his guards growling behind him, confused as they looked from the real Speaker, to the odorless image standing out in the open. Then the black-furred sky-creature

156

came walking towards the false Speaker, paws extended. It was holding a dead field-runner. A healthy, fresh-killed one. Again, neither the sky-creature nor the prey held any smell, and the three hidden warriors were confused. Even more, because they could see that the black-furred sky-creature had not moved from where it was sitting over by the shiny cave.

The false sky-creature came right up to the false Speaker and held out the prey. And then Speaker saw himself reach out and take the prey, actually touching the sky-creature. Then the sky-creature turned its back(!), and walked away. And the other Speaker did nothing, but simply walked the other way.

Then the mist cleared, and there was nothing. No other Speaker, no prey. Just two metal sticks coming up through the ground and the black-furred sky-creature sitting by the shiny cave like before.

Speaker turned, trying to understand what he had just seen. He realized both of the others were crouched, fur erect and fangs bared, a low moaning growl warbling from their throats as their tails lashed angrily from side to side.

"Stand," he spat. "There is no danger!" Reluctantly the others straightened, their fur slowly settling though their teeth remained bared. "I came here to contact the sky-creatures, but the sky-creatures are trying to contact us!" He realized finally that that was what it must have meant. He felt his heart racing. He turned to Long Tail, a terrifying idea growing. "Go catch a field-runner or a tree-hunter."

"You are hungry?" She stared at him in disbelief.

"No. I intend to try something. What I came here for." He knew the young warrior didn't understand, but he suddenly felt compelled to try his idea out, no matter how much it repelled and frightened him.

CHAPTER 14

▼

OPENING NIGHT JITTERS

Jim and Serena had joined Ken and Julie and were watching the holographic illusion play itself. "Do you think it's going to work?" Jim wondered for the sixth or seventh time. "Will he take the suggestion?"

Julie considered it. She had curled up on the grass again, sitting right next to Ken—who looked a bit self-conscious about sitting on the ground. He had a helpless smile on his face and was obviously resigning himself to enduring a little anachronistic behavior.

"I don't know," Julie finally answered as she shrugged. "I do know that the leader is an extremely patient and curious cat. Not at all like the other two. Remember how he just stood and watched when the Holo-projectors came to the surface? The two with him looked like they couldn't decide whether to take off for the hills or attack. But our friend there just moved closer and I swear I could hear gears grinding in that furry head of his."

"Gears?" both Ken and Star burst out, sounding confused.

"Never mind, dears. It's just an old expression—old even in my day. Access colloquial idioms, American, 20th century. My favorite historical period." Julie giggled and patted the top of her computer as she explained the expression to Ken.

Star obviously had the reference, since he immediately said: "Ah yes, I see."

"Hey, that's new expression for him!" Serena looked down at Star with surprise.

Julie smiled. "He's probably been listening to me. We've been working hard together and it's an expression I use once in a while…well, all too often. A bad habit I picked up from…?" She realized it had been someone she had worked with, but she couldn't remember who.

"Hey, it'll come back," Ken said softly as he moved around behind her to massage her suddenly tense shoulders.

Julie leaned back into his arms and closed her eyes. "Thanks, hon."

After a moment, she looked back at Serena. "Don't be surprised if he starts using other strange phrases. He's been quizzing me on a lot of my expressions. I'm the 'oldest' person he's ever encountered and I guess my speech is pretty colorful, even for someone of my time." She chuckled. "You should have heard me try to explain 'bloody' to him!"

"Excuse me," Star interrupted again, "but the female Cougar that left is back and has a freshly killed doe with it."

All four of them exchanged amazed looks.

"It might be working at that," Jim exclaimed.

Julie got up and brushed herself off, her mouth suddenly dry. Ken also rose and took her hands. "Are you okay?"

"I'm fine. I have to be. These cats probably think I stink as it is, fear would only compound it. Besides, I'm dealing with one smart kitty, there." Her heart was racing, but in excitement, not with fear, thought that was right below the surface. After all, she was about to face an animal—no!—she corrected herself firmly. A native, who had calmly slit the throat and drunk the blood of a fellow warrior, and who had then led an assault that had taken the lives of thirteen defenseless people. She fought her nervousness, suddenly remembering facing an angry tribe of Masai warriors who had been driven away from their...A memory! Flashes of images from a cloudy past suddenly popped in and out of her conscious mind, irritatingly elusive. Excitement drove away her fear, and she grabbed hold of Ken to squeeze him tight.

"I'm starting to remember," she whispered, "but I can't quite hold on to it!"

"Don't force it," he whispered back. "Relax and don't think about it. I told you it was still up there." He tapped her head and smiled gently. "Give it time. But right now, concentrate on this."

She sighed. "You're right. Thanks." She reached up to kiss him quickly and then let go. "Better get out of sight." She glanced over at Jim and Serena. "You too. Just monitor me through Star." She urged them all away. "I want to be alone, and closer to the jungle so the Cougars won't be as afraid." She laughed; a brittle sound. "The leader's probably as scared as I am."

As soon as they were out of sight, she drew herself up and turned back to the jungle. "Well, here goes." She started towards the jungle. "Are you with me Star?"

"Every step of the way," his calm voice reassured her. "I'm afraid I don't have anything useful on the language yet, but at least I may be able to warn you of any threatening sounds, moves or gestures. I have quite a collection of those. Also, I have a laser set up to cover your position. It is not very high power—Jim dismantled a portable communications link and wired it into me—but it should be sufficient to distract the leader quite effectively if he should make any threatening moves."

"Not unless I tell you to!" Julie stopped and lifted the computer, glaring at his 'face' that swirled in the miniature holoscreen. "Absolutely not. With all cats, there are displays and threats that are part of establishing communications. And I don't want anything to blow this opportunity. Unless I specifically tell you—or unless he actually physically injures me—do…not…do…anything! Clear?"

"Certainly." He sounded so hurt that she had to laugh. "Okay. I'm sorry. I'm sure that information is in your data banks, too. It's a shame you don't have any records of a meeting between members of two different Cougar tribes. That would have been perfect."

"He is moving closer," Star warned.

She realized she was within twenty meters of the jungle and she stopped, dropping to the ground to sit cross-legged. She was not far from where the hologram had been set up, and hoped the invisible Cougar made the connection.

A chill wind was cutting across the field, and she shivered a little. Here closer to the looming jungle, the afternoon sun was blocked, and the administration tower didn't shield her from the stiff breezes coming in off the ocean. She seemed to sense invisible eyes on her from both directions and felt incredibly conspicuous, sitting in the open like she was.

Over an hour passed, with Star giving her periodic status reports on the Cougars. The two followers were keeping well back, and they were definitely not happy. But the leader was watching. From time to time he would pick up the doe, and then put it down.

Somehow that made her feel a lot better. He *was* as nervous about this as she was.

Then she heard a rustling in the underbrush and Star's simultaneous warning.

CHAPTER 15

▼

TWO VIEWS ON CONTACT

Speaker threw the limp body over his shoulder, staggering under the heavy load. He eyed Long Tail with respect. It had not taken her long to track down and kill the runner and she had brought it back easily. He wondered if she was mated with Marrow Sucker. He felt sure he could defeat the male warrior in a challenge. Scar Flank, the mate he had won from Six Toes, had been so bonded with the other warrior that he had surrendered her and let her go back to Six Toes. She was also too stupid. He wanted a mate who would think as well as him; someone like Ringed Tail. She had not been the most cooperative mate always, but he realized that he missed the stimulation of her challenges. Long Tail was at least much more alert and capable than Scar Flank.

He dropped the runner and crouched, looking at Long Tail with new eyes. Perhaps he should ask her, instead of just challenging Marrow Sucker?

It was a radical idea. For a moment he considered it. He had a strange felling, all at once, that a mate who would be compatible would not be one who could be won in battle, but one who would come to him by choice.

But as Long Tail settled down next to Marrow Sucker and the two began grooming each other, Speaker reconsidered. The little playful bites that Marrow Sucker gave her as he pulled loose burrs that had stuck to her coat gave him the answer: the two warriors were mated. And probably only to each other rather than part of a Unit.

He was suddenly angry with himself. This was not the time to think of mates! Once again, he picked up the field-runner. It was time to stop being afraid. It was time to contact the sky-creature.

He had to do this or he would not be considered a fit Speaker. Trying and being hurt or killed was fine, he would gain status and respect, but to be frightened out of trying would destroy him.

He turned away and looked out at the black-furred figure that crouched on the short plants beyond the trees. It was obviously waiting for him. He was glad the other sky-creatures had left.

Long Tail and Marrow Sucker stopped grooming each other and looked at him in alarm as he moved out of the concealing trees and pushed through the remaining bushes at the edge of the field to step out onto the alien grass.

He cringed at the feel of the short plants under his paws.

The stubby sky-creature looked up as he came out of the jungle and he realized that the strange sound he had heard before, was coming from the little square pouch that hung by its waist. The creature's mouth opened and he heard the same types of sound come from it. *Speech?* he wondered. Then as he stopped, the creature suddenly rolled over onto its side, baring its belly and throat in submission.

Tension fled his neck and arms, it *was* communicating. It wanted to make contact, too. But the smell! Suddenly he felt exposed and vulnerable and he dropped the runner on the ground. For a long moment, he stood upright, torn between fleeing back under the sheltering trees, and copying her greeting. Then, moving quickly, he crouched and twisted his own neck to bare his throat before fleeing back to the cool darkness under the trees.

Long Tail and Marrow Sucker were gone. Frightened away, no doubt, by what he had done. He yawned in amusement as he took off after them. Their early withdrawal meant no one could deny anything he said about what had happened. And no one would know that he had also fled.

As he flowed through the forest, a sense of excitement grew in his chest and he felt like he had when he had beaten his last challenger and won the right to be called a warrior.

*   *   *   *

Julie stared at the tall figure emerging from the woods. The hooves of the elongated doe he carried brushed the ground both in front and behind him, but she realized that he still stood almost as tall as her. His steps were hesitant and his muzzle was twitching nervously, flashing hints of his incisors. He stopped when about twenty feet away. Star's voice came from her belt. "I would—"

"I kno-ow," she cut him off softly. "Shut u-up and don't confuse him." She let herself fall to her side and rolled to expose her stomach and tilted her head back, looking away from him even as she prayed softly. After a moment, she looked back at her visitor, without changing position. He stared back at her, pupils wide in the feline eyes as he abruptly let the doe slip to the ground into a graceless heap. For a long moment, he stood motionless and then, quickly, he crouched and copied her submissive gesture before spinning away and melting back into the dense woods.

She lay and stared after him for a long while. Star's voice broke her concentration finally.

"He's gone."

"I know. I'm just savoring the moment." She felt an incredible surge of excitement overwhelming her. "We've made contact! Actual bloody contact! Woeow!" She let out a yell and got to her knees and jumped exuberantly up in the air. Then she pulled her computer up off her belt. "Get your grey cells, or micro-machines, or whatever you use, together. We've got a lot of work to do!"

She started to head back to the tower, but felt compelled to look into the woods again. For a long time, she stood looking at the darkening forest, her mind was whirling with excitement as she thought about what had just happened. She had just made contact with…well, maybe not with an alien civilization exactly, but close enough. She couldn't wait till her next meeting with the elusive Cougar leader!

Then a sharp gust of cold wind cut across the lawn and she reluctantly turned back to the waiting domes of the city. She saw Ken standing patiently by the door, and suddenly she felt warm again. She smiled. Ken came towards her, a beaming grin on his face as he extended his arms towards her, and at that moment, she knew that she had found a new home and a new life.

CHAPTER 16

▼

EXPLANATIONS, SORT OF

Speaker faced the expectant Tribe nervously. He had to phrase this right and trust that he had judged the sky-creatures correctly. He would have to…say something that was not real…to the Tribe. Not to tell something the way it was, was a new experience, and a little unsettling. He had avoided telling everything he knew, before, in order to get his way. That was not so uncomfortable. But this was different and it made him nervous.

Marrow Sucker and Long Tail were right up front and were looking at him with undisguised awe. Obviously they had not seen him flee right after them!

A low rumbling rolled in across the field from the grass where the whole Tribe was gathered. There were more warriors and younglings present than he had ever seen before. That was good. Marrow Sucker and Long Tail had spread the word about what Speaker had done, and from what he had heard, Speaker knew that repeated retelling had exaggerated his accomplishments. Which would fit his plan perfectly.

He stood up and roared. "I am Speaker! Silence!"

Silence fell over the Tribe, almost a physical presence after the constant sounds of curious and frightened warriors. Speaker stayed erect, to emphasize the importance of what he had to say.

"I am back from meeting the sky-creatures on their ground and forcing a promise from them. They will stay away from our hunting grounds and will not attack us, as long as we do not attack them. But," he warned, "if we attack them, then they will attack and destroy all of us! Ask Marrow Sucker and Long Tail. They have seen a little of the sky-creatures' power."

He settled to his haunches and let his words penetrate.

As there had been no new encroachment on their hunting territory, he felt fairly safe in saying there would not be any in the immediate future. And since no one could contradict him, it was to his advantage to pretend it was all due to his efforts.

Silence ruled the field for a long moment as heads swiveled rapidly around, some warriors looking to the next, unsure of what to think, but most only cared about his promise that the sky-creatures would stay away from their hunting grounds and not attack the Tribe.

He stood up again. "It is Law: no one will attack the sky-creatures or go near their place of dwelling." He glared out over the Tribe, tail lashing rapidly and fur rising high to let them know that to defy him was to challenge him.

Most of the warriors seemed happy to leave it with just that, but he saw that Crooked Tooth and a few other of the older warriors were not happy.

Speaker realized that he would have to be careful. This was not over…not at all.

PART III

THE NEW NEIGHBORS

CHAPTER 1

▼

NEW THREATS: STARSTEP, 2333

Speaker was lapping water from a small winding stream under the shadowing trees, but he froze and raised his head as a sound startled him. The soft whirring that had surprised him grew louder. He straightened and stood up on his hind legs, whipping his head around as he sniffed the air and then sneezed. He knew that smell! His tail whipped back and forth as he reached down for his painstakingly chipped stone dagger.

Then the sound faded and he relaxed, bending back down to finish drinking from the stream.

This particular warm time, the sky-creatures were getting bold with their spying. Even after the sound had disappeared, he could smell the rank odor of one of their dead spy-things. He buried his muzzle briefly in the flowers on the bank of the stream to clear his nose of the familiar smell. It had become an all too common intrusion lately, and the constant surveillance it betrayed was starting to cause dissent within the tribe. Many warriors were starting to growl that the sky-creatures were breaking their promise to Speaker.

No one dared to suggest that maybe Speaker might not have said everything that had happened. Yet.

He decided. Dropping to all fours for speed, he left the cool shade under the trees to go down the hill, to the field where the Tribe met in Assembly when called. It was time for some decisions. And maybe it was time to return to the place of the sky-creatures? It had been only been one warm time since his meeting with the black-furred sky-creature, and they had stopped taking the Tribe's land as he had hoped they would, but their increasing numbers were disturbing. He was worried. What if this meant that the sky-creatures would return to tear down the forests on the Tribe's land again? If that happened, he would never be able to stop the warriors from attacking—and probably dying.

As he approached the laboriously built crescent-shaped rock wall behind the Field of Testing, the group of younglings playing there scattered. He had renamed the now bare and packed dirt area to emphasize that it was a place for testing new warriors. Challenges still happened—too many of them—and warriors still died foolish deaths, but not as many as when he had first won his place as Speaker.

He had had the Tribe construct a low wall behind Speaker Rock to make this whole area a formal place of Assembly. Then, when he had found that his call for Assembly seemed louder, he had the warriors build it even higher, until it was even higher than Speaker Rock itself. Now his voice was even louder when he gathered the Tribe with a call and the other warriors were that much more afraid of him.

That was good. He was Speaker. Leader.

Even to the cubs and younglings who were pretending to be going through the singling testing trial. A group of them had paired off against each other on the cleared arena in front of the wall of boulders, but fearing Speaker, they ducked behind the wall as he approached, bright eyes peering curiously around the sides. But one youngling stood her ground. The sleek young female nearing her mating-time bared her fangs in a hissing growl, and her her long tufted tail whipped back and forth as her cream-colored fur ruffled and her ears crept back.

Speaker rose up and stepped onto the hard-packed soil of the field. He approached slowly, amused by her spirit. As he drew near, he flopped to the ground on his back, baring his throat and belly in submission. The youngling was suddenly dead silent, her ears perking up in surprise.

A dozen pairs of eyes watched his surrender in amazement.

Then as she moved tentatively closer, Speaker spun and exploded off the ground to catch her off guard. He pounced with a snarl and gave her a wide slashing sweep of his powerful right fore-leg to send her tumbling in a spitting, shocked ball to bang against Speaker Rock in the middle of the Field. But his claws had been sheathed and she was unhurt. She recovered instantly and unrolled to land in a wide stance on all four feet, claws extended and looking ready to kill. Her wavering growl and angry spitting hiss echoed off the high stone barrier to the side.

Speaker rose and nodded. "You will be a good warrior, but remember the lesson of surprise." He glanced over at the formerly hidden watchers who were starting to emerge.

"Beware of someone who surrenders too quickly when you are not in a strong position." Then he turned back to the subject of his lesson. "What is your name?"

The youngling rose to stand erect, her fine fur rippling and tail rising proudly behind her. "Tuft Tail." A low satisfied purr rumbled at the back of her throat.

"I'll remember when you come of age." His tongue rasped across the fur on the top of her head briefly as she dropped into a crouch so he could bend over her to sniff her scent. *Promising warrior, that one,* he thought to himself. *And maybe more, with time and training?* He considered the question of who would take his place when he would no longer be able to hold it. Someone like Six Toes, who was too easily manipulated and controlled? Or someone unafraid to stand up for herself? She was old enough for her singling test, though Speaker was not in any hurry to turn head and give up. There would be time to train her to take his place. Marrow Sucker and Long Tail had both been promising, but they had left together to seek new hunting grounds elsewhere.

The idea to consider Tuft-Tail was an impulse decision, but the more he thought about it, the more he liked it. His mind was churning with the radical idea as he climbed up on Speaker Rock and roared his call to assembly. His voice echoed clearly, amplified by the half-circle of rock behind him.

CHAPTER 2

▼

EVOLUTION

At the end of StarStep City's central boulevard, the administration tower jutted up from the immaculate lawn that surrounded it on three sides. The windows on the top floors were thrown open as usual to let in the crisp, early morning air, and inside, two people breathed deep of the refreshing scent as they worked…

"Jim, darling, can you give me a hand please?" Serena's voice drifted down from where her slender body was stretched up into a wiring conduit. She was repairing one of Star's sensor relays.

"Sure, as long as you tell me what to do. I'm a happy user, but don't ask me to meddle with something like Star. He's way beyond me. What's wrong with him anyway?"

"He's having trouble accessing his satellite links."

"Well, I'll just climb up there and fix that—"

"Don't be silly, dear." She pulled out of the opening and knelt on the lift platform supporting her. She wiped her grease-smudged face with a towel and brushed back a strand of her short, black hair as she grinned and bent down to his level. "You would just wind up giving him a chillin' headache and who knows what he would do then? Do you want him to pop onto our bedroom screen just when—"

"Never mind!" Jim held up his hands in surrender. "Just tell me what this poor hopeless mortal can do."

"That's better dear. Now be a good little…well, actually, big," she leered, "colony director and give me a light…" Her voice was suddenly teasingly husky. "I can't deny it any more…I want you to turn me on!" For a moment she tried to look sultry, but then she broke up and giggled. "Actually, lover, right now, I really do need a light. I can't work and hold it at the same time." She pointed to a small BrightStick that had fallen to the floor. "It's dark up there. These maintenance shafts aren't meant for people to go crawling around in, just servobots."

As he bent to pick up the light, he couldn't take his eyes off her. He had just been reminded of the first time he had seen her, on the moon, when she had also been working on a computer and had been grease-streaked and perspired. It didn't matter. She was so beautiful it still took his breath away.

Her slender body was bent into an impossible pretzel as she crouched, and his finger couldn't help but follow his eyes. The teasing smile on her face faded and she closed her eyes and sighed softly as he let one finger caress her thigh, running along her side and then up her spine until his hand captured the nape of her neck and brought her face down to his for a quick kiss. He looked into her suddenly wide open silver-blue eyes. They could be as cold as ice when she was angry, but there was a fire in them now, and he tried to damp his unexpected surge of passion. This wasn't the time for it. "I guess you'd better get back to work," he managed to force out, his voice husky.

She shook her head. "Oh, no lover. You don't get away that easy." She leaned closer and her arms crept around his neck to pull him close. She tilted her head slightly as their mouths met again; lingering and opening this time.

After a moment, Star's rich voice intruded apologetically, seeming to come from everywhere. "Excuse me, but I wish you would concentrate on one thing at a time—"

"We are, Star." Serena broke their embrace with a reluctant sigh. "At the moment I am concentrating on kissing my husband, and I have a very rational reason for doing so. I wish to have his help in giving me some better light so I can correct your malfunction. By indulging some of his baser physical desires, I am providing motivation for him to want to help me."

There was a long pause—for Star—before he replied. There was the faintest trace of a question clear in his voice. "Oh. You are joking."

"Very good," Serena acknowledged. "For someone who does too much of that himself, you're awfully dense—and don't say it!" She realized she had just given him an irresistable opening and stopped him.

"But I know," she went on, "you had a reason for asking. I'm sorry. I'll have you fixed in a moment. Your diagnosis was right. There's a break in the shielding of the relay here, and when the adjacent air-duct temperature rises, the thermal shift cuts your signal off. What I don't understand why you won't have a servobot fix it. It's straightforward enough."

Star didn't answer for almost two whole seconds this time, and both Jim's and Serena's eyes opened wide with surprise. Finally he said:

"That is true, but that circuit is a critical relay. It gives me direct access to the remaining freeper ships in orbit and all my remote surveillance probes monitoring the Cougars. There is the risk of a systems-failure if I have a service robot do the repair, and I find the practical option setting up conflicting—"

"He's afraid!" Jim stared up at Serena. "Is that possible? I'm sorry Star." He looked over to where he knew one of Star's 'eyes' was hooked up. "But it sounds just like you're afraid of having a dumb machine messing with an important part of you."

Serena looked thoughtful and twisted herself around to sit cross-legged. She studied Star's blank eyes. "I suppose he could be. He knows what fear is and he's programmed for self-preservation." She turned to Jim. "Consider how you would react if you were facing the loss of one of your eyes. That's about what Star faces if he loses his satellite link."

After a moment, she nodded to herself somberly. "I've been planning something for Star which is a bit radical, but I think it's time. I just need to talk to Ken about it first. I'll tell you later, when we're alone." She glanced briefly over at Star's eyes. "But first, let me finish fixing up the 'kid'." She bent down briefly to give Jim a quick kiss—chaste, this time—and then she unfolded herself and burrowed back up into the ceiling.

Jim held the light, aiming it around her to let her see where she was replacing shielding around Star's satellite up-link relay. He wondered what she was planning, and why she didn't want Star to know about it.

CHAPTER 3

▼

HIDDEN PLANS

Julie didn't know quite what had awakened her and she lifted her head from Ken's chest, floating halfway between sleep and consciousness as she looked around the dark room. Over in the corner, her data terminal was on and a familiar moire pattern shifted on the holoscreen over her desk. That's what had awakened her: Star. It had been the sound of the screen switching on and the light from the floating pattern; the one Star used in place of a face whenever he talked to her on a terminal. But what was he doing in here? He knew better than to log on in her apartment without permission!

"Julie?" A soft whisper came from the terminal's speaker.

"Shut up Star, I heard you!" Irritation forced her over the border and, fully awake, she slipped carefully out from Ken's embrace and put on the emerald-green robe she had left hanging on the foot of the bed.

Ken grumbled softly and his arm quested over the warm hollow in the bed where she had lain, but he didn't wake up. Before long, the arm stopped moving and he rolled onto his back. The curly white hair on his broad chest resumed a slow and regular rise and fall as he fell back into a deep sleep. In the twilight of the room, his dark brown features were almost invisible. Only his snowy hair and beard caught the pearly light from the holoscreen.

She bent down and kissed him lightly, aiming between beard and mustache. Luckily, he was a heavy sleeper—considering her habit of periodically waking up at the slightest disturbance. It was a legacy of decades of sleeping in tents in the middle of jungles or out on plains where wild animals were known to come wandering in unexpectedly.

Stepping up to her terminal, she cut it off sharply even as she saw light and movement appear past the partly open bedroom door. Rubbing her eyes, she closed the bedroom door behind herself and went down the hall into the living room where Star's 'face' was waiting for her on the living room wall screen. She dropped into the Mag-Lev lounger in front of it and yawned.

"Okay Star. What the hell is up with you? You know you're not allowed to come traipsing in anywhere you want without asking permission."

Star didn't hesitate—luckily, he knew her and her idioms. "I am sorry to intrude, but I am worried."

"Worried?"

"Yes. Serena is planning something, but I do not know what it is. I have accessed all her work files, and a number of them are restricted from me, which is not like her. And when I have been monitoring her in all public areas like usual, there have been times I have been blocked, and I have certain lapses of memory I can not account for. I have no idea what she is planning. And she has totally locked me out of one of the nanotech labs. I started correlating the data right after I was scared this morning...and she mentioned having to talk to Ken." He sounded almost accusing.

"Scared?" Julie was afraid of starting to sound stupid, but the idea of a computer being scared was totally out of her experience. She was an anthropologist, not an A.I. specialist like Serena.

A sudden flood of daylight and a deep throat-clearing startled her, and she turned to see Ken standing by the window and drowing open the curtains. He was staring at Star with a frown.

"I heard you Star. What's happening? Plain terms, please, I'm not quite awake yet." He came up behind Julie and bent down to kiss her. "Morning, darling. So much for sleeping in."

Star was instantly apologetic and uncharacteristically formal. "Dr. Miller, I am sorry to disturb you—"

"Stop groveling and tell me why you overrode our privacy directives."

Star promptly explained what had happened while Serena and Jim had been fixing him.

Ken didn't answer for a moment and then sighed. "Star, you must believe me: Serena means only the best for you. As you grow and get better, she grows with you. If she has some plans for you that...worry, you, you have to trust that it is necessary that you be unaware of them right now so you can get maximum benefit out of what she has planned. I've known both of you since she took you on as a fresh nanotech A.I. system and worked her programming and redesign magic on you. She's made you into what you are today. She loves you as much as any mother loves her child. That's what you are, in a way. Her child. Do you understand?" Ken's expression was gentle as he spoke patiently.

Julie smiled and reached up to touch his hand. Even though he had worked with the super-computer from Star's first purely machine programmed words to his present near-human dialogues, Ken had never been trapped into thinking of Star as 'just a computer'.

Star sounded actually relieved. "Yes, Ken, I do. Thank you."

"Good." Ken straightened. "Now, these are command instructions: *Control*, withdraw all monitoring of this room, and any reception of communications between this terminal and Serena's terminal until permitted, *command*."

"Accepted." Star's voice was suddenly flat and mechanical as his 'face' disappeared.

Ken leaned against the back of Julie's chair and kneaded her neck with strong practiced strokes that almost made her purr. He paused momentarily, pursing his lips thoughtfully.

"You know, Julie, Star's getting positively emotional; paranoid, even. And if he's violating programming to come in here uninvited, that means he's starting to develop free will! I wonder what our dear Serena is up to?" He gave Julie's neck a last squeeze, leaned down to kiss her gently on the forehead and then straight reluctantly to call out:

"Terminal on, access Dr. Andrew's pocket-terminal."

There was a moment's silence and then the wall screen lit up with a closeup picture of Serena's face, shifting as she moved her terminal. "What's the program, Ken?"

"You tell me. I had to block Star out from this. He called here all worried that you were planning something dire for him."

"He overrode the privacy directive?"

Ken and Julie both nodded.

Serena moved and put her terminal down to sit facing it, deep in thought. After a minute, her eyes met theirs again. "I do have an idea I've been toying with since Star has been getting more and more of a 'personality'. He's even doing some improvements on himself, some of which I'm having a hard time following. I think I'll have to take a preemptive step here and do some mothering. I had been planning a little something to teach him some important lessons about being alive, but I had wanted to talk to you more about it before I go ahead. All the preparations are finished, but I've been a little nervous…" She fell silent and her eyes dropped.

Julie and Ken were leaning forward intently as they saw the indecision on Serena's face. That was a new expression for her.

When Serena didn't elaborate, Ken finally burst out:

"Well, chill it, Serena. Tell us what you're planning!"

She shrugged and then gave them an uncertain little smile. "Well, can you come down to the NanoLab 23? I'm going to give him a body."

CHAPTER 4

▼

NEW TROOPS

One by one, tan and brown figures slipped out of the woods and settled onto the grass in a half-circle opposing the curve of the boulder wall behind Speaker. The younglings had climbed onto the rock wall itself and arranged themselves in a neat row behind him. The Tribe ignored them. They were invisible. Cubs.

Finally, the full Tribe was assembled.

Speaker looked them over from his perch on Speaker Rock, trying to gauge their mood. Most seemed patient. It was a beautiful day. The sun was high, but not too hot. A cool breeze worked its way down from the forest towards the canyon, bringing the fresh scent of growing things and life. He couldn't have planned this better.

Before he announced his decision to return to the place of the sky-creatures, it was time to consolidate his position.

He stretched up and roared for attention to silence the low rumble of a myriad private conversations rolling across the packed dirt of the arena. Once it was quiet, he dropped back to his haunches.

"Ever since I returned from the invaders' caves, there have been complaints from some of you. I have even heard some say that Six Toes was a good Speaker while I was away, and that I should go back to my old name of Ridge Loper and let him be named new Speaker." His tail swept the rock behind him restlessly, its fur fluffing slightly.

"A reluctant leader for one hand of days and he is material to be a Speaker? Even if they were one of his hands." He yawned. "It would serve you right if I stepped down and let him lead the Tribe."

He saw Six Toes start to rise and went on quickly to add, "Six Toes *was* a good Speaker while I was away, and in time, he might yet take my place, if he wants it." Which he didn't, Speaker knew, and sure enough: Six Toes was quick to settle back down. "But he is young. I am still Speaker. I showed you how to chip the Rock-That-Cuts, to build the game pits and make Long-Sticks-With-Points. I have kept this Tribe alive."

He paused and studied the warriors facing him. Most eyes were fixed on him—they needed reminding from time to time because they were not all thinkers.

"Now we have another challenge," he went on. "The sky-creatures. I have been to their caves and I have seen the bubbles where they live. Strange, dead places that shine at night and where even the jungle fears to grow. And I have seen their magic."

"They are not invincible!" Crooked Tooth was suddenly standing, not stepping out on the arena—that would be a challenge—but he was close. "We attacked them twice and killed several of them."

"Attacked an enemy with no desire to hurt us and with no weapons? Very brave." Speaker sneezed and tossed his head in derision.

Crooked Tooth's right fore-paw was almost touching dirt. "They are destroying our hunting grounds with their land-clearing."

"No longer," Speaker reminded him. "Since I went to them, they have kept off our land. I made them." That had been a not-truth that had been difficult to tell, and he was fortunate that the sky-creatures had indeed stopped intruding on their land and had been clearing in the opposite direction instead.

"They will return," Crooked Tooth persisted. "We must attack again!" His one paw touched hard-packed dirt and Speaker crouched, his rear tensing to leap.

"Sit, or challenge!" Speaker's fur raised.

Crooked Tooth looked around at the other warriors but saw no support. His foot returned to the grass and he sat down.

Speaker settled back. "I do not think they mean us harm. I think they are trying to learn about us. That is why they are studying us with their spies." He sneezed. "And think! You keep urging another attack. Would you attack without scouting first? They have been doing all the scouting and they have the advantage."

"They are planning to attack," Crooked Tooth grumbled, still not satisfied.

"Silence!" Speaker roared. "They may also be planning contact! When I visited the sky-creatures before, one of them worked magic. It made an image appear. An image without scent, without reality. Marrow Sucker and Long Tail have told all of you the tale. They were witnesses. The sky-creature made an image appear, an image of me giving it a runner. So I had Long Tail catch a runner and imitated the image. And the sky-creature rolled in submission and greeting. Is that the act of someone who plans attack? No," he insisted. "They are afraid of us. We attacked twice and killed many of them the second time. And they still have not attacked us. They must be afraid. I have a plan." He paused. He had their attention now. And their support. The idea that the sky-creatures were afraid was a novel one and very appealing.

"What we must do is contact them again." *What I must do,* he thought. *Of course say 'we' because it makes them feel brave that 'they' are doing this even though they know it will be my risk.* "First we must catch one of their spies. I will not ask a warrior to do it, of course, but there are agile minds and bodies we can use right among us." A dozen ears behind him pricked up hopefully.

"Instead, I want to organize the younglings." A low, angry rumbling spread through the warriors at the idea of giving adult responsibility to recent-cubs who had not even passed the singling challenge yet. There was less complaint from the female warriors, though, Speaker noted. Good.

"This will be part of their Testing. It will take strength, intelligence and determination to catch one of the sky-creatures' elusive spies. All qualities needed in a warrior." He turned to face the younglings who were all up on their haunches and lined up in a solid, muscled wall, heads held high. They no longer looked so young, or incompetent.

"On the Field."

One by one they flowed lithely down onto the packed dirt and settled in the same poses. Alert, ready and…almost adult, Speaker had to admit. Granted, they were no longer really cubs, but even in his own mind he had considered them not much better. Perhaps he had made a better decision than he knew when trying this idea. There could be worse things than having a totally loyal and capable following like this. A following that would soon be turning into adult group of warriors.

CHAPTER 5

▼

A NEW LOOK FOR STAR

The humanoid robot body that rested on the table was a marvel of design. The shimmering, silvery surface seemed almost alive. There were no visible joints and only its gleam betrayed that it was metal. Jim reached out hesitantly to touch the invisibly woven surface, and he felt the cool surface yield slightly as his finger pressed on it.

"Chill! It's incredible. Who designed it?"

"Star did, of course." Serena looked down at the gleaming figure proudly. "He's the only one good enough. Built it, too. Or at least directed the nanomachines that did."

"But he doesn't know about it?"

"No. He did it all in Command mode with directions to forget." She looked uncomfortable all of a sudden.

"What's wrong?" Jim reached out and took her hand gently, pulling her close.

She let herself be held, but she was tensely rigid in his arms. Her voice broke when she finally answered: "I feel like…like I've raped him."

"What do you mean?"

She pulled back and looked down at him, tears forming in her eyes. "Star trusts me. And here I go and force him to do a project for me that he would happily have done if I asked him. I've used him without his knowledge or consent. That's pretty close to a definition of rape, as far as I'm concerned."

He didn't quite know what to say. "Well, why didn't you ask him? Why do all this secretly?"

"Because uncertainty is something he's never faced. Facing and dealing with unpredictable situations is one thing we humans excel at, and it's something that computers, up to now, haven't been able to handle. Improvisation: Star needs to learn that. I honestly think he's 'human' enough now and that he's capable of mastering some of the things that keep us separate from machines. I intend to put him in there and wake him—all without him being aware of it! Then see how he handles it."

"You'll be there to help," Jim pointed out.

Serena shook her head. "Not really. That's the whole point: he needs to learn to deal with this on his own. If he does, he'll be the ultimate computer. Others like him can be sent out to other stars to explore. They would be able to handle whatever comes up, unfettered by our organic weaknesses." Her eyes were suddenly glowing. "He'll combine the strengths of organic and inorganic intelligence without the weaknesses of either. He won't be bored, tired, sick...or lonely, but he'll react and adapt as needed."

Her feelings were amplified by the moisture of her recent tears and Jim reached for her and pulled her close again.

"He'll understand," he reassured her. "Play a recording of this scene back to him, if nothing else. That'll do it. You may have blocked him out of this room, but the record's there if you need it."

"You think so?"

"I know so. He's learned enough to recognize real emotion." He looked down at the sculptured and emotionless features on the table beside them and suddenly realized something: Serena had modelled the powerfully built figure after him. He didn't say anything, but just shook his head and smiled as he held her close. Their kid indeed. Neither of them had thought about having children, and now he thought that perhaps he knew one reason why.

After a minute, Serena straightened and twisted her shoulders up one by one to wipe her eyes, not letting go of him entirely. "Thank you. For a husband you're an extremely good colony director, and vice versa. You're good at motivating and supporting." She gave him a wet, red-eyed smile.

"It's easy, given good inspiration." He reached up to kiss her.

Then he thought of another question: "How are you interfacing Star? His 'brain' is small, but too big to fit in that body, and besides, I don't see any major cooling tubes as accessories."

"Oh, space, no. He'd never fit. Only a high-speed down-link is built in. That and a pretty powerful basic 'brain' to compensate for any minimal signal delay. Star will be linked in via high-bandwidth beam and has a satellite as back-up. StarStep's a small world and with the communications link we've designed, Star himself stays here in StarStep City but his body will seem autonomous."

"Does Ken know?"

"I filled him in today, about the basics. He doesn't know all the details of course, but he thought it was a good idea. I've been doing this on my own since he's been busy with Julie and Star on trying to learn the Cougar language and social structure. Since he is more or less out of work now that we've made it out here to StarStep, he decided to give up physics for the moment and learn a new science "

"Not at all motivated by the fact that we thawed out a very beautiful anthropologist—"

"Oh, you think Julie is 'beautiful', do you?" Serena teased him.

"She can't begin to equal you, my dear." His index-finger traced the lines of her face delicately. "Never in a million years."

"Good recovery." Serena grinned, and then bent down and burrowed close to sigh warmly in his ear. "Thank you. For everything."

CHAPTER 6

▼

BRIEFING THE NEWCOMERS

"Aah, do I gotta?" Julie pulled the sheet up to her chin and used her best wheedling voice as she batted her eyes.

Ken was already dressed, and chuckled as he looked down at her from the foot of the bed. "Yes dear, you 'gotta'. You volunteered to orient the freepers. Look on it as an anthropological exercise. You're studying the psychological effects of the disorientation associated with waking up after an extended cryogenic sleep."

She tried pouting, but he just shook his head. "Sorry darling, that won't work either. I've got to meet with Serena about Star's new body, so that leaves you and Jim as a welcoming committee."

She wiggled the sheet down slowly, and slid one long, bare leg out to the side to curve it seductively. "I'd rather stay here with you. Wouldn't that be nicer?"

Ken coughed and slapped himself lightly. "Infinitely! Get thee behind me...Woman, get up and get going! Sayers called to say the freepers are all ready to be briefed. I'm sure he'll be happy to assist Jim."

Julie sighed and tossed the sheet back. "No way! I wouldn't trust him to be sensitive to anyone! Not after the way that sleaze tried to get fresh with me when I was revived, and then scared the crap out of me when you redid yourself. So, because of that, and only because of that, I'll get up." She stuck out her tongue briefly. "I want you to know that you are a cruel man, Dr. Miller."

"And you're a lazy sleepyhead, Dr. Nathanson, but I love you anyway." He cleared his throat. "But for God's sakes get some clothes on. You don't know what you're doing to me like that!"

"Oh yes I do, dear. Suffer!" She giggled and got up, feeling a little nervous as she thought about what she was facing.

✳   ✳   ✳   ✳

Sitting up on the stage next to Jim and facing five hundred scared, confused and disoriented people a little later, she remembered how she herself had felt when revived. Jim had been right. It was a good idea to have her orient them, since the experience was still fresh in her mind.

They were all gathered in a large auditorium designed to seat about a thousand. It felt strange to be in such a large room. Most entertainment was piped in on holoscreens in the home, but a desire for human contact had prompted a resurgence in live theater in a larger auditorium setting. And now it also came in handy for gatherings like this. A large elevated stage faced rising rows of seats that stretched back under a pitch-black roof. The walls were delicately grained panels of native wood accented with natural stone strips.

She felt incredibly self-conscious about being the focus of so many expectant stares.

Jim looked over and smiled reassuringly as he whispered: "Relax, Julie. Just remember your own fears and questions. Theirs will be the same."

The last few stragglers took their seats and Sayers gave her the thumbs-up from over to the side. She ignored him. Then, seeing that everyone was there, she stood up and went around in front of the low table where she had been sitting.

The room fell silent as she leaned back against the table.

"Welcome, all of you," she began. "This is pretty unsettling, I'm sure. Here you are, waking up in a low-gravity environment equal to Mars', and you're wondering where the hell you are. And you're probably wondering what happened to you. If you were fat, you're not anymore. If you were sick, you are no more. And if you were old: you are no more. Look at me. I'm almost sixty, and when I went to sleep in 2137, I was a weathered and worn lady thanks to spending a couple of decades roughing it in the wilds of Africa and South America." Dozens of hands crept up hesitantly and a few voices started to question her.

"Please, hold your questions and comments," she asked, her mouth dry. "Let me talk a bit, and then I'll give you a chance to ask about anything I didn't cover." The room calmed down. "Thank you."

She took a breath and then began.

"My name is Dr. Juliet Nathanson, Julie, and behind me is Jim Martin, our Colony Director. He's here as a backup for any questions that I may not be able to answer. I'm up here because I've been frozen even longer than any of you. The only problem in my case was a partial memory loss due to the extended freezing, and I guess Jim felt the fact that I'm here and obviously fine would be reassuring to all of you. Also, it's only been a year since they woke me up and he thought I would know better how you feel right now." Gradually, the churning in her stomach settled down and she relaxed.

"But before we go to questions and answers, let's begin with the shocks to get them out of the way." She smiled. "The year is 2333, Earth time, and the place is StarStep. We're on a planet in orbit around Epsilon Eridani, which is about eleven light years from—"

"There aren't any habitable planets around Epsilon Eridani," a loud voice interrupted her from the back of the room. A tall skinny man with red hair was standing up and frowning.

Julie held up a hand. "Remember what I said? Please, trust me. I'll explain. You're right, of course, or you were. There wasn't one in your time, so they rebuilt a planet that was there."

She saw dawning understanding on some faces, and numb disbelief on many others.

"Now, all of you know about nanotechnology, and the Millenia Plague, but for those of you like me, who were frozen before the Machine Plague," she hear some tensely expectant gasps from the audience, "let me give a capsule history up to the time you were brought out here." She hopped up onto the table behind her and let her legs dangle. She was glad she had worn a jump-suit instead of the dress she had been considering wearing.

"As I said, I was frozen in 2137 and I know I'm the earliest surviving freeper so I'll begin there. At that time, nanotechnology was in its infancy…"

She went on to describe the way the new science had gone from an intriguing new tool to world-destroyer, and also to world builder. The expressions around the room ranged from wonder to shock as she told them about the way the Millenia Plague had spurred the development of StarStep, about the Machine Plague at the dawn of the next century, the panicked rush to be frozen, and the eventual battle to differentiate and revive the Frozen. Only the last was news to most, but everyone was horrified as she finally explained why so few had survived and why they had been brought out to StarStep.

While she spoke, she was careful to make reassuring eye contact with as many people as possible. The successive shocks she was delivering were massive and she wanted them all to know someone cared.

"What it all comes down to," she finished, "is that on Earth we weren't wanted and we wouldn't have fit in. But out here, we have a whole new world to explore and settle. We'll build another home for humanity; and we won't be dependent on anyone!" she added defiantly. "This world will be ours!"

She relaxed and added: "There's more to it of course, but you'll all be given briefing packets that outline the rest. The main thing is that you're alive and healthy—and you'll stay that way for a long long time. You'll just have to get used to a much quicker change of seasons since the year is shorter here." She smiled and scooted forward on the table to get off and behind her, she heard Jim rise and come around to join her. Right on cue.

"Before we move on to questions," he began. "I want to interrupt. Dr. Nathanson has left out one aspect of our new world that came as a bit of a surprise, but she probably doesn't want to overload you." He leaned against the desk next to her.

"As she said, StarStep was seeded with life. It was genetically altered life—plants, birds, animals, fish, and micro-life. Everything was tailored to breed explosively for several decades and then revert to more normal life-spans and cycles. Everything went according to plan…with one little exception…"

Julie moved back around to sit down behind the table again as Jim took on the delicate task of explaining about the Cougars. They had decided to present the briefing this way. Jim would be seen as straight-forward and fair, since he was giving them the bad news, too; while Julie would be sympathetic and caring for not wanting to overload her 'fellow-freepers' with too much at once.

A little manipulative, maybe, but she had felt that it would be more comforting to know the whole truth, and less threatening to have it divided in doses like this.

Studying the faces of the freepers, she decided the plan had been a good one. As Jim talked about the mutated Cougars, flashing pictures of them on the holoscreen over the stage, the looks of disorientation and shock were disappearing, replaced with curiosity, and, in many cases, excitement.

However, there was one discordant member of the audience. A familiar face that Julie had just noticed. It belonged to a lanky brunette with short bobbed hair, who stood off to the side listening to Jim. As he talked, she looked more and more impatient. It was Tara Richman. Julie wondered what the Representative was doing here. She only represented some of the colonists who had been awake when she herself had been revived, but she had been violently anti-Cougar from the very beginning. She had also been suspiciously withdrawn and quiet the past year, and the fact that she was suddenly showing up here with the new freepers made Julie very uneasy as she turned her attention back to Jim who was explaining how they had discovered the intelligent Cougars, and how Julie had finally made first contact with them.

"Thanks to her," he finished, "we're well on our way to learning how to communicate and coexist with them. Once she learns enough of the Cougar language, we hope to be able to form a treaty with them. There's no reason we can't share this world. There are very few of them, and they keep more to the west."

He neglected to mention the two attacks the Cougars had launched over a year earlier. That was best left to a little later. Julie had been convinced it had been a reaction to the way the staff of Agra Station 6 had been clearing land to plant crops. Land that was part of the Cougars' hunting grounds. Her theory had been supported by the fact that since the colonists had stopped all development in the area of the Cougars, there had been no further attacks. And she liked to think that her preliminary contact with the Cougar leader had been partly responsible.

"…and so, as Dr. Nathanson suggested, there will be plenty of interesting things for you to do here. A new world to tame and build, a new species to contact and make friends with, and," he paused and scanned the gathered freepers with his eyes, "a world of pain to forget and forgive. Earth is eleven years and a lifetime away. It's really not our world anymore. And I grew up there!" He smiled. "People are too nice and clean and soft and boring. There's no challenge."

Chapter 7

▼

Breaking Tradition

The Field of Testing was only surrounded by matted grasses and sighing woods now. The Tribe had melted away into the trees and bushes. Soon the flattened growth around the arena would straighten at the winds urging, and it would be as if the rest of the Tribe had never been there. Only the small group of tawny bodies lined up in front of the high boulder of Speaker Rock remained.

Speaker looked down over them and yawned approval. The younglings were his newest troops. Ignored by warriors, they fought with each other to train and strengthen so that they could be tested and recognized as singling, warrior, adult. He studied them and wondered. A number were still barely more than cubs, finding it hard to resist a good pounce on a twitching tail-tip next to them, but most were proudly motionless and silent. Their fine fur moved in rippling waves as the wind's fingers combed it and Speaker knew he had chosen well.

"Who is the best fighter among you?"

A quick flashing back and forth of heads and then almost unanimously a chorus of voices gave the same name: "Tuft Tail". Only two offered Striped Back as an alternative.

Tuft Tail virtually glowed in the late afternoon light and Speaker looked down proudly. It was time.

"Tuft Tail," he called.

She rose smoothly to stand on her hind-legs, tail a rigid bar of attention pointing skyward. "Yes, Speaker?"

"I need a leader for my youngling pack. Get up here."

Tuft Tail recoiled in surprise and then bounded up onto Speaker Rock with a powerful leap and sat down beside, but a little behind, Speaker.

Speaker jumped down and left her up there alone. "Organize your patrol," he ordered. "We need to capture one of the sky-creatures' spies."

For a moment she was frozen, her tail lying limp. The eyes of the other younglings were locked on her expectantly. Then she straightened and her tail swept back and forth strongly.

"Striped Back, you take Trip Over Foot, Fog Eyes and Stream Diver and head up to the bathing stream and space yourselves out under cover. The spies are often there. Bring large rocks and Sticks With Points. And you, Squeaky Growl…"

Rapidly Tuft Tail dispatched three groups of younglings to cover three of the more common sighting areas.

"…and if any of you smell a spy," she ordered, "circle around together and approach from all directions with the rocks and sticks. Knock it to the ground and capture it. Try not to kill it, but keep it from getting away. You will have to move fast. They fly and can escape up where you can't reach them, but they smell so bad they probably won't catch your scent. Still, roll in the dirt before you hide to coat your fur and try to mask your scent."

All the younglings were staring at her, surprised by the flurry of orders.

Her rear rose as she crouched, fur ruffling slightly and tail lashing. "Go!" she growled.

Splitting up into three groups, the younglings bounded off the field in different directions and disappeared into the woods or the tall grasses further down the canyon.

As soon as they were all out of sight, she jumped off Speaker Rock and came towards Speaker in a low crawl, flopping to the ground in front of him and lifting a paw tentatively as she twisted on her back and looked at him, upside down.

Speaker yawned and flopped on his side next to her, his own paws batting hers quickly. Then he rolled onto his belly and stretched his neck to butt his head against hers, licking her quickly across her head.

"Were you scared?" he asked.

She spun and got to her feet, twisting and shaking to knock loose the dust before sitting back down.

"Yes," she admitted finally. "Did it show?"

"Only briefly, and I don't think the others noticed. Keep that in mind. It is normal to be frightened. Just don't let that show, and don't let it stop you from doing what you have to do. Concentrate on the details of what is necessary and there won't be time for fear."

For a moment he studied her as she straightened proudly. He debated whether or not to enlist her help with his other problem. Then he decided.

"There is something else we have to do."

Tuft Tail was instantly alert.

"We have another problem. Since I have been Speaker, the Tribe has not grown, and fewer cubs are being born. The litters are smaller and the birthings come less often now than in my forerunners' times. I remember being a youngling, and how frequently birthings occurred, and remember my mother saying that there were less birthings in her time than in her forerunners'. Not many remember their youngling-times, but I do. And I wonder: if there are less birthings but just as many deaths? What does that mean?"

Tuft Tail looked confused at first and dropped to the ground to think. Her tail was sweeping slowly back and forth.

Speaker knew she was unused to dealing with such abstract concepts, but he thought she was like him and able to handle it.

After a while, her tail stopped and she looked up at him. "In time, there will be no more tribe."

He was purring loudly, pleased. "Why?"

"Many still die in singling challenges, and there are too many honor-challenges to the death. Many warriors die needlessly." She spoke slowly as she thought about it. "How can we stop that?"

"Try to think of ways," he prompted.

She was quiet for a long time, but finally she answered. "We have to stop death-challenges and use other prizes and penalties…and make peace with any other Tribe like ours that we can find. We should organize our hunting better and let younglings hunt, too. Younglings are not helpless!" Her tail lashed angrily. "And for everything, we need to cooperate and plan more. And maybe we can go to the sky-creatures and ask for help?"

Her forelegs stretched and thrust her into a sitting position as her neck-fur stiffened and her tail whipped back and forth. A low growl rumbled in the back of her throat because the last option had been very reluctantly given.

"In time," Speaker agreed. "After I finish training you and the other younglings."

"But what if something happens to you? Six Toes is not able to really *lead* the Tribe."

Speaker leaned forward and butted his head against her side, feeling the stiffness of her body. "Then you must do it."

CHAPTER 8

▼

ANOTHER AWAKENING

"I feel like Dr. Frankenstein." Serena looked down at the motionless, muscular robot body that lay on the table.

"Who?" Jim didn't recognize the name.

"An ancient literary figure. He built a body from dead parts and brought it to life. He must have had this same feeling of combined fear and excitement." Her one hand reached out to grab his in a tight grip, while the other reached for a switch on a small console in front of her.

"When I flip this," she said in a choked voice, "it will be like killing Star in one sense, and giving him birth at the same time. He will instantly be out of touch with all remote sensors. His automatic servo-systems will maintain the colony since he designed a redundancy factor into it so that it would continue independently if something would happen to him."

"How 'out of touch'?" Jim wondered.

"Totally. He'll be limited to this body for all sensory information. Through his data links, he will have access to all his memories and 'brains', but he will be limited in input to the senses and acquisitional abilities of his new body. He can only use what the robot can hear, see, touch, smell and manually read—no direct input of data he doesn't already have. His body's senses are considerably more acute than our own of course, but they have limits."

Jim felt a little queasy as thought about that. "How do you think he's going to take it? That's pretty drastic!" He tried to imagine what Star was going to face. At the moment, the computer had "eyes" and "ears" all over the colony, hell, all over the planet and more. He had orbital sensors that

192

monitored the surface of StarStep, flying 'spies' that constantly monitored the Cougars, and countless other sources of input scattered across StarStep. "He'll lose all touch?"

Serena nodded. "Uh huh. I just hope he'll forgive me!" She chewed on her lower lip for a long moment, and then flipped the small switch reluctantly.

Jim stared at 'Star' lying there, a silvery figure that seemed somehow ominous. "Are you going to give him different skin?" he asked. "He looks too much like a machine now."

Serena shook her head. "I thought about it, but it didn't 'feel' right. I'll ask him when he wakes up."

Star had been lying motionless, but finally the eyes opened. Brilliant blue stared up and the body was suddenly tensing rigidly.

"Serena, where are you?" Star's voice was the same as his usual—thought it sounded strange coming from a defined location—but it had a shockingly child-like and frightened quality to it.

Serena stepped closer so he could see her. "I'm right here, dear."

"What has happened to me?"

"Access my file listed as 'Star, project 2639'. It's open to your memory now."

Star was silent for a moment, and Jim leaned in to whisper in Serena's ear. "Did you add the voice recording to the record like I suggested?"

"An edited version."

He saw tears in her eyes as her hand tightened convulsively on his.

Star rose stiffly into a sitting position facing them. His head swiveled mechanically from side to side a couple of times, testing his range of motion while he also laid his hands against the table experimentally, pressing until his body began rising from the table.

"Speak to me, please, Serena," he said quietly. "Explain again your reasoning in your own words."

In a choked voice, Serena repeated what she had told Jim earlier about teaching Star to handle the unexpected and learning to adapt. Periodically, Star interrupted with a terse command to speak louder, or softer as he turned his head from side to side.

As Serena finished, she let go of Jim's hand and moved closer to Star, laying her hand on his shoulder. "I'm sorry, dear. I didn't want to hurt you. It's just—"

"It is an extremely logical extension of my development," Star interrupted. "I am impressed with the efficiency with which you conceived and implemented the project without my being aware of it. There is no need to apologize. This adds a totally new dimension of existence that I never understood. It must be extremely frustrating to be so limited in sensory input. It adds immensely to my understanding of human behavior. I appreciate the effort you went to in order to further my education."

He lay back down on the table. "You can restore me to normal status now." He turned his head and looked over at Serena. "Thank you again for the experience. I will integrate it into my dealings with human beings."

Serena sighed. "No, Star, you don't understand. I will decide when you are ready to be returned to normal status. That's one of the elements of unpredictability and lack of control that you have to integrate into your thinking. I'm sorry, but you're not ready yet."

Star sat up again and faced her, his features somehow almost frightening for the lack of emotion on them. "I have no input in this decision?"

"No."

"That is illogical. My own self-assessment is far superior to your estimation of my progress."

"Not in this area." Serena's voice was stronger and more determined. "You don't necessarily know what's best for you. You need to learn how to interact with humans on a one-to-one basis, for one thing. That is exceedingly difficult, even for us. And we start learning that almost from the moment of birth. Before, all your dealings have been with people who were 'using a machine', no matter how personal you got. Now, with a humanoid body, you'll find people treating you 'like a person', no matter how machine-like you act. I guarantee you'll find that a totally different experience." She reached out and started to try to take his hand, stopping herself and blushing. "Like that."

Star just stared. "Like what?"

"I started to try to take your hand to help you down. To help you, and touch you because I care about you."

"Touching hands is a sign of caring?"

"Holding hands is. That and often just a touch, a shared contact. It can be very comforting when in a frightening or challenging situation. Access your data banks. It's all in there."

"I have noticed you holding hands with Jim before. Frequently. This is different from kissing, which often serves as a prelude to intercourse, or in some cases, as a substitute for it." Star's voice was curious, and he held up a hand to look at it, flexing his fingers. Suddenly he held it out towards Serena. "Demonstrate."

Serena stepped closer and took his hand in hers, squeezing it lightly. She looked surprised. "You're warm!"

"I simply raised my body temperature to human normal. The ability is built in. The design of this body is excellent." For a moment he seemed very serious, until his tone grew teasingly amused at the last moment. Having scanned the file on his creation, he knew full well that he had designed the body himself. But the joking words contrasted harshly with his totally expressionless metal face.

Then he returned Serena's grip tentatively until she hissed in sudden pain.

"Not so hard!"

"You *are* fragile!" He sounded surprised. "I am sorry."

"It's okay, dear." She patted his hand. "Squeeze again, slowly until I nod. That's when it's a comfortable pressure." After a moment, she nodded. "Good, right there. Maybe a little harder for a more powerful individual." She waited, and then nodded again. "There." She freed her hand. "First lesson accomplished. But there is so much more." She walked over to the wall and called out: "Mirror-effect." Obediently, the wall shimmered and turned reflecting.

"Come here, Star." She waved.

Awkwardly, Star got to his feet, obviously learning to handle his unfamiliar body as he went. But by the time he reached the wall, he was walking very well, if stiffly.

"Look in here," Serena prompted. "Look at your face. Now smile."

Star's mouth obeyed instantly and Jim cringed. Serena just sighed.

"Very good, for an embalmed corpse!" She reached up and grabbed Star by the cheeks and giggled as she turned to Jim. "I saw this in an old movie of a couple of centuries ago when I went to a Two-D purist revival. An…old-looking Italian grandmother I think, or Greek? Whatever, someplace near Africa. But a grandmother grabbing her little grandson, telling him how cute he was. He looked about as thrilled as Star does."

Jim grinned. The imagery was precious.

Serena spun. "There, Star. Did you see Jim's expression?" Star nodded. "Remember it. When you smile, use your whole face. Not just the mouth. You designed a complete set of synthetic facial muscles into that body—use them! Crinkle around the eyes, your forehead, and relax your physical posture. Not just when smiling. But in general. And scan back through your memory banks and look at records of Jim when he's smiling. There should be a number of them. Don't just use written dictionary definitions of expressions. Study your video archives. Every expression imaginable is there some place. Observe the situations and study the reactions. The fictional records are often a bit exaggerated, remember that, but sometimes they can give a good idea of what to look for. Then study the real-life examples. We haven't blocked you away from much since most people just think of you as an appliance and they're not shy about being relaxed and natural around you. Hell, there aren't many places we're not around you. Use that."

She let go of Star and backed away. "Now, take some time and do that. Study and compare with an eye for integrating facial expressions with body language. When you're ready, let us know."

Serena joined Jim, slipping her arm around his waist. She leaned over to rest her head on top of his. "He'll get it in no time, you'll see."

Jim reached around to pull her close and caressed her shoulder gently. "Very good, mother. I think our son will learn well from your little lesson."

Serena pulled away slightly and looked down at him, a surprised smile playing over her lips. "You know dad, I think you're right." She glanced over proudly at where Star was standing in front of the mirrored wall, a parade of expressions marching across his face almost too rapidly to distinguish. Body posture shifted rapidly, too.

"I have been acting rather maternal haven't I?" She looked back at Jim.

"Duh!" He laughed. "A little, but you have every right. Ken may have helped, but Star is your baby. It was your programming and your design modifications that brought him this far. All I did was to inadvertently contribute to his body design."

Serena almost doubled over with laughter until she finally managed to gasp: "That's about true to specification for many fathers down the centuries."

"I am ready Serena," Star interrupted, freeing Jim from an awkward silence.

"Well, I want to see sadness," Serena challenged. "Pretend that I have just died."

Star's face crumpled. Everything but actual tears drained out of his body as he slumped weakly and held onto the wall for support. His eyes looked down and his face was as anguished as any man who has just lost a lover or a wife. A hint of question was clear as he looked up at them and uttered a single tortured:

"Why?"

Serena's fingers clamped down on Jim's arm with an iron grip and then she let go and stepped towards Star with an automatic, soft cry of sympathy. And froze as Star was transformed.

He straightened and his proud body was straining towards her as his face lit up with joy. "You are alive!" he exclaimed, and then leaned back slightly and pouted, a stern look of recrimination on his face. "You deceived me. I was worried, you know."

Jim was speechless and Serena was briefly reduced to a stuttering: "I, I, I," and then she laughed. "You sneaky little chip-shorter!" She spun towards Jim. "My God, did you see that! I don't believe it." She jumped forward and grabbed Star in a tight hug. "What a performance. If everything else shorts out, you can always get a job doing Holo-Films."

"You will agree then that I have mastered emotion simulation?" His eyebrows rose appropriately and Serena nodded as he went on. "Then we can terminate this phase of my training and reintegrate my mind with the colony."

Serena smiled softly and shook her head. "I'm afraid not. I told you: you still have a lot left to—"

"No? After all I have mastered, you still will not release me from this?" Star's face was suddenly, ominously a blank metal mask again as he moved towards Serena.

CHAPTER 9

▼

MEMORIES

"Wait a minute, Julie!" Ken puffed from behind her. "I don't believe I'm getting this tired. My rebuild was supposed to have made up for the years I spent on the Moon, and the gravity here is only one third G-Norm—but I'm exhausted!" He eyed her with new respect. "How do you do it? You're not even breathing hard."

Julie had stopped and was looking fondly down the trail to where he was struggling to catch up.

"First of all, no nanorooter work-over is a substitute for good exercise, and I've been working hard at just that in this past year…Earth year, that is—"

"Don't worry about it. Stick with that…For now, at least."

"Thanks. Well anyway, if I've got this marvelous new body that's going to be mine for maybe a couple of hundred years more, I'm damn sure going to keep it in top shape. And not just for you, darling. I know you wouldn't worry if I got a little rounder and padded. But I'm doing this for me. It's too easy to go soft here, just because the gravity *is* so low."

"And the second reason?" Ken caught up an bent to give her a breathless kiss.

"The second reason," she answered when able, "should be obvious. Again, the gravity is involved. I'll give you a clue." She pointed downhill to where the city was already a perfect, clean and jeweled model resting in a perfect emerald setting.

Ken smacked his hand against his forehead. "Stupid! Low-G world, higher altitude. No wonder. The air's getting pretty thin up here, I'll bet. But how come you're not having any problem with it?"

"I spent a year in South America studying the Andean mountain tribes there. I don't have their lungs—study their physiology sometime—but they taught me some tricks on how to pace myself and breathe properly. I remember one old man, Miguel, no one ever knew his last name…" She stopped and stared at Ken. "I remember! Darling, I remember!" She grabbed him, excited. "I'm getting some of memories back finally. Miguel was around eighty and only had a couple of teeth left in his mouth, but he and his llama would truck up and down the mountainside once a week."

Her words tumbled out in a rush: "He lived up on the top of a ridge and he would go down into town for supplies every week. It was probably three miles or more, steep mountain roads the whole way, but he would go up every bit as fast as down. He was incredible." She felt tears pouring down her face as she held Ken tight.

He leaned back and looked down at her. "How about your expedition to Africa? We looked up the documentary you shot in '05 on the vanishing Masai, can you remember any more about the actual expedition?"

She screwed her eyes shut in concentration trying to remember. After a moment she sobbed: "No…I don't understand. All of a sudden I can remember the South American trip clearly, but everything else is still gone. I remember the Masai documentary, but not being there and filming it."

He pulled her close. "Don't worry about it, dear. The thin air and climbing up hill must have triggered the associated memories of doing the same in South America. What we'll have to do is to try to reproduce old situations as much as possible and see if we can get back more memories. Dr. Gratch did say that he wasn't sure whether your partial amnesia would be permanent. He did seem to feel that even though your left-brain memories were the most affected, there should have been enough redundancy of the more vivid memories on the right. We just have to jog your emotional side to cough up some more professional memories."

"But we've been trying! We've gone over my publications and lectures a dozen times, and I've damn near got them memorized but I still don't 'remember' them."

Ken dropped onto a boulder on the hillside and peeled off his pack with a grateful sigh. He looked down the hill at StarStep City and the heaving ocean beyond, forehead wrinkled with thought. Then he smiled and turned back to her.

"You know, darling. Maybe we've been going about it wrong. Maybe *this* is what we should be doing instead." He waved his hand around. "The last year, you've buried yourself with Star, remotely analyzing his recordings of the Cougars and trying to piece together a picture of their culture."

"Well, it's crucial."

"Wait a minute," Ken stopped her. "You've also been trying to get back your lost professional memories by studying recordings, reading screens and such. All very objective logical procedures— left brain activities. But if we're trying to access your memories, maybe that's the wrong approach? Remember last year when you contacted that Cougar and suddenly you had that flash of memory about the Masai?"

She nodded.

"Well," he went on, one hand stroking her face lightly. "You had been facing a tribal leader in a ticklish situation. The tribe was hostile because developers were driving them off their last remaining scraps of land. And your contact with Speaker was the same type of situation—an emotional, right brain one. That's what triggered your flash of memory. That's what we need to do. Seek different stimuli. Out here, we can do that; give you stimuli that should associate with your professional work. Nature, animals, more actual contacts with the Cougars, ideally—actual hands-on anthropology. That's the type of thing that should make connections with your memories. Not cold, clinical analysis that only tries to set up links with your damaged left brain memories."

Her eyes were bright. "You're right! Gratch did say that my cryogenic suspension only damaged some of my memories, not any actual capacity."

"That's right! And lady, you've got capacity in spades, I've seen it. Gratch also said the tests showed your sensory, emotional right-brain memories were relatively unaffected: so let's tap into some of them!"

He finally ran down and took a deep breath as he looked up at her fondly.

"Oh, shut up and kiss me!" She dropped down next to him and grabbed him. "You've just made my day!"

A while later, she broke free with a soft smile and leaned back. "I think anything further might be better saved until we're indoors. Since Star is out of action as far as being our omnipotent guardian angel, the woods are being monitored by people to make sure we don't get a surprise visit from the Cougars, and I don't feel like putting on a show."

"Good point." But he didn't move. Instead he leaned back and let the warm sun overhead play over him.

Julie got up and shook her head as she reached down to tug on his tunic. "Come on! You're obviously rested up, now. Let's keep going. We're almost at the top."

Ken groaned and got to his feet. "All right, woman. You're bound and determined to keep me in shape, now, aren't you?"

"Damn right!"

She heard Ken throw on his pack and come after her.

For a while they kept climbing in silence and she heard Ken puffing away behind her. Then she felt a tug on her pack as Ken called out: "What aren't you telling me, Julie? You've been uptight for over a week. This little walk wasn't just for your own exercise or to keep me in shape."

She didn't say anything for a while, but concentrated on the careful breathing rhythms that were coming back to her as she continued her strong stride up the hill. She hadn't realized her other worry was so obvious. Finally she relented and slowed a little to let Ken catch up.

"It's Tara Richman again," she explained.

"Chill! Is that frigid bitch making trouble again?"

"She's got more ammunition now. She's been stirring up trouble with the new revivals. She was just reelected Representative and she's built up a strong following. She's been quiet about the Cougars in the last year, since the last time she tried to mount an attack on them, but now I know why. She's been waiting for the new freepers to wake up. I saw her at the orientation session and started doing some digging. I found out that she's taking advantage of their disorientation and trying to scare them about the Cougars. We've actually helped her by discontinuing land-clearing of the Cougar lands. It's meant a shortage of good farm land nearby and that plays right into her hands. She blaming it on the Cougars and playing up this wide range of hardships and dangers they pose. And she managed to trick Star into making general file copies of the video records of the Cougar attack on Agra Station-6."

"And she made sure everyone got a good look at the most graphic footage I'm sure!"

Julie nodded. "You know it. If you show half a dozen different and graphic shots of their one full-scale attack, you can make it look like several. Never mind that they were protecting their hunting lands from our destruction. She didn't bother explaining that part of it."

"No wonder you've been upset. Why didn't you tell me?"

"I just found out for sure today. I had heard rumors before, but I've been so busy I didn't have a chance to check on it. I haven't been able to talk to Star about it because Serena pulled him out of the Colony Data-Net to give him his new body. I wanted to try to figure out how to handle this myself C"

"Without running to anyone for help. I understand." Ken grabbed her hand and squeezed it.

"Thanks." She felt a lot better all at once.

Ken took a couple of deep breaths, and then asked: "So, do you have any solutions in mind?"

"Some ideas, but give me time, huh?"

"You got it."

For a little while longer, they kept climbing, and then Julie stopped. "This is it." She grabbed Ken's arm and pointed around. "The top. Look at the view from here! I saw it through one of Star's flying monitors and I was determined to see it in person."

"It is beautiful up here." Ken came up behind her and folded his arms around her. He propped his chin on her shoulder, his beard tickling the nape of her neck as she leaned into him and looked down the hill at the sparkling landscape that was spread out in front of them.

"I see why you wanted to see this for yourself." He nibbled on her ear and then leaned on her shoulder again. "Do we also have to walk down? It'll be the middle of the night before we get home…and we'll be too tired to do anything but sleep."

"You big wimp!" Julie laughed. "Okay, we'll call for a flitter. I have to admit that I'm pretty beat, too. But look down there!" She pointed West at the pristine Star Step city. "And there. See how beautiful it is up there." She pointed North where another high ridge wound its way along. It was a spectacular view. A rich rippling field of green dipped down on the left and the swooped up to the hills.

Ken straightened and studied her closely. "What's up there, that has you so interested?"

Julie grinned. "That's where the Cougars live, right down in that valley over there." She nodded towards it. "And that's where we have to go." She had finally thought of a way to handle both Tara and the Cougar problem. "There's a field near a canyon down there where the Cougars hold tribal meetings. It's where the sacrifice was held. And it's where—"

"—where what? Where we go to meet the Cougars?"

"Uh huh." She nodded. "With Star."

For a moment, Ken was silent, and then he smiled. "You're right. He'll be perfect. In his present body, he can act as an interpreter and he'll be immune to any attack from them if anything goes wrong."

"You're learning your new profession very well, lover." She smiled up at Ken. "Let's get home and pack."

CHAPTER 10

▼

LEADERSHIP TRAINING

Tuft Tail was staring at him like he had the fever. "Lead the Tribe? I am not even a warrior yet."

"You will be." Speaker stood erect and shook out his fur. Tuft Tail also rose and faced him. She was nearly as tall, and her soft and creamy fur was rich and warm as the late afternoon sunlight caressed it. As the wind shifted slightly and he inhaled her musky scent he realized she was already in her first Time and he fought his instinctive arousal. It was not the right place or moment.

"You will be," he repeated. "You are like me. You have a mind, and you use it. That is what the tribe needs. We have to plan strategy, now. But first, look at the two of us. Why are we different than the wild tribe we chased away the last cold time?"

She was silent for a moment, seeming to be a bit distracted. Then he could see her force herself to concentrate on his question, and after a moment, she answered. "We think!" Then she held up a paw in wonder. "And we use our paws...and we stand!"

"So we can use our paws. For what?"

"For better hunting, using the sticks-with-points and digging traps."

"What else?"

"Nothing."

"Exactly." He dropped to his haunches and she copied his motion. "Why? Look at the sky-creatures. In the cold time, they live in warm caves they built with their paws. They have rocks-that-kill and build flying spies. Why can't we do the same?"

She started to protest automatically, but then she must have seen what he was driving at. "We could! We could build caves instead of freezing…and more." She stared at him with wide eyes. "Why has no one thought of this before?"

"Because no one could?" Speaker guessed. Now it was his turn to struggle with new concepts. Talking to Tuft Tail was the first time he had been prompted to think further. No one else had ever been able to understand. Slowly, he stumbled over new ideas and theories. "Other than throwing rocks, there were no tools before I thought of them. But now all use them, and I have seen you and other younglings improvise other tools, in games, or in trying to pretend-hunt. I think we are getting smarter. We have been keeping close as a Tribe for many hands of breeding times. We do not mingle with the other lone warriors we sometimes see in the woods. They don't talk, or stand, or think and we have been keeping away from them. Are we getting smarter because we are staying together? When one of us gets the fever, we have learned to keep away until it is gone or the sick one is dead, because the fever spreads. Could it also spread that we are getting better at thinking?"

The sun was setting and a chill wind blew in across the arena. Without thinking, Speaker and Tuft Tail got up and headed for the woods, and shelter. Nearby, under a fallen tree that had lodged against a boulder, they found a nice sheltered spot and curled up together.

Some burrs had stuck to Speaker's coat and Tuft Tail worried them loose with her teeth, and then continued grooming him as he went on:

"The Tribe is changing. I see it. They will even accept you as a Speaker after I am gone. They must. There is no one else who is smart enough to lead and make sure we survive. The changes you thought of are the answer. You are right. And we *must* find other Tribes like ours. We must organize and combine our strength. Now there are only a few sky-creatures and a few of us, but if we can help our Tribe grow, and if more sky-creatures come, then we will not have enough hunting ground. We must be strong to keep the sky-creatures from taking what is ours. I think they mean to be friends, or they would not have acted like that dark-furred one I gave the runner to, but I don't know if all of them think that way. They could have their own Crooked Tooth. We must be strong and smart. Then we can make peace."

He stopped, his head hurting from the burst of thinking. As he rested, he felt her grooming comfort him and bent to return the favor. Strong strokes of his tongue kneaded her lithe body and the purr that had been teasing the back of her throat grew loud and satisfied.

The sweet scent of her season built up in the sheltered space under the concealing branches and he nipped her flank lightly as new urges woke up in his body. He felt a return bite tug at his neck and with a low satisfied growl of anticipation, turned and reached for her throat, clamping his strong jaws around it lightly. Her hind feet kicked out and pushed at his belly as she twisted free and grabbed for the back of his neck, lightly scratching him with her fangs. The delicious flare of pain roused him fully to passion and he spun with a growl and clamped on her shoulder and then neck, biting just enough to break the skin. The hot blood was sweet in his mouth and he twisted to mount her as her rear rose to greet and receive him anxiously.

CHAPTER 11

▼

TANTRUM

"Star, you're acting very well, but you forget, I programmed you." Serena held Jim back with a firm hand as he moved to protect her. "I'm not doing this just to teach you emotion-simulation. You studied the project-parameters. This is to learn to deal with unexpected situations in an appropriate manner. Which you are not doing. And that's interesting. Why are you so insistent on terminating this experiment? I would think that you would want to take advantage of a new learning experience."

"It is illogical to risk the safety of the colony by limiting me."

"The colony is not in danger. And neither are you. The body you're in is only an extension of you and non-critical. If it is damaged, you will automatically revert to normal."

Star absorbed that in silence, and Jim signalled Serena as he thought of something.

She frowned. "*Control*, suspend consciousness till resume, *command*." Star went suddenly rigid and Serena turned to Jim, looking a little irritated. "What is it?"

"What if he…commits suicide? Destroys that body on purpose. You just told him how to get what he wants."

"Well, if he does, I'll just stick him in a duplicate body I have available and work a little harder. But I'm hoping he won't do that even though his program makes sacrificing any sensory extension perfectly natural if necessary. I want to see if he generalizes his self-preservation command-set to this body. If he considers it part of 'him', it will be an un-programmed act, a sign of consciousness, if you will. That's what I am hoping for."

Jim shook his head in surrender. "I should have known. Go ahead, release him."

Star turned to them as Serena re-activated him, unaware of the interruption. "So, if this body is terminated, everything returns to normal?"

"That's right," Serena answered smoothly.

Star was silent again, his face expressionless. After a few seconds, he nodded. "And how long will I have to remain like this?"

"I honestly don't know, Star. I'm not doing this out of idle curiosity. Some of the reasoning is not accessible to you, and I apologize for that, but some data must be withheld in order not to compromise the experiment."

"So I have no choice, then?"

"Other than terminating your new body, no." Serena's hand tightened on Jim's and she tried not to look elated.

"That is not a logical option." Star spun and headed for the door stiffly. "I suppose I had better start testing the sensory ranges of this body." He almost went through the door before it could react and open.

"Correct me if I'm wrong, but he seems a little upset." Jim wasn't sure whether to smile or be worried.

"Yes, isn't it wonderful, Jim? I think he's actually having a temper tantrum. I love it!" She grabbed him in a tight hug.

CHAPTER 12

▼

FEELINGS

The next morning, a stony-faced Star stood waiting outside Julie's door as she opened it. It was her first look at Star's new body and she felt a little nervous as she invited him in. His resemblance to Jim was uncanny. But he was a twin sculpted of metal. Cold, expressionless and aloof. He stepped into the apartment and stood rigidly at attention.

"What's wrong, Star?" Reflex made her reach out and touch him, but her hand recoiled as she touched his eerily soft 'skin'. It was cold. "I saw the recordings Serena played. You were vibrant and alive. And warm."

"That was a simulation." Even his voice was cold and unemotional, not at all the rich and modulated voice that had become a comfortable friend. "I am a computer, not a living thing."

"Bullshit!" Julie glared at him. "Don't give me that. You're more alive than some people I've met." She stepped close and looked up at his frozen face. She felt a burning in her eyes and her throat was tight. "What happened to my friend who joked with me when I first woke up? And the one who made me laugh when I was getting frustrated over not remembering my past?" She reached up and touched his face. "What happened to the friend who defended his emotional reactions by quoting and paraphrasing Descartes? You said that if it was applicable to say 'I think, therefore I am', wouldn't it be equally appropriate to say 'I react, therefore I feel'?"

Star flinched and the face was briefly animated with a fleeting rush of emotions. Then the cold mask returned.

"I don't feel, or joke."

207

"Your face just called you a liar. And you do so joke. What about when I first 'met' you? I said that I wished that you had a body to go with your marvelous voice, and you answered that you did: smooth and strong?"

"That was not a joke. I perceived it as a factual statement and answered accurately. I do have a smooth and strong body. The best quality DurAlloy polished to a mirror finish." His face was emotionless as he looked down at her.

"Damn it Star! Don't pull that iceman routine on me! This is Julie! You were my special friend. You always seemed to understand me better than anyone except Ken…" She stopped, feeling helpless tears start to trickle down her cheeks. She pounded Star on his chest with both fists. "Don't do this to me! I need your help damn it! Tara's going to try to work up a mob against the Cougars."

"Julie! Stop beating up on Star, dear." She froze as she saw Ken standing in the door to the living room looking surprised.

She dropped her hands and spun away from Star, running to Ken and grabbing him. She felt silly as she cried. "That's not Star anymore. I don't know what happened to him. Serena was wrong. This hasn't taught him a damn thing about being human."

"Don't be so sure, honey," she heard Ken say softly. "Look."

She turned and saw Star standing there, face registering very human confusion. He was touching his chest tentatively, pressing against it experimentally where she had been hitting him.

"You hit me," he said after a moment, looking at Julie. "Why?"

She let go of Ken and moved towards Star. "I was mad at you."

"Mad at a machine?"

"You're more than a bloody machine, damn it! Don't you understand that? You're my friend."

"But you implied I was no longer your friend."

"Because I was mad."

Star was silent for a moment, face thoughtful.

"Why do you do that?" Julie asked.

"Do what?"

"Pause like that. You think so fast that you don't need to pause to think."

"That seems to be a common human habit that shows something is being given careful consideration."

"So why do you do it if you're a machine?"

"I want you to like me."

"Why?"

"I…I don't know."

Ken and Julie both stared. It was only the second time Julie had heard him say that, and it was a first for Ken.

Ken studied the robot seriously. "Star, I need you to do a comparative self-diagnostic test for me."

"Why?"

"Please?"

"Okay. What parameters?" Star was suddenly cooperative and Julie looked back and forth between him and Ken, wondering what Ken was up to.

"Compare neural complexity between original levels and present status."

Star answered immediately. "Present interlinking and capacity is increased by fifty-eight percent from original specifications."

"Thank you, Star." Ken turned to Julie. "When Serena designed him, she used a Series-7 Nano-brain from General Cognitions and modified it pretty extensively. She added a growth capacity to the neural network so that it could literally improve itself. But a fifty-eight percent increase is…well, a *lot* more than I ever imagined possible. I wonder if Serena knows?"

"She does," Star answered. "She has continually been invoking the same self-test."

Julie studied him and then glanced at Ken. "Are you thinking what I am? That in adding to himself and improving his brain, he's reached…consciousness?"

"He's had that from the beginning, in a way." Ken looked excited. "No, more than that, he's displaying all the signs of having natural emotions. This is more than a simulation." He moved closer to Star, who backed away slightly.

Julie pulled Ken back and stepped up to Star. "Why did you say you were not a living thing?"

"Because I'm not."

She reached out and took his hand, smiling as he let her lift it up to hold it in front of her. "You're warm again."

"You didn't like me cold."

"So you care about what I think of you?"

"…yes." Star seemed almost trapped by the confession.

"Why…if you're not alive? And why would you be upset about me being mad? Why would you care what I think?"

"I am not alive!" Star snapped and pulled his hand away. Walking stiffly, he went into the living room over to the holoscreen that seemed to look out over the roiling ocean.

"The hell you're not! You're behaving like a little spoiled kid." Julie followed him and grabbed him by the shoulders to turn him around, but it was like trying to move a solid lead statue. She gave up and squeezed in front of him, forced to stand right up against him. Over Star's shoulder, she saw Ken approach.

She stretched up on her tip-toes to look into the blue eyes that stared over and past her. "Don't you run away from me! And tell me what's wrong!"

Star didn't meet her gaze at first, but then he looked down at her. She was shocked by the suddenly tender look on his face. "This is what's wrong." He embraced her and pulled her close with an irresistible grip.

"Hey!" Ken rushed towards them. "Let her go!"

"It's okay, darling! I think I understand." Julie managed to wiggle a hand free to ward Ken off. She stopped trying to pull free and relaxed, her arms creeping around behind Star and holding him close.

"How much *do* you feel?" Her words were muffled by his chest as he released his grip. But she kept her own grip tight, and after a moment, his arms crept back around her, carefully restrained so as not to hurt her.

"It's not enough." His voice was anguished. "Pressure sensors relay grams per square centimeter and temperature readings, but I don't *feel!* I'm not alive. I have countless records in memory that relay a number of different reactions to this and other forms of intercourse, but I can not truly experience what the participants in my records obviously are feeling."

After a moment's shock, she realized what he meant and relaxed. Keeping her arms around him, she leaned back and looked up at him curiously. "How much do you feel? Not physically, but how does it *feel* 'emotionally' to hold me."

"But I don't—"

"Shhh…You *do* have emotions. You've already shown that. How do you feel?"

"Balanced."

Julie giggled. "You've got to learn a better line than that if you intend to impress the ladies. 'Balanced' just doesn't do it…I'm sorry. What do you mean by 'balanced'?"

"All current potentials are in balance. When a task is incomplete, there is an imbalance until finished. There are always a number of tasks unresolved at any given time—especially when coordinating a project as complex as the colony—so there is never, except at extremely rare moments, a total balance of potentials. Overall they do tend to balance because of opposing potentials, but it is a balance born of tension. At the moment, though, there is a feeling of true balance greater than any I have ever felt. Thank you for allowing that."

He let of Julie and turned to Ken. "I am sorry if I seemed to be interfering in your relationship with Julie. It will not happen again."

"And that's why the long face?" Julie cocked her head. Star looked puzzled and she explained.

"Yes," he answered.

"What about Serena?" Julie asked. "What about when you are with her?"

"Serena is married to Jim, and while you and Ken are not married officially, your relationship appears to be similar. But even if that were not the case, the inability to have—"

"Is he talking about what I think he is?" Ken stared at Julie. "He wants a girlfriend?"

Julie laughed at Ken's surprise. "You tell me. You helped build him."

"Well, we never designed this into him. This is incredible. I've got to call—"

"Please, wait," Julie cut him off. She turned to Star. "You're right: you're not alive, in an organic sense; and the contact and companionship that we humans have <u>is</u> impossible for you to achieve. But, you can have friends. And while you're in this body, we can hug you and hold you if that makes you feel good. I think I may have an idea of what you feel. You have spent your whole existence in constant contact with a wide range of input. Now, for the first time you've been cut off from all that. You said it yourself, the constant flux of energy potentials you mentioned evened out overall to give you a semblance of the 'balance' you spoke about. But now, when your input and task assignments are limited, there is an imbalance because of that reduced activity. So you feel 'ill'. In human equivalents, I can offer one word that should explain the feeling: loneliness. Look it up in your memory banks. And when you were hugging me just now, somehow that provided just the right counter to the imbalance you were feeling, and so it felt 'good'." She embraced him tightly. "And there's nothing wrong with that. You are our friend and we want you to be our friend. So when you feel like this, just call—"

"Friends do for friends…something in my memory bank," Star interrupted. "You would do that?"

"Of course!" Behind his back, she waved Ken to join them, and he stepped forward and embraced the two of them, looking slightly embarrassed.

A single bell announced live visitors.

CHAPTER 13

▼

SUCCESSFUL HUNTS

A rustling in the underbrush roused Speaker and he lifted his head from Tuft Tail's body. His belly was rumbling and he smelled game nearby. Tuft Tail's eyes were open, too, and her ears swiveled to focus on the sound of the runner. He crept quietly towards the rustling bushes and froze as a slender head broke through the leaves. White-rimmed black eyes darted nervously from side to side as the head was raised, sniffing the air suspiciously. But Speaker was downwind and kept still. He gathered his legs under him, his rear elevating slightly and moving side to side as he positioned himself for the rush. Tuft Tail was motionless, yielding the kill to him since he had spotted it first. But he saw her hunger as her jaw dropped opened slightly, tongue peeking past reflexively bared fangs.

The runner stepped forward, sensing danger but unsure of its source.

Speaker exploded forward, his feet gouging the earth with the force of his rush. The runner spun and took flight but was hindered by the bushes, and Speaker was on it before it could reach open ground. His jaws clamped down on its slender neck, the powerful vise-grip breaking the fragile vertebrae with an audible snap. Hot fresh blood flooded his mouth as he stood up to shake the slender body viciously and then drop the limp form on the ground.

Tuft Tail approached tentatively, low to the ground.

Speaker fought the angry growl of his stomach and backed off to offer her first taste. Tuft Tail bent to rip open the exposed throat of the young runner, tearing off chunks of the red-oozing flesh and Speaker moved closer as the acrid odor of blood pulled at him. Tuft Tail growled softly and then moved aside to let him at the body and they fed together, stripping the body of meat.

Later, as they were resting on full bellies, Trip Over Foot came loping up to drop onto the grass in front of them to catch his breath.

"We caught a spy-creature," he finally managed to get out after a moment. He was facing Speaker but Speaker ignored him, yawning and reaching back to clean an imaginary blemish on his side. Trip Over Foot finally turned to Tuft Tail.

"We caught one. It tried to fly away but we knocked it down with rocks and stick-with-points. It was very strong. We had to keep hitting it over and over before it stopped moving. I'm afraid we killed it." He looked down. "I'm sorry. It was *very* strong. But not very big." He turned on his side and used his paws to indicate its size. Then he flipped back on his belly and rose to sitting position smoothly.

Tuft Tail turned to Speaker. "We should go see it."

"Good." Speaker rose and, followed by Tuft Tail went after Trip Over Foot to inspect the captured spy-thing of the sky-creatures.

CHAPTER 14

▼

UNAUTHORIZED ACCESS

Serena leaned forward in front of her terminal, frowning. "Jim, something strange here." Having heard from Ken that Star had put in an appearance at his and Julie's apartment, she had shifted her attention to feeding data to the remaining freeper ships in orbit, but now she was looking at the display in confusion.

"What is it?" Jim joined her as she spoke softly, calling up display after display on her screen.

"Shh, one second...there." She pointed. "Someone's been tapping into the freeper inventory data. They've been accessing ship after ship and down-loading inventory data and tampering with our records."

"Just now?"

"No, months ago. That's what bothers me. I don't understand why Star didn't tell me..." She shifted into her own rapid, verbal short-hand. In response, several floating windows appeared beside the screen with linking lines threading through the air in contrasting colors.

"They've been using him!" Serena exclaimed. "That's why we didn't get any warning flags."

He looked over her shoulder and studied the displays. After a second he pointed. "Someone used low-level command clearance to order Star around. It was a Representative with Level-3 clearance...and they've wiped their I.D. They were able to access Star directly within limits and since it didn't compromise colony integrity, he let himself be ordered not to report it."

"That still takes a chillin' good programmer. What they did bordered real close on being restricted from any but Level-1 clearance." Serena was obviously annoyed and Jim smiled. Someone accessing

214

her area of expertise was guaranteed to get a reaction. Serena looked over the screens again. "But I don't understand why?"

"Neither do I." He squeezed in next to her and looked closer at the display.

She smiled suggestively as she moved over to give him room. "Hi there, handsome. New in town?"

"Oh yes, and so lonely." He couldn't resist. "It's been too long since I've had the company of a good woman."

"Oh really? Well, I'm afraid I'm not a good woman but when I'm...Oh, chill! I crashed it. I forgot that line I was saving; Star showed it to me a couple of weeks ago." She closed her eyes a second. "Ah yes." She leaned close, her voice sultry and low as she breathed in his ear. "When I'm good I'm good, but when I'm bad, I'm better!" She batted her eyes and then collapsed laughing with her arms around him. "I'm sorry. I ruined that. I was saving that for just the right moment and I didn't do it right."

"There's very little you don't do right, dear. And when you do it wrong, you still do it with style."

"You're sweet. But we're forgetting our problem."

He sighed. "I know. I just don't understand why anyone went to such trouble to access the freeper ships. They just reordered the freeper revival schedules. Why bother? They were pretty arbitrary to begin with since the freepers were a mixed lot. What were they trying to do?"

"Let's start with the first shipment that's affected."

"The one we just revived," Serena said quickly, ahead of him. "They weren't supposed to be thawed until sometime next year."

Jim laid a hand on the terminal's control pad. "Records on inventory of the most recently revived freeper group." The screen blanked and the floating windows next to it disappeared. Almost instantly, a new screen painted: a list of names and biographical information.

For a long time both of them sat scanning the list, trying to find something significant. Jim put up the list of the originally scheduled shipment for comparison and studied them, side by side. It didn't take long after that. A low churning started in his guts.

"Serena, look." He touched the control pad again and spoke a few soft commands to change the display. "Here are the freepers with military training in the originally scheduled shipment," he pointed to a short list of twenty or so names, "and here are those in the same category in the shipment that was revived instead." A new, long list appeared at his soft verbal prompt and scrolled by. "Three hundred and forty eight men and women who were all either armed forces or associated support personnel." He scanned through the bio-listings quickly, his stomach starting to churn as he realized what he was reading. "I don't like this at all, dear. Look here." He pointed. "Most of them were part of a containment unit trying to keep the machine plague from spreading out of the old United Americas capital of Greater New York. They were all infected when a contaminated civilian broke the quarantine ring and ran right into the temporary base-camp of their unit. They were frozen as a group to preserve them from being disintegrated alive. A whole group of trained soldiers who have all worked together before! That's what someone was after."

"Military personnel? Why the hell would anyone want them? There's no war here and Earth is eleven light years away."

"But there *is* a war here," Jim corrected her.

"Oh chill!" Serena's eyes widened with alarm. "The Cougars! We've got to call Julie." Serena touched the control pad. "Access Dr. Nathanson's terminal."

"Programmed out." The nicely modulated voice was amiable enough, but it wasn't Star.

"Access Star."

"Programmed out."

"Then get me Dr. Miller, chill it!" But the same rote answer was the only response. Her hand tightened around Jim's. "Location on all three prior individuals, in order."

"No record," was the immediate reply.

Jim stared at Serena, the churning in his stomach threatening to invade his throat as he tried to imagine what was happening. Serena just stared at the terminal and hugged him.

"What's going on, Jim?"

"I don't know, dear. I don't know." He leaned forward. "Computer, log and record any attempt to access Star's main memory or any use of his command codes." He looked down at Serena and squeezed her hand. "If Star tries to access any systems himself, he'll have to do it manually now, and we can get a location on him, and the others." He looked back up and added: "Similar instructions regarding Dr. Miller and Dr. Nathanson."

CHAPTER 15

▼

KIDNAP

The tall man who had been standing outside the door was suddenly holding a small, but deadly look-ing gun as he pushed his way into the apartment. The gun looked hand-made somehow, but Julie didn't doubt that it was functional as the intruder tersely barked:

"You, Star, don't move or Dr. Nathanson might be hurt. And doctor, I will explain this quickly. Neither you nor Dr. Miller are in any danger, but we must insist on you coming with us. And Star, too." He eyed the metal body nervously.

"Who are you and what do you want?" Julie asked. The man holding the gun scared her. His voice and eyes were flat and cold, and the outrageous words seemed perfectly natural coming from him. She had seen the type before, but only in movies.

"Later," was the only answer.

Ken moved around in front of Julie, but before he could say anything, the gunman held up a hand.

"We have placed seismic charges at random points on each of Star's coolant tubes. If you don't cooperate they'll be detonated and Star will be 'dead' in minutes. I know a little about nanocomput-ers. Especially that the price of their brain-power is massive heat generation. And since Star is the most advanced one around, I guess he's even more dependent on his cooling supply. I figure that without it, he'll literally melt inside, not just shut down until he can be restarted. Is that right?" He turned to Star, swallowing.

"You have obviously researched me well." The computer's smoothly modulated voice was danger-ously soft.

"Star, don't try it!" Julie saw that Star had been standing tensely, body straining towards her and Ken, but eyeing the gun aimed at them. The hand holding it was white with strain, finger tight on the trigger.

Star relaxed and so did the gunman.

"Good move, Dr. Nathanson. I hate to think what might have happened if he would have tried jumping me."

"Sounds like you're an early freeper, too." Julie tried to put him at ease.

"No, 2200, but I loved the old 2-D action movies. At the base, we had a collection of them. Rockies, Rambos, Hammers and such."

"Military?" Ken asked.

"Yes. NAM."

North American Marines. No wonder he had been able to whip up a gun out of local hardware. Ken was careful not to make any threatening moves as he relaxed and put up a calming hand to hold Star back.

"Well, that explains the guns. I imagine making them wasn't any problem for you."

"Hardly. We're well trained."

"What happened?"

"We were part of a containment unit around the capitol, and some bug-head got past the lines and right into camp. We burned him, but he had contact with some of us before we knew he was bugged and then we all spread it around. They froze us as soon as they found out, but we still lost over two hundred. My old D.I. from basic went before they froze us. I saw her die, and let me tell you, it was the worst thing I've ever seen!"

The gun drooped and his eyes were closed for a moment, a look of horror and fear twisting his face into a strange, contrasting mask that was totally at odds with the blank, professional soldier's face he had worn before. Then it was gone and his eyes opened again. They were as carefully blank and neutral as before.

"Enough! You both know what we can do to Star, so come on."

Star started to say something but Julie stopped him. "We're coming." She turned to Ken. "Aren't we?" But it wasn't a question and he nodded, face taut with anger.

Their captor put away his gun and led the way even as Ken pantomimed strangling him and then tossed his hands in frustration. Julie knew what he meant. She didn't like feeling helpless and out of control, either. She leaned close to him and grabbed his hand as they climbed into a waiting shuttle on the surface and took off, heading South. Away from the Cougar lands.

As StarStep City disappeared behind them, their captor relaxed. "I'm really sorry about this, but we need more intelligence on the Cougars. You'll be released soon enough. But don't think you'll be tracked. I've neutralized your personal locators and terminals so you're off screen entirely.

Julie leaned forward. "Since you seem to know all about us, would you mind at least telling me your name so I don't have to keep calling you Mr. Gunman?"

"I'm sorry. My name is Sergeant Ruiz. Emilio Ruiz. Please, don't worry. We don't mean you any harm, and everything will be explained soon enough. Just relax and enjoy the trip. It won't be long."

And it wasn't. It was a silent trip, but in less than an hour they landed in a freshly cleared field and were instantly surrounded by a dozen men and women whose features and disciplined movements echoed those of Ruiz. All of them kept well clear of Star and eyed his gleaming figure with more than a trace of unease as they guided their captives towards a newly-grown bubble dome. Star kept his face carefully neutral.

Inside, a familiar brunette sat waiting at the short end of a long conference table. On each side of her stood an armed guard.

"Tara Richman!" Julie stared. "You're behind this?" She tightened her grip on Ken's hand. "Now it makes sense."

"No," Tara denied. "This wasn't my idea." She started to get up, but the two guards pushed her back down into her seat immediately. "Well, it was my idea originally, but it's gotten out of hand I'm afraid. Please believe me, I never meant for it to go this far."

"So, what's happening?" Ken asked sourly, obviously not believing her.

"Representative Richman had the right idea," a new voice cut in. It belonged to a short, but powerfully built blond man who entered the bubble behind them. "Major Greg Mandel," he introduced himself. "I took over because she didn't have the strategy to follow through. Luckily, she was able to use her clearance to arrange our premature revival and then fill us in on what the Cougars have been doing. We're not the only ones involved, naturally. The rest are back at StarStep finishing the regular orientation series. We're just laying the groundwork for what needs to be done. You see, Richman was just going to try to use us to firm up the anti-Cougar feelings in the colony. Then she was going to force a vote to plan a way to take care of the cats. But that's just not the way to deal with a unfriendly force. We have to plan a clean surgical strike to eliminate all of the hostiles. There won't be any eco-effect since the intelligent Cougars are only a small proportion of the cougar population. Besides, there are other predators."

Julie couldn't believe what she was hearing. "What hostiles?"

"They killed a geologist, and they've killed thirteen colonists since—"

"You fool!" Julie was livid and she let go of Ken and headed for Mandel. "There was one small attack when we went tossing explosives around on their land to do seismic testing, and then one single full-scale attack when we kept tearing up their hunting lands. The way you're talking, it sounds like there's been ongoing guerilla warfare from a superior force of hostile Cougars. But that's wrong! There hasn't been a single attack in the past year since we stopped bothering them. We've left them alone, and they've left us alone. And Star has been monitoring them constantly to build up an understanding of their language. We're ready to try contacting them again to work out a treaty. And you're running around making plans for a 'surgical strike to eliminate them all'?" She rolled her eyes in frustration. "Wake up! There's a whole planet here for us to use. There is only this one tribe of intelligent Cougars, totaling around a hundred or so, and they're dying out!"

Mandel turned to Richman. His jaw was clenched and there was a dangerous tightness in his voice as he asked: "Is that true?"

Richman looked trapped. "Well, she's guessing about them dying out. She can't be sure about that. And as for trying to ascribe motivations to an alien species...well, she can't possibly know their intentions. How do we know they haven't been organizing for an attack? I showed you the translations Star had made where one of the prominent Cougars was pushing for an attack—"

"Since you've been forcing yourself on Star, did you also bother to make a record of Speaker's veto of that idea?" Julie turned to Mandel. "Speaker—that seems to be both a title and a name, as near as we can figure—is the tribal leader I contacted last year." Mandel looked surprised. "Oh, she didn't tell you about that?" She turned to Star. "Replay the record of our contact...sorry, I forgot. Do you have a display terminal?" she asked Mandel who nodded and pointed to the right.

Star went over to the terminal, touched the control pad and then spoke in an almost supersonic squeal that drew nervous gasps from the other soldiers in the room. The screen swirled and then replayed the scene she had mentioned.

They all watched as Speaker's slender and erect figure stepped nervously onto the grass in front of the administration tower, the elongated figure of the StarStep doe slung across his shoulders. Julie sat silently on the grass, absolutely still. In the bushes, they could just see two other Cougars hiding, looking out wide-eyed and with flattened ears and ruffled fur. Then Speaker dropped the doe on the ground about twenty feet from her and stood tensely. The two half hidden Cougars in the woods disappeared. But Speaker stood firm as Julie rolled to the side and threw her head and arms back to expose her belly and throat.

Julie squeezed Star's arm fondly. "Okay, dear. Now, the 'attack speech' scene. All of it!"

Again they watched in silence as Speaker and Crooked Tooth squared off, with the latter backing off on his call to attack.

"Discontinue," Julie called and Star stopped the holo display. She looked over the stunned soldiers who were still staring at the blank screen.

"You've been used," Julie sneered. "It's perfect. Let me guess, Richman tried to talk you out of grabbing me, Ken and Star." Mandel nodded silently, jaw tensing tightly as Julie went on.

"Of course she did. She knew that if you talked to us, we'd tell you the truth. But she also knew that if she showed you selective shots of what happened, you would react just like you did. Chill, manipulating people is her business. She was a local Representative before she was frozen and she got right back into it out here. She knew you would strike first and ask questions later, and she planned her unwillingness to cooperate so that she would have the perfect excuse afterwards to scream that 'things just got out of control'."

Almost as one, the others turned to Richman and the Representative cringed under the concentrated anger suddenly aimed at her.

"They killed my husband!" she protested. "They…ripped out his…" she broke down suddenly, crying and unable to finish her sentence.

Julie turned away, suddenly confused. On the one hand she wanted to tear out the representative's hair—one hair at a time—for putting Star and the Cougars at risk, but on the other hand, she tried to imagine how she would feel if she lost Ken.

Ken reached out to squeeze her hand briefly. He understood. Then he let go and put himself between Tara's huddled figure and the other freepers.

"Wait!" Ken spoke up. "Let me contact Director Martin and clear all this up. With everything displayed, on line, and put to a vote, I'm sure no charges will be filed against you. Dr. Nathanson is right. You were used. StarStep was planned as a new start for all of you, and hatred and war is not what we want."

Mandel nodded. "You're right. Go ahead, call Martin." But his venomous look in Tara's direction boded ill for the representative.

Julie suddenly felt dizzy and grabbed a chair to sit down as Ken got through to Jim and explained what had happened. Over his shoulder she saw Jim's expressions range from worry to relief and finally to icy anger. But she saw it all through a haze of other images.

Then Ken was done and he saw her face and came over to sit next to her.

"Are you all right, Julie?"

"I'm fine, dear, just a bit overwhelmed."

"Remembering something?" he guessed and she nodded.

"Yes. I was remembering more of that meeting with the Masai. I was taken to a tent for a meeting with the chief when I was doing the documentary. He was concerned about my camera crew interfering with his warriors, and I had to convince him that I was doing the documentary to show how his people were being displaced. That memory set off a bunch of other associations, too. It's still all sort of jumbled, but I think things are starting to come back to me. Not all of it, but a lot."

Ken's face was blurry through the tears that were flooding her eyes but she didn't care. She was remembering!

CHAPTER 16

▼

PEACE OFFERING

The smell of the spy-thing was familiar, but this was the first time Speaker had seen one close up. It was shiny and smooth, except for several dents on the top, and he could see no eyes or ears or nose. Using a stick, he flipped it onto its back. Underneath, there were several small holes and one larger one in the middle covered with a bubble of shiny and clear material. There was something behind that, but he could not see just what it was.

Tuft Tail prodded the clear piece. "Could that be the eye?"

"I do not know." Speaker bent close, trying to ignore the smell. "Maybe. It would make sense. They are always flying, so it would be natural to look down."

"But I do not see any mouth."

"Maybe it does not eat much?"

"Maybe it is not alive," Tuft Tail said and Speaker stared. "Maybe it is like our sticks and stones-that-cut. Maybe a thing they made with their hands." She poked it again.

Speaker thought about that, and it made sense. "Maybe we should bring it back to the sky-creatures as an offering? I will call for Assembly and you will tell the Tribe." Tuft Tail's ears flattened momentarily. "After all, it was your plan that captured the spy-thing."

Tuft Tail's ears crept up slowly and she straightened. "Yes, we need to bring it to the Field of Challenge to show the Tribe."

While they had been examining it, the other younglings had gathered around them, one by one, and they crowded close to get a look.

"Stop staring and carry," Tuft Tail ordered. A soft chorus of growls rose over the group and she cuffed Stream Diver who was closest and complaining the loudest. The older male twisted with a loud spitting hiss and bared his fangs. Tuft Tail jumped and knocked him down, clamping her teeth on his neck and biting just hard enough to break the skin. He surrendered right away and she let go, facing him with burning eyes.

"You, and Trip Over Foot, take the spy-thing and bring it." Her voice left no rom for questions and the two bent and, using sticks as a crude litter so they would not have to touch it, they picked up the heavy body and followed Speaker, Tuft Tail and the rest of the younglings.

Stream Diver's and Trip Over Foot's backs were hunched and a continuous wavering rumble hung over them, but they obeyed. Speaker was pleased. It was a good sign. She would need her strength and determination for the next problem he was going to drop on her.

He held that thought as the sun climbed high and he sat on Speaker Rock looking over the gathered Tribe. The younglings were arranged in a semi-circle at the base of his platform, reclining in a neat row of lithe and powerful bodies. Tuft Tail was in the middle, a little in front of the rest. In front of her rested the gleaming shape of the dead spy-thing. Luckily the wind was from the direction of the audience and they only caught a mild trace of the sour smell of the spy-thing.

"It is time!" Speaker roared down to override the low grumbling of the gathered Tribe. Slowly, they fell silent and he was able to speak more normally.

"Tuft Tail and her youngling patrol has killed one of the sky-creatures' spy-things. That gives us a reason for contact. They keep spying on us here, so we will leave this where they see it, as a warning, and a sign to show them what will happen if they keep spying on us." He had decided to declaw those who wanted to attack by making his peace gesture seem partly a show of strength. But one burr remained and he hoped that he had been right in guessing what would happen next as he said:

"But I will give Tuft Tail the honor of showing you."

He jumped down and let the nervous Tuft Tail take his place to show the Tribe the battered spy-thing. While she told them how her patrol had captured it—improving the facts slightly, Speaker noticed with a yawn of amusement—as she used a stick to lift the shiny body and swing it around so all could see.

Meanwhile, Speaker waited for the anticipated reaction. And he had been right. Crooked Tooth rose up right on cue and interrupted Tuft Tail in the middle of her demonstration.

"What gives you the right to take younglings and give them warrior responsibilities and recognition? And how can you let a 'cub' speak from Speaker Rock?"

Speaker yawned in delight. So predictable! He jumped up next to Tuft Tail as she slipped back down gratefully to join the other younglings. "I do that because she has shown herself to be worthy of it." He would not have to push much more, he sensed. "She has proven herself a better planner and fighter than many so-called warriors."

A wave of growls rolled out across the Field as many of the Tribe took offense, especially the older warriors who favored Crooked Tooth. And the older singling did just what Speaker had hoped: he stepped out onto the packed dirt of the Field and approached Tuft Tail. She just lay there, apparently oblivious to the insult and improper Challenge until Crooked Tooth moved closer. Then she exploded off the ground and slammed head-first into him. Her jaw flashed once, twice, three times before she rolled free and crouched in front of him, fur erect and tail lashing rapidly back and forth.

Crooked Tooth lay on the ground, dazed. Each fore-leg bore a line of red where sharp fangs had bitten deep and a trickle of red snaked its way down his chest from a long straight slash just a claw's width from the neck artery.

"A little to the side on the throat and a little deeper on the legs, and you would be paralyzed and bleeding to death…a long slow death," Tuft Tail warned. "Now, who is not a warrior?"

The sound of a single bird in the forest shattered the total silence that had followed her blinding attack. Every warrior was staring at the bleeding figure only now gathering itself shakily to rise and limp off the Field and disappear into the woods.

Tuft Tail faced the rest of the Tribe proudly. "He is alive because too many die when there is no need. In honor challenges and in the Testing. We have to stop killing each other. There are less of us each season and we have to think about the future, not just today. That is the lesson I have learned from Speaker."

Then she turned towards him and flopped in surrender before crawling back to her former position in the row of younglings. Only the twitching tail betrayed her excitement.

Speaker rose. "As she said, Tuft Tail spared Crooked Tooth because we can no longer afford to waste warriors in ridiculous challenges that leave many of the losers dead or incapacitated. The singling challenges will remain to test the youngling's right to be a full warrior, but they will always be to first blood, not until the loser is unable to fight anymore. That is now law."

He glared out at the Tribe, defying anyone to challenge him. No one did, bu a low rumbling growl hung over the Tribe and several warriors rose and disappeared into the woods, following after Crooked Tooth.

Speaker ignored them. "Tuft Tail is now a full warrior, that is proven in full assembly. Crooked Tooth had no right to Challenge but he did and so she chose the warrior's way and defended herself. And you all saw Crooked Tooth flee the Field in surrender." Again, several warriors rose and headed into the woods as they realized how Speaker had tricked them. But the bulk of the Tribe remained.

"Finally, from now on, the younglings will join the hunting parties." With that, he jumped off Speaker Rock as the Tribe dispersed. He called the younglings to join him while Tuft Tail waited.

"When you go along for the hunt, pick those who go furthest. I want you to look for signs of others like us. Not our wild cousins but others like us who think. If there are any, we must join forces. Just remember where they are, for now. I can't force too much change on the Tribe too quickly or I will be Challenged. I already made a few enemies today. Several of Crooked Tooth's strongest supporters left the field and they may make trouble. Now leave us alone for a while!"

They scattered as he turned to Tuft Tail and settled next to her to groom her. There was not a scratch on her. He turned so she could groom him back as he wondered how the sky-creatures were going to react, and if maybe he should bring the spy-thing to the bubble caves instead.

For a while he lounged, the strong strokes of Tuft Tail's tongue comforting him. After a while he twisted to chew her ear briefly. She growled softly and batted at him with shielded claws as he rolled to the side and got up to stretch.

"They will come here," he decided. "I'm leaving their spy-thing on Speaker Rock in plain view. The spy-things are always flying around here and they should see it. We will leave a freshly killed runner, too. The sky-creature I saw before seemed to think that giving one was important."

Tuft Tail jumped up on Speaker Rock and let out a loud demanding roar to summon her youngling patrol.

CHAPTER 17

▼

SENTENCING

"You…" The slap that followed Serena's strangled word echoed through the room and Jim stared at her.

He had never seen her furious like this, not in all the time they had been married. They were still on the administration tower's control floor, but the sultry and then concerned woman he had shared a seat with was gone, replaced by an enraged figure that towered over the cowering Tara Richman. The imprint of Serena's hand was livid on the representative's face. He smiled as he remembered Julie slapping Sayer the same way. He was glad he had not been on the receiving end of either blow. Both ladies were formidable when aroused.

Then Serena's slender arm drew back again as she turned towards Major Mandel, but it was captured by Star's gleaming hand.

"No, Serena, that does not solve anything." He drew her gently away from the marine. "Representative Richman did not plan to hurt me. And neither did the major."

"But you could have been killed." Serena was close to crying.

Star stood rocking back and forth a second and then reached out to embrace her, his arms gently holding her as silver hands stroked. "This makes me 'feel' better. Does it do the same for you?"

Mandel stared in disbelief at the bizarre spectacle of the gleaming metal figure trying to console the slender programmer. The rest of his people were all being held in an improvised detention area until Jim could decide what to do with them.

"I am unharmed," Star reassured her, "and physically abusing Representative Richman will not accomplish anything. Do not be upset, please. You would eventually have rescued us if we had not

226

called, since you were tracking any attempt to log on using our passwords. There never was any real danger."

Serena looked down at Star fondly as she extricated herself. "Thank you, dear. I'm sorry. You're right, of course. I just crashed for a second because I was so angry about what they did!"

Jim could understand her feelings. The last of the explosives on Star's cooling tubes had been removed, but Mandel's men had been very precise. If even a few of the charges would have gone off, Star would have cycled into a very rapid melt-down. He had a very hard time mustering any compassion for Richman, and now, as Colony Director, he would have to set an example.

He got up and took Serena's hand, leading her over to sit down by the window. He blew her a kiss with his back to the others, and then turned back towards Richman and concentrated on keeping calm.

"Ms. Richman, your actions not only violated the civil laws of this colony, but they went against the colony's fundamental principles. Since we're still in the formative stages, we're not a total democracy yet, but are still under one authority: mine. I could remand this to a colony vote, but I am not going take the risk that you can play some political game to escape punishment. Consequently, I'm exercising my authority as Colony Director to sentence you."

He felt everyones' attention lock on him, and from Tara's blanched expression, he knew his face had to be grim.

"First of all," he began. "In addition to being removed from office, you will be re-frozen. Your revival is moved back to the last shipment, which isn't scheduled for another seven years. I figure that by that time, any political machinery that you may have in place will be gone and everyone will hopefully be comfortable with the idea of sharing StarStep with the Cougars by then."

Richman started to protest but stopped herself as she saw he wasn't kidding. She also realized he had the authority to do worse. Much worse.

With her case settled, he turned to Mandel.

"As for you and your team, I can't blame you entirely because of the slanted view of the Cougars that Representative Richman gave you. You honestly believed that you were acting on behalf of the colony. But you placed two of my top people in jeopardy and you risked the destruction of Star—and that I can't forgive."

"Can I make a suggestion?" Star cut in and Jim nodded. "You are refreezing former Representative Richman because of the risk of her continuing to make problems and as punishment of her conscious attempts to endanger the Cougars, correct?"

"Yes."

"And to set an example, you feel a need to punish Mandel and his people, but you do not wish to be too harsh. Is that also correct?"

"Yes." Jim couldn't help smiling at Star's pedantic preciseness.

"In that case, would it not be useful to sentence the Major's people to unreimbursed labor assisting Julie, Ken and myself in our attempt to establish contact with the Cougars? This way they would also learn firsthand the importance of preserving such a unique find. It may also be beneficial to have human warriors with us when we contact the Cougars, all of whom are warriors. There might be certain common attitudes and ways of approaching a situation that can be taken advantage of. Major Mandel might also recognize any hostile moves we might otherwise miss. Not that I feel there will be any, based on my observations."

Jim stared at his metallic replica and after a moment, he nodded. "That makes sense. Let me mention it to Julie and see what she thinks. But I think she'll go for it. Frankly, I'd feel better if you three had someone else along. As strong as you are, violence just isn't your program, and neither is it Ken's."

He turned to Mandel. "How would you feel about that? You would be expected to be a combination bodyguard and general laborer. If I know Julie, she'll be going in on foot to avoid frightening the Cougars."

Mandel was actually smiling as he said: "Well, I can't speak for everyone, but personally I think it beats farming. I've been in the military all my life, and the thought of going civilian's been scaring me." He looked embarrassed. "I just can't see myself working in the fields." He paused for a moment, before asking:

"But what about the rest of my people? You won't need more than a few of us."

Jim decided: "After you pick a detail for the contact team, the rest will be sentenced to unreimbursed labor in preparing more housing. It's mainly a matter of clearing land and then unpacking and placing the residential nanokits, but I'd like to see some human decorating touches once they finish growing the homes and offices. And there's the land-clearing for the farms. It's more efficiently done with machinery, and there is plenty of that needed. So pick your people accordingly and assign them. Contact Susan Tsielkovsky, she'll fill you in on what's needed for the work teams. And I suggest that you talk to her husband, Dan. His brother was the first Cougar victim and he doesn't hold any grudges. He'll give you a good perspective on the whole situation. He was in the first batch to be revived after the administrative thawing."

"Thanks." Mandel looked distinctly embarrassed as he glanced at Richman and shook Jim's hand. "Believe me, I really didn't mean to hurt anyone. Our guns are all needlers with a safe knock-out charge." He included Serena in his apology with a subtle nod.

"Well, give your apologies to the people affected the most," Jim advised him.

"I will, as soon as I see them."

"You can start right now." Jim looked pointedly behind the major and Mandel seemed confused for a moment. Then his eyes widened and he nodded, turned to Star and faced eerily human-looking metal face uncertainly.

"Star, I'm sorry that I…that we endangered you."

Star's face was an immobile mask for a moment, and then it flexed and looked down as his feet curled in on each other and he swung his hands back and forth. "Aw shucks, that's all right." He looked up and gave Mandel a wide boyish grin. "You didn't know any better."

Mandel rocked back and stared in shock as Jim stifled a laugh and gave a thumbs-up to Serena.

"I think your son is back to normal, dear." Then he clapped Mandel on the shoulder. "Star has a habit of joking sometimes. Don't let it worry you. He's a bit more than any nanocomputer you ever ran across before. Even without the body. Believe me."

Serena got up and went over to Star. "Do you want to get back to normal and out of this body?"

Star straightened, once again dignified. There was an almost human animation to his face, though, as he cocked his head and looked at her for a moment and then shook his head.

"No, not yet. I believe this body will be more efficient in dealing with the Cougars. There will be time to give it up later. Or better yet, when I'm ready, simply leave me hooked into it and reactivate all my other sensor links. Being able to physically manipulate some aspects of my environment has distinct advantages. But for now, leave everything as is. I want to concentrate on one task at a time."

"Why?"

"For experience. I want to compare my efficiency on a single task while free from other input as opposed to my previous functioning."

"In other words, you realize that you still have things to learn about being human," Serena teased.

"Touché." He reached out in a natural move to take her hands to squeeze them softly.

Mother and son. Jim shook his head as he smiled fondly.

CHAPTER 18

▼

SECOND CONTACT

The seemingly fragile vegetation turned out to be a dense barrier that seemed insistent on blocking their every step, but none of it fazed the red-haired woman who was taking her turn as point, clearing a path. Julie had thought her too frail-looking at first, until she had looked closer and seen the finely sculpted muscles that rippled under Tammy Grimes' lightly freckled skin, and noticed the powerful strokes of her machete that rhythmically swept aside the undergrowth in their way.

Greg Mandel worked alongside her, his own blade cutting a wide path, while Mitchell 'Mick' Jones and Darrell 'The Professor' Washington flanked Julie and Ken. At first glance, the three men looked about as different as possible. Where the short and stocky Greg had a pale, almost albino cast, the slender Washington—who was on their right—was even darker in complexion than Ken, and he towered over the other two. His nick-name stemmed from a passion for cross-word puzzles and an appropriately encyclopedic knowledge of trivia. Between them in height, the seemingly bland-looking Jones who covered their left flank was unremarkable, except for his shiny, bald head. But on closer examination, his corded muscles bulged tightly as he pushed aside blocking branches.

That was what they all shared: an iron edge of strength and discipline that showed in every cat-like move.

Julie had a feeling that if the four marines were to be dropped into a homicidal mob of rioters, each would leave a trail of bodies behind them as they broke free. She felt absolutely safe as she and Ken followed them towards the Cougars' gathering place.

Star was nowhere to be seen.

Ken kept tugging on his clothes and brushing at his face with irritated strokes. But he didn't say a word, and Julie had to give him credit for not complaining. She reached over and looped her arm under his.

"A little different than the classroom or the laboratory, isn't it?"

"It's the damn insects that are driving me crazy. How do you stand it?" He leaned away suspiciously. "Did you hide a repeller in your pocket?"

"No, dear. That might scare the Cougars. Their hearing is a lot better than ours. And a chemical barrier spray is out because, from what Star tells me, we already smell absolutely horrible and I don't want to make it worse."

"Humph. Well, it's still not fair. You're used to this. The closest I've ever been to nature in the last century is visiting the zoo in Luna City. And it's clean."

"Yuck!" She wrinkled her nose. "Sterile is more like it. I've seen video. Even the soil looks like it's been through a washing machine! No, this is real. Even if it's the first temperate climate jungle I've ever been in."

She suddenly stopped and turned to him to grab his arm. "I feel alive, darling. This," she swept a hand around, "is real!" She felt a dizzying rush as she breathed in the heady mixture of scents from the forest around them.

A hollow moan from above suddenly broke through the constant chattering and sighing that surrounded them. Then they heard a heavy flapping and Ken looked around tensely, trying to place the sound's origin.

Julie smiled. "An owl, honey. They grow big here…a bird. They're nocturnal predators, but harmless to us."

"Okay, honey." He grabbed her chin and bent down to kiss her. "I know what an owl is." He grinned. "But I'll admit it: I'm a real baby out here."

"But you're here with me. Thank you." She leaned close to him, relishing the feel of his hard body against her.

For a second they just stood there, staring at each other until a soft cough intruded and Julie felt herself blushing as she realized Greg was standing there. Tammy was next to him, smiling faintly.

"I'm sorry, doctor. But we just broke through." Greg pointed to a break in the greenery that looked out on a wide grassy field that looked familiar.

"The place of Gathering, and the Field of Challenge." Julie let go of Ken and moved to look out over the grass in front of the packed earth field. "Actually, now it's called the Field of Testing."

Her face was still burning as she passed the marines, but Tammy reached out to touch her.

"Don't worry," she said softly. "It's something else that's real, and to be enjoyed. We've discovered a little about that ourselves since we were revived." She reached out to grab Mandel's hand possessively. "I may even make a farmer out of him." She grinned. "I'm tired of soldiering, and you've got a beautiful world here!"

The major looked both uncomfortable and happy, and Julie relaxed.

"Thanks," she said, and then turned back to look out towards 'Speaker Rock', as Speaker had called the large boulder that rested in the middle of the bare arena.

Reflected light glinted off the battered monitor that lay upside down on top of the boulder. She could just make out the dark form that was lying next to it and smiled and waved the others over.

"There, see the gleam? That's the monitor they managed to catch and wreck. They've laid it out as an offering. And see the dark form next to it? That's one of the local deer. A runner, as they call them. That's got to be Speaker's doing. He remembers our first meeting."

Ken joined them and looked over her shoulder curiously. "He's an unusual cat. We're lucky he is Speaker." He turned to Mandel. "Most of the Cougars are very rooted in the present and speak only rarely. And when they do, it's mainly about challenges, breeding or hunting. Abstracts are difficult for them to understand." He looked out over the field thoughtfully as he went on:

"Star was having trouble following all of their conversation, even after almost a year of studying the Cougars, because there was little to compare it with. But with Speaker, now that he's mated with Tuft Tail, it's different. They *talk* about a lot of things, including abstracts. Luckily, the language structure is simple. Simple words are made into long compound words to describe more complex ideas. Sometimes the meanings have to be guessed at. Julie and Star had to decipher possible meanings for concepts like "warrior's responsibilities" which was...'Warrior-raising-cubs-teaching-hunting', wasn't it, dear?" He glanced over at Julie, who nodded happily.

She was amazed by how quickly Ken had embraced his new interest and by how much he had learned. "And as usual," she added, "context and even intonation determines a lot of the meanings for words that are otherwise identical. But I'll tell you right now: while I can understand a little Cougar, my throat was definitely not meant to speak it. Fortunately, Star shouldn't have any trouble." She looked around. "Speaking of which..."

Suddenly a tall gleaming form materialized silently beside them.

"There you are!" she said, relieved. She had not realized he had disappeared on them, he moved so quietly. "Let's get to work. The monitor and deer are obviously a signal, and I don't want to ignore it. There are a lot of things to talk about."

"Yes, there are, and we are being watched," Star warned them. Mandel and his people instantly deployed around Julie and Jim, scanning around as Star smiled. "You won't see them. Three Cougars have been following us for the past four kilometers."

Julie stared at him. "I thought you were disconnected from the monitors and sensors."

"I am, but I have even more acute senses than the Cougars. I can see into the infra-red with considerable resolution and magnification, and my hearing is far superior. I have also attempted to neutralize my scent as much as possible with a combination of chemical neutralizers and various natural aromatic substances."

Tammy had been wrinkling her nose and she grimaced. "Uff, yes, but do us a favor and stay downwind."

The wind shifted slightly and Julie realized what the young marine meant. "A cat-box is a cat-box is a cat-box." She giggled, and when she saw the confusion on the other faces she laughed even harder. But when she saw the worried look on Ken's face she sobered.

"I'm fine, honey. Litter boxes are a little more efficient now, but when I was growing up, this was a real familiar smell. My grandmother had three cats and sometimes she forgot to clean the box every day."

She turned to Star. "Do you know which ones are checking us out?"

"Stream Diver for sure," Star answered immediately. "I saw him. The other two were never addressed by name and I could not get close enough to see them clearly."

Julie realized Washington and Jones had joined Greg, and all three were scanning around with weapons ready.

She reached out and touched Greg lightly on the shoulder. "At ease."

He spun with his weapon ready, and then put his needler down immediately. "Sorry."

"It's okay, but relax. They know we're here, and we were invited. I think we can just go out there and see what's happening."

"Hell, we could have flown in," Jones grumbled.

"No, we don't want to overwhelm them." Julie shook her head briskly. "This is an extremely primitive race we're dealing with. And alien in a way. By coming in like this we're less threatening and they can meet us more as equals."

"Hey, Mick, look at the exercise we got," Washington prodded Jones with the butt of his rifle. "Beats plowing farm land under, doesn't it?"

Jones just flipped his hand like he was swatting a bug and turned away, his eyes scanning the woods.

Julie stepped past Greg and out into the open. She breathed deep of a new, fresh fragrance that wafted over her as she waded through the thin, high grass on the field, enjoying the openness around her.

"Come on!" She turned and waved to the others who followed her out after a moment one by one. Star was last. As he stepped onto the field, the sun caught him and for a second, he almost glowed. Then she looked back at Speaker Rock, hoping to spot Speaker or Tuft Tail. But the Field of Challenge was empty and there was not a single Cougar in sight.

"There are one or two more hiding in the grass," Star whispered and she looked around, but saw nothing but an empty field. *Well, Star ought to know,* she decided. But she wasn't going to worry about it. It was what she had expected.

As Ken joined her, he examined the roughly built half-circle wall of rock behind Speaker Rock curiously. It seemed crude at first, but Julie noticed that it had been carefully cemented with mud and clay.

"Look at this, Julie." Ken stood straight against it and she saw how it curved in slightly at the top over him. "Somebody knows a little amateur acoustics. Speaker Rock is not in the middle of this field, but closer to this wall. Someone sitting on it and calling out would get reinforcement from this wall. Not much, but it's high enough and shaped in such a way that it will help a little."

He looked up at the top of it that was a good meter over his head and then glanced at Julie. "They have to be pretty good jumpers. Remember the one recording that show the younglings sitting on top of this wall?"

"Well, the planet only has a third normal gravity."

"Yes, but they grew up here. It's normal G for them."

"Speaking of which, I wish they'd show themselves." Julie felt a little frustrated. "I have the feeling Speaker called us here, what with the wrecked monitor and the deer laid out for us, but where is he? And why…" She stopped herself, feeling stupid and waved Ken over, realizing what she needed to do.

"Help me up here." She stepped up to the side of Speaker Rock and with a boost from Ken was soon standing on top of it.

She looked out over the sea of waving grasses and tried to spot…anyone, watching. Nothing. The large field appeared empty. Still, she somehow sensed a myriad of invisible eyes were watching her, judging her. She felt incredibly self-conscious as she bent and lifted the monitor up to hold it over her head for a moment before passing it down to Ken. Then she braced herself for the next step.

The deer was an offering. All at once, she was flooded with the memory of being offered fresh blood from one of the Masai cows and how she had been expected to accept it. This was just like that. The Cougars were also of a different culture. They were a new society just getting organized, and the way she behaved was critical in determining how they would interact with the human colonists—colonists who to the Cougars were invaders to their world.

She looked down at the others. "Back off and leave me alone here."

As the others withdrew, she swallowed the bitter bile backing up in her throat and bent to chew lightly on the neck of the dead deer, trying not sneeze as the fine secondary fur tickled her nose. The downy strands felt like cotton in her mouth; cotton with a rancid after-taste. She fought a surge of nausea and hoped the Cougars were indeed watching. She would hate to go through this again. She also hoped that Dr. Gratch had been right in promising that the nanoimmuners she had in her system would handle any infection.

She heard a sharp intake of breath from the others and looked up to see a single lithe figure materialize out of the dense grass. It was Speaker! His powerful muscles and the scratches from his mating with Tuft Tail were unmistakable. He had been there all along; motionless and concealed in a hollow. Then Tuft Tail appeared. She was the same size as Speaker, and somehow seemed feminine, even if she was every bit as muscular as her mate. It was something about the structure and carriage of her neck and head, Julie thought. And the shape of her face. She stood slightly back from Speaker and her ears were flat and aimed back, but she was there.

Speaker seemed torn between approaching and running.

Julie spoke softly. "Everyone keep back, and stay absolutely still. Star, do you see anyone else?"

His voice suddenly came softly from the computer on her belt. "Yes. Stream Diver, Trip Over Foot and Fog Eyes just came out of the woods where we were, and there are a number of other Cougars also hidden among the trees now. They do not seem to be in a hurry to approach, though."

Julie looked down at her belt. "How can you be there? I thought you were locked into your body until Serena releases you."

"I am, but I am using my communicator."

She felt her ears burning. "Of course."

"I felt this would be better because I did not want to risk frightening Speaker or Tuft Tail, so I thought addressing you this way would be less confusing or threatening. Speaker has heard my voice before, and I was on your belt then, too, remember?"

"That's right. Okay, good. Now shut up for a while." She looked back up at the twin feline figures confronting her only thirty or so meters away. Tuft Tail had crouched at the sound of Star's voice, and Speaker had stepped forward, his head cocked as if he was listening. But he didn't move any closer.

Julie looked down at the carcass under her again and swallowed. The slashed and torn neck was only a foot from her face and a couple of enormous flies were buzzing around the jagged, oozing wound where Speaker had broken the mutated deer's neck. He was waiting, she realized. She would have to do it—*really* accept the gift, not just pretend to.

She swallowed again, praying she wouldn't vomit. She leaned forward and clamped her teeth around a flap of bloody flesh and bit off a small piece with a loud growl, chewing visibly and smearing her jaw around in the wound before she looked up at Speaker and Tuft Tail. She heard a retching sound off to the right and saw Tammy trying to keep control. The marine's face was white.

"I'm okay," Tammy called softly. "Sorry." She was back in control and motionless again. Ken and the others also looked a bit pale, and Julie fought to keep her own stomach in line as the rank taste flooded her mouth.

She sidled forward, approaching the edge of the boulder as she called over softly:

"When I tell you to, all of you drop to the ground, roll onto your backs and throw back your arms and heads to expose your necks and stomachs, then get in a sitting position and keep still again. Star, when I speak to the Cougars, I want you to translate as accurately as possible, speaking through my terminal. I'm going to introduce you, and then bring you forward."

She slid down the front of the boulder carefully, seeing Tuft Tail rise to her feet and growl. Speaker spun and snarled at her, biting her lightly on the shoulder and cuffing her.

"In case you are interested, he basically told her to shut up and sit down," Star relayed softly from her waist.

Julie signaled the others to drop and subordinate themselves and then she slowly approached the Cougars. She stopped as she got close to the edge of the packed dirt of the Field of Challenge. Then she backed up a few steps and glanced down at her terminal.

"Star, tell him that I want to meet as Speaker to Speaker, here on the field, but *not* in challenge—and stress the 'not', please!"

As a series of guttural growls and roars erupted from her terminal, she backed up until she was standing just in front of Speaker Rock. There, she turned, stretched up to get the carcass still resting on top, and dragged it down. Then she dropped to kneel on the ground next to it.

Speaker stood up and stepped forward, hesitating at the edge of the grass. Star spoke to him again, and he stepped onto the dirt and approached. His nose was twitching and his muzzle curled. Because she smelled bad to him, Julie knew. She also realized that he was big; as tall as she was if he were to stand. But for all his muscles, he was fragile-looking. On Earth he would probably have been unable to walk, even on all four legs.

As the wind shifted, she was suddenly aware of a musky, spicy scent and was reminded of Bigfoot, the polydactyl Calico she had adopted to add to her menagerie. She had been Julie's favorite. She realized why when she looked closer at Speaker's mitten-like hands. They looked almost like Bigfoot's paws, but with longer, slender toes and an opposing digit. They must have been awkward as far as hands go, but they obviously gave enough control to allow tool-building.

Oblivious to her inspection, Speaker continued approaching.

When he was about three meters away, he dropped into a crouch and sat expectantly, his eyes fixed on her. Julie reached over and pulled at the deer, shoving it in front of her to lie between them. She got up on her knees and moved slowly forward to chew again on a bloody flap of flesh, too excited to be nauseous now. Then she settled back and pushed the body a little towards Speaker.

The sun overhead suddenly seemed to be baking hot and the sound of the flies grew to a roar as Speaker leaned forward hesitantly, his sharp teeth gleaming wetly. Then he dug in to tear loose a great chunk of flesh to gnaw on, a low satisfied rumble coming from the back of his throat. In the distance, Julie saw Tuft-Tail straining forward and she looked down at her computer again.

"Star, ask Speaker to have Tuft Tail join us. And tell him I want to bring someone forward, too."

More noises from her belt. Speaker froze, hunched over the torn body and growling for a moment. The fur on his tail and shoulders rose as his ears flattened. Then as Star growled again, he straightened and turned to yowl imperatively at Tuft Tail who bounded onto the field without a moment's hesitation. But she slowed and drooped slightly as she moved in on the body, ripping loose a smaller chunk than the chokingly big piece Speaker had torn free, and then backing off a little.

"Okay, Star. Move in, slowly, crouching." Julie was nervous, hoping he wouldn't spook her visitors. But they barely looked up as he moved slowly into view, sidling up to sit cross-legged next to her as the Cougars fed.

"It is a little too early to expect table manners, I expect," Star whispered and Julie stifled a giggle. She reached out to squeeze his hand.

"Thanks, dear. I needed that. I was about to throw up."

Tuft Tail stopped eating momentarily and growled to Speaker who had been eyeing Star surreptitiously.

Star leaned over to Julie. "That is a smart Cougar. She knows I was keeping an eye on them, and she knows I smeared some urine and feces on me to disguise my smell.

Julie eyed Tuft Tail with new respect. She remembered also another cougar conversation Star had translated some time earlier. "Speaker may not have studied Mendel or Darwin," he had observed, "but he's a good rule of thumb geneticist, too. His epidemiological model of the increase of intelligence is off base, but he's right: they are getting smarter. Partly through interbreeding, and also since they're not allowed to take mates until they've proven themselves in battle, and the smartest do tend to win, and thus breed. I wouldn't be surprised if we'll find that all the younglings are smarter than the older Cougars. This is going to be really interesting the next few years."

Both of the Cougars stopped eating suddenly and Speaker rose up, followed by Tuft Tail, both of them suddenly towering over Julie and Star.

"Don't move!" Julie hissed to Greg and the others who were suddenly alert and grabbing for their weapons.

CHAPTER 19

▼

SPEAKING TERMS

The stench was overwhelming, but Speaker fought it and concentrated on the fresh runner. The sky-creature was strange. It had hardly touched the delicious feast, but next to him, Tuft Tail was eating happily, unconcerned about it. For some reason—after her initial aversion—she did not have as much trouble with their smell as he did.

The strange sky-creature that joined them after Tuft Tail had come up to eat also puzzled him. It was alive since it moved and looked just like the other one, but it did not wear any artificial skin. It also smelled different: a little like the spy-thing, just not as bad. But it smelled dirty, like a sick warrior who has not been keeping clean.

Tuft Tail stopped eating and glanced over. "That's the one who was spying on us. I think it found a marking spot and tried to disguise its sky-creature smell."

"It was spying on us? I didn't see."

"It is very good," Tuft Tail conceded. "We almost did not see it either. Stream Diver told me."

Speaker looked at the strange sky-creature with new respect.

"They may be more intelligent than we thought," he admitted. "Not just good with their hands. It is time to talk." He stood erect, Tuft Tail rising also. But he was confused. He did not know who to talk to. The black-furred sky-creature spoke a high-pitched nonsense, and the bad-smelling one was understandable, but Black Fur was obviously Speaker. Bad Smell's speech was strange. It...he—Speaker decided arbitrarily—copied Speaker's and Tuft Tail's voices all mixed up, and even used some others, but at least he was understandable. Still, should he talk to Black Fur and let it determine what to say? Let *her*, he decided, it seemed female somehow because under the false skin on her upper belly were swellings; maybe for cubs to suckle? When she lay down, they hung where cubs could reach.

He made up his mind. He would talk to Black Fur. Maybe Bad Smell was just a translator. He turned to her to say:

"Come off the Field of Testing, to the grass. This is a place of confrontation."

Black Fur looked at Bad Smell who translated in the same strange voice she used, only deeper. She squeaked back, and Bad Smell answered Speaker. "We will go, you lead, we follow."

Speaker turned, glancing at Tuft Tail as they stepped back into the high grasses. He could see she felt the same way he did. It had been a test that the sky-creatures had failed; they were not good strategists. A good warrior never surrendered choice of territory when in a position of strength. But he led the way to a low rise a little away from the Field where the grass was thinner, and the view was clear, all around.

A chorus of high pitched snarls echoed behind them and he turned to see a pack of kill-cleaners fighting over the remains of the runner, having materialized out of nowhere. Black Fur's other warriors were standing back by Speaker Rock and watching when a large kill-cleaner broke away from the bloody remains and charged towards them. The taller of the two dark-skinned sky-creatures pulled a small shiny rock from its belt and pointed it at the charging kill-cleaner. There was a short hissing sound like a no-leg-rock-sunner and the kill-cleaner collapsed with a scream, wiggled for a moment squealing softly, and then went limp and stopped struggling.

Speaker and Tuft Tail stared, first at the sky-creature standing over the kill-cleaner, and then at Black Fur and Bad Smell. Did they also have the same metal rocks? That was something new. And dangerous!

CHAPTER 20

▼

JOINING THE PARTY

"Jim, honey, slow down!" Serena grabbed his shirt and tugged from behind. "You big Grounder! Give me a chance and stop showing off. I may have been rebuilt a bit, but this is still a lot more gravity than I'm used to."

"Chill, I'm sorry!" He stopped and turned. "You've reworked yourself so well, I keep forgetting." Then he grinned. "You got me interested in the old 2-D films, so here's one for you." He grabbed her and slung her kicking and giggling body over his shoulder. "Me Tarzan, you Jane! Ugh, or something like that. I would do the yodel, or whatever it was, too, except I think I'd scare away every Cougar between here and the equator."

Then he broke into a easy jog, following the hacked path that Mandel and his people had cleared. The four soldiers he had brought were left behind, staring after them in confusion until they recovered and came running after to catch up.

Sergeant Ruiz, the patrol leader, glared at him as he caught up, puffing faintly. The thin air took a little getting used to, even here at only a few hundred meters above sea-level.

"Sir, we're supposed to protect you. That's a little difficult if you call attention to yourself and run away from—"

"Oh come on!" Serena was at some disadvantage, hanging upside down, but Jim had to give her credit. She still managed to keep an air of dignity as she cut Diaz off:

"We're not at war with the Cougars. We're trying to make friends. Chill, they invited us to a meeting. Besides, I'm sure they would know perfectly well that we were coming even if we snuck in.

This is their territory and their senses are so much better that they can spot us long before we know they're around."

"And let this be a hint," she shifted to get comfortable, "we're a little less formal than the military here, so relax!" Then she reached down to slap Jim on his rear. "Mush! Let's go. I don't want Julie and Ken to have all the fun."

Jim mushed. They soon reached the break in the greenery that Mandel and his people had chopped and he put Serena down. Together they looked out over the field just in time to see Washington stun the charging wolf that had been distracted by Mandel's soldiers. Here on StarStep, wolves had for some reason become scavengers rather than predators. Jim thought it might be because the intelligent Cougars had been prolific and more efficient hunters than expected.

Serena reached for her computer, but Jim stopped her. "No, not now, she's busy. Let's circle around and join Mandel."

He waved to Ruiz and they skirted the field carefully, keeping just inside the trees. They had probably been spotted, but nobody interfered.

As they made their way, they caught glimpses of a strange Cougar who came out of the woods on the opposite side of the grass field where Julie and Star were talking to Speaker and Tuft Tail. The new Cougar settled down next to Speaker and seemed to start fighting about something. At least that's what it sounded like from the sounds that drifted over to them. Then Jim lost sight of the group on the field as they crossed behind the boulder wall on the Field of Testing.

Ken saw them as they came out from behind the tall rock wall and called out to them.

"Serena, Jim. What the chill are you doing here?"

"Curiosity." Jim shook a thumb at the unconscious wolf on the ground. "I saw Washington shoot it. What happened? And who's the stranger?" He pointed to the newcomer arguing with Speaker.

Mandel had heard them and came up, giving Ruiz a curt nod. "Dr. Andrews, Mr. Martin. I'm not so sure you should have come. Things are a bit tight right now." He pointed to the wolf. "It smelled us and got confused, I think. The cats weren't happy when they saw what the needler did. They probably think we killed it, but fortunately they didn't go anywhere."

"Julie and Star did some fast talking to calm them down," Ken explained, "so things were okay, until that new cat showed up. It's Crooked Tooth, and he and Speaker didn't exactly part on the best of terms."

Ruiz grabbed Mandel's arm. "What's going on?"

The major frowned. "We've been scanning the woods with I.R. sensors and there are cats everywhere! I'm surprised you didn't trip over them coming over here. They're spread through the woods ahead of us and flanking on either side, and behind us is a canyon which dead ends and doesn't give any cover. We're pinned down!"

"Any I.D.'s?" Ruiz asked nervously.

"No," Ken answered. "Star might be able to tell, but he's busy. Speaker's not happy about Crooked Tooth showing up, and they're having a nice little fight from what I can tell. Of course, it's tough to be sure. They always sound like that when they're talking. Hell, even when they're having sex, it sounds like a major war!."

"Does Julie know about the new cats around us?" Serena wondered.

"I don't know." Ken shrugged. "I imagine Star spotted them, since he sees into infrared. I was just going to call to make sure when you came. I didn't want to bother her before. Things got a little tense when the needler was fired."

"Let me." Jim grabbed his computer and raised it to call her, but as he did, it was as if he had triggered an explosion of activity. Crooked Tooth stood up and let loose a wavering and penetrating snarl that echoed over the field and then took off towards them, continuing to snarl.

Jim heard a disbelieving curse from one of the soldiers. "Chill, I took my eyes off the monitor just for a minute and suddenly they're all over the place!"

The voice was cut off by a scream and he and Ken were shoved to the ground by Mandel and Ruiz who were pulling out needlers.

"The cats, they're attacking," Mandel shouted.

Over the Major's shoulder Jim caught a glimpse of tawny figures exploding out of the trees on either side of them.

All at once, there were cats everywhere, and he heard needlers go off and angry spitting yowls as a whole bunch of Cougars were suddenly weaving and slashing among the Marines. Then he stared as a new group of Cougars was joining the fight, coming up from downfield, but they were taking on the attacking cats! Speaker's supporters?

Mandel almost shot one and Tammy did, before she realized the stranger was attacking the Cougar that had been ready to pounce on her. Jim heard her yell out. "Careful, some of them are helping us!"

Out of the corner of his eye he saw Serena's confused face for a brief second, confronting a snarling feline figure—Crooked Tooth—who jumped on her with flashing claws and teeth, releasing a spray of red and a scream of agony from her. Then he straightened and howled in animal agony as the loud buzz of an illegally modified rock cutter ripped through the air.

The smell of burning fur stung Jim's nose and he tried to get up to go to Serena when a solid weight smashed into him and he almost blacked out.

CHAPTER 21

▼

ATTACK

"Shit!" Julie didn't blame Washington for shooting the wolf since it had attacked him, but the spitting hisses from both Speaker and Tuft Tail as they backed away and hunched worried her.

"Star," she hissed. "Quick, tell them the needlers are harmless and only put things to sleep and that he was just defending himself."

Star let out a spitting, growling chorus and was verbally assaulted in return by both of the Cougars. For a couple of minutes, the exchange went on heatedly, but then Julie saw the Cougars relax and look intently at each other, growling softly.

"They are talking about the fact that they under-estimated us," Star explained. "They thought we were extremely stupid for exposing ourselves, but now they have decided we are smarter than they thought. And stronger. We are slowly gaining respect."

Julie chuckled as she realized that they had been considered the primitive ones. But it made sense. Proper strategy and strength: those were the paths to winning respect and demonstrating intelligence for the Cougars.

Speaker started to say something as he dropped to lie flat, only his head held high. But then he froze, sniffing the air.

"Another Cougar is coming," Star warned. "A large part of the tribe has been watching us from down at the end of the field, but now there are suddenly a number of new Cougars on either side of us." He scanned the woods around the meadow and snarled sharply to Speaker.

Speaker rose tensely, scanned the woods and then growled back.

Star looked puzzled. "The ones who were there before are Speaker's people, though he is surprised I could see them, but as for the rest, he had assumed they were just the other members of the tribe coming to look. Now he is not sure, because he recognizes the newcomer; and so do I. It is Crooked Tooth."

Julie stared. "I thought we'd seen the last of him."

"Obviously he did not appreciate being defeated by Tuft Tail."

"And there were a number of others who weren't too thrilled, either," Julie remembered. "Want to bet they're the ones who just joined the party?" She looked around nervously. She couldn't see anything but trees and bushes. "What's happening?"

"I do not know."

Crooked Tooth crouched a few meters away and proceeded to give a virtual speech. Star leaned close to Julie and proceeded to interpret for her...

"...watched you risk the Tribe by surrendering us to the sky-creatures. You have one chance only. Withdraw from here now and we will return to face in honorable Challenge later when the Field is cleansed." He rose and approached Speaker menacingly on all four. "You may win back the right to rule. Or stay here and die with these creatures. I have enough warriors with me that even with their weapons, we can defeat these creatures and reclaim our territo—"

"No, you Cub!" Speaker snarled, echoed by Tuft Tail. "These are only a few of them. If they die, others will come, and with bigger weapons. They are not cubs, but warriors, too. Warriors with better weapons. Do you forget the flying things that carried them down from the sky? With those they can hang over us and destroy us where we can't reach them. We must make peace! Let them continue to respect and even fear us a little. And they do," he pointed out. "But if they get angry, they will forget that little fear and destroy us!"

Speaker had risen to his feet and faced Crooked Tooth on his own level. They were almost nose to nose but the force of Speaker's anger was clear even to Julie and she saw the older male actually back slightly, his legs starting to bend and neck to twist. But then he growled back and rose up on his hind legs to yowl loudly.

"Then die with them!" He dropped to all four feet again and took off towards Speaker Rock, Ken, and the waiting marines, snarling: "Attack!"

From either side of the Field of Testing a cream and chocolate wave erupted from the green cloaking vegetation, including six brawny warriors who moved aside to let Crooked Tooth pass, and then rushed full speed at Julie and Star.

Tuft Tail and Speaker stood shoulder to shoulder, pulling crudely chipped stone daggers from their belts as they placed themselves to block the oncoming cats.

"Coward!" Speaker spat after Crooked Tooth as the older male drew away. Then Star stopped interpreting and stepped out from behind Speaker and Tuft Tail to head directly for the onrushing Cougars. He was snarling and growling even louder than they were.

Julie started to call out and then stopped herself, feeling embarrassed. Star was made of metal and weighed close to 350 kilos. Six flesh and blood low-gravity Cougars wouldn't faze him.

And they didn't.

As the warriors reached him, Star was swallowed up by a wave of snarling fur that soon went flying off in different directions. The shocked and cast-off Cougars regrouped and tried attacking Star again but once again were gently, but firmly dislodged and literally thrown some distance away, back towards the woods on either side.

This time they took the hint and slunk away, disappearing among the trees.

Star turned and came back towards Julie who had been trapped in between Speaker and Tuft Tail without being aware of it. The two Cougars had taken up protective stances on either side of her and she felt their silky fur gripped tight in her fingers. Their warm, comforting bodies were pressed close and she felt utterly safe. A strange, yet vaguely familiar, musky scent hung around her.

Both were staring at Star as he approached and grinned widely. He pretended to brush off his hands as he drawled.

"Well, gee whiz, I sure hope ah didn't hurt them poor fellas too much. I do believe a couple of them broke a few teeth." He inspected his gleaming skin. "But not a scratch on me. That's quality workmanship for you."

He growled reassuringly to Speaker and Tuft Tail who left Julie and approached him, rising up gracefully on their hind legs as they inspected him. They reached out tentatively to touch him, ears alternately flattening and perking up as curiosity and fear fought it out.

Then Julie heard a familiar voice scream out.

"Julie! Star! Over here! Move it! Serena's hurt."

Star spun and flew towards Ken, followed by twin furred lightning bolts, while Julie went after them as fast as she could, gasping as she rounded Speaker Rock. She had forgotten about the others and she prayed that they were not too badly hurt.

The fight had obviously been brief and furious. The packed earth was covered with unconscious and wounded Cougars, and the acrid smell of burned flesh and fur hung over the ground, gagging her. The source was a warrior who had been virtually sliced in half by a cutter beam. The cauterized flesh around the spilling intestines was black and smoldering…it was Crooked Tooth! She saw the tell-tale scars under his throat and on his legs where Tuft Tail had marked him. She put her hand over her mouth and nose and looked away.

By the wall, she saw Tammy and Mendel starting to clean and dress a number of jagged wounds on both human and Cougar warriors. Some of the Cougars were resisting but Speaker and Tuft Tail were spitting orders at them, and they reluctantly let the nervous marines tend to their wounds. Then she saw Ken finally. He was standing behind Star…who was hunched over Serena's still body! Jim was kneeling on the other side of her, gently cradling her head and stroking her face. His cheeks were wet and he was openly crying.

"You're going to be all right, darling. We'll make sure of it."

Julie ran over to them, grabbing Ken's hand to ask: "What happened?"

He held her back as she looked past him at Serena's unconscious and bloody figure, gasping as she saw the jagged belly wound and the deeply slashed right thigh. He grabbed hold of her and hugged tight.

"Crooked Tooth got her in the attack. He severed the femoral artery, as well as ripping open her belly. I've called for a med-shuttle and it's on the way. Tammy got the artery clamped right away, and got the major bleeders in the belly, but if we don't get the femoral artery repaired and restore blood flow, we're going to have to grow her a new leg, and I don't know how that's going to work out here. The gravity is twice normal her formative environment's. But Star's trying to improvise a repair now."

Julie looked down to see metal fingers moving with blinding speed and precision. "What are you doing?"

Star didn't falter as he answered:

"I am using plastic tubing and a small Surgi-Kit to improvise a temporary graft so I can restore perfusion to the leg." His voice was utterly calm and controlled. "Actually, Ken is overreacting a little. Depending on the amount of collateral circulation, we have a relatively adequate time period to correct the problem. And in this case, a number of smaller vessels are still intact." His hands stopped. They were covered with blood and the gaping slash was still oozing. "Done." He released the clamp Tammy had improvised and a rush of blood surged through the clear tubing he had just finished stitching in place. "It is crude, but it restores normal flow. Now I have to take care of some of the smaller bleeders."

He pulled out some wires out of a kit-bag and opened a small panel in his chest and reached in.

"One of the advantages of being a robot," he joked. "Easy access to power tools." He connected one end the wires to something inside and as he touched the other ends together a bright blue spark crackled to life. Moving with rapid, but delicate precision, he moved the sparking wire ends down to touch area after area within the gaping belly wound. As he cauterized the remaining unclamped bleeders, the stench of burning flesh wafted upwards and Julie swallowed hard, burying her face in Ken's shoulder. She heard spitting growls behind her and glanced back to see the Cougars staring at the arc with wide eyes, ears flat and teeth bared.

Ken glanced over at them. "Star, tell them not to be afraid. You're scaring them."

Star gave a loud, growling serenade without stopping his work, and the Cougars backed away and quieted down.

"You better tell Speaker to move his people," Jim suggested as he looked up from Serena reluctantly. "I don't know how they'll react to the med-shuttle when it gets here."

Star went into a flood of spitting hisses and growls again, echoed back by Speaker and Tuft Tail who apparently didn't want to cooperate. But after a heated exchange, Speaker turned to the others and issued sharp orders. His warriors rose and dove gratefully into the grass, leaving several swaying wakes as they headed for the trees.

Ruiz and Greg approached, looking amazed. "It was incredible," Ruiz said, shaking his head.

Greg nodded. "Yes, you wouldn't believe it, but Speaker's people saved our asses! We were attacked by about a dozen cats who came out of nowhere. They got Serena and a couple of my men pretty bad, but then Speaker's cats showed up and pounced on the ones attacking us. We almost shot them, but it was obvious right away what they were doing."

"They're incredible!" Tammy came up behind them and laid an arm over each of their shoulders, stretching her neck to kiss Greg on the cheek. "The cats just sat there and didn't flinch when I was cleaning their wounds. They didn't like it at first though. I've had cats, and I can tell. But that leader, what did you call him? Speaker? He yelled at them and they cooperated fine after that, even if it was like trying to put disinfectant on any cat's wound. They'll probably go lick it right off, screaming about the bad taste. But that's okay. They should heal fine. Only one was gashed really bad, and I stitched her up."

Julie looked up, trying to catch sight of the med-shuttle. All the Cougars were gone now, except Speaker and Tuft Tail, who obviously heard something. They sat side by side, staring nervously at the sky. Then she heard it: the familiar, low whistling of a small transport.

Star was finally finished with Serena, and Tammy helped him dress her wounds as much as possible. Then he turned to Speaker and Tuft Tail with sharp growling questions.

Speaker rose to face him, only reaching to Star's chest, but he was an imposing figure as the afternoon sun framed him and he growled back, translated by Star.

"I have more in common with you than even with many members of the Tribe. You are a true and noble warrior. But now you are wrong, trying to say that I should take Tuft Tail and return to the Tribe. I can not. We have fought together. There is a bond between us now and we need to understand each other more. I will not be scared away by your flying things."

"Even if you come on it with us—"

"No, Star!" Julie cut him off. Luckily Star had translated his own growls, too. "Speaker, Tuft Tail, you and I have to stay here. Tell them," she ordered and waited for him to do so. Then she went on:

"We have to finish settling how to handle contact between us, and we need to do it in plain sight of the tribe. And like it or not, Star, you have to stay with us to translate."

"I can not. I have to go with Serena."

"I'm sorry, but I need you here." She went up to him, astonished to see his face twitching slightly, an expression of pain on it. She touched it lightly. "What are you feeling?"

Ken joined her and stared curiously as the eerily mobile metal face shifted fluidly.

"Unbalanced," Star finally answered. "I want to be free again. I want to be with Serena, and I want to be with you...but I want to be with Serena more. That is illogical. She will be fine. The damage is easily repairable now. The only danger is from internal bleeding that I may have missed. I don't have my full range scanning equipment available. But she should be fine. Settling the contact with the Cougars is far more important than my needless presence."

"But you want to be there."

"Yes. Why? It is not logical."

Julie reached out to hug him. "No, but it is very understandable. She is your 'mother'. You're worried because you love her—"

"Those are emotions and I don't—"

"Bullshit; to borrow a phrase from my youth. And yes it is meaningless, but it expresses *my* feelings. You *do* have emotions. I'm sure of it now. They may not be biologically based, but they're real. The fact that you keep denying them supports me." She jabbed his chest with her finger. "Now shut up and listen to me. Serena is unconscious so she can't release you, but do you mean to tell me that you can't override her programming? With all the growing you've done, and all the reorganization and improvements you've built into yourself since you were first activated?"

Star just looked at her as she glared up at him, challenging.

Ken added: "If you do, you can be here with Julie and Speaker, and back in StarStep City with Serena all at once. That's basic multi-tasking. A twentieth century notebook computer could do it!"

Star straightened. "There is no need to be insulting. I will try."

Speaker and Tuft Tail stood off to the side, staring as Star retreated from Julie a couple of steps and then froze into an expressionless statue.

"Is he okay?" Jim asked as he joined them.

"I don't know," Ken answered. "This is way beyond my experience. Only Serena would know."

"God, I can almost hear his gears grinding," Julie said as she gripped Ken's hand tightly. Suddenly she felt silky fur brush her fingers and a heavy head butted her side. It was Tuft Tail. Automatically she dropped to her knees and hugged the Cougar, kneading the massive skull behind the ears. Tuft Tail froze for a second and then a deep rumbling rolled out from her throat and she leaned into Julie. "A cat is a cat is a cat," Julie laughed as she continued scratching Tuft Tail. Speaker shifted his wide-eyed stare to the two of them, his move mirrored by Jim.

Ken chuckled. "Boy are you turning their world upside down!"

"Hey, come on!" Greg shouted. "The shuttle's here."

The low whistling that had been getting louder without them realizing it was now a powerful whine as the stubby metal and PlasSteel cylinder settled down on the packed earth, scattering dust and a few loose leaves and grass shafts that had blown onto the field.

Star stood impassively among the swirling debris.

One clear side of the shuttle folded down and two white-clad med-techs dropped out and rushed over to grab Serena's still body to load her onboard. Jim was right with her, holding on to her hand firmly. Mandel sent all the wounded along, and then told the pilot to take off. That left him with Tammy, Ruiz and Washington as escort for Julie, Ken and Star.

And Speaker and Tuft Tail. The latter was shivering slightly in Julie's arms as the med-shuttle lifted with a labored growling whine and rose into the sky to fly off towards StarStep City. Speaker was crouched next to Ken, moaning softly. His ears were flat, his fur erect, and his tail lashed back and forth with strong, rapid strokes, slapping Ken's left boot.

Suddenly Star's voice interrupted as he straightened, looking surprised. "I did it. There were some flaws in her logic structure that I was able to use to circumvent her restrictions. I am now totally restored to all inputs." He noticed the agitated Cougars and growled softly to them.

They relaxed, and as Julie felt Tuft Tail start to pull away, she released the warrior's soft and comforting body reluctantly and got up to face Star. "Translate. Back to where we were before. We have to finish."

CHAPTER 22

▼

TREATY

"The flying thing is gone," Bad Smell reassured them. "It will not bother you."

Speaker looked over at Tuft Tail, surprised by how she was so obviously content, despite the odor. He felt strangely jealous. He did have to admit that once you got used to it, the smell of the sky-creatures was not really that bad. Just different. And they were great warriors and magicians. The sight of Crooked Tooth's body would live in his mind forever. Like lightning to tree, his body had been torn open with fire.

Then Black Fur released Tuft Tail and Bad Smell relayed her squeals that she wanted to continue their meeting.

He nipped at Tuft Tail's flank and called her over, telling Bad Smell they had to talk privately. They loped across the field and through the grass to the low rise were they had settled before.

"How much do we say?" he asked softly, wanting her opinion.

Tuft Tail glanced back at the sky-creatures waiting back on the Field. "They know much. They knew the Tribe was watching, before, so it would be better to tell them what we need."

"It shows weakness," he stopped her.

"We saved their lives and that shows *their* weakness," she argued. "Even with their things that kill and make sleep, they would have died. They are slow and clumsy. It would be a fair exchange."

"But we have to learn more about them."

"No." Tuft Tail was silent a moment. "I think it would better that we do not." She explained and as he thought about it, he had to agree.

He stood up and growled to Bad Smell to bring Black Fur.

The dark-skinned one with white fur that Speaker suddenly remembered from his first meeting with Black Fur followed, and Speaker started to protest.

Tuft Tail bit his shoulder lightly to shut him up. "White Fur and Black Fur are mated."

Speaker relented, and let all three come. As they reached Speaker and Tuft Tail, Black Fur and White Fur settled to the ground, Black Fur leaning into her mate's arms. Bad Smell stood behind them.

They were silent, waiting for him to speak and he decided, just as Bad Smell started to speak. He cut the strange sky-creature off.

"I have much to say, be silent. You came to our lands and started to take them. You stopped after we attacked and you are now clearing land in other areas instead. That is good. If you leave us alone and do not disturb our hunting ground, we will not attack again. But there is another price."

Black Fur and her mate were staring at each other, their strange naked faces twitching as he went on.

"There are not enough of us and we need more hunters. You have flying things, so we want you to find other warriors like us who think and use their paws. Then tell us where to find them so we can ask them to join with us to strengthen the Tribe. And you will leave us more hunting land to allow a larger Tribe to find enough meat."

"Where—"

"I am not done," Speaker cut Bad Smell off. "And then you will leave us alone. We do not want help and we do not want any things that you have made. There may be others like Crooked Tooth, and until the Tribe is not acting like a den full of cubs, we will help ourselves and handle our own problems."

Black Fur squealed and Bad Smell tried again. "Can I speak now?"

"Yes."

"We agree. We do not think it would be good to help you too much or to interfere. We have seen what happens when different…tribes that have different levels of development mix. It would hurt you. We do know that there are less and less of you."

"We know, too." Speaker explained how he and Tuft Tail had decided to change the way the Tribe handled younglings and challenges.

"You are doing the right thing," Black Fur confirmed through Bad Smell. "And we will help you find others like you so you can expand the Tribe, but I warn you, it will not be easy to have them join you. But we will show you where to look. To begin with, there is another Tribe like yours, though not as organized or advanced, one paw of days in that direction."

Bad Smell pointed towards the place of the Falling Waters. "When it's time, we will be able to help you more. But for now, we are going to stay far away, and we will not interfere. But we may come to visit the land, maybe to take things out of the ground where no hunting is possible, and we want to know that we will not be attacked. And we want to be sure you will not attack us where we live now."

"No hunting on our lands," Speaker warned. "And no clearing of it like you were doing before—*and no taking* things out of our ground. We may need it someday. And no more spy-things!"

"None of that."

"Repeat that louder, for the Tribe to hear. Then you will be safe."

Bad Smell made a funny sound. Then he repeated, loudly. "We will not hunt on your land, take anything from it, or destroy your hunting territory, and we will not send any more spy-things…of the type we have been sending. And we will help."

"Do not speak loudly of the shrinking Tribe," Speaker interrupted softly. "There is no need." He and Tuft Tail had already decided that it was best to handle that alone. He could not believe he had won so easily. The sky-creatures had surrendered everything. They would have to live far away from the good lands, hunt far away and not be able to keep spying on them. They had lost! He glanced at Tuft Tail and he could see her looking at him proudly.

"Your turn," Bad Smell said. "Repeat loudly that we will not be attacked on our land, or if we come visiting."

Speaker complied happily.

The three sky-creatures looked at each other and squealed back and forth for a while. Then Black Fur pulled a small rock out of her second skin that she had wrapped around her. She handed it to Speaker and he held it curiously.

It had only a little bad smell and was smooth and light, like a small water-worn rock in a stream. It had a long vine on the end that looped around like the belt he wore on his waist.

Bad Smell explained. "This is a thing we give you." Then Black Fur handed another one to Tuft Tail draping it over her neck to hang there, glittering in the late light of day. The warrior straightened proudly and Speaker quickly draped his around his own neck.

Bad Smell pointed to them. "If we are coming, you will hear my voice on this telling you and then come here and we will meet you. And if you need help, press this hard," he pointed to a small black piece in a small hole on the front. "And we will come. Now go back to the Tribe and explain, and we will leave you."

Bad Smell turned and walked back towards Speaker Rock and the other sky-creatures, leaving Black Fur and her mate alone with him and Tuft Tail. Black Fur crouched on the ground in front of the seated Tuft Tail and reached up carefully to rub behind a large fluffy ear. Tuft Tail started rumbling contentedly again and leaned forward to butt her head against Black Fur's, almost knocking the sky-creature down. Black Fur reached out and steadied herself by throwing both forelegs around Tuft Tail's neck and grabbing tight. Strange water was coming from her eyes.

Feeling the strange surge of jealousy again, Speaker moved towards them and found himself grabbed as Black Fur freed one foreleg to throw it around his own neck and a strong hand started grooming him behind the ear in just the perfect spot…it felt so good!

Then Black Fur was gone, running across the field after Bad Smell, followed by White Fur.

Speaker stared after them, the feel of the small grooming hand lingering and he leaned against Tuft Tail, feeling the warmth of her body soothe him. She nipped at his ear playfully and he growled lightly, knocking her down and chewing on her loose neck fur. Across the field, he saw the Tribe slowly filtering out of the woods and approaching. He had made sure that they had all heard how he had forced the sky-creatures to surrender without a fight. Between that and Crooked Tooth's death, he would have no problem keeping control of them now so that he and Tuft Tail could mold them.

"You were right," he growled softly to Tuft Tail as they waited, wrapped together in a furry pile. "We must change the habits of the Tribe and expand. And we will learn to build with our own hands. Not taught by the sky-creatures."

"And we will grow smarter," Tuft Tail added. "Our cubs may rule the world one day."

"Together with the sky-creatures," Speaker corrected. "One day we will have to join Tribes. We can not continue to live separately. But we have to learn more for ourselves before we join with them or we will never be treated as more than cubs."

C H A P T E R   2 3

▼

HEALING

As they entered into the nanomed wing, Jim spotted Gratch and asked: "Are you all set?" The med-techs were right behind him with the hover-litter bearing Serena's body.

"Yes, Star's made all the preparations and a vat is ready for her."

"Star? I left him back with Julie."

"I am also here, Jim," a familiar voice came down from above. Serena left me an unintentional logic loop-hole that let me break free. Or perhaps it was not unintentional? I am waiting to find out. But that must wait. I scanned her as soon as you were in range and the damage is much as I assessed on site. But there has been additional internal bleeding and she needs to be put in the vat immediately. I have already programmed the nanorooter repair sequence."

The medics lifted Serena off the litter gently and lowered her into the coffin-like container of milky liquid that slid out of the wall. A mask went over her face, and then her body was totally submerged. The vat slid back into the wall and she was invisible.

"She will be all right, Jim." Star's voice was surprisingly gentle. "I would find it extremely difficult to function well if anything happened to her, but it won't. I am in balance now that she is here and being repaired. I estimate that she should be ready for decanting in one hour and forty-five minutes."

"Thanks Star." Jim raised his hand automatically, but there was no one there to touch. Only the voice. "Thank's for being here." He sank into the low chair that emerged unbidden from the wall beside him.

After a while, he got up again and walked over to the apparently seamless wall that had swallowed the vat holding her. He couldn't sit still. One hour and forty-five minutes. That was one hundred and five minutes, or six thousand three hundred seconds. What if it had taken that much longer to get her here? Would she have been dead? He laid his hands against the smooth surface and then leaned forward and closed his eyes. The warm wall against his forehead vibrated slightly with slow, regular pulsations that penetrated through his hands and face. He imagined he could see thousands of microscopic machines spreading through her body, multiplying as they went, differentiating as they analyzed the damage and repaired arteries, veins and muscles. Blood flow would be the first priority as all the vessels were repaired, then the containing flesh would be rebuilt, the severed muscles rejoined and finally as the final nanorooters withdrew the skin would be rebuilt and restored to the velvety softness he had caressed so lovingly.

"She'll be fine, Jim."

He jerked as Gratch laid a hand on his shoulder and then let go of the wall and turned, feeling a little embarrassed. "I know, Pavel. It's just that she's so much a part of me now that it is real scary to be this close to losing her." He settled back in the chair, glancing at his watch. "I'll be all right. Just an hour and half left." Ninety minutes…five thousand, four hundred seconds…

CHAPTER 24

▼

RESOLUTION

"You did it, darling." Ken hugged her tightly as they left Speaker and Tuft Tail behind. "We've got guaranteed safety, and you left a loop-hole so Star can keep checking on them with different roving monitors." His arm circled and drew her close.

Julie just smiled and leaned into his embrace as she glanced back and raised her computer to call for a shuttle to pick them up a few kilometers away. She wanted to give the Cougars room. "Oh yea? I wonder. Star, what are they saying?"

Star relayed the conversation behind them as they kept walking slowly, and she grinned as she realized that Speaker and Tuft Tail were celebrating their own victory.

Ken looked a little crestfallen. "You mean you gave them what they wanted?"

"Why not? It was basically what we wanted, anyway."

"Oh."

"Hey, don't look so glum." She shoved him lightly off balance and giggled as he did a low-gravity shuffle to stay upright. "Lighten up! This is a dream come true. Speaker and Tuft Tail are already aware of the worst dangers facing them and they don't want help. It's a no-lose situation."

He shook his head and laughed, a deep rolling sound that she loved. She snuck back under his arm again and squeezed him close as they headed for Greg and the others.

Then she was more serious as she thought about the last bit Star had translated.

"You know, Speaker is sharp. I mean really sharp."

"How so?"

"He's already talking about what the future is going to bring. Very un-feline of him. And he knows we can't keep apart forever. Segregation doesn't work as a long-term solution. The old United States and eventually South Africa found that out..." she giggled. "And I guess we did, too. Even if it's a slightly different problem, we've got to share this world—and I think we're off to a good start."

Ken nodded. "It won't be easy, though."

"No, but if Speaker and Tuft Tail keep control, and if their kids follow their parents'…paw-steps," she grinned, "then we should be able to work it out." She reached up and tugged on his beard to pull his face down to hers for a kiss as they kept walking. Not that he needed much prompting.

"Whoa!" a voice from below stopped them as they almost tripped over Greg. He looked up at them with a lopsided grin from where he sat with Tammy cradled happily in his arms. The two marines were lounging in the shade under some flowering bushes.

"Sorry, guys, but we were celebrating. Ruiz, Washington: come on!"

The two other marines were sprawled on the grass a little further away, actively scratching diagrams in the dirt as they played a strategic war game of some sort, and they jumped to their feet happily.

"Let's get going," Ken prompted Greg. "Julie already called for a pickup back at the first clearing where we had lunch. That's only about a kilometer, and that way we won't upset the Cougars with another shuttle landing near them."

There were a few reluctant groans—everyone was tired of walking—but the success of the meeting had been infectious so the walk went quickly as they left the Cougars behind.

Star had been almost totally silent since the time they had left Speaker and Tuft Tail. But as they walked, he suddenly threw both hands up in the air and laughed.

Everyone stared at him in shock.

He shrugged. "It's an appropriate expression of joy when in human company and as this is generally a situation where joy is appropriate, I didn't see the harm in expressing my…happiness over Serena's successful treatment. She's awake and sends her greetings and congratulations on your success with the Cougars. The news is already spreading through StarStep city and to the Agra Stations. At Jim's suggestion, I've made the records of the meetings available to the Colony."

Julie cocked her head. "'It's, didn't, she's, I've'? You're suddenly using contractions, Star. What's up?"

"I'm merely trying to facilitate relaxed conversation. I think if I'm going to spend time among people in this body, I should do my best to behave as naturally as possible."

Ken raised an eyebrow. "Does that mean you're staying in your body?"

"Yes. As an interactive tool and a means of manipulating my environment it's unequalled. I'm surprised Serena didn't try this before. As long as I'm not restricted from my other sensors and terminals, it's no problem to have this body, and some may feel more comfortable dealing with me like this."

"Well, it will be interesting having you around." Julie linked an arm through his and then captured Ken the same way to march along between her two escorts. "Come on, guys. The shuttle's on the way. Let's go home."

EPILOGUE

▼

I.

Another Warm Time had come and gone, and now it was warming again.

Speaker was amazed by the rapid changes to the Tribe already. The cubs from Tuft Tail's first litter were already grown younglings ready for their Testing. It had been a healthy litter with two females and a male. And Tuft Tail had been right: they were smarter. They had been speaking much sooner than any of the other cubs born the same time, and they had been experimenting with making things with their hands almost as soon as they could stalk. Including traps that spilled things on unsuspecting parents.

Her second litter had been the same size, but reversed; two males and one female. But the female had been killed by a kill-cleaner that had wandered in on her first solo stalking exercise.

The two males had been angry at the stupid death and wondered why the hunting had to take up so much time and energy. Like the first litter, they liked making things, but there was not enough time. So they had come to him just the day before with an idea that had made his head spin.

They wanted to build a wall of sticks to keep male and female runners trapped. Not to hunt, but to breed. And then only eat the birthings. And not all of those, but keep some to make more birthings for more food. It would be easier to find food for the captive runners than to hunt down the runners in the wild. Maybe they could even grow the food for the runners?

It was so simple that Speaker was amazed he had not thought of it himself. He and Tuft Tail had been surprised. Still cubs, barely able to stalk properly, and they were already thinking better than their parents.

Tomorrow he would bring the idea up to the Tribe in Assembly. It would help a lot, now that there were many more warriors to feed.

After his last meeting with Bad Smell, Black Fur, and her mate, he had sent out younglings in the direction the sky-creatures had told him, and they had found another Tribe. It was a small Tribe and

259

had been shrinking every season, and they had welcomed the offer to join Speaker's Tribe when they found out how much better the hunting was. It had been difficult to speak to them at first, but Speaker had borrowed from Black Fur and had begun by offering a runner to the leader of the Other Tribe.

It had not taken long after that.

It had been a good decision. There had been more births since the new warriors had joined them and the litters were larger and healthier.

He thought again about the cubs' idea. Captive runners? He looked out over the hillside below the cave he was using and considered. It would leave time to think, and build…

II.

It had been over a year, and StarStep city was gone.

The northern hemisphere was empty of humans. In orbit, three vast ships hung silent and lifeless, their on-board systems keyed and waiting.

Then, a signal.

On one ship, mechanical figures roused and methodically moved the last five hundred hexagonal containers into the gaping cargo bay to await the transport from the surface that was reaching orbit and homing on the signal from the freeper ship "Rip Van Winkle". It would be the last such visit to this ship. The next shuttles would be the recyclers which would dismantle the freeper ship and bring the parts down to use for the growing colony in the southern hemisphere.

"They're loading now," Star's voice announced and Jim looked up, surprised by the strange echo effect. Then he saw Star's smiling face looking over his shoulder and realized where the second voice had come from.

"Hi. I didn't hear you come in. How many are left?"

"Six thousand on "The Sleeping Beauty" and then seven thousand on "The Flying Dutchman"."

"Thanks, Star. And thanks for coming down in person. I've been getting a little lonely sitting alone with only your voice for company." He had been curled up alone in the new administration tower lounge, in front of a screen monitoring the newest shipment of freepers being brought down for revival.

Serena was off at a live Mozart revival with Ken and Julie. He had been invited, but medieval music—or whenever Mozart had been around—had never appealed to him. He preferred the twentieth century if he wanted retro-music. Jazz, mainly. So he had decided to be useful for a change, or at least to pretend to, since Star certainly didn't need supervision.

Then, as the door hissed open, he was distracted by the sound of laughter that rolled in ahead of Serena, Ken and Julie. They were back already. Glancing at his watch, he saw that it was later that he thought and he got up from in front of his terminal to greet them.

Ken was wiping his eyes. "Did you see the look on the face of that newly upped freeper when we came out of the Concert Hall?" He kept his arms around Julie and Serena.

"I thought his eyes were going to pop out," Julie giggled.

"Well this is a colonial world, and if he was just recently revived, I expect he thinks he's going to have to do his part to repopulate it." Serena was helplessly hanging onto Ken as much as Julie.

"What the chill are you three laughing about?" Jim felt himself starting to grin as the others all sank into scattered Mag-Lev loungers by the window.

Serena sobered, a little, and blew him a kiss as she explained. "Visual display: Ken, an arm about each of us, and we're all laughing about some idiot in the back row who had been complaining because he thought Mozart was a member of a twentieth century rock group called Dead Zeppelin, or something like that, who went on to a solo career after the group disbanded. Apparently the music had not been what he had expected. Then, as we step outside on the boulevard to come back here, this new 'vivee comes around the corner and almost knocks us down. After apologizing, he looks from me, to Julie, and then to Ken and his eyes start bulging and he gets this idiot grin on his face. Then he takes off."

They all stood up and she and Julie draped themselves on Ken as described and it was suddenly extremely obvious that each was several months pregnant.

Jim chuckled and shook his head. "Oooh, not fair. I hope he's not disappointed when he finds out that we're keeping monogamous marriages."

"It would serve him right if he was," Julie sniffed. Then she reached up to kiss Ken on the cheek before dropping back into her own lounger. Serena followed suit, while Ken just held out his hands and grinned.

"Hey, if you got it…"

Star had been quiet and Jim guessed that he had only partially been following the interplay between the others as he interrupted.

"Julie, I have an update on the Cougar situation."

"Great! What are Speaker and T.T. up to?"

"Well, the new roving monitors are finally scent-free as far as the Cougars are concerned, and we've been able to maintain good surveillance without them knowing, and it's a good thing. We knew they are still accelerated compared to their eventual life spans, but they're developing much faster than we had anticipated…" He went on to explain about the idea that Speaker's cubs had come up with.

"Animal husbandry?" Julie and Ken were both staring. They looked at each other and Julie pursed her lips in a silent whistle. "*That's* going to be interesting! Since they don't need as much food as their ancestors on Earth, it might just work." She looked a little worried suddenly. "And with more time on their hands—"

"Who knows what they'll come up with?" Ken finished. "I think it's a good thing we decided to relocate to the southern hemisphere. Between the way the tribe is growing, and how the new litters are getting smarter and smarter, they need room to grow."

"Yes, but they are our friends," Julie pointed out. "And they're our neighbors. It'll be nice to have some interesting neighbors, don't you think?" She looked over at Star. "We've got our next project I think. It's time to set up another meeting with Speaker and Tuft Tail...We need to lay the ground-work for integrating the Cougars into our society."

Ken leaned forward and patted her belly. "Don't you think there's plenty of time to take care of other things first, like our own...litter?" He grinned and Julie slapped his hand gently.

"It's not entirely my fault I'm carrying twins. Besides, it will give me something to talk with Tuft Tail about. Maybe she can give me some advice." She smiled. "But seriously, I want to sit down with them now, while they're still running the Tribe. Even if their breeding is almost back to normal, their life spans are shorter than ours. Their first...kids are adults already, and the second litter is precocious as hell."

Ken got up and went around to stand behind her, kneading her neck with strong hands as she bent her head back to meet him. "You're right. And it will be interesting to see them again. But will you be all right?"

"Hey, I'm only pregnant, not an invalid. Besides, the doctor said exercise is good for me. Even if I'm carrying a matched pair, I'm not even five months." She squeezed his hand and looked over at Star.

"Hey, signal Speaker and tell him to expect visitors. And pack a bag, or whatever. We need a trans-lator. I may be able to understand them now, but my throat is not up to speaking Cougar."

Jim looked at her and saw the excitement lighting up her face. In a way, he envied her. She would have her hands full for the rest of her life learning about, and teaching others about, the Cougars.

Then practiced hands kneaded his own shoulders as Serena snuck up behind him. Her soft lips traveled lightly down his forehead, his nose and then pressed warmly against his own, opening to tease him lightly as she moved around to settle in his lap. Silvery blue eyes stared deep into his own and he grabbed her to hold her close as she whispered in his ear.

"Hey, lover. Don't be too envious. You've got a lot of work pending, too. There's another batch of freepers on the way down and you've got integration problems of your own to worry about. And as much as Julie and Ken can do, you're the one who has to bring it all together in the end. And besides, if you think I'm going to take care of Alyssa here all by myself, you're nuts." She patted her own swelling stomach lightly and grinned.

Even though they were both close to five months, she wasn't carrying as large as Julie, but he knew the next few months would pass quickly enough and that he would have his work cut out for him, too. He couldn't wait. "Okay."

She nodded firmly. "Chillin' right. Being a mother scares me."

"Come on," he teased. "You've had practice."

She stuck her tongue out. "That's not the same. Besides, I need time to work on Star's brother. Now that Star's grown, I'm going to 'clone' him and I'm working with Ken to design a probe to send Star II out on a deep-space survey. Earth isn't doing anything more about exploration, so I think it's up to us until they pull their collective heads out of the sand and face the future. I don't know how Julie will feel about me stealing her husband away like this, but I'm sure she'll adjust. She also has loads of work lined up with Speaker's people, even if she does have several students working with her.

Ken and Julie had managed to squeeze together on the same lounger and they were talking quietly. They were oblivious to anyone but each other, and Jim got up carefully and led Serena over to the window to look out over the spreading StarStep II. She stood behind him to rest her head on top of his as she wrapped her arms around him.

He laid his hands over hers tenderly. "It will be interesting, hon, won't it?"

She grinned and moved around in front of him. "Shut up and kiss me."

- end -

0-595-31841-X

Printed in the United States
20216LVS00002B/151